Praise for *Answer Creek*

"With faultlessly authentic perio........... ....g twists of fate, *Answer Creek* puts the reader right on the Oregon-California Trail in every sensory and emotional aspect imaginable. This compassionate but utterly realistic telling of the story gently crushes the sensationalized versions and releases something that feels much closer to truth. Ada is hope personified—it takes wing, soars, crashes—and survives."

—Ellen Notbohm, award-winning author
of *The River by Starlight*

"So well researched, one can almost feel the cold of winter and the stifling pain inflicted upon the heart and soul of these courageous pioneers."

—K.S. Jones, award-winning author of *Shadow of the Hawk*

"Ada Weeks is an unforgettable character, authentic and true, created by the deft hands of author Ashley Sweeney. Together they provide a possible answer to the question 'how might I fare in a time of trial?' But this is only one question of *Answer Creek*. Full of distinctive language, fresh images of overland travel, and the challenge of choices, Ada Weeks is a woman to cheer for while we explore our own journeys toward meaning no matter the century nor trail. Be prepared to burn the night oil to discover more."

—Jane Kirkpatrick, award-winning author
of *One More River to Cross*

"*Answer Creek* is brilliant, masterfully written."

—Frances Simmons, editor

"Majestic, moving, and layered with beauty and horror, *Answer Creek* is a bittersweet and satisfying historical novel."

—*Foreword Reviews*

"If there can be beauty in horror, Sweeney has managed it in the writing of this book. Doom hovers on every page—in the sunsets of the western sky, in emaciated cattle, in boots worn down to shreds—yet the human spirit radiantly perseveres in the form of young Ada Weeks, who is determined to find love despite an avalanche of losses and sorrows. Her harrowing physical and psychological journey grips the reader in a tightly woven web of suspense. Impeccably researched, *Answer Creek* is a triumphant re-telling of a mythic American tragedy."

—Laurel Davis Huber, author of *The Velveteen Daughter*, winner of the Langum Prize for American Historical Fiction

"Intimate, engrossing, and personal—this novel is so much more than the story of the Donner Party. It is the story of a budding young woman: her loves, her hopes, and her generous spirit in the midst of an unfolding tragedy. As I read this engrossing novel I forgot I knew—or thought I knew—the story that inspired it. Sweeney captures both the highs and lows of human behavior with each gripping scene."

—Martha Conway, author of *The Underground River*

"In *Answer Creek*, Sweeney rescues the story of the Donner Party from its fate as salacious anecdote and delivers a harrowing tale of resilience, folly, loss, and hope."

—Mary Volmer, author of *Reliance, Illinois*

"The author is a master of vivid descriptions, dragging readers along every wretched mile of the trail, sharing every dashed hope and every dramatic confrontation, with Ada as their guide. Ada is a marvelous creation, twice orphaned and both hopeful and fearful about a new life in California, the promised land . . . A vivid westward migration tale with an arresting mixture of history and fiction."

—*Kirkus Reviews*

Answer Creek

Other works by Ashley E. Sweeney:

Eliza Waite

Answer Creek

A Novel

Ashley E. Sweeney

SHE WRITES PRESS

Published 2020
Printed in the United States of America
ISBN: 978-1-63152-844-6 pbk
ISBN: 978-1-63152-845-3 ebk
Library of Congress Control Number: 2019914838

For information, address:
She Writes Press
1569 Solano Ave #546
Berkeley, CA 94707

She Writes Press is a division of SparkPoint Studio, LLC.

Map design by Ruth Hulbert
Layout by Kiran Spees

For my children

We are troubled on every side . . .
Persecuted, but not forsaken; cast down,
but not destroyed.

2 Corinthians 4: 8–9

DONNER PARTY
Cast of Characters

Ada Weeks: 19, stepdaughter of Augustus and Inger Vik; from Noblesville, Indiana

Breen Family: Patrick and Margaret; children: John (14), Edward (13), Patrick, Jr. (11), Simon (9), James (5), Peter (3), Isabella (9 months); from Keokuk, Iowa

Eddy Family: William and Eleanor; children: James (3), Margaret (1); from Belleville, Illinois

Reed Family: James and Margaret; children: Virginia (13), Patty (9), James, Jr. (6), Thomas (4); from Springfield, Illinois

George Donner Family: George and Tamsen; children: Elitha (13), Leanna (11), Frances (6), Georgia (4), Eliza (3); from Sangamon County, Illinois

Jacob Donner Family: Jacob and Elizabeth; children: Solomon Hook (14), William Hook (12), George (9), Mary (7), Isaac (5), Samuel (4), Lewis (3); from Sangamon County, Illinois

Graves Family: Franklin and Elizabeth; children: Mary (19), William (17), Eleanor (14), Lovina (12), Nancy (9), Jonathon (6), Franklin, Jr. (5), Elizabeth (1); from Marshall County, Illinois; traveling with married daughter Sarah (and husband Jay Fosdick)

Keseberg Family: Lewis and Philippine; children: Ada (3), Lewis, Jr., (infant); from Germany

McCutcheon Family: William and Amanda; child: Harriet (1); from Jackson County, Missouri

Murphy Family: Widow Levinah; children: John (16), Mary (14), Lemuel (12), William (10), Simon (8); from Weakley County, Tennessee; traveling with married daughters Harriet and husband, William Pike, and children: Naomi (2), Catherine (1); and Sarah and husband, William Foster, and child: George (2)

Wolfinger Family: Jacob and Doris (no children); from Germany

Single Men (friends, teamsters, drovers, helpers, jacks-of all-trades):
Karl Burger (30); teamster for Lewis Keseberg; from Germany

John Denton (29); teamster for George Donner; from England

Patrick Dolan (35); teamster for Patrick Breen; from Ireland

Milt Elliott (28); teamster for James Reed; from Kentucky

Luke Halloran (25); joins Donner Party near Bridger's Fort; from Ireland

Wilhelm Hardkoop (60); travels with Lewis Keseberg; from Belgium

Walter Herron (27); teamster for James Reed; from Virginia

Noah James (18); teamster for Jacob Donner; from Illinois

Hiram Miller (30); teamster for George Donner; from Kentucky

Joseph Reinhardt (30); travels with Jacob Wolfinger; from Germany

Samuel Shoemaker (25); teamster for Jacob Donner; from Ohio

James Smith (25); teamster for James Reed; from Illinois

John Snyder (25); teamster for Franklin Graves; from Illinois

Augustus Spitzer (30); travels with Lewis Keseberg; from Germany

Charles Stanton (35); travels with George Donner; from New York

Jean-Baptiste Trudeau (16); joins Donner Party at Bridger's Fort; from Canada

Antonio Velasquez (20); joins Donner Party at Bridger's Fort; from Mexico

Baylis Williams (24); travels with James Reed; from Illinois

Single Woman:
Eliza Williams (31); cook for James Reed family; from Illinois

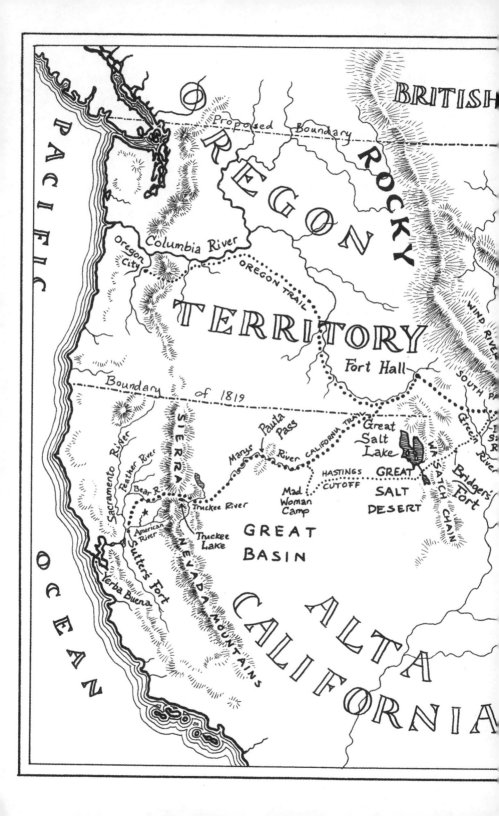

A MAP of the EMIGRANT ROUTE from Independence, MO. to CALIFORNIA
POSSESSIONS
IOWA TERRITORY
UNORGANIZED TERRITORY
Missouri River
Sweetwater River
Independence Rock
Beaver Creek
Fort Laramie
Scotts Bluff
Chimney Rock
Ash Hollow
North Platte River
Platte River
South Platte River
Big Blue River
OREGON-CALIFORNIA TRAIL
Independence
MISSOURI
INDIAN TERRITORY
ARKANSAS
MOUNTAINS
NEW MEXICO
TEXAS

Part One

THE PLAINS

1

May 31, 1846
Big Blue River, Indian Territory

From sundown to sun up, the Big Blue River thunders through the night. Torrents of debris twist and collide as the river races downstream: upended roots, splintered boards, trees the size of an ox. Guards posted at the river's edge swing lanterns, measuring the river's depth at thirty-minute intervals with mud-coated poles. By dawn, the Big Blue subsides eighteen inches.

The Russell Party, a day delayed because of high water, wakes to bugle call. It's a rush of oxen and horses and mules and milch cows to get the wagon train across—a cold hitch, they call it, fording a river before coffee or bacon or beans.

"Steady, now," Ada murmurs. Her jittery mules whimper as she leads them toward the roiling river. Wet to the knee, skirt plastered to her calves and ankles, she goads Rosie and Bert onto the rough-and-ready rope ferry. The air is oppressive and there's no hint of wind. Ada wipes sweat from her forehead.

The angry river still flows at twice its normal rate. Root balls and branches bob and heave in the foam. Carcasses of deer—their antlers reaching out of the water like ghastly arms—pitch and roll in turbulent water. Ada plugs her nose. The river smells of ruin.

After the risky pull across, the sullen ferryman dislodges passengers to return for the next set of wagons. Ada waits there on the steep, muddied riverbank for Augustus and Inger Vik to ferry across. They're still three wagons back on the opposite side, biding their time with a yoke of travel-weary oxen. Ada knows Inger will be grousing by now, Augustus not so much.

Ada strokes her mules. Her stomach grumbles—it's near noon, for God's sake, and no one's eaten yet today. Minutes later, Ada squints toward the eastern bank. *Can it be?* Sure as salt, it's the Viks, passing wagons waiting their turn for conveyance. They plow into the Big Blue like marauders.

Ada isn't sure if they're impatient or frugal, or both. But the river's running too fast, and *anyone with eyes in their damned heads* can see it's still choked with debris. No wagon can expect to ford the Big Blue River today without assistance.

"Wait for the ferry!" Ada roars, her arms waving wildly. Her words dissipate in humid air that hangs, heavy and full, like a thick bedspread that covers the vast, treeless prairie.

"Haw!" Augustus Vik yells, as he whips his yoke of oxen. The oxen's bellies disappear in swirling water as Vik attempts to dodge oncoming wreckage. Inger Vik holds tight to the splintered wagon seat, her mouth set like a rattrap. The oxen lose their footing, and their massive, long-horned heads plunge below the river's dark surface.

Clutches of reeds slide around the Vik's wagon, but leafy branches cluster and mount against sideboards, unable to dive beneath. When the wagon is a quarter way across the swollen river, Augustus Vik swerves to avoid a gnarled root ball barreling downstream.

"*Herregud!*" His wife's piercing cry carries across the muddy ribbon of water.

Vik grimaces, pulls tight on the reins. In the chaos of managing oxen and detritus and screams—and with what he himself would have termed *rotten luck*—Augustus Vik mistakes a tree bowling down the middle of the Big Blue for a dark shadow on the face of the river.

Ada gasps. She can't form any words that resemble prayer, so she's left to watch and worry.

"To the left!" someone yells from the near shore.

Too late, Vik cannot change course mid-stream when the trunk is upon him.

"Mamma! Pappa!" Ada screams. Seconds slow to hours as the monstrosity broadsides the wagon. Even above the *whoosh* of the river, Ada hears desperate bellowing as oxen thrash in their futile attempt to right themselves. Tree, wagon, and oxen entangle and spin, and then the wagon rolls, driven by the river into deeper water.

"Quick, man," one of the teamsters yells. Ada can't recall if his name is Foley or Dolan or Moran. Panicked men run down the banks after the Viks.

"You, on the ferry, take us back across. We'll pay your damn fee," another teamster hollers.

Ada stands, rooted like an oak, eyes wide and wider, dry and dryer, until everything blurs.

In what could have been two minutes or two hours, Ada feels a gentle tug on her arm. It's Margaret Breen, a stout Irishwoman in the Russell Party. "This way, Ada. Come and sit. There's nothing to be done standing there. I've got coffee on."

"My mules . . ."

"Edward! Now!" Mrs. Breen yells to one of her sons as she leads Ada to a three-legged campstool. Rosie and Bert follow the Breen boy to a shaded spot away from camp.

Ada sips black coffee and waits. And waits. "My mamma always says: 'Our vays are da best vays, Ah-dah.'" Ada does her best imitation of Inger's Norwegian. "I'm not so sure of that now."

"Don't give up hope," Mrs. Breen says. "St. Jude is always with us."

Edward Breen ambles into camp and loiters by the campfire. Ada estimates he's twelve or thirteen: all arms and legs and fine-looking, like his Black Irish brothers.

"You got a notion why your folks didn't wait?" Edward asks.

"Enough!" his mother scolds. "Give the girl her peace."

"Hell bent for leather, I guess," Ada answers. "I got no other idea." She looks down, shakes her head. *"Our vays are da best vays."* She eats what's offered, and thankfully (she'd eat anything, she's that hungry). She mops up juices with a heel of bread.

"Thanks for the fixin's, ma'am." Ada hands Mrs. Breen her plate and holds out her mug.

"More?" Ma Breen asks.

Ada nods. By now, she's downed seven cups of strong, bitter coffee.

At nightfall, the Breen's teamster strides into camp. "They're gone, I'm afraid."

"What do you mean, gone? Where have they gone to?" Ada asks.

"Scoured both banks of the river," the Irish teamster reports. "Found the . . ."

"You found them?" Ada sits forward on the stool, her eyes crazed.

"No, miss. Found the wagon about a half-mile downstream snagged on a sandbar." He accepts coffee from Mrs. Breen and nods his thanks. "Wagon was half above water, on its side, tangled with that giant of a tree," he continues. "Sorry to say the oxen were still snarled in their harnesses. We put them out of their misery."

"But what about my pappa? And my mamma?"

"Couldn't get to the wagon, miss—water's way too high. We called and called, but got no answer. Maybe got knotted in the bonnet. Or pinned underneath. Might never know."

Ada drops her head into her hands and rocks back and forth. *Mamma. Pappa.*

"Even went another two miles downstream, Baylis Williams and Milt Elliott and me," the teamster continues. "But all we recovered was this." He hands Ada a soggy blanket. "Wish I had better news."

Every minute or two, Ada cranes her neck and checks the riverbank, as if, by some miracle of St. Jude, Augustus will lumber up the bank with Inger in tow. After all, they had survived a harrowing ocean voyage from Norway as newlyweds (Ada had heard the story countless times). *Surely they can survive this unremarkable river,* she thinks. But all she sees is debris—and more debris—careening down the Big Blue on its race toward the Missouri.

The next morning, Patrick Breen cobbles together a small wooden cross with wagon slats and twine. He pounds it into a high spot on the riverbank near the place the Viks disappeared. Ada stands by the cross, a slight breeze rustling her red wool skirt. There's no time to waste. They'd buried old Mrs. Keyes a couple of nights ago and moved on in the morning.

Ada sweeps clutches of dark brown hair from her face and casts her eyes down. Ordinarily, emigrants don't leave grave markers along the Oregon-California Trail. Instead, they trample over gravesites and leave no trace; it's the only way to ensure the dead aren't defiled. If grave robbers seek to despoil this gravesite, they'll come up woefully empty. There are no bodies buried beneath. Ada dribbles a handful of dirt over the phantom graves. *"Gud velsigne deg, ha det bra,"* she whispers. *God bless you, goodbye.*

Ada accepts condolences, a piece of cake, more black coffee. She's nineteen and stripped bare: no parents, no wagon, no oxen. She's hardly skilled at driving mules, nor does she have funds enough to hire a mule driver. And tomorrow, wagons roll again, no rest for man or beast. All she's left with is a hotchpotch of supplies buried in two mule packs.

What of her oversized trunks heavy with clothing and commodities? And food enough for the five-month journey? Gone are sacks of flour, barrels of bacon. Cornmeal and pickles, coffee and tea. Guns and powder and lead and flint. Choke chains and ground cloths. Laudanum and bandages. Seeds and starts, boxed in Indiana soil, and books on animal husbandry. In short, everything she and her mamma and pappa jam-packed into their wagon when they forked over one thousand dollars, pulled up stakes, and banked that this train of hope would deliver them to the Promised Land.

Paltry offerings straggle in the next morning: an extra trunk (missing its lock), two wool skirts (colorless), a handful of rags (*thank goodness for rags*). Ada doesn't know what she'll do with a trunk; after all, she doesn't have a wagon, or anything to fill it with. What she pines for most is a new pair of boots, but there are none to spare. She'll have to tie her flapping soles together with odd bits of string, whether she goes forward to California or turns back to Indiana.

But why would Ada go back? Noblesville, Indiana, is the gateway to nowhere. She has no sisters or brothers, no aunts or uncles to take her in. And what would she do there anyway, an orphan with no connections? Take a room? Apply as a teacher? Work as a clerk? No, she'll press on toward California and take her chances there.

"Could use your help," Margaret Breen says. "Got six rambunctious boys and the babe. Travel with us, we'll see to your rations."

Ada nods. It's as much of an assent as she's able to offer.

"Father, heft up Miss Weeks's trunk."

Patrick Breen grunts and heaves the chest into his wagon. The Breen's teamster hands Ada a long rifle. "The way I see, it, a girl traveling alone's got to have a good piece," he says. He tips his grubby hat. "Name's Dolan, Pat Dolan."

"I'm obliged," Ada says. *Dolan.* "What do I owe you?"

"No need to pay, miss," Dolan says. "Here, take it."

Ada takes the heavy Hawken in her rough hands. She's never shot a rifle before, but no one needs to know that.

"Wait. Don't have any use for these." Ada reaches into Bert's pack and pulls out a pair of worsted wool trousers, a blousy shirt, galluses, socks, and a handful of handkerchiefs. "Belonged to my pappa," she says. She bites her lip. "In case he had to go on ahead for any reason."

Before she hands the bundle to Dolan, she shoves one of the hankies in her apron pocket.

Later that evening, after more salt pork and beans and dry bread and coffee, Ada spools out her bedroll under the Breen's wagon and extracts Augustus's handkerchief from its dark hiding place. She fingers the large embroidered *V* stitched onto the corner. Before they left Noblesville, Inger Vik sewed their initials onto all their clothing. Maybe it was her way of ensuring posterity. Maybe it was nervous habit. Either way, it's all Ada has left of her pappa. She presses the hanky up to her nose. It smells of tobacco and turpentine.

2

June 23, 1846

Near Chimney Rock, Unorganized Territory

"Git, you stubborn son of a jack." Ada slaps the john mule on his wide rump and wipes sweat from her forehead. The sun she can sometimes get away from, shaded by her hand or her slatted bonnet, but still her face is sunburnt, her hands like leather. Perspiration dribbles down her neck and between her breasts.

Ada's boots *flap, slap,* feet oozing with open sores. It's one foot, then the other: six, twelve, eighteen miles per day through clouds of black gnats and dust. Each step is painful, but she's learned to keep her mouth shut. It's no worse than ague and broken bones, boils and lung fever, dysentery and sunstroke, pressed down and shaken together in this gallnipper-infested bottomland. If anyone has reason to complain, it's Philippine Keseberg, who's heavy with child. Ada hasn't heard Mrs. Keseberg utter a single complaint, even with a sour husband.

The thin, jagged spire of Chimney Rock looms ahead. The closer the wagons get to the spiky outcrop, the farther away it looks. Ada squints at the strange monolith and wishes she could ask her pappa how to calculate miles, especially in this near-treeless prairie. *Twenty? Twenty-five?* But her pappa's not here.

In wide tracts of grassland deep in Unorganized Territory—that no-man's-land west of the States and months before California— snaking troupes of lurching oxen-yoked wagons stretch in length for more than two miles, the coaches' loose off-white bonnets swollen in warm, constant wind. When they travel single file—finding purchase on hard packed dirt or at a pinch point between river and cliff—sometimes the dust's so thick they can't make out the wagon in front of them. So when they can manage it, wagons fan out over the wide, flat prairie, flocks of them making ruts in scrubby grassland so as not to swallow another's dust, that unremitting menace of the trail.

And in pursuit of what? And where? By the end of each day, swatting at insects and camping by unnamed creeks, everyone—everything—is grimed with brownish-red powder as fine as newly milled flour. Where the harsh sun hasn't turned Ada's angular face and long, sinewy arms nut brown, sand and dirt pack the crevices. Her sweaty forehead and itchy scalp are caked with it, her grimy clothes rimmed with it. If she's ever needed a bath, today would be that day, although yesterday and tomorrow she's bound to say the same. She hasn't had a proper bath since Indiana, won't have another until California, if they even have bathtubs there.

It's late June and they've broken into smaller parties now, about a hundred and fifty in Ada's company, give or take single men who hover around the entourage like flies. Lilburn Boggs, former governor of Missouri, leads Ada's group after William Russell's sudden resignation in mid-June. Boggs is gruff, and an anti-Mormon crusader. Ada steers clear of him. Two of the other wagon leaders, George Donner and James Reed, travel with large families, multiple wagons, and a slew of dogs and horses and cows between them. Reed, assiduous to a fault, stands six feet tall, gaunt and bearded, with deep crow's feet at the edge of his eyes. He's a veteran of the Black Hawk War and a born leader. Donner's an inch or two shorter and unusually fit for a man of sixty with a voice that carries over two states.

"Wagons, ho!" is the rallying cry at dawn, and again after nooning. "Gee, haw, walk on, steady now," these, too, are trail words. And underneath these commands, there's rarely a moment a teamster's not yelling or a child's not bawling or someone's not complaining. Or cursing. Or shoving. Or swilling rotgut whiskey "for spiritual consolation." At night, there's fiddle playing. Ada taps her feet and hopes Dolan will ask her to dance.

Less than a week ago, just past where the Platte forks into two stems, the overlanders forded the South Platte and traveled north over a wide plateau to attain the North Platte. In the crux between rivers, they faced California Hill, rising starkly above the valley floor. The emigrants unloaded carefully packed wagons and double-teamed oxen before tackling the rise. A lone mockingbird perched atop a straggly juniper chastised the entourage as they bested the summit: *hurr-eep, hurr-eep, hurr-eep.* Ada thought it sounded like *hurry up hurry up hurry up.*

The next day, they found themselves at the north edge of the plateau, the North Platte almost in sight. Windlass Hill, dense with needle grass, yucca, and thistle, posed the emigrants' first difficulty. How to get the wagons down safely? And in one piece? At the crest, all Ada could see were a series of endless, undulating hills like a golden coverlet spreading clear to the horizon. There, she helped Ma Breen unload their wagon again, this time for the descent into a shady dell named Ash Hollow.

Ada carried a heavy Dutch oven in one hand and a jug of molasses in the other, careful not to slip on the steep downward slope. She's as strong as any woman (and taller than them all). Although it's not done that way—*and more's the pity*—Ada could have been of great use assisting men maneuver the wagons. But instead, she joined the caravan of women and children stumbling down the slope with prized possessions as testy wagoneers and cussing teamsters rough-locked rear wheels and inched empty, teetering wagons down the decline.

When all the wagons reached the grove, the overlanders rested for two days of wagon repair, laundry, and hoof trimming; hymn sings and gossip; shade and blessed naps. After their respite, the travelers grasped the North Platte, their river highway for four hundred miles west through Indian and buffalo country. At the juncture, the North Platte's a half foot deep and more than a quarter mile wide meandering over a bed of quicksand. Water's not fit to drink without filtering, and watch your children, dear mothers—this river's too testy to swim in.

Between sandy bluffs clothed in sage and greasewood, Ada's group goes full chisel (or, as fast as oxen can manage, two miles an hour on a good day, less on a fair day). Emigrant wagons follow a well-worn trail on the south side of the wide and muddy river. It's been three years since the trail burst wide open for westward travelers in 1843. More and more come west each year—thousands this year alone.

This morning, the emigrants are barely west of Courthouse Rock. Ada does a head count of the four eldest Breen boys: John, Edward, Patrick, Jr., and that rascal, Simon. The younger boys, James and Peter, stay close to their mother, who's toting Bella in a sling. They ford here at a narrow spot of the North Platte. Ada grits her teeth as she leads the mules across. She counts in Norwegian—*en, to, tre, fire, fem*—to keep her mind off the unpredictable river. Every crossing churns up fright. A person can disappear so fast.

"Watch it, now," Ada says. She grabs the mules' halter lines at the far side of the river. It's still at least an hour before the train rests at noon. Ada traces the sun's arc as it rises weightlessly in the sky. Flies buzz around her head as she walks to the left of the team—they all walk to the left, it's easier to keep track of one another that way. Too many children and dogs get caught beneath rolling wheels and there's not a damn thing to do about it.

"C'mon Bert. You, too, Rosie. Step it up."

The mules' long, pointed ears angle sideways as they listen and assess their surroundings. They fall in beside the Breen's wagon on the flat terrain, their doleful, fly-crusted eyes cast down.

When the train halts at noon, Ada stakes Bert and Rosie under a stand of cottonwoods. Why she's leading pack animals across the country is up for debate, but she doesn't want to let them loose—that would be tantamount to throwing good money away. No good Norwegian would do that. Plus she loves them; Rosie anyway. She could sell Bert at Fort Laramie or Fort Hall to swell the forty dollars Inger sewed into the hems of her skirt before leaving Independence. As Ada rummages in Rosie's pack, she feels a small package—*What is it?* She unrolls the cloth. *Ah, yes.*

Ada helps Ma Breen with the noon meal: another unremarkable round of bread, bacon, and beans. Bella's asleep under the wagon. The mutt, Muzzles, curls up beside Bella's cradle. James and Peter scamper through camp.

"Away, boys!" Ma Breen scowls. "And see to your brothers!" She turns to Ada. "And you go fetch Mr. Breen and Mr. Dolan. Tell them dinner's going cold."

Ada walks to the Reed wagon looking for Dolan. He's with a handful of teamsters and saddled horses.

"Dinner's on," Ada says.

"Be back in an hour," Dolan says. "I'm off to Chimney Rock."

Ada wades through a wake of dust in search of Breen. James and Peter scamper past with Simon and Patrick, Jr. in tow. She sees Patrick Breen talking to George Donner by the Donner camp and turns toward the men. Edward Breen stands by his father, chewing a long stem of grass.

"Ma says dinner's on, and gettin' cold."

"Be there when I get there," Breen says.

Edward walks back with Ada. When they return to camp, Ada

tells Ma Breen that Dolan's off with some teamsters and Breen will be along soon.

"I confess! I've half a mind to let Mr. Breen do his own cooking," the older woman says. "And Dolan'll be begging for vittles when he gets back. See if I save him any this time."

Ada brushes grime from her forehead and starts to dish up. Breen strides into camp and takes a plate. Ada serves him first. "Your turn, now," she says, as she hands out tin plates. The boys line up in order of age, oldest first.

"Did John go with Dolan, then?" Ma Breen asks.

Patrick Breen grunts. "Likely with the Reeds again."

"John's sweet on Virginia," Edward says. He puts his spoon down and pouts.

"You're sweet on Virginia, you mean," Simon interrupts.

Edward scowls at his brother and sticks out his tongue.

"Enough of that!" Ma Breen says. "I don't want to hear a whit more about anyone being sweet on anyone, you hear? Not until we're good and settled, wherever in Joseph and Mary's name that will be." She shakes her head. "A fine mess you've gotten us into, Mr. Breen, moving us again."

Ada waits for Ma Breen to serve up, and ladles the last of the meal for herself. She leaves a smidgeon for Dolan. Just as she is about to sit, a group of riders thunders into camp.

"Back so soon?" Ma Breen asks.

Ada puts her plate down, wipes her hands on her soiled apron, and stands with her hands on her hips. She squints into the sun. "It's not Dolan."

The riders pull up near the Breen's wagon.

"Who have we here?" Patrick Breen says. "I'd swear you've come from the west."

"Right you are," the leader answers. "Darwin Stakes, here. My friend, Verly Morse. Have any coffee for thirsty travelers?"

Ada tends the fire. "In a minute." She grabs the boys' tin mugs.

"Miss Ada!" Simon whimpers. "What're you doing that for?"

"Shush, young man. Don't you see we got company?" She rinses out the mugs, pours coffee, and hands steaming mugs to the men on horseback. They have not dismounted.

"Thank you, miss," Stakes says. "You're sure a tall one, aren't you?"

"Heard that before." *String Bean. Daddy Long Legs.*

"Where're you coming from?" Breen interrupts. "Better yet, where is it you're going?"

"Me and Morse here, we're headed back to the States." Stakes nods to the man beside him. "Went partway west for the adventure, plan to sign on to lead a westering party next year." He points to three grizzled horsemen, who linger behind the two men. "These fellas are headed back to Independence. Got in a scuffle with another party, you might say."

"Kicked out, you mean?" Edward pipes in.

"Let the man do his talking," Ma Breen scolds.

"You might say that, young fella. Don't want to mess with another man's woman."

"That's quite enough," Ma Breen snaps.

"Sorry, ma'am. Just telling the boy the God's honest truth. Met up a few days back and decided it was better to travel in numbers. Sometimes you can't trust another man, but you can't never trust Indians." He slurps the dregs of the coffee and thrusts the mug at Ada. "I'll take another cup if you're offering."

Ada takes Stakes's mug and returns to the fire. She pours to the brim and walks back to where Stakes sits, still mounted on his horse.

"Thanks, stick girl." As he reaches down for the mug, he pinches Ada's nipple. She swats his hand away and narrows her eyes.

"Got any letters to send back home to your sweetheart?" Stakes leers at Ada's soaking blouse and laughs. He's missing his two front teeth. "We'll deliver them for two bits. Or maybe you'd like to ride along with us? Deliver them yourself?"

Morse erupts in laughter. By now, other emigrants have assembled. Stakes and Morse are peppered with questions. What's the road like ahead? Have you seen any buffalo? How many wagons you reckon are ahead of us?

"I'd say five hunerd wagons, give or take, wouldn't you, Morse?"

Morse removes his grimed hat, runs his hand through thinning hair, and pumps his head. "It's not too rough ahead," he adds. "But you folks are a-ways behind."

"The forward party, how far ahead are they?" James Reed asks.

"Maybe a hunerd miles," Stakes says.

"More like a hunerd twenty-five," Morse adds.

Reed shakes his head.

George Donner joins the conversation. "What of the Sioux?"

"Won't bother you if you're traveling in a big company like this," Stakes says. "Just watch your horses at night. And your women."

He swipes at his mouth and laughs.

"Thanks again for the coffee, stick girl." He spits at Ada's feet. "Wish you was coming along with us. We like our girls big"—he puts his hands under his chest and hoists them up, like he's cradling large breasts—"and tough. This girl here fits the bill on both accounts, don't she, Morse?"

The men ride out of camp in a wake a dust. Ada coughs and swats at air. As she rinses out dishes, she spies a lone vulture circling in the distance. *If those ruffians have met with trouble, it wouldn't bother me none.*

The night of the fire, Ada awoke with a start, and nothing—not even the taste of milk—was the same ever again.

Augustus and Inger collected her the next day from the minister's house, where neighbors delivered the wide-eyed child, who they found huddled in her parents' room clutching her mother's housedress.

"She'll do," Inger Vik had said. "Ve can use da help." Ada was eleven at the time, big boned and awkward and not particularly pretty. That was eight long years ago—days and months largely defined by three plain meals a day and little conversation. But it saved her from being shipped to the orphan's asylum, which Inger reminded her daily.

Ada learned early on it was better to do what Inger asked of her; otherwise, there would be sour looks, mutterings, smaller portions at supper. Inger only once alluded to Ada's hazy future. "You'll need to find yourself a husband."

Husbands were the last things on Ada's mind. It was all she could do to keep up with her studies—and help Augustus in his business (Inger pronounced his name *Ow-goos-tus).* Sundays were for church— devout Lutherans the Viks were, although Ada wondered secretly if Augustus was all that religious. He told bawdy jokes and passed Ada snuff on the side. He also teased her mercilessly about her bookkeeping skills. "Vit a mind like yours, you could go to university. But not for mathematics!" Maybe that was Augustus's answer to having Ada leave home, without the threat of a finding a husband.

Two months before, Ada had prescience that something was wrong, very wrong. Was it the absence of sound from Inger's kitchen? Or the way the wind lifted her curtain to reveal a dark stain of rainclouds overhead? Was it the smell of a distant thunderstorm, humid and sour? Or the crackle of the air, like invisible fireworks? For the first time in eight years, Inger had not woken Ada with her severe, "Is morning, Ada," as she pulled the covers from Ada's bed (Inger pronounced her name *Ah-dah).*

Ada shimmied into her plain clothes and descended the narrow stairway to the kitchen. Inger was packing kitchenware.

"Ve are leaving, Ada. Going vest," her mamma said.

Ada stared at Inger. She would be on her own again.

"So you'll be Ada Veeks now," Inger continued.

"Veeks?" Ada countered. Her mind was spinning like a child's top.

"Veeks, vit a double 'v'. Ve must be more like Americans, have a name people recognize. Is nice, no? Veeks."

Ada Weeks. So she would be going west with the Viks after all. She'd have to get used to another name, though. First, she'd been Ada Hubbard. Then Ada Vik, and now Ada Weeks. *Can't get too attached to a name.*

Within days, the Viks headed west in a newly minted wagon pulled by two strong oxen. They reached Independence, Missouri, late on a Friday. At this last bastion of civilization at the knife-edge of the country, men lined up at feed stores, saloon doors, and ill-concealed bawdy houses; women bent their bonneted heads as they hurried up and down noisy and crowded wooden sidewalks; children scampered between wagons and jangling harnesses and dung.

Over the next few days, Ada helped Inger lay in supplies: eight hundred pounds flour, six hundred pounds bacon, two hundred pounds beans, and a hundred pounds coffee. Augustus extracted two hundred dollars from a hiding place in the false floor of the wagon box. "Ve need some pack mules. If da vagon gives out, or I need to go on ahead, ve'll still have a vay to go on."

At night, Inger painstakingly sewed forty dollars of silver coin into the hems of Ada's skirt. "Is not much," Inger said. "But—*Gud* forbid it!—you vill have enough in case anything happens. And it vill keep your skirt from—vat is da vord?—*hatching* up."

"You mean hitchin' up?"

"Vat I mean is it von't show your unmentionables ven you valk." Inger glared at Ada as she bit off the end of the thread. "Ven ve make it to California"—(Ada can still hear in her memory how Inger elongated the syllables: Cal-ee-forn-ee-ah)—"*da er det værste bak oss.* Dat is ven all da hard going vill be behind us."

Inger handed a small package to Ada. *"Om det blir for ille, åpner vi den.* If ve hit hard times, ve open it."

"What is it?" Ada asked.

Inger made that clucking sound that signaled worry. "Is jerked meat. Yust in case."

When the Viks crowded in as much as they could transport, they set their eyes on the Overland Trail due west to Oregon or California. The choice to turn around and go back home didn't cross their minds, or, if it did, they only whispered it.

So it was, on a balmy Tuesday that might not have signaled any remarkable occasion on a Tuesday back home, the Viks signed on with the William Russell Party headed to California by way of Oregon Territory. They signed the register: Augustus Weeks, 51; Inger Weeks, 49; and Ada Weeks, 19.

When their company left Independence, there'd been a thousand in the westering party, mostly farmers and businessmen, from places like Springfield, Illinois, and Woodsfield, Ohio, and Keokuk, Iowa. Most of the overlanders traveled with families and teamsters and enough lowing and bleating animals to scare up God himself, heirlooms crammed in next to the mundane. Every jockey box rumbled as ironclad wheels crunched over rough dirt; every kettle and butter churn and lantern and scythe clanked against wagon sideboards. Almost all of the westerners walked. Only the sickly or elderly rode in jarring wagon boxes that creaked over uneven ground.

Ada doesn't have much hope for the sickly. She regrets her parents didn't do more for the widow Keyes. All they could do was help bury her. They were good at that. *And now they are dead, too.*

Dolan pulls into camp an hour later and tips his hat to Ma Breen. "Sorry to miss dinner, ma'am. But it's not every day you can climb a column like that. Could see halfway to Ireland, I could! Scratched my initials into it, too: *J-P-D.*"

He winks at Ada. Ada's in no mood for flirtation. She packs the last of the plates and utensils and avoids conversation.

"I saved you some eats," Ma Breen says.

"Knew you would," Dolan says. He winks at Ma Breen, then.

"Don't you get cozy with me, young fellow. Won't get you nowhere. And I thought you went by Patrick. Why the *J*?" Ma Breen asks.

"John, after my grandfather."

"So it's John Patrick Dolan, then?"

"Indeed. Born County Clare, 1816."

"We've had visitors—" Ma Breen begins.

Bastards, Ada thinks.

Dolan looks up. "Who?"

"No account hooligans," Ma Breen answers. "Headed back East, and good riddance. They weren't too mannerly with Miss Weeks."

Dolan shoots Ada a concerned look.

"Weren't nothin' I haven't heard before," Ada says. *Stick girl.*

Ma Breen continues. "Word is, it's not too rough the next hundred miles. That's good news for the animals, anyway."

"Wish I'd known," Dolan says. "I have a letter for my ma, could have sent it along with them. What about you, Miss Ada? You sent any letters on?"

"Don't have anyone to write to."

Captain Boggs rides past the wagon. He doesn't stop as he hollers, "Wagons, ho! Step it up, now, boys!"

Ada stuffs the last of the kitchenware into the wagon and runs for the mules. She untethers Rosie and Bert and ushers them toward the dusty trail. She's tempted to look back at Chimney Rock, but it's bad luck, like the biblical story of Lot's wife when she gazes back at Sodom. Ada is superstitious enough, so she doesn't tempt fate. It's always eyes to the west along the long, uncertain road.

Everything in California will be better, she reminds herself: the climate, the abundance of water, the soil. Lansford Hastings said so. Three or four well-thumbed copies of Hastings's *Emigrants' Guide to Oregon and California* circulate among the travelers. Before they died, Ada read aloud to the Viks:

> *You will find in California the most extensive plains, beautiful prairies, and fertile valleys . . . in one day's ride, you will pass over every possible variety of soil. The California mountains are covered with a great variety of vegetation, as well as by their affording in many places, a great abundance of good timber: fir, pine, cedar, 'red wood,' spruce, oak, ash, and poplar.*

"That will surely help, will it not? For the coffins?" Augustus Vik had grunted.
"And Mamma, Pappa, listen."

> *The climate is that of perpetual spring, having no excess of heat or cold; it is the most uniform and delightful . . . running water never freezes . . . both the climate and the soil are eminently adapted to the growing of wheat, rye, oats, barley, beans, hemp, flax, tobacco, cotton, rice, coffee, corn, and cane . . .*

Inger Vik looked at Augustus. "Did you hear dat? Ve can grow coffee!"
"I heard tobacco," Augustus said, winking at Ada.
Inger swatted at her husband as Ada continued reading.

> *. . . and there you will find a great variety of grapes . . .*

"I reckon I'll dream of grapes," Ada interrupted.

Tasting a grape is one of the reasons Ada keeps plodding west. *That, and a bath. And a feather bed. And . . .*

As the wagons get underway after nooning, Ada straps Isabella Breen to her chest. To protect Bella from the relentless sun, she covers the baby's head with Augustus's hanky. Now, hanky-less herself, Ada breathes in an inescapable stream of dust churned up by wagon wheels and oxen and horses and mules.

James Reed pulls up from behind on his large mare, Glaucus. He reins her in and yells across four wagons. "Put your shoulders to the work, boys. Another eight miles to go. Scotts Bluff's straight ahead."

Teamsters nod, and hurry the animals. There's no rest to be had, except for a few hours' uncomfortable sleep each night under wagons, or, if you're lucky, on lumpy bedrolls inside sagging canvas tents. There's no room in wagons.

Five miles west of Chimney Rock and closer to the next monolith ahead, Ada hands Bella back to Ma Breen. The Irishwoman—like all the women on the train—wears haggardness on her face like an assault. It's nothing but cooking and tending children and laundry: wash, rinse, dry, repeat. Maybe at night, after coffee and beans and storytelling and fiddle playing, there's time to knit or mend or write a few scratches in an overland journal, if you can keep your eyes open that long.

Ada kicks rust-colored dirt and raises a small cloud of dust. It settles on her battered boots and bare ankles. Roughly five hundred miles are now behind the emigrants, and there are more than a thousand to go. Each step is fraught with uncertainty—there are pregnant women, sickly infants, and shuffling old men, including a near-deaf Belgian named Hardkoop. Will any of them survive this journey?

That's a question that surfaces with every revolution of the sun. Today could be the day. Or tomorrow. Death comes knocking without an invitation. One never knows. If there's one thing Ada's sure of, it's that she hasn't seen the end of it.

First, and without warning, she lost her parents, the ma and pa who tried their best to raise her. Then, in a flash of mud and panic, she lost the Viks, the mamma and pappa who took her in after the fire. She is, as Scripture says, well acquainted with grief.

Now she's tagging along with a family of Irish Catholics like a poor postulant, although she's not Catholic or Lutheran or Episcopalian, like many in the westering party (and she's certainly not a Mormon—Captain Boggs would have seen to that). What she is, is ambiguous. She's got a rocky relationship with God, and for good reason.

Ada shades her eyes as the sun fades below the wide, western horizon. It's the close of another long, scorching day and she's tuckered. She rambles into camp, stakes the mules, and pauses before going to help with supper. By now, the sky is awash with copper and salmon and gold. She inhales, holds her breath, and exhales. That there can be such beauty and such sorrow in one life is perplexing.

"Ada!"

She reties her limp apron and pins up her straggly hair. "Comin'!"

As she hastens to camp, Ada glances once more to the west, that place of destiny and doubt. All bets are off where any of them will end up. If at all.

Dyin's gonna get us all in the end, one way or the other, she thinks. *But dyin's not the hardest part. Livin's a lot harder than dyin' any day.*

3

June 29, 1846
Alta California

The man swings his arms above his head and brings the ax down with a forceful thud. For one so used to seeing from horizon to horizon, he's hemmed in here in the foothills of the Sierra Nevadas. His clearing houses a small cabin, lean-to, and woodpile. It's the woodpile that's cornered his attention today, his chopping stump surrounded by splinters. His sleeves are rolled to the elbow and beads of sweat cover his temple. Stringy, dark hair droops over his face. When he focuses on a project, his tongue lolls to the side of his mouth. If he knew, he would pay attention to it, but he doesn't realize he pants like an overheated dog when he's working. It's been so long since anyone's noticed anything about him—his long legs, his lean waist, or the large scar running from his left eye and disappearing in a scraggly beard down to the jaw.

The creek burbles in the background and the wind soughs lazily through cottonwoods. A chorus of frogs, the chitter of squirrels—these are the things that keep the man company as he labors, one hour sliding into another until he realizes he's downright famished. He wipes his brow and sets the ax down.

After the panic of 1837, he'd shelved his plans to farm in Wisconsin

Territory. And there was that other sadness, the one so great he thought he'd suffocate from surviving it. He often wished, in the years that followed, that he, too, could have shriveled and died. But no, he was condemned to the living, and with it, the brutal realization that once someone—someone you loved beyond breathing—no longer draws breath, that each time your lungs fill with air, the world does not contain that which sustained you before, and the simple, involuntary act of inhaling is as painful as if someone has kicked you in the gut and knocked the wind clear out of your lungs and you struggle, there on the ground, knees writhing, gasping for thin reeds of air.

He left Wisconsin Territory soon after, and did what he could to make two nickels. Frost on his beard, eyelashes frozen together, he'd pick trap lines with cracked fingers to extract muskrat and wolverine. Back aching and thighs bowed, he'd ride a thousand miles doing more of the same, eking out a living by cheating the seasons, earlier in the spring, later in the fall, more of the same, the ground his bed, the constellations his ceiling. He'd meet familiar faces on his travels east or west and spend a night or two trading tobacco and ammo and sharing stories and meals, and once, an Indian woman. She had been fine, very fine.

But he much prefers being alone. It's easier, this semi-monastic life that it is. He stacks logs in neat rows, chest high, then lugs an armful to the cabin's porch, where he drops the load with a thump. There's a large carved sign above the cabin's crude door. He'd carved it the first winter he was here, 1845. A pair of vagabonds passing through had laughed when they read it. Good one, they said. Rufous, his only neighbor, can't read, so he'll never get the pun. Others who have passed by—trappers and gold seekers and military men—either haven't thought to ask him, or can't read themselves. Well, he can't read, either. He'd asked someone at Sutter's Fort to spell it out for him, and the clerk wrote it out on a piece of brown paper. As the man labored over the letters, he recognized the letter *A*. It was a start.

It suits the man, the simplicity of it all: the clearing, the cabin, the creek. He's lived on and off the land the past nine years, and this is as good—maybe even better—a home as any he has ever known. It's blue oak woodland, peppered with grey pine and western redbud. Cottonwoods choke the creek. In a grove of pine, he's cleared an area fifty yards on each side of the cabin to keep pinecones and leaves and branches from crashing onto the roof. And game and fowl are plenty. It's a place that suits him perfectly. One thing's for sure, he can't keep running away—any further west, and he'll be in the great Pacific Ocean, over his head in sea foam. And he's not much for swimming, never has been.

The raven's "*barrrrh*" disturbs his thoughts. At first, the pair of birds were more like old friends, living high in the scrub pine at the edge of his property. Old One, he calls the male; The Missus, the female. Lately, he's soured on them. Some mornings he can't get his thoughts straight, the ravens bicker so much. They mate for life, he remembers. Got to be a squabble now and again. But now and again is every day now, so much so the man's taken to heaving a rock in the general direction of the nest to shut them up. He'd never harm them, just gives them a scare—anything to quiet their incessant barking. The female's left the nest this week, so abrupt calls from the raven's perch are more profuse and harsh. *Could be calling for her,* the man thinks. *Could be hungry, who knows?* Although he knows it's madness, he empathizes with the raven. He's known loneliness and hunger and pain, too.

If it hadn't been for Rufous when he hobbled into the clearing last year, he might've died from the knife wound. Paiute. Poor bugger didn't live to see the sunset. The man left the body there in the Sierras; the boy's people would know what to do with him.

It had been two weeks of hide and seek with the young brave. Once the man realized the Indian was tracking him, he made a game of it. Fleet of foot as any, hostile or not, the man swung down into gullies and back up ridges, sleeping without benefit of firelight. But for all his stealth, the Paiute found him every morning. The brave kept his distance.

"Aren't afraid of you," the man yelled into the stand of trees where the Indian stood, silent and resolute. "If you got some business with me, better you tell me, 'cause I'm getting tired of your company."

For thirteen days, the Indian followed him. On the morning of the fourteenth day, the man changed course. He placed his bundle under his blanket in the form of a man. He placed his hat where the head would be and left his unloaded rifle beside the sleeping phantom. He lit a smoldering fire to bring the Indian in. Then he circled back into the woods and waited. He didn't take his horse, which was his biggest gamble. When the Paiute appeared at the edge of camp at dawn, the man tiptoed toward him and grabbed him around the throat. The boy swung around, his knife brandished, and he struck the man in the face, slicing him from eye to jaw. Dripping blood, the man lunged and knocked the knife from his attacker's hands.

"Is that how we say hello?" The man wrestled the native to the ground and pinned him to the moist earth. The Indian did not register fear. He peered at the man with utter calm. He wasn't more than eighteen, thin and muscular, with piercing brown eyes. The man had expected something different—pleading or panic. They locked eyes.

Why had this Indian followed him for two weeks? Was it a vendetta for another white man's wrongdoing? A ploy to steal his horse? Or an honor killing to prove he was a man? The man wasn't sure. But it was him or the Indian, and he was going to make darn sure it wasn't him. Even when the man forced his knife flat across the Indian's throat, the young brave did not flinch. It was over in a second, as the Indian's soul flew to the spirit world. The man wiped blood off his knife before he mopped his own face.

"Whoa, there," the man heard when he rode into Rufous's clearing. "What the devil?" Rufous helped him down from the horse, washed the wound, trussed him up right. "Got a shed for ya," Rufous said. "It ain't much."

"Don't need much," the man said.

"Welcome to stay as long as you like. But it ain't free. Need some fences built. Could use a fella like you. I don't ask no questions."

"You've got yourself a deal, then," the man said. He has been on the creek ever since.

The man resumes his chore. He's got his own place now, spitting distance from Rufous. They trap together, go to town once every couple of months, sometimes go on a bender, laughing and carousing into the night like a couple of hawbucks, one white and one dark.

The raven ruffles its feathers and launches from the pine, its iridescent wingspan near four feet across. The feathered ends of its tapered tail gleam purplish as it wings west. The clearing is quiet now except for a crack as the ax head finds purchase. The man is glad the raven has gone off to hunt. It's quieter now. But, like clockwork, he knows the great black bird will be back before nightfall, issuing jarring calls to empty report. Long after midnight, they'll each settle in, nursing their loneliness in the untamed foothills of the vast and formidable Sierra Nevadas.

4

July 3, 1846
Beaver Creek, Unorganized Territory

Ada strides to keep up with the wagon, her legs as long as any man's. The North Platte is never out of sight. They stick to the south side of the wide, treeless river. It's maddening that timbered islands choke the length of the Platte. All that willow! But braided channels and treacherous quicksand make for difficult crossings, let alone forages for firewood. And the water's still so muddy, it's unfit to drink without filtering or settling.

Yesterday had been a rough, difficult stretch over gravel and cobble. Patrick Breen tied a red handkerchief onto the spokes of one of the rear wagon wheels in a crude attempt to count miles. Simon and Peter counted the revolutions as they walked: *forty-one, forty-two, forty-three,* before they got tired of that game and ran ahead to chase the Reed girls. Breen muttered, and continued the count. It was the surest way to know how far they'd traveled on any given day.

Today, the dry, sandy soil along the river takes its toll on oxen. Teams are tired and sweaty. Wheels sink eight or ten inches with each turn as teams slog up the river's edge, sixteen miles since sun up. Breen resorts to the whip for the first time. At the junction of the North Platte and Beaver Creek in the high prairie five days west of

Fort Laramie, the wagon train lumbers south to lay over a day. It's the day before Independence Day, a good enough day as any to take time off trail driving.

Ada walks shoulder to the sun, swiping at buffalo gnats as she swishes through tall grasses. Above the quiet prairie, she spots another butterfly, this one close enough to touch, its spotted ginger wings a stark contrast to the tired yellow of weathered grass. Each dry, dusty day brings its share of whining black-winged blue bottles, droning dragonflies, and pesky flies. Ada makes a game of counting butterflies—it helps pass the time. She counts thirty-one before noon and more than fifty afterward, but gets distracted at fifty-three when she trips over a prairie dog hole. Her boot plunges into the soft earth, and she wriggles it free. Ada hopes Simon doesn't see that butterfly hovering ahead. If he were to spot it, he'd be quick to pounce, his long-handled net crashing down to capture it.

"Waste of time, boy," Patrick Breen ridicules Simon. "Leave it to those useless scholar boys, not a one of them worth shite. Reading science or letters? What's the good in that? Don't put food on the table. Pray that you don't make that mistake."

If only I had the chance, Ada thinks. *What does prayer have to do with it anyway?* Best-laid plans shiver before plain dumb luck, like a broken axletree or a tear in the bonnet, a crushed hand, or worse. Ada spurs the mules, stops to wipe out their dusty nostrils. But she can't linger: it's rise and shine, move on, git yer lazy ass up and goin', dammit. *Pray all you want,* she thinks. *In the end, it's all up to chance.*

A long "whoaaaaaa!" rumbles down the train. The emigrants suspend their trek near a conical hill covered with buffalo grass along the banks of Beaver Creek. For the first time, they don't circle wagons up. Instead, wagons dot the large, bowl-shaped valley, each family seeking as much privacy as traveling in a group of more than a hundred allows. As Ada pins the mules by the creek, she spies chokecherry at the base of the hill. *Never know when you'll need it. Wards off fever.*

Ada scurries to help with supper. First, she digs a short, narrow trench, sets the tripod, and hangs the Dutch oven. She's tired of dry bread, beans, and bacon for breakfast and noon. Supper's the same fare as last night—salt pork and the rind of this morning's loaf. At least, there's fresh water.

The Breens have seven mouths to feed, same as Jacob and Elizabeth Donner. Lots of big families with four, five, six children apiece. Other families have one or two children. Only the German couple, the Wolfingers, is childless. For all their blessings, children are also a liability. There's snakes and drowning, illnesses and separation, and the constant worry of falling under unforgiving wagon wheels.

Ada can't keep track of all the single men, stock handlers and wagon drivers. One looks like the next, dressed in drab trousers, filthy shirts, and scuffed boots. Always a grubby hat, a tired belt (rope, even), and a face smeared with grease and grime. More often than not, they're arguing—fighting some nights—marking their territory, like dogs. She hears them called by their last names only—Spitzer, Herron, Reinhardt—as if their mothers never gave them proper Christian names. Last week a handful of these single men decided to trade in their wagons and oxen for mules to move quicker along the trail toward California. Ada was heart sore to see the newspaperman Edwin Bryant go along with them. His stories at night were worth cheating sleep.

Ada tiptoes to the edge of Beaver Creek. She throws her boots, now cobbled together with twine, in the matted grass behind her. She sits on a ledge, her bare feet dangling in cool water. Two of her blisters have popped, and the water feels refreshing as it rushes over her dust-caked soles. Mayflies hover above the creek's surface and bits of debris float down the narrow channel. Creeks don't bother her much; you can't drown in one too easily. And the water's much clearer than the muddy Platte. She cups her hand and takes a sip.

Ada listens as wildfowl settle in for the night along the sluggish tributary that winds back on itself in large, lazy esses through this flat spot in the hollow. Ducks and sandpipers and geese nest nearby. In the distance, just to the south, a large red canyon rises from the high prairie, an anomaly in the otherwise flat plains.

"Care if I join you?

"Mr. Bryant! You're back!" Ada's heart quickens.

"Couldn't miss the Glorious Fourth with old friends. Turns out we were only a few days ahead of you. Not surprising we can get along faster without wagons."

"Without women and children, you mean."

"You said it, not me. But I'm still getting used to mules."

"I've got two of them. Bert and Rosie. My pappa bought them in Independence. Fellow there said they were about twelve, maybe thirteen. 'Best age for a mule,' he said, although I don't know if we could trust anythin' he said. He said they were siblings, but I rather doubt it. Bert's cranky as an old man, and Rosie's sweet as honey."

"Mine's named Frank. Maybe he's Bert's brother. Hee-haws every time I try to get him to move along faster."

"Oh, they got a mind of their own, mules do. Can I let you in on a little secret?"

"And that would be?"

"They love sweets. That's somethin' the fellow said that's right as rain."

"Aha. I'll pack in loaf sugar when we're off again tomorrow," Bryant says. "And off we'll be. I am beginning to feel alarmed at the tardiness of our movements, not so much for myself, but for you women and children, Miss Weeks, isn't it?"

Ada nods. "Yes, sir."

"Well, Miss Weeks, I'm fearful that winter will find us in the snowy mountains of California, or that we shall suffer from the exhaustion of our supply of provisions if we don't make better progress on this trail." Bryant saunters to the creek and stands above her. He is mid-height, yet stately, with crinkles around deep-set eyes. "'No man ever steps in the same river twice, for it's not the same river and he's not the same man.'"

"Heraclitus?"

"A-plus. You must have paid attention in school."

"Didn't have much else to do, sir. Exceptin' readin' and studyin' and helpin' around the house."

"Heaven to my ears. But you don't talk like a book, Miss Weeks. Ought to watch your g's. You leave the last letter off of your words and people think you're from Tennessee."

"But my pa were from Tennessee. That's how he and his kin talked. I never thought I were talkin' funny 'til my ma harped on me." Ada feels a pang in her chest. *Ma.* "I don't think about it now that's there's no one naggin' me on it."

"We've all got our rough edges, you might say," Bryant continues, interrupting her thoughts. "Not a bad idea to straighten some of them out. Like chewing tobacco. A habit I just can't seem to shake." He spits a yellowish brown dribble into the grass. "Say, I'm off on a jaunt. Aim to explore a natural wonder of the world, not a mile from here."

"A natural wonder?"

"See those rocks there?" Bryant points upstream to where the wall of red rock bursts out of the high prairie. Ada nods. "Seen on maps there's a rock bridge spanning the gap up that canyon," he continues. "Natural, not the work of man or beast, but carved over time. Any newspaperman worth his salt wouldn't let a chance like this slip away. A miss is as good as a mile, Miss Weeks. Some people turn that phrase to mean they've avoided disaster. Way I look at it, if we don't take advantage of every opportunity, *poof,* it's gone, like breath you can't get back in again." He tips his chin upward and blows into the air.

"Mind if I tag along?"

Bryant scratches his chin. "You're traveling with Breen?"

Ada nods.

"Give me a minute. I'll ask him if I can unburden him from one or two of those boys of his for an hour or two. Wait here."

Ada colors. Of course, she'll need someone to chaperone her, going off into the wilds of Indian country with a man she hardly knows. *And a famous one, at that.* She laces her boots over her tender feet. The thought of walking two extra miles tonight—one upstream and another down—is about as tempting as walking on shards of glass. But to see a natural wonder . . .

Simon Breen bounds into the grass with Edwin Bryant close behind.

"We have a taker! Breen says be back before long. Not exactly a hail fellow well met, is he? Here, may I?" Bryant takes Ada's hand and helps her up. As soon as she's standing, Bryant drops her hand as if it's a hot coal. Simon runs ahead.

Ada matches Bryant's long strides as they amble alongside Beaver Creek toward the canyon.

"That was a right shame your parents disappeared on the Big Blue."

"I miss them," Ada says. "Maybe not as much as I thought I would, though. Sometimes . . ." She pictures Augustus sharing his tobacco. "Never mind."

"Don't get off that easy, Miss Weeks. Do tell."

"I were just thinkin' of my adoptive father. He were good to me, in a stern way. Knew how to make me laugh. But the Viks—they weren't my real parents. Lost them to a fire. 1838." She looks away. "You might say my ma and me were close. Not my pa, though. He were rough."

"Rough with you?"

"No, not so much. With others. With my ma."

Bryant sets his mouth into a fine line, nods. "I know something about that myself, Miss Weeks. Hardly knew my father. Mother's name was Silence, if that gives you any indication. What do you mean, close to your mother once?"

Ada takes a moment before she answers. Her first eleven years she spent at the farm, her mother dropping babies every year, and not a one of them living past the first three months. Milk fever. Bouts of depression. And then the accidental smothering. Her mother had not been right in the head afterwards. Ada put all the baby clothes, newly laundered, pressed, and folded, away again in the cedar chest under her mother's feather bed, until the next time. "Lost too many babies. Melancholia."

"Was she sent away? To an asylum?" Bryant asks.

"No, thank heavens. But my pa didn't know what to do most days. More often than not, we ate cold beans, and then he'd try to make things right, tell me a story. My ma would say, 'Your pa, he can go on 'til the candles burn low. Not a word of truth to any of it, Ada.'"

Yes, her pa was a great storyteller. But her ma ignored her pa's shortcomings. *Is that what love does to a person? Overlook the bruises? Forgive once, and again, and again?* Ada noticed little things, like how her pa stiffened up the day after he rolled the wagon. He'd lost his best horse that day and never walked straight again. He was a master of cutting corners, especially when he thought no one was looking—strangling a deformed calf, tying his crusted saddle together with strips of old leather, cheating his neighbor by three dollars after haying. He hadn't secured the lantern the night of the fire. It still haunts her. Her mother had been expecting again.

"Should be against the law, a man committing his wife without her consent," Bryant says. "Almost had my hide ridden out of Kentucky for saying so. Lost more than a few subscribers to the *Louisville Daily Courier* over that editorial. Among others."

A tapered red-rimmed canyon looms ahead. Ada scans the chokepoint in the ruddy rocks and sees a tight opening from where the creek escapes and rushes toward the North Platte. Deep cracks and fissures line the craggy cliffs, as if they could crumble at a sneeze. Simon wades in the shallow streambed through the narrow slot in the wall of red rock. Ada holds her breath. As Simon passes through the tight gap, a trickle of pebbles falls into the stream from somewhere high above, but the cliffs still stand. Ada squeezes through, her hands on either wall to help her keep her balance. She breathes shallowly, hoping against hope she won't upset the delicate balance of nature. Bryant brings up the rear, his booming voice behind them.

"Hoo-ey, Miss Weeks! Have you ever seen anything like it?"

Ada wonders if a voice alone can cause a canyon to crumble. If it could, Edwin Bryant has such a voice.

Inside the gap, gorge walls rise several hundred feet, striated in uneven layers of ochre, salmon, russet, and tan. It's as if someone's made a rock pancake over thousands of years and left it to dry, smoothed and ironed by wind and water and time. Ada follows the tawny ribbon of rough-edged rock as it winds deep into the canyon, multi-colored layers streaked with blood-red smears of cinnamon.

As Ada rounds the corner, she gasps. Rising more than fifty feet, a natural archway spans the width of the canyon, straddling the creek. Ada moves up the gravelly bank of the stream, mesmerized. Simon runs ahead and splashes in the creek under the formation, shouting. His words echo off the underside of the bridge: *heloo heloo heloo.*

Ada's boots are sopping. She'd love to kick them off, but that would mean putting them back on again. Soon she's shaded from the sun in the underbelly of the bridge. She leans against the cool side of the red sandstone and lets out a long, whistling exhale.

"Never."

"Excuse me?" Bryant asks.

"Never have I seen such a sight."

"You must remember Vermillion Creek."

"That rainbow?"

"Yes," Bryant says. "No Roman general, in all his gorgeous triumphal processions, ever paraded beneath an arch so splendid and imposing." Bryant waves his arms. "And now this." He leaves Ada in the cool of the bridge's underside and splashes upstream. "Be back in a moment." He rifles in his pocket and produces a sheaf of newspaper. "Here. Never know when you'll need it."

Ada colors. She uses grass to wipe herself. Newspaper would be a luxury.

Simon cavorts in the stream, gathering armfuls of water and tossing it upward. He stands underneath the droplets as they fall, like a rain shower. He is soaked through and laughing. "Look, Miss Ada! I'm wet as a new lamb!"

Ada waves to Simon but doesn't budge from underneath the arch. She breathes in and out, eyes sweeping the scenery. After the dust and heat of the day, this is a refuge, a heavenly oasis if she's ever seen one. If she could put down roots like cottonwoods lining the creek, she would be happy to stay here for the rest of her life.

When Ada was six, she wandered back behind the milking shed on her ma and pa's farm outside Noblesville. As she crossed the long meadow, the sun glinted off the tops of dewy wildflowers and grasses. She waded through the pasture, singing, her long arms and legs keeping beat with her tune. When a monarch caught her eye, she followed its flitting, meandering path to where the meadow angled down to Butler's Creek. When she reached the banks, she splashed in the shallows, and sat—clothes and all—and cooled off. The butterfly lit onto a branch and stilled its orange and black wings. Ada watched the beautiful creature until shadows swallowed it. When she squinted, she could still see it there, regal and motionless. Ada went to the creek every day to visit her new friend and to get away from her mother's sadness, as weather (and her mother's moods) allowed. Ada imagined building a fort and living there by the creek, away from crying and screaming and dead babies. So she began building, gathering rocks for the foundation and branches for the walls. But she never got to finish. Her dream of life on the creek fizzled after the fire.

Staying in that place, or in this place under the natural bridge—*or any place,* she thinks—is as likely as ice cream for supper, so Ada revels in the coolness here until Bryant signals it's time to go and she picks up her pace to follow him back to camp. This time, she does look back. She won't turn to salt like Lot's wife. Or will she?

As she turns, Ada catches her breath. By now, the canyon is awash with radiant color, swaths of corals and salmons where the sun still beats on age-old walls. As soon as the sun abandons the rock face, the colors change abruptly to deeper shades of russet and burgundy. Deeper into the canyon, that place of shadow between light and dark, the walls have already turned to maroon and chocolate where the sun has long left tail. The image of all these shades of red burns itself into her brain, one used to only the burnt shades of yellow and brown.

When they are almost back to camp, Simon slips. He falls sideways and lands on his leg. "Ow!" he yells. Bryant lifts the boy from the water and carries him to the side of the creek bed. He palpitates Simon's ankle and calf, squeezing and prodding the young boy's leg. "Studied medicine for a short time," he says. "Not two weeks back, I was called to a neighboring train on account of my reputation. Misguided, at best. I'm no physician. Nasty business that day, taking the leg of a young boy."

Simon's eyes widen.

Ada kneels next to Simon and props his back. She reaches down to palpitate the boy's leg. "Not broken," she says. "Might have a sprain, Simon. When we get back, I'll wrap it up tight. Don't go puttin' any stock in what Mr. Bryant's alludin' to. There'll be none of that here." She gives Bryant a sidelong glance.

"Hoo-ey, Miss Weeks. If that doesn't cap it all. Chastised like a schoolboy. But you saved me from ripping my shirt plumb off to save the boy's leg." He lifts Simon from the bank. "Looks like you'll live to see another day, young man." He carries Simon like a baby, even though the boy is almost nine.

"Where'd you study medicine?" Ada asks.

"Apprenticed under my uncle, Peter Bryant. You may have heard of my cousin, William Cullen Bryant? The poet? His father taught me physicking. How is it you've learned so much about anatomy?"

"Some book learnin'. Learning," she corrects herself. "And my pappa were an undertaker. I've seen more bodies than I can count." Ada splashes in the shallows, cleaning dirt and grass from her soles.

Bryant places his hand on Ada's elbow. "Can't step in the same river twice. Remember that, Miss Weeks. If you don't take advantage, you'll miss all this changing world has to offer. You've got to be willing to stray off course, see the opportunity, not the obstacle." He scuffs his boots. "Why, a couple of weeks ago, I saw a death and a funeral, a wedding and a birth, all in the space of two miles and two hours' time. Such are the dispensations of Providence!—such the checkered map of human suffering and human enjoyment. No choice but to keep on at this life before our Maker deems fit to take us." He reaches for tobacco and stuffs a wad into his cheek. "Do you consider yourself bold, Miss Weeks?"

"Can't say that I do." Although she had just risked turning into a pillar of salt. But not bold enough to ask for snuff.

"Girl like you, big-boned, tall, if you don't mind me saying. Many a fella's going to pass you by on account of your height."

Stick girl.

"Hell, you're a half-foot taller than most. Put some grit behind it, that's my advice. No excuse for weakness."

"I don't consider myself weak," Ada says. "Not particularly."

"Then live boldly, like a man."

The sound of Patrick Breen's fiddle steers them into camp.

"Be saying my good-nights now." Edwin Bryant tips his hat. "Think on what I've said, Miss Weeks."

Ada sets Simon on a campstool. She begs strips of cloth from Ma Breen and works the cloth around Simon's leg until it's tight. After she's satisfied with the wrapping, Ada says her good-nights, hobbles the mules, and prepares to bed down.

She crawls under the wagon to look for a flat spot. Her head almost touches the bottom of the wagon as she tosses rocks from a level patch of dirt and grass. If only she had hay to line the ground (and she doesn't have a tarpaulin anymore). Ada unfurls her bedroll, shakes it out, and lays it on the cleared spot. She wedges against the large rear wheel of the wagon to ward off elements and memories and listens for wolves howling at a distance. Atop the bedroll, Ada rubs her aching feet with balm. After she worms inside, she stretches out and rolls her neck in a slow circle. She pulls out the newspaper scrap Bryant had given her an hour before. An advertisement catches her eye: *Eggs! Eggs!—dozens for sale at 10½ c. Call and examine for yourselves. At A. Thompson's, corner of 4th and Green streets, L'ville.* Ada's mouth waters. She hasn't had an egg in two months. *Oh, for a scrambled egg. Or an egg fried in lard. Or poached egg on toast.* Ada licks her chapped lips. Muzzles noses in beside her, his gentle breathing comforting as she cozies in for the night.

"Your turn, Breen," she hears someone say. Breen puts his fiddle away. He's on watch tonight. The camp settles into night, soundless now except for the last crackling embers of the fire and muffled boot steps. But Ada cannot sleep. Like Eve tempted by the apple, Ada is enticed to return to the natural bridge again tomorrow. It nudges at the edges of her mind, pulls at her with invisible strings. Can she risk setting out alone? And on a holiday? *See the opportunity, not the obstacle,* she thinks. *Why not?*

5

July 4, 1846
Beaver Creek, Unorganized Territory

Ada opens her eyes. It's not yet dawn and the encampment is silent. Most days the bugle would have sounded already, but today's a layover day. From her vantage point tucked under the wagon bed, she peeks through splintery spokes of a chest-high rear wheel and watches dewy grasses sway gently in the near distance. There's colorful rudbeckia and coneflowers among the grasses, although the sun hasn't yet hit them with its fury. It's even too early for birds. A hush, somber and still, hovers over camp, soon to be broken by all the morning sounds: coughs, muted voices, clank of kettles, tantalizing smells of fresh ground coffee and sizzling bacon.

It's both high and dry here on the banks of Beaver Creek, a wild, virgin country flecked with hills and hollows. Soft, rolling knolls surround the encampment, two months and more than eight hundred miles from Independence and who, in their right mind, would want to leave, ever?

Ada shimmies out of her bedroll, changes to a fresh blouse, and walks a hundred yards away from the wagon to pass water. A hiss, and then a puddle, forms beneath her as she squats. Before breakfast, Ada checks on Rosie and Bert, picketed at the edge of the creek. As she approaches, Rosie turns her head and then returns to her task hoarding grass. Ada unhobbles them and secures the picket. She glances upstream. If she hadn't followed Edwin Bryant last night, oh, what she would have missed.

A loud boom shudders through camp. Someone's up and shooting off firearms already to mark Independence Day. Men gather by the livestock, and smoke, spit, laugh. Women hurry to do their business before setting coffee to boil. Children, still sleepy eyed, stumble over stools to await breakfast. Meadowlarks and magpies chatter overhead.

"Here, take this, will you?" Ma Breen hands Ada the hot iron kettle.

Ada grabs it with the edge of her apron and pours boiled coffee into five mugs, one each for Patrick and Ma Breen, another for the eldest, John, one for Pat Dolan, and the last one for herself. She's careful not to spill on her fresh blouse. She empties the dregs and returns the pot to its hook on the side of the wagon.

"Don't touch," she says to Peter.

"No, miss, I won't."

"Do you know what today is?" Ada asks.

"No, miss. Is it Sunday?"

"No, it's the Fourth of July, silly."

Patrick Breen gulps his coffee. "Let's be at it, then. Along now, boys." With the Donner brothers, William Eddy, and others, Breen spends the morning breaking down wagon beds and propping up rough planks on sawhorses to form an uneven line of board tables. By the time they are through, Ada guesses tables stretch for a quarter-mile across the pleasant valley. Ada covers the planks nearest her with an off-white tablecloth.

Virginia and Patty Reed skip by the Breen wagon, their hands filled with lupine and larkspur. "Tin cans to spare?"

Ada hands them an empty tin.

"Thanks, Miss Ada," Virginia says.

Simon and Peter dart under a table to hide.

"All ye, all ye, outs in free!" Edward Breen yells. He uncovers his eyes and prowls around camp, searching for his brothers.

"They're under the table, Eddie," Virginia says.

As Virginia walks past the younger boys' hiding place, Simon sticks his leg out to try to trip her. She stumbles, but doesn't fall. Simon explodes in laughter from somewhere under the tablecloth.

"Sorry, Miss Virginia," Edward says. His face reddens.

Sorry, Miss Virginia, Simon apes. He's still laughing. "Eddie and Virginia, sitting in a tree—"

"Shut yer trap!"

Simon runs off, with Edward in pursuit.

"I've been warning you," Edward yells.

"For the life of me," Ma Breen says. "I don't know why the Good Lord gave me six boys."

The girls pretend the boys had never been born as they place their posies down the center of the tables.

"What do you think, Miss Ada?" Virginia asks.

"I think you've got the knack."

Ada turns her head toward the east like a wild sunflower seeking warmth. The sun has edged over the hills with long, slanted rays. It promises to be another hot day here at the end of the earth and the beginning of the earth, with a sky wide enough to hold all the constellations at once. It's arguably the most perfect spot Ada has ever seen. And tomorrow they will pull up stakes and move on out of here, west, west, always and ever west. A hawk screeches overhead. For all the mumbo-jumbo in camp this morning, Ada's keenly aware of other sounds, ones that don't emanate from the rising chorus of human voices, sounds that will linger long after they've moved on. The wind will still whistle through tall grass, hawks will screech high above the grassland, and crickets will warp their limbs until there's nothing left to rub to produce song.

The animals are let out to graze instead of being penned up within the circle of wagons. Simon and Peter dump buffalo chips in a heap by the fire pit. Ada peels potatoes, mixes cornmeal with lard, stokes the fire. The *bois de vache* is odorless, and repels mosquitoes. Ada singes her fingers and shakes it off.

At a quarter to twelve, a bugle sounds. Ada grabs Bella and follows the Breens to where overlanders gather at a central spot near the Boggs's wagon. Captain Boggs begins reading:

When in the course of Human events it becomes necessary for one people to dissolve the political bands which have connected them with another . . .

Ada gazes up at the fluttering flag atop a long pole braced against the Radford wagon. Last night, women pieced together the ragtag banner, strips of red and white stolen from assorted sheets, jackets, and skirts. Thirteen red and white stripes representing the original colonies set off the dark blue square where twenty-eight white stars peek from the dark background. She's heard if President Polk's obsession with what he calls "manifest destiny" comes to fruition, soon there will be more stars added to the flag. *Maybe this land beneath our feet will become the next state.*

The recitation of the Declaration of Independence drones on. Ada's mind wanders. *What to call it, this state that's not yet a state? Mandan? Dakotah? Sioux?*

When the reading is finally over, a young man whoops, "Hurrah for the nation's seventieth birthday!" Ada counts by tens, using her fingers, beginning with 1776 and counting off the decades. She's never been good at math; that's why Augustus was always aggravated with her bookkeeping. All those number and columns. Ada uses both hands to count by tens, her right pointer finger touching the tips of her left hand until she counts fifty, and then switching hands to count sixty and seventy. Seventy years old! *Old enough to know better than entice people to take this blasted journey.*

At precisely noon, James Reed brandishes a stout brown bottle.

"Gather 'round, men. Boys, too." He passes the jug around. "Here's to Illinois and Missouri and Ohio. Or wherever your kinfolk be." He takes a long draught when the bottle returns to him. *Or Indiana,* Ada thinks. *Though I don't have any kinfolk left.*

Women shake their heads at their men and head back to their cooking pots. Ada sets down mismatched tin plates, cups, and forks at each place setting at the Breen table. The wind is light today (for once), but it's habit to plop a small rock on top of each cloth napkin. She counts again to see if she has reserved a place for everyone in the family, including Dolan. Eleven, all together.

When the signal sounds to sit for prayer, Ada wedges between Ma Breen and Simon and bows her head. She wishes she were sitting next to Dolan, but he's three down on the same side of the bench across from Patrick Breen. After the interminable prayer—*the food's goin' to be cold afore it's over*—she swats at flies as she dishes up: corn bread, boiled carrots, roasted potatoes, rabbit, sage hen, elk, and antelope stew. As she ladles butter onto a warm roll, a yellow stream splatters on the front of her blouse. She dabs it with her napkin. The table buzzes with lively conversation, laughter, the slow hum of a bee. She sips sweet tea.

"You ladies have gone whole hog here," Dolan says.

Ma Breen nods. *Is that the hint of a smile?*

"What do you think, Simon?" Ada asks. "You like this spread?"

He mumbles a reply. "At least, there's no beans."

"Now there's somethin' to celebrate."

There are more desserts than Ada's seen so far on the trail—a basketful of fresh wild strawberries, a jelly cake, a peach pie, even a fruitcake Mrs. Mink baked back in Ohio and saved for the occasion. Ada chooses pie and scrapes the edge of her plate to finish the last morsel.

"Three cheers for Uncle Sam!" one of the teamsters yells. Ada thinks he's called Elliott.

"And let's not forget the ladies!" Pat Dolan adds. "Haven't had a meal like this since Illinois!"

"Or Missouri," another drover says.

"Yeah, or Indiana," another pipes in. *Home.*

A faint rumble jars the ground. *Must be buffalo?* A great cloud of dust confirms Ada's suspicions and a group of teamsters takes to their horses and races out of camp.

Smaller children rush to join sack jumps, three-legged races, and tug-o'-war. The younger men organize a shooting match. Clutches of adolescent girls linger at the edges of the marksmanship competition. Ada fixes her disheveled bun and walks toward the women washing up. She picks up a faded dishtowel and begins to dry tin plates. Little as she puts weight to most of the offhand talk, Ada is addicted to camp gossip.

"I'm as certain as corn in July," Arlys Mink says to a group of six or eight women within earshot. "Marcie's young Lucas has set his sights on my Amelia." She turns to Marceline Radford and nods. "Say it's true, Marceline."

"She could do much worse," Marceline replies.

"Guess I wasn't much older than fifteen when my Silas proposed to me, poor as Job's turkey, he was. My pa didn't have any objections."

"And why might that be?" Marceline laughs.

Married at fifteen? Ada feels like an old maid, nineteen and no prospects. She stacks dry tin plates on a nearby table and reaches for two tin cups. She steals a glance at Dolan, who's tuning up his fiddle by the Breen wagon.

"Someone catch your eye?" Eleanor Eddy asks, pinching Ada's arm. "Pat Dolan, perhaps?" Eleanor's not more than a couple of years older than Ada, married to handsome William Eddy. She's got two children already.

"Maybe," Ada smiles.

"I've had my suspicions," Eleanor says.

"Shame on Charity Borden and that Carlisle girl," Arlys Mink continues. "Went off with a couple of teamsters last night, and not back until last call. Saw you, too, Miss Weeks, going off with Mr. Bryant. Do tell."

Busybodies. "We went to see a natural bridge, about a mile from here." She cocks her head in the direction of the red-rimmed canyon. "Had Simon Breen with us, if you were wonderin'."

"Prudent thinking on your part."

Can't spit without anyone noticin' or commentin' on it.

"If I figure correctly, Miss Swain must wed, *and soon,*" Marceline Radford interrupts. "Don't tell me you haven't noticed!"

"Another reason I'll be happy to see Amelia good and married off to Lucas before she's in the family way," Arlys Mink retorts. "I'm thinking there'll be a penny wedding tonight."

Eleanor tugs at Ada's arm. "If there's to be a penny wedding tonight, my bet is Amelia's in the family way already," she whispers. "You agree?"

The unsaid is as pregnant as the said. Being a wife and mother is multi-layered. *Like sweaters in fall,* Ada thinks. There is no question about wives following their menfolk. Where their husbands and brothers go, they go, no question about their opinion or their health or the number of children they lug along. Why, George and Tamsen Donner have moved across state lines four times already in their married life! Who says this will be their last move?

Leta Bradley joins the group, washcloth in hand. Arlys Mink stops her with a hefty pull on the elbow. "Now what's this, Leta? Another black eye?"

"Clumsy is all."

"Claptrap! No one is *that* clumsy."

Ada casts a sly eye at the other women washing and drying dishes. *Is that a welt on Mrs. Wolfinger's arm? Or a burn?* She's used to seeing Mrs. Keseberg's arms covered with bruises. Ada knows the signs. Her pa struck her ma plenty, especially after she'd lose another baby. Her ma blamed herself.

"What do you aim to do for the rest of the day, Miz Eddy?" Ada asks.

"Why, I think it's a good a day as any for a nice, long nap," the young woman replies. "And you, Ada? Canoodling with that beau of yours?"

"He's not my beau. At least, not yet."

"Well, let's see if we can't change that," Eleanor replies.

Ada strikes out alone around the camp in search of Dolan. It's time she was wed. *But one can't be wed by just thinkin' about it. What to do?*

Should she fix her hair like Amelia, braids woven around her ears? Ada pins up her straggly hair. *No, too much trouble.* Should she loosen her blouse like the Carlisle girl to reveal her generous cleavage, and then bend over so Dolan can sneak a peek at her breasts? *No, too brazen. I'll just have to talk to him. Ask him about Ireland or mule handlin' or how to shoot that blasted gun.*

Gnats swarm around her face and neck. Her bonnet, rendered limp by prairie thunderstorms, sags over her forehead. *At least, my nose is shaded from that blazin' sun.* Once she could have gone to the kitchen cupboard and found starch, right next to the lye. Here, in the middle of Unorganized Territory, she has what she has, which isn't much. *And my arms look like an Indian's, brown as a biscuit.* Ada's surprised hostiles haven't threatened the train, and she hopes their luck holds. There had been the two Sioux who trailed the train for a few days and joined the entourage one night for supper. But the next morning, two horses went missing, so it's common knowledge that any invitation to other Indians, hostile or not, won't be forthcoming any time soon.

Lively shouts emanate from beyond the wagons. Older children play at three-legged races and tug 'o war. Ada watches as John Breen's team pulls Joey Radford's team over the line in the dirt.

"Watch out, Miss Ada!" Simon runs past, his homemade toy buzz saw whizzing in the air. Ada ducks to avoid being hit. As he runs, Simon bumps into his brother, Peter.

"Look what you've done!" Peter shouts. "I almost had it." He focuses again on a ball attached to a string tossed in the air.

Ada claps as the ball falls into the cup. She spies a cluster of young girls playing cat's cradle on a quilt spread over prairie grasses. Two younger girls—*twins maybe?*—play a button game in the dirt. Virginia Reed is in deep conversation with her clothespin doll. Ada stops and squats by William Hook, who's whittling a small wooden figure.

"Nice job, William. Who taught you how to whittle?"

"My pa. My real pa. He's dead now."

"I've heard, and I'm sorry for it. My pa's dead, too. But today's not a day for sadness. Why don't you go on, play with the others?" She shoos him toward the boys.

Where is Dolan?

At the western edge of camp, a group of men and mules gathers. Ada squints to see if Edwin Bryant is among them. He is. Farewells echo through the camp as he addresses a swarm of men. *Is that Hiram Miller? One of George Donner's teamsters, joinin' the mule party?*

"A miss is as good as a mile!" Bryant yells in her direction.

Ada waves. She's relieved that Dolan is not among the group departing. *Where is he?* She swats at more gnats. Finally, Ada hears Dolan's voice near one of the Reed wagons. As she approaches, Dolan's got his back to her. Teamsters and young women her age surround him. His hands are flying in the air as he spins another tall tale. Ada steps out of the way to let Amelia Mink and Lucas Radford pass. *Will there really be a penny weddin' tonight?* She enters the circle, but Charity Borden and Edna Carlisle turn their backs to her.

By now, Dolan's hopped up onto the rear gate of one of the Reed's wagons and dances a sloppy jig. A raucous jumble of harmonica and jaw harp pierces the air. Ada taps her foot. *Maybe he'll ask me to dance.* The other teamsters slap their thighs and whistle, egging him on. Dolan motions for Edna to join him and pulls her up onto the buckboard. He bends to whisper in her ear and encircles her waist. Ada slinks out of the circle. Her face is hot. She knows where she's going, *Dolan be damned.*

George and Jacob Donner sit on the bank of Beaver Creek, fanning themselves with newspaper. "Miss Weeks," George Donner says, scrambling to stand.

"No need to get up," Ada says. Both men are now on their feet.

"Why aren't you with all the other young people?" Jacob Donner asks.

"I thought I might be goin' up the creck a-ways." *Going up the creek a-ways,* she reminds herself.

"Mind you don't go too far," Jacob Donner adds. "Haven't seen any Sioux today, but they're always lurking."

Ada nods. *I can watch out for myself.* She rambles up the creek and gathers chokecherry. Forty-five minutes later, she reaches the narrow gap in the canyon again. She slips through and looks right and left. No one is about. *They're all busy drinkin' and dancin' and canoodlin'.* She pictures Dolan embracing Edna Carlisle.

Ada places the chokecherry in a shady spot and sits at the edge of the stream. She tosses her boots on the bank and bathes her bare feet in cool water. *Oh, what the hell,* she thinks. She fumbles with her blouse, and slips off her skirt. She hangs her top over a nearby shrub, careful not to prick her fingers on the thorny bush. Stripped down to her chemise and bloomers, she wades into the shallow water. She glances up, taking in red striated cliffs, billowy clouds, and cobalt sky. Ada doesn't know what the Garden of Eden looked like—or if there really was such a thing—but she doubts Eve ever lived and breathed in a place as beautiful as this. Ada is acclimated to the cool water, so she strides deeper into a pool beneath the red rock arch until the creek brushes her waist. She leans back against a larger boulder, her head nestled in a wedge of rock. The sun slants through the slot canyon and a soft breeze rustles sparse cottonwoods. She calls a tentative "Heloo!" and then a louder one, her voice pinging off red canyon walls.

After a long soak (she can hardly feel her feet by now, the water is that cold in the deepest pool), Ada clambers on a boulder and sits with her legs extended and her back arched toward the sun. Within minutes, her bloomers and chemise are almost dry. High above her perch, a lone tree hangs precariously from a crack in the red walls, clinging for its life by shallow roots. Its silvery-grey leaves shiver in the afternoon breeze. Ada's skin prickles.

She knows her party should've been to Independence Rock by today, but, according to James Reed, they are still a good week away from that landmark. Sure as anything, this day's been a welcome respite from the drudgery of walking, and, *sure as snot,* there'll be a lot more walking before this journey's done. But it doesn't erase the nagging feeling that maybe Edwin Bryant and his entourage have the right idea to hurry along the trail.

Between the dry heat of the rock and warm wind, Ada is able to dress within a half hour, layering her blouse and skirt over her now-dry chemise and bloomers.

A rumbling of voices catches Ada unaware. She freezes. *Indians?* She clutches her hands to her chest and slinks behind the boulder.

"Miss Weeks!" It's George Donner's voice. Ada unfolds herself from her haunches and stands as a group of men and boys thunders into the canyon. "There you are! You've been gone for hours," George Donner yells. "It's been the talk of the camp."

Ada's mortified to have brought attention to herself, and more so that the wagon master has almost caught her in her underclothes.

"I didn't mean no harm, sir," she says.

Donner glares at her. "Don't go off like that again, do you hear me? I thought we warned you."

Oh, you did. But I don't always follow directions. Like the night of the fire . . . Ada dredges up memories. Her pa had called her to the barn, but she hadn't come. Her book was just too good, and she couldn't break away. And if she had been in the barn . . .

"Pa, can we stay?" one of the boys asks George Donner.

"A minute, no more."

Patrick Breen enters the clearing with John and Simon.

"There she is!" Simon yells.

"Mrs. Breen's beside herself," Breen says, his face set in a grimace. "You'll owe her an apology, Miss Weeks."

As they march down the creek, Ada is careful not to slip on slick rocks in her wet boots. A gilded flicker's cheery *wicca-wicca-wicca* interrupts her thoughts. She remembers the mockingbird's *hurr-eep.* She picks up her pace and crashes through the stream, water wicking up her just-dry skirt and clinging to her ankles. She avoids conversing with the Donner brothers or to Patrick Breen; they've shamed her enough for one day. *Talk of the camp?* There will be more eye rolling and gossip, for sure.

At the edge of camp, the sun casts a copper glow over the escarpment, where pronghorn antelope dart in packs of twos and threes. Ada raises her arm to shield the sun and wonders how far Edwin Bryant traveled already today. By the time she reaches the Breen wagon, the sun has slipped behind the farthest hill, its golden fingers clawing to the horizon until they lose their grasp.

Ada murmurs a weak apology to Ma Breen. She eats another piece of pie and calls it supper. By the time the fireworks show begins, Ada sits with her back against the Breen's wagon wheel and drapes her blanket over her shoulders. Her hair is still loose around her shoulders.

Pop, pop, pop. Boom! Ada covers her ears as deafening fireworks shoot into the night sky. "C'mere, pup. All them fireworks got you scared up? Worse racket I've ever heard in all my born days." Ada scoops up the mangy dog and nestles him in her lap, giving long, slow strokes across his quaking back. The day has cooled off fast, and Ada draws her shawl tight. Getting any sleep tonight will be a miracle.

Young men still whoop and holler. She hears Dolan's animated voice two wagons away. Ada feels a flash of jealousy. "Bet they've all bent an elbow tonight, pup. Imbibin' in that rot-gut again. Well, we've got our tobacco." Ada doesn't know any other women who dip snuff, so she does it on the sly.

She picked up tobacco at Fort Laramie a week before. Wouldn't be able to get more until Fort Hall, more than a month away on the trail. Within the fort, trappers, traders, and emigrants mingled. Outside, thousands of Sioux camped in preparation for a war with their rivals, the Crow. It was quite a sight: tipis, colorful dress, and brown-skinned children running naked. Overlanders traded fabrics and beads and mirrors with the natives for buffalo hide. Ada had nothing to trade.

Prices at the trading post were sky high. Ada purchased five cents' worth of tobacco for a buck and a half. *A buck and a half!* Sugar was two dollars a cup and bullets seventy five cents per pound. Everyone grumbled. When she approached the counter, the shopkeeper didn't blink. Did he think she was purchasing snuff for her husband? Her brother? Her beau? Or didn't he care one way or the other? That's where she caught the tail end of a conversation between James Reed and a grizzled stranger. When she overheard the beginning of the conversation, she loitered to catch the rest.

"I'm of half a mind to believe you, Clyman, but the other half is fighting what you say. Lansford Hastings guarantees his shortcut will save miles and time. We're already behind schedule."

"Your choice, Reed. But I'm telling you, I've just come that way east and the route is, well—seeing as the womenfolk aren't around—I can tell you it's *hell* coming over the Great Salt Desert. It won't be easy on the oxen. Wouldn't be surprised if it kills 'em all. That's if you get to the desert at all with them wagons. Even on horseback, I had a devil of a time this side of the gap. Take my word and don't be tempted by Hastings's folly. You'll be sorry."

Ada shudders when she thinks about the conversation. She has no intention of taking any other route than the Fort Hall route. Surely everyone else will come to the same conclusion. Reed and Donner and the rest of the men will see to it. She spits, clamps her eyes shut, and listens as rockets fade into the night. The dog shivers again, and she pulls him closer.

Ada recalls the Fourth of July when she was eleven, just before the fire, when she had hoped to go to town for the parade. Her pa said they couldn't go. Ada doesn't remember the excuse he used that day. There had been so many.

6

July 4, 1846
Alta California

A loud boom ricochets in the forest. The man's in a mood to celebrate. He wheels around and fires his rifle again, straight up. The whiskey's clouded his mind a bit, but not enough to numb him. Old One squawks at him from fifty feet above.

"Quit your screeching. Sorry The Missus hasn't returned. Just me and you here tonight, neighbors gone for the holiday. Oh, bugger it. Let's make a ruckus."

He fires off another round into the cloudless sky. He could have gone with Rufous to Yerba Buena, but he'd just been there and didn't relish the idea of traveling back late tonight. And Salina's gone to see her people and took the kids with her, so there's no one else on the creek today. Not even strangers passing through.

As the afternoon wears on, he regrets not going with Rufous. They could have had a grand time. Could've eaten pie. Drunk whiskey with other lonely bachelors. Maybe got a pound of flesh. He's partial to Miss Fay, the madam at Fay's Boarding House. Better to lose yourself in generous folds of flesh, not someone who looks like a younger sister, all angles and bones and pouts. Fay doesn't entertain regularly, but she makes an exception for him, sees his needs are deeper than his member's. When he cries out, he says, "Bet!"

Lisabet, everyone else called her. Elisabet Marie Duchette. Her slender hands. Her narrow waist. Her jet-black hair. Bet caught his eye in Prairie du Chien in 1830 when he first left home, twenty, raw, and ready for life. She was sixteen then, daughter of a French-Canadian trapper and his native wife. He first saw her in the school-yard, a willow-wisp of a young girl tasked with teaching the town's *métis* bastards like her.

He's too proud to say he was smitten, but if that's what brought him to lurk around the schoolhouse, place himself in Bet's path late afternoons, lust over her at night in the boardinghouse, let him call it whatever he wants to call it. She was a beauty. And he was a virgin then, and tempted to remedy that. But he couldn't bring himself to go to the bawdy house outside of town. He wanted one woman only—Lisabet.

It didn't take long to win her. He was one of the only young men unencumbered in Prairie du Chien at the time. And he was indus-trious, trapping until his hands were raw to bring in peltries, six, ten at a time, not stopping for weather or Sunday. They were wed in late December, a lively affair put on by her father and attended by all the trappers wintering over and a few of the townsfolk who braved the afternoon, minus ten and blowing. They spent their wedding night in her parents' cabin, and all the days after until he built a small home a hundred yards away where they made love and laughed and made love some more. She tried to teach him French.

Others might have given in long before the marriage bed, but he was glad he waited. At the time, he had no one to compare her with, and he doubted any could do to a man what Lisabet did to him. Looking back, he knows she was divine. He often thinks he wouldn't have minded even if the coupling had not been as robust. Bet was *his, all his*, and if she merely sat in his presence he would have been satisfied. Trudging through the woods, laying traps, skinning beaver and fox and muskrat, all he could think about was getting home, drowning in Bet's soulful violet eyes and putting out the lamplight. In the dark, he was transported by her hands, her tongue. He wondered if all men were as lucky.

Her death rattled him, gutted him, threw him into such a frenzy that when her father found him, outside, naked, shivering, his hair shorn to the bloodied scalp, Dom Duchette took the battered coil of a man back to the bed where he'd spent his wedding night with his daughter and nursed him back to health with broth and tea and silence. He had lost his own wife by then, so they were two bachelors getting along as best as they could until the man was well enough to go.

He spilled this all out one night to Fay. Since then, she's let him into her bed whenever he comes to Yerba Buena. Sometimes, they don't make love at all. They spend the night side-by-side, and she strokes his hair until he falls asleep.

If Rufous had stayed at the creek, or Salina and the kids, they could have had a real celebration, and his mind wouldn't be focused on sadder days. He wonders what people in Prairie du Chien were doing tonight, or in grander places like Chicago or New York. If what he's heard is gospel truth, large caravans of westering folk—maybe upwards of five thousand of them—would be celebrating somewhere out on the wide and dark prairie tonight.

He imagines what the caravans look like, miles of wagons and oxen and horses and mules. Families, mostly. He'd like a family someday, but that someday is unraveling faster than a ball of twine on a hillside. He's more likely to live on the creek alone for the rest of his all-born days than take another wife and have a passel of young'uns.

"All them travelers might have more powder and whiskey than we do tonight, Old One—and more than a few might even get lucky behind a wagon tonight—but, by God, you worthless old son of bitch, we're here in California already and they're not."

He shoots off a last volley into the burgeoning purple of dusk. "Yessiree," he calls into the curtain of night. "We're here and they're not!"

"*Barrrrh*," is the only answer.

7

July 12, 1846
Independence Rock,
Unorganized Territory

Fifty-nine days. Ada makes another tick mark on the side of Rosie's worn leather saddlebag. Augustus said it would take roughly one hundred fifty-three days to reach California. If his reckoning is correct, the emigrants are about one-third of the way to the Promised Land and, if all goes to plan, should reach California by late September—early October at the latest. But here she is, fifty-nine days into the journey without Augustus to help count the long, dry, dust-filled hours.

Ada saunters around the mile-long perimeter of Independence Rock. The whale-shaped granite outcrop shoves up from the center of the plains, named for the spot overlanders aim to reach by Fourth of July if they're on schedule. *And that was a week ago, blast it!* She swishes through clumps of high bunch grass and spooks a lizard, which scuttles away, wriggling its long tail. Ada finds a shaded spot under a low overhang on the west side of the hundred-fifty-foot high monolith. *Must be a hundred degrees.* She flips her bonnet onto the grass and fingers indentations and markings in the hard granite where others have left their mark, some with a chisel and others with white chalk or tar: "E. Whiting, Boston, Mass., 1843"; "Francis E. Long, 1845"; and one carved just this year: "M. Anderson, I'dence, '46".

A couple of weeks ago, the emigrants set up camp at Register Cliff, a narrow spot pinched between the North Platte and surrounding jagged cliffs. Ada didn't have time to inscribe her initials while they camped there. There'd been some thieving going on in camp that day, and Ada didn't stray far from the Breen wagon while Ma Breen went to the river to wash. Someone had pilfered Patrick Breen's ax; Ma Breen's heavy ladle had also gone missing. The interlopers had meant to take the whole Dutch oven, too, but thought better of it and left it in the ashes. Someone would be sure to see a thief make off with a cast iron pot. An ax, not so much. Nor a ladle.

When Ma Breen returned, it was Ada's turn to wash and Ma Breen's turn to keep watch at camp.

"It's those Germans, I'm sure of it," Ma Breen said.

"How can you be sure?" Ada asked.

"I just know it. Never have liked Germans. And there's six or eight of them in this party. Probably in cahoots."

Ada's not sure if it's Germans or Indians *or hooligans,* but she doubts it's Mrs. Keseberg. She's quiet, keeps to herself most nights— not the kind to go off and take a man's ax or a woman's cookware or anything else, for that matter. Mrs. Keseberg has a young child named Ada, who had been a twin. Ada laments that Mrs. Keseberg already lost a child and now is showing with another. *She must be reminded every day of the little one she lost. Like my ma.* Ada vows to show Mrs. Keseberg some kindness; goodness knows Mrs. Keseberg doesn't get too much of it from her husband. *Who might have stolen the ax.*

Ada washed her spare blouse in the Platte, rinsed it twice, and set it over brittlebush to dry. As she walked up from the river, she ducked, avoiding swooping rock swallows whose nests covered the lip of the cliff. A baby swallow, tossed from its nest too soon, landed on the hard dirt in front of her. Ada picked it up gingerly and coaxed it to fly, even to live. The bird shuddered in her hands. When its tiny body stilled, Ada placed its limp carcass under a cottonwood and left it for scavengers.

Ada likes Ma Breen. The Irishwoman is different from her ma and from Inger. Her ma was lively and talkative when she was well, but scrabbled into a cave so deep and dark when she had melancholia that Ada wondered if she was the same woman. There were sparks of joy when the layette would come out again, little linen sacks and bonnets and socks, all washed and bleached and hung to dry in the Indiana sun. That's how Ada knew her ma was expecting again. But after another difficult birth, signs of darkness clawed into the farmhouse again, then her pa would go to the barn and hammer out another white pine coffin, six in all buried under the oak trees at the far edge of the farm. Her mother would go out to the oaks and lie down in the grass and weep; her pa would take out his frustrations on his wife, leaving bruises the size of flatiron up and down her arms, which is all Ada could ever see, anyway. It would be weeks, months even, before her ma appeared in the kitchen again, cheeks bright and hands busy, pecking Ada on the cheek as if nothing had happened and a "Here's the pail, bring in some water now, will you?"

Inger was steady, if that is the word for a woman who worked morning to night without complaint, except for clucking sounds and mutterings in Norwegian. She wasn't quick to smile, but that didn't mean she wasn't happy. *Content,* Ada thought, with a good strong husband and a home in town and a thriving business and a girl to call her own. "You'll be our girl, now," Inger said soon after they brought her to town. Ada knew then that her allegiance to her ma was something of the past and that now when Inger asked for help in the kitchen or the garden or to run to the drygoods store she must follow Inger's instructions and commands without so much as a peep of disagreement. She did not want to go to the orphan's asylum, so she tried her hardest in school, too, winning prizes and praise for her recitations. It was the only way to assure they'd keep her, to be obedient and good.

And she made sure Augustus never left the lantern burning after he went to bed. The fire that consumed her pa's barn—and her pa and ma in it—haunts her every night. Ada can't count the number of midnights she fumbled through clotted mounds of furniture and around silhouettes of ghostly lamps in Augustus's storefront as she wended her way to the embalming room at the back of the establishment to check the lantern. Her cue? As soon as she heard Augustus mount the stairs and roll on top of Inger and grunt (that was the surest sign of all), that was her signal to throw off the covers and tiptoe downstairs on her singular mission. One cannot be too careful.

And then there's Ma Breen, chubby and capable and firm. She treats Ada like a peer, not a child, so that's a shift that Ada wasn't prepared for when Margaret Breen issued the invitation for Ada to travel with the Breen family. It doesn't change Ada's sense of duty, however. She does what's she's asked, and more. She and Ma Breen have the camp routine down so that little needs to be said. They weave around one another without words as they set up and take down camp three times per day. The wages of sin may be death, but the wages of Ada's work are hard-earned smiles and the occasional thank you. But Ada doesn't need a thank you. She needs something else—to be wanted.

The wagon train has reached the Sweetwater now, a long tributary of the North Platte with the Great Divide at its headwaters. They'll lay by here for a day by the calm river. It's hot, and the wagon master calls for a day of rest. The country here is full of curiosities, like this erratic rock named for the Fourth of July smack in the middle of the high prairie. Most of the men are out on a buffalo hunt past Devil's Gap, five miles away. All of the women have stayed in camp to do wash and gossip and try to keep cool with soaked rags wound around their necks. The children cavort with boundless energy, even in this heat.

Ada reaches into her apron pocket and holds her knife at a right angle to the rock. Not that she'll pass this way again or that anyone in years to come will seek her initials. No, what she's attempting to do here is strictly for posterity: *Veni, Vidi, Vici,* I came, I saw, I conquered. Slowly, she begins to gouge the rock surface. Others have left their mark with chalk or tar; she intends to leave a lasting mark. Rock dust coats her fingers, and she is careful not to let the knife slip and pierce her hand. Ada labors for more than an hour, her hand cramping more than once. She concentrates as two large ornate letters begin to take shape. When Ada finishes the letters, she carves the year. When she's done, she steps back to admire her work:

AW
1846

"You'll be Ah-dah Veeks now. Veeks, vit a dobblt 'v'."

A long, sweeping prairie folds out from Independence Rock, phlox and redbud amid thick grasses. *It's what an ocean must look like,* Ada thinks, stretched as far as one can see, a mass of slow, undulating waves rolling across the prairie. But Ada's never seen an ocean, nor heard a seagull, nor smelled the tang of salt air. Landlocked in Indiana, she's known rivers and creeks and lakes and swamps, but nothing resembling an ocean.

This sea of grasses is fit for no mariner on land or water. Today, thunderclouds mass in the distance and rumbles shake the earth. Although the unadulterated prairie fans out horizon to horizon, there is no getting away from the enormity of the weather. Nor can she avoid the stink of animals and campfires and unwashed bodies or the *tedium* of the journey.

Unless, of course, one just started walking or riding away from the entourage, away from Mrs. Keseberg's screams and Mrs. Reed's whimpers and Ma Breen's scolding—ever scolding—as the boys cajole and cat fight and carouse. Ada is envious of Edwin Bryant and the entourage who rode out last week. *Too slow. Too encumbered. Too many rules and regulations.* The wagon train slowed them down. So they up and left their wagons and supplies and took off on pack mules, nine of them, and not a woman among them. They'd get to California, by hook or by crook, and on their terms. Ada takes out Patrick Breen's pocket compass and watches as the little needle spins as she turns west. She'll be sure to return it later in the day from where she swiped it, a little pouch tucked in Patrick Breen's jockey box.

"To the left, Miss Ada!" John Breen shouts.

Ada moves to her right to let a long line of boys pass. "Sakes alive, boys!" She ruffles Simon Breen's hair as he passes. "Faster now, Simon! You can do it! You, too, Peter!" Poor little James Breen lags far behind.

John Breen examines a crevice and begins to scramble up the rock face. Patrick Breen, James Reed, and Charles Stanton are already atop the monument waving the boys up. None of the women will scale the rock, *damn their skirts.* Ada's drenched with perspiration and her blouse chafes her chest. She untucks her blouse and flaps it in the still air. A *whoosh* of cool air travels up her midsection to her breasts. She does this three times before retucking her shirt. Her skirts are loose now at the waist. She'll have to borrow a paper of pins, a needle, and thread to take in a generous fold. But not from Ma Breen. She's been irritable lately. Maybe Tamsen Donner? She's tidy and organized and would be sure to have needle and thread. She wouldn't bark at Ada for the asking, would she? Maybe better to ask sweet Eleanor Eddy.

Ada stops at the Eddy camp after carving her name for all time.

"How are you getting along, Ada?" Eleanor asks.

"Good, thank you, considerin'. And you, Miz Eddy?"

"Baby's fussy. Teething, I suspect."

Ada pats Margaret on the head. "Do you ever wonder if we're ever goin' to get wherever it is we're goin'? We're fifty-nine days today already. I've been countin'. But I've heard grumblin's we should've been here a week ago."

"Never you mind, Ada. No need to fret. My granny told me to pay attention to each day. 'Tomorrow's got its own worries,' she'd say. Can't count on tomorrow, is the way I look at it."

"Guess I can't help worryin'. Like about the Sioux. There are stories . . ."

"We're getting along. Better not to think about it and then thank the Lord each morning we've seen another day. But I do wish we could stay at this spot a day or two in the shade and cool along the Sweetwater. Just look at them men and boys playing in that river. Though there's not much choice we have in the matter, when you get right down to it, is there, Ada?"

Has Ada ever had a choice? After the fire? After the drowning? Choice today is winnowed down to no grits, thank you, or can I help wash or dry? Should I sleep on the left side of the wagon tonight? Or the right?

When Ada reaches the Breens' wagon, she overhears another argument. Sometimes, the Breens argue two, ten, twenty times a day.

"If there's anything to bring out the worst in a man, it's a trip across this blasted continent with a yoke of goddamned slow oxen," Breen complains. "Bryant and his men, now they had the right idea: leave everything behind and get on with it."

Ma Breen counters faster than a jackrabbit. "You go on ahead, Mr. Breen. See if I miss you for even one day."

A lone cloud drifts over the high plains, casting a shifting shadow. Ada wishes she could live under the shadow, to be shaded from the ruthless sun. Her nose is peeling again, and her lips are dry and cracked. She avoids the Breens and pees behind a dense clump of brush. The blood's back, so she'll have to dig out her rags. And she's glad she still has the scrap of Bryant's newspaper to wipe with. She saved it for a day like today. Not that her monthlies were ever regular, but here, walking every day thirsting for water, her menses are irregular, a little blood one month, none the next, and then an unexpected hemorrhage. No amount of cold compresses or concoctions of herbs can dull Ada's abdominal pain—not even essence of peppermint.

Tomorrow, when the wagons roll again, she'll stuff her discomfort and take her place in the long line of travelers, spurring her smelly mules west. In this treeless prairie, she'll rely on other women when she needs to change her rags. A nod of the head indicates the call, and then women gather, circle, and turn outward, their skirts fanned out to safeguard privacy while the one inside does her messy business. Ada hopes this month she won't be in as much pain as last month, when she could hardly keep up with the wagons. *Two miles an hour doesn't sound fast until you get behind,* she thinks. Being left behind, that's one of the things Ada dreads most, like disease and dementia. And drowning.

All over camp, conversations turn to arguments turn to shoves. Even the weather is testy, hail the size of large stones pelting wagons three days out of ten. When it rains, it doesn't trickle; it pours buckets. By late afternoon, Ada dives under the wagon and watches the sullen sky dump hail the size of gold coins. It pummels the ground beyond her hiding place, drumming up earth as high as her ankles. Little Peter Breen cuddles up to Ada. "Won't be long now, Peter. See that you don't slip gettin' out from under the wagon. That mud's slick."

Ada re-emerges after the hailstorm, changes her rags, and helps with supper. Her clothes are stiff with dirt and grime. Her feet are blistered. Her hands are sunburnt. As for her boots, what's left of them still flap when they're not secured with twine.

"Trail meeting after supper," Breen says. "Donner says we need to be there."

What Donner? There are so many Donners: George and his wife Tamsen and their five children, and Jacob Donner, his wife Elizabeth, and their seven. Ada dishes out salt pork and beans. She sits on a campstool and chews the tasteless supper. After washing up, Ada and Ma Breen amble over to the lip of Independence Rock. George Donner stands a few feet up the side of the monolith.

"Come closer," Donner yells.

There are forty or more adults gathered, some sitting, others milling around. Patrick Breen smokes his pipe. Dolan joins him. Simon and Peter play jacks in the dirt. Ada squeezes in next to Eleanor Eddy.

"What now?" Ada asks.

"Shush now and listen," Eleanor says.

"No telling where we'd be by now if we'd reached this rock by the Fourth, like we should've," Donner says, his voice loud and strong. "We're a week behind schedule."

Men grumble, women murmur.

"You can ask my wife, I'm not one to make hasty decisions," Donner continues. Tamsen Donner covers her mouth, hiding a smile. Her stepdaughters Elitha and Leanna, nod between them. "But I'm concerned about the calendar. Can't get days back, ones that have slipped by."

Ada looks at Dolan. *Can't get days back. Got to get his attention, and soon.*

"Now, many of you have read the *Emigrants' Guide.*" He waves Lansford Hastings's *The Emigrants' Guide to Oregon and California* above his head. "Hastings himself says his shortcut will shave hundreds of miles," Donner says. "You can read it for yourself. It says right here . . ."

"You heard Clyman urge us to avoid the shortcut," James Reed interrupts. "He's just come that way, talked to him at Laramie. Can't say I agree with him, but we ought to consider his words. Says it's impassable in parts. Especially for wagons."

And women, Ada thinks.

"Hogvash. It's clear ve'll do far better taking Hastings's route than vasting time on da old trail," Lewis Keseberg says. Other Germans nod.

"Simmer down. I hear you all right square. That's why we're all gathered here," Donner says. "I'm of a mind to take the chance, but I want to hear from all of you."

Well, not all of us, Ada thinks. She nudges Eleanor. "Thinks he's the biggest toad in the puddle."

"Shush, Ada. Not another blessed word."

"Vat have ve got to lose?" Keseberg says.

Donner reads to the crowd.

> *The most direct route, for California emigrants, would be to leave the Oregon route . . .*

"Hear, hear!" By now, more travelers have gathered at the foot of Independence Rock. Even portly Mrs. Radford has come out from her wagon. Mrs. Mink stands beside Mrs. Radford, an ample arm woven through her friend's shawl. It's only been three days since Tommy Radford was smashed under a wagon wheel, life oozing out of him in front the whole train, his head almost unrecognizable. His father buried him in an unmarked grave, no cross or inscription, nothing but wagon wheels and oxen hooves tamping out any vestige of the gravesite. His mother took laudanum and retreated inside the wagon that crushed her only son, trying to escape the same fate by her own hand.

Donner continues to read:

> *A very good, and much more direct wagon way, has been found, about one hundred miles, southward from the great southern pass, which, it will be observed, lies principally through the northern part of California. The California route, from Fort*

Hall to the Sacramento River, lies through alternate plains, prairies, and valleys, and over hills, amid lofty mountains; thence bearing west southwest, to the Salt Lake; and thence continuing down to the bay of St. Francisco, by the route just described.

"You heard it," Jacob Donner says. "A very good, and much more direct wagon way. All those in favor of taking the new route, say aye."

Ada shakes her head. Certainly no one will agree. Around her, there's a chorus of *ayes,* as both Breen and Dolan raise their hands in ascent. She can't believe her ears. Others grumble *nay,* Radford and Mink among them. They shake their heads and murmur, hats and beards close together. Mink turns towards his wife. With a jerk of his head, he signals for Mrs. Mink to follow him. Mrs. Radford disappears into her wagon again.

Within moments, the entire group disbands. It's clear some of the travelers do not agree with Donner's vote. They'll likely take the known trail via Fort Hall and turn their back on any talk of a cutoff. Ada's torn about splitting the caravan. It will be yet another parting of the ways for the travelers. What should she do? The Minks and Radfords—*and anyone who has any sense in their brains*—will follow certainty by taking the established course toward Fort Hall. Those who side with Donner will hedge their bets on promises.

Promises. Ada thinks of all the promises her ma made to her: a puppy when she turned eight, a cheap necklace for Christmas, a little brother or sister on the way. All of her promises went up in flames one hot August night in 1838. There are little promises now, except for the Great Promise of California.

We're goin' on little more than promises, Ada thinks. *But I've had plumb enough of promises—it's gotten me right nowhere, except maybe a big heartache.* So, no, Ada decides. The route to Fort Hall is the only route. She will not be tempted.

The sound of Patrick Breen's fiddle draws her into camp. He goes

through all his favorites: "Home, Sweet Home"; "Ole Tare River";
"Turkey in the Straw." Ada taps her foot. Dolan does a little jig, and
Ada laughs. "You're a sight, Mr. Dolan."

"You want to try it?"

Ada shakes her head. "Don't know any jigs."

"Come from Ireland, you're born doing it." He kicks his heels one
way, then the other.

"Well, I were born in Indiana," Ada says. "My pa were from
Tennessee so I know the reel. He taught me in the barn." She remembers her pa sweeping hay out of the way and taking his great paws of
hands into her own and practicing the steps on happier nights near
Noblesville.

"We'll have to see about that, Miss Weeks. Haven't seen you at any
of the dances."

"Oh, I've been there."

The wagons creek westward early the next day. Ada lugs Bella and
walks beside Eleanor Eddy. They walk on through larkspur and
indigo and Indian paintbrush. Some afternoons, Ada wonders if the
sun will ever set. It hangs in the sky and doesn't seem to move—just
sits there and scorches them like a red-hot poker. Buffalo is plenty,
and they eat well. Ada listens as Breen and Dolan tell tales of bravado,
one upping the other about heroics of the kills. Ada doesn't care
much for the details. But she loves the meat, especially of a fat calf.

Late afternoons, when the sun finally dives for the horizon, hundreds of insects flit in the still air like snowflakes. On every side, the
high plains stretch wide, dotted with carpeted hillocks thick with
sage and prickly pear and poison ivy. Ada walks until the wagon
master calls for the day's halt. After supper, she marks the sun's
descent until all that's left is a golden glow above the horizon. Like

clockwork, the lustrous gold quickly dissolves, sliding into apricot, into rose pink, into violet, and then, after five minutes of deep amethyst, settling into a dusky, dull grey. Twilight lasts deep into the evening. At last, all's that left of this day are the blue-black shadows of rounded, distant bluffs under cold, flickering stars.

Tonight, large strips of buffalo meat dry over a slow fire. It'll be desiccated and stuffed in pouches for use as pemmican—eaten raw or mixed with flour for sustenance. Ada's still got Inger's jerked meat saved if she needs it. She hopes to throw it over her shoulder when she reaches California.

"Why anyone would turn down a clear saving of even a hundred miles is beyond my reasoning," Breen says.

He and Dolan calculate merits of the new route as they sit smoking after supper. Ma Breen's back from tucking in the younger boys and sinks onto a campstool, her knitting needles clicking in the firelight. Ada is drying the last of the supper dishes.

"Got my doubts," Dolan says.

Breen shoots him a sour look.

"But I'm with you, sir," Dolan replies. "Won't be sliding out like some of the others."

"I've got my doubts, too," Ada interjects. She's sitting now, peeling a wild pear with a rusty knife. "Heard it's not a known road. Maybe just passable by horse or mule, but not by wagon."

"Quiet, Ada," Ma Breen whispers.

"Why? We're goin' along, too, and without an opinion. Well, at least, not one we say aloud."

Ma Breen gives Ada a sideways glance.

Ada continues, "I'm thinkin' of hitchin' on with the Minks or the Radfords goin' the Fort Hall route."

Silence descends on the foursome.

"It'd be a right shame if you left us, Miss Ada," Dolan says. "You're like family now."

"Don't mean to be ungrateful." The knife slips out of Ada's hand. She bends to retrieve it in the dirt and wipes it off on her soiled apron. "You've been kind to me, especially after . . ." Her voice trails off.

"Think we'd let an orphan girl fend for herself?" Ma Breen says. "Our Lord Himself says we're to look after widows and orphans. But if you're all bent on taking up with the others, I'll see to it that you've got supplies."

"One less mouth to feed," Breen says.

His wife glares at him. "Don't never mind Mr. Breen, Ada. He's a sourpuss tonight."

Ada inhales a mouthful of gnats, chokes, and spits. "I'll think on it; let you know my druthers in the mornin'. I'd surely miss the boys. And Bella. And you, Ma Breen."

She doesn't mention Patrick Breen. She longs to mention Dolan. "Maybe I'll come around."

By the time Ada wakes up, she knows she's staying. *You're like family now,* Dolan had said. That was enough to persuade her, although she still has a nagging inkling that it's the wrong decision for the wrong reasons. Every day is full of decisions. She hopes she made the right choice. She shakes her legs free of cramps and wriggles out of her bedroll to greet another long slog of a day: harnesses jangling, men yelling, and women grousing over bygone pleasures.

Ada heard enough of well-stocked kitchens and heirloom linen and china saved for Sunday dinners. She wonders why all the complainers didn't stay in Illinois or Missouri or Indiana reading Mrs. Beecher's Receipt Book and tatting. But women don't have much say in the matters of picking up and moving on, so Ada turns her mind to simple joys, things she misses most—tender shoots of scallions in spring, the first bite of a juicy summer peach, *an egg!*

All left behind, and for what? More of the same, day after day after dry, dusty day—undergirded always by bacon, dry bread, creek water coffee, and beans, beans, *and more blasted beans.*

8

July 18, 1846
The Great Divide

Ada spins slowly, the Antelope Hills to her south, the Wind River Chain to her north, and a wide, flat endless plain of sagebrush ahead and behind her, nothing but earth and sky. Wind prowls over the divide, and wisps of dark hair fan out behind her as she turns in thin, dry, mountain air. She closes her eyes and catches her breath. Her heart beats fast, as if in anticipation. For all their traveling—all the mornings chaining up and tolerating dust, all the windstorms, hail, torrents of rain, deaths, arguments, *and beans*—the overlanders have crossed the backbone of the continent. They are halfway to California, standing here on this remote treeless steppe, more than seven thousand feet high under a cloudless, sapphire sky.

After the relative ease of crossing the Great Divide through a low, wide shoulder of the Rocky Mountains at South Pass, a wall of peaks in the distance is as formidable as any geographic barrier Ada has ever seen. Sure, there had been California Hill and Windlass Hill early in their travels, and the steep descent in a *V* west of Scotts Bluff, that sandstone outcropping that rose out of nowhere from the flatlands, where rear wagon wheels were locked with chains and a downed tree dragged behind the wagons to diminish speed on the sharp decline. Now that the emigrants have crested the spine of the continent, ahead are the jagged peaks of the Wasatch Mountains, powdered with snow. Ada longs for her winter cloak, now submerged under the mud of the Big Blue River. The only consolation (Ada wonders if there is any consolation at all) is that the East is now squarely behind them. All rivers from now on will flow west, to the Pacific.

The sun has barely reached its zenith as Ada watches clouds of dirt and dust churn up behind the Minks and Radfords as they veer north toward Fort Hall instead south toward Bridger's Fort and Hastings's shortcut. *Should I follow?* Ada reaches out toward the dust at this newest parting of ways. Dust filters through her fingers and settles on her wrists. No, she's made her decision. Her head pounds. She waits there, feet rooted, until the last of the wagons becomes a mere speck in the distance and her headache begins to subside.

She kicks her long, muscled legs at the brown grass to scare up rattlesnakes as she lopes to recover ground behind the train. If she were in Noblesville, she could walk into Prince's Drygoods and purchase a pair of new leather boots for three dollars. She could touch bolts of calico and consider which of the many options would do for a day dress. She could eat pork roast every night. She could sleep in a room with a feather bed and a wardrobe and a simple chair. She could pass her days without imminent mishap. But she couldn't appreciate it all then like she can now, in the absence of it all.

There is no chance of finding any source for new boots until the group reaches Yerba Buena, eight hundred and fifty miles west now, unless, if the gods are smiling, she finds a pair at Bridger's Fort. Ada does mental calculations: at more than five thousand feet per mile (counting every three feet with her long, manly strides), she has more than a million and half more steps to cover in these ragged boots.

Can't be right. She recalculates, counting out the zeroes. *A million and a half?* She doubts her math. Whatever the number, her boots will not last that long. If rendered useless, she'll have to wrap her feet in cloth, or—*heaven forbid it*—walk barefoot over the Sierra Nevada Mountains this fall. For now, she will mend her boots again to stave off the inevitable. Her soles are already worn through so she's laid some leather on the inside that she's cut from the flap of one saddle-bag. Next, she'll be packing them with grass.

It's nothing but time, now, time and weather, pressing from all sides. After a celebratory toast at the nooning (and the dispensing of so much gunfire her ears ache), Ada gorges herself on gooseberries, a decision she later regrets. Dust billows around incoming horses as today's outriders veer into camp. After looking at maps and consulting with the scouts, George Donner and James Reed point toward the distant mountains. The emigrants plod on now toward the southwest, as the crow flies, only deviating from the path when met with craggy, upturned rocks and deep swales. Maybe Lansford Hastings will still be at Bridger's, and they'll have a reliable guide to shepherd them across the little-known section of the trail. Ada has her doubts. Snake oil salesmen are rarely found after peddling their goods. She wonders if there are really grapes in California.

Ada trips over a clump of grass. A barb of a prickly pear impales itself in her big toe, and she is forced to sit on the ground away from the caravan to yank it out with her forefingers. By the time she's finished, she's three wagons back and dashes to catch up. Virginia Reed catches the edge of Ada's apron as she hurries past.

"Miss Ada?"

"What is it, Virginia?"

"It's something I can't ask my ma about."

"The curse?"

Virginia bunches her eyebrows. "Is that what you call it?"

Ada takes the young girl's hand as they keep a steady pace. There is no stopping from sun up to noon or after the nooning to dusk. To combat thirst, Ada's learned to chew on a small green twig or leaf as she walks. "Have you started to bleed, that is?"

"Just spots."

"There's no avoidin' it. Sign of bein' a woman, they say. See if you can gather up some rags. If you want, I'll show you how to fasten them. Maybe after supper? But you should consider tellin' your ma."

Virginia squeezes Ada's hand. "Thank you, Miss Ada. Thanks much."

"Oh, Virginia?"

"Yes, Miss Ada?"

"I think John Breen is sweet on you. And maybe Eddie, too."

"Well, I'm not sweet on either one of them," Virginia says. "I'm never getting married."

Ada never told Inger Vik about her menses. Some things women didn't talk about, no matter how close. And Inger wasn't her real ma anyway, nor close. Ada had collected her own rags, figured out how to attach them to her bloomers with pins, and rinsed them out at night in her washstand. They dried, hanging in the dark wardrobe in her bedroom in Noblesville.

When Augustus got the wild hair to abandon their life in Indiana, Ada bundled all her rags at the bottom of her satchel. Within a week, the Viks were on their way west. Augustus sold both the undertaking business and their apartments above the furniture shop to another young Norwegian who planned to take over where Augustus left off, with two dead bodies still stiff in the back room.

And now they're gone. Everythin's gone. Except the mules.

Ada walks into the sun, her eyes itchy and red. The land is increasingly barren. Eighteen miles today. Rosie and Bert plod along, their ears erect. As the wagons circle loosely at the banks of the Little Sandy River, tongue to rear axle, the oxen are corralled inside, chained to the wagon wheels by their heads. Ada waters Bert and Rosie and sets out to help with supper. After the evening meal, Ada looks for Virginia Reed, but can't see her among the heads surrounding the Reed camp.

Ada feels gritty, down to her crusty private parts. At twilight, she wends her way to the edge of the Little Sandy, arms stretched out before her as she tangles with crooked branches and wayward vines. The mules graze downstream, front legs hobbled. Ada sits upstream from a clump of rushes, its susurrus calming. Her toes squish in cool, muddy shallows of the river.

Ada bends down and rinses out Augustus's handkerchief with the monogrammed *V.* She makes a pouch of it and holds it above her mouth to let the filtered water drain into her throat. The sky is starless at this early hour, except for Venus, the Evening Star, gleaming low on the western horizon.

Rosie and Bert perk to attention, their heads raised and ears projected forward. A shiver climbs up Ada's spine. She senses a slight rustling on the opposite bank. *Wolf?* Ada stares across the Little Sandy. The train's been dogged by wolves lately, some slinking into camp at night. She waits for the yellow eyes, the growl. Nothing. Any thrashing in the thicket she thinks she's heard dissolves. Ada lifts her skirts to reveal calf, knee, and thigh. She dips her hands into the creek and splashes water up her legs to clean her crotch. Mosquitoes bunch around her ankles. She flails her feet, making soft splashes in the silence. She hums, more as a deterrent to any wolf or coyote than to render a tune.

Ada keeps her eyes trained on the Evening Star as she bends her right leg and rests her ankle on her left knee. She kneads her sole, then switches legs to massage her other foot. For all the supplies the emigrants drag west, there is little that can be transported without being hauled in wagons or carried. Of all the commodities—foodstuffs, china, books, tools, ammunition, the kit and cargo of everyday life—none is so precious as feet.

Ada stands and walks barefoot back toward the camp, her tattered boots dragging behind by long leather laces. The scouts have selected a sensible place for the night, where wagons don't tilt and tents are pitched on flat ground. Grass, water, and fuel are the requisites for camp—and this spot has all three. Water is the utmost concern, followed by grass for the animals. The trail has been pitifully low on fuel, but medium-sized saplings border this place. They're thin and green, but they'll do. Boys scout behind rocks and brush for any source of dry firewood, as *bois de vache* is all but non-existent now that the overlanders have moved out of buffalo territory.

Ada avoids a pronghorn antler jutting into the pathway. Its once sharp points are now partially covered with decaying leaves. She can't afford to re-injure her toe. She already filched axle grease from Patrick Breen's larder without asking and smeared it on her toe to protect it. That's not all she swiped. She stole heels of bread late at night and even some of Breen's tobacco. She hasn't even returned Breen's compass yet. No, she's not proud of it.

Now she's got a nagging cough, can't get in a full breath in this thin mountain air.

If only she had *Jones' Guide* or *Bassett's Herbals for the Home*, she could paw through pages to find something to stop this infernal hacking. *Hyssop? Wild cherry?* She took all Augustus's books for granted when she worked alongside him, flipping through Cheselden's *Osteographia* page by page to see illustrations of bone structures and human organs, or skimming Dr. Rush's pamphlets on medical opinions. Even though she doesn't have Augustus's books at her disposal, she's got his medicine pouch filled with physicking pills, calomel, castor oil, vials of peppermint essence, and a sleeve of headache wafers, which are almost gone. She'll step in when she needs to, offer her limited knowledge, if it can save a leg or a life.

Picket guards saunter at the edge of the encampment. Ada ducks between two sentries standing at ease, smoking. She nods at the men.

"Evening, miss."

"Might've heard a wolf across the creek," she says. "Maybe I'm just hearin' things, but better to be safe with the animals and all."

Dolan stands on the near side of the wagon, honing his knife. Ada marches toward him, one goal in mind by way of another.

"I'm wonderin', Mr. Dolan, if you can teach me how to shoot."

Dolan spits tobacco juice to the side and smiles wide.

"Why, I'd be obliged, Miss Weeks. That Hawken is an old friend of mine."

"Tomorrow, then?"

"Tomorrow it is."

9

July 20, 1846
East of Bridger's Fort

At dawn, Patrick Breen strikes the tent while Margaret gets breakfast on. Dolan lugs the yoke from its resting spot against the wagon and sets it on the grass. He goes to the corral, calls for the oxen, and goads the huge creatures back to the wagon. First, he secures the curved frame over the burly neck of the off-ox and then coaxes the lead ox into the yoke. Ma Breen scours dishes, and the boys rush to clean up camp, tying bedrolls and loading items into the battered wagon box. Ada leads Rosie and Bert to the rear of the Breen wagon and ties them there. The Breens are in the lead platoon today, so there's no time for dillydallying. The sun's not even up yet.

Before they leave camp, George Donner stops at each campsite. He's captain of the train now that the Boggs Party has decamped for Fort Hall. Ada is surprised the men didn't elect Reed; he normally sent scouts out by morning and called the halt each afternoon. But men resent him, his military service, his wealth, his arrogance. Now that the men have voted Donner in, Reed must defer to George Donner, his friend from Illinois. It's not a democracy.

Ada passes the Reed wagons on her way to get water when she hears Reed and Donner arguing.

"Been sold up Salt River," Reed mutters.

George Donner looks exasperated. "We'll have no talk of that," he says. "Vote was fair. We'll be to Bridger's in three days. No time to waste."

Reed scowls. "Just remember, it wasn't my idea to take Hastings's route."

"It was the decision of the whole group," Donner says. "Let bygones be bygones."

Ada hurries back to camp to sort out the mules.

"Giddap!" Dolan yells.

Amid the jangling, snorting, and lowing, the oxen shake their cumbersome heads and settle into a slow, steady rhythm, tilting their great horns side to side as they walk like lumbering oafs. Ada swats at Bert's backside and slings Dolan's old rifle over her shoulder, butt end down. There won't be a shooting lesson today.

Families are spread out, bound for Jim Bridger's, seventy-five miles south of the main trail. When they reach the Big Sandy River, the land opens up, sun scorched and arid, dotted with alkali pools. Wagons cross the Big Sandy without trouble, their beds greased to protect supplies inside. *As soon as we get to Bridger's,* Ada thinks, *I got to see about some new boots.*

Today it's a turbid, murky sky. Ada smells rain. "What do you see today, Simon?" Ada looks up at the angry cloud formations. "I swear I see a rooster. Do you see the cockscomb?"

"It's just a cloud."

"Look closer." She squats, puts her arm around Simon. "Yesterday, you saw a castle, remember? Well, today we have a rooster."

Ada hopes the ballooning clouds bring rain, if, for no other reason, to keep the dust down. There's been no rain now for more than a week, although the sky's been moody. Huge buzzards circle overhead, hanging on warm air. Then, a faint rumble. Ada tracks the thunderstorm as it approaches across the wide, grey sky: maybe fifty, then thirty, then ten miles off. The sky darkens, and a deep roar emanates from somewhere behind them. The oxen snort, sidestep. Donner calls for a halt, and the wagons come to a creaking stop. Ada and all the Breen boys take cover beneath the wagon before the deluge. Patrick and Ma Breen scramble into the wagon to wait out the storm. First tentatively, and then with a vengeance, hail the size of quail eggs begins to pelt the wagons, fast and faster yet, a torrent from heaven. It sounds like a drum, percussive and short. Rosie lets out a long, loud call from behind the wagon; it starts out as a whinny, followed by a loud bray.

"Hang on, Rosie," Ada yells. She squeezes Peter's arm. "She's afraid, but there's nothin' to be afraid of. Look!" Ada says. A lizard scampers for cover to avoid pounding hail.

"Is that a lizard?" Peter asks.

Ada nods.

"If I were a lizard, I would want to be called Leroy," Simon interrupts.

Edward sneers. "That's a stupid name."

"You're a stupe," Simon shoots back.

Ada tries to hide a smile. "Maybe his name's Leland."

"Leland the Lizard," Peter says.

"I wonder if there's a Mrs. Leland Lizard," Ada says. She bites her lip to avoid laughing. A heavy deluge of hail pounds the ground just beyond the wagon wheels. *It's goin' to be a sea of mud here in a jack's minute.*

Rosie continues to bray, louder now.

James stops up his ears.

"I never!" Ada says. "Rosie! Quiet!"

The wagon jolts as Patrick Breen stomps above the children's heads.

"What in heaven are you doing, man?" Ma Breen yells.

"Grab it!" Breen yells. "We're losing the cover!"

Ada pulls Peter and James closer. She wants to peer out from underneath the wagon to survey the damage, but there will be time enough for that, after storms (and arguments).

"I don't ever want a missus," Simon says. "Even though Eddie does, don't you, Eddie? Eddie and Virginia, sitting in a tree, K-I-S-S—"

"Shut yer trap," Eddie says, as he swipes at Simon.

"Now, now, boys," Ada says.

The hems of Ma Breen's skirt appear by the rear wagon wheels. Soon, her face peers beneath the lip of the wagon bed. "Up and out," she roars. "Think it's nap time?"

Simon looks at Ada. "See what I mean? About not wanting a missus?"

Now that the hail has stopped, Peter slithers out from underneath the wagon, and Ada follows. Her hands are muddy and her hem drags in brown muck. She helps James as the rest of the boys shimmy between wagon wheels to untangle themselves from their hiding place.

"Off with you!" Ada says, and goes back to check on the mules. Rosie thrusts her head into Ada's chest. Ada rubs the molly mule on the crown of her head. "Sorry if you were scared there, girl. It's all over now." She sinks her face into Rosie's fuzzy cheek.

Bert glares at Ada. His ears are pointed straight back, the sign he's angry. "It's not like it's my fault," Ada says. "You best put it behind you, Bert. But that's like askin' you to do a cartwheel." She knows mules don't forget, not bad weather or bad treatment or bad water.

By the time the Breens pull into the trading post, it's nearly sundown on the third day of blazing hot travel. A dozen men—including James Reed, William Eddy, Charles Stanton, a couple of teamsters, and the Germans—circle George Donner outside the palisaded gates of the fort.

"And where's Hastings?" Breen demands.

Donner looks grim. "Not here." He looks down, kicks the dirt, clenches his fists.

"What in tarnation?" Breen shouts.

"Left for California with a forward party. Four days past," Donner says.

Patrick Breen's lips clench. Lewis Keseberg swears and leaves the circle. Jacob Donner shakes his head. James Reed's face looks to explode. It's bad news all around. If enmity had a name, it would be Lansford W. Hastings, this is one thing Ada is sure of.

"I'll get the mules," Dolan offers. He ruffles Bert's mane. "C'mon, Bert. Got an apple for ye." Rosie eyes Dolan. "You, too, Rosie."

Wordlessly, Ada and Ma Breen set up camp: tripod, Dutch oven, campstools; the unwieldy crate of utensils, plates, and cups (they never touch Ma Breen's good china). Ada's arms are strong from all the hefting. Ma Breen shoos the younger children away. It's beans, biscuits, and weak coffee for supper, this morning's grounds used for the third time today.

"What I'd do for a fresh sack of coffee," Ma Breen complains. "Tomorrow, we'll get as much as our purse allows."

"A big sack of flour, maybe?" Ada asks. "I've got a hankerin' for an apple pie. Or a peach pie. Or a . . ."

"Quit your mumbling and get these biscuits on."

Secretly, Ada's glad for the rest. Wagons need repairs. Wooden wheels need soaking. Iron tires need hammering. Clothes need washing and mending. Animals need reprieve from their labors. And she's just bone-tired, having walked halfway across the continent. Maybe she can even nap in the middle of the day, right here by the creek. Ada unlaces her tattered boots and dips her toes. The creek runs swiftly over her sore feet. She recalls lazy days along Butler's Creek back in Indiana and the fort she aimed to build there when she was six. It seems like a lifetime ago.

The next morning, Ada extracts coins from her hem and counts them out. She's got thirty dollars left. She stuffs five silver dollars into her apron pocket and sews the rest of the coins back up into the edging of her skirt. That leaves twenty-five dollars for California. It will have to do. She's still got the sewing notions she begged from Eleanor Eddy back at Independence Rock. She squints, threads the needle, and pulls the strand through. As she makes small, even stitches in her hem, Ada makes out a mental list: *boots, flour, tobacco.*

She crosses the meadow and enters the gates of the fort, now open for business. To the right, a long, low, log building houses a dim trading post. Ada's eyes adjust as she enters the store. There's not a square inch that's not covered with something for sale: coffee and whiskey, syrups and digestives, guns and hides. Cans and sundries line the narrow shelves: candles, soap, tools, patent elixirs, and matches. The interior is rimmed with barrels of flour, cornmeal, rice, and salt. Even saleratus, a luxury now. All their cakes are flat without it. She breathes in the scent of licorice. *Will I have enough left over to buy some? Or camphor?*

Ada meanders up each aisle and adds items to her basket. She worms her way to the back of the store, scouting for boots. Two pairs are left, pinched between buffalo robes and fur hats. Her heart quickens. She can't wait to discard these boots and wear a new pair as soon as *right now.* She knows without trying them on that one pair is much too large. Even if she wedges rags into the toes, it would make the going rough. She'd trip every other step. She tries to cram her foot into the other pair, and finds them woefully small. *Rotten luck.* Somewhere between dainty and a giant and all she's got are boots not worth two bits. All she can hope for now is that someone will die so she can claim the boots right off the body, like Augustus used to do when a stiff had no family. Got a pocket watch and fifty dollars once for his trouble. She adds a stick of licorice and a large ball of twine to her purchases and goes back for camphor, now that she won't be buying boots today.

Virginia Reed waves to Ada from across the store.

"Been lookin' for you, Virginia."

"I just wanted to tell you I did what you said. Told my ma. She helped me with, you know."

"Well, you let me know if you've got any more of your questions."

"You know what's good for a toothache? My pa's got one and he's been mighty ornery."

"Could try a pinch of pepper with clove oil, if you have it. Otherwise, pack the tooth with pepper. Worked for my pa every time."

A line snakes to the register where Bridger's partner, Louis Vasquez, tallies up. When it's her turn at the register, Ada plunks down coins on the counter.

"And add a long plug."

"For the mister?" Vasquez says.

"You can be sure of it." She tucks the snuff into her apron pocket and signals to John Breen. "John, take this flour to the wagon, will you? I've got my hands full."

Ada sidles over to a group of men and women huddled around Jim Bridger. From the corner of her eye, she sees Lewis Keseberg pocket a small tin of mustard. *Cheatin' bastard.*

"From here, it's a level road, with plenty of water and grass," Bridger says. "Seven weeks to the day you'll be at Sutter's. Hastings said he'd leave notes along the way, in case anyone was still traveling this late in the season."

Who's to argue with Bridger's advice? Explorer, mountain man, Army scout, and experienced guide? Bridger's head almost reaches the low-slung ceiling, and he stoops forward as he speaks. If Bridger says the way is navigable, the emigrants can be assured of his counsel. His word is like Moses's.

"We'll lay over two days, maybe three," George Donner says. "Get to what needs doing. Check your yokes, axles, tires. Look for hairline cracks. And see to it all your oxen are shod proper. I'll leave it to you ladies to do what needs doing in the wagons. Still a long pull ahead."

Ma Breen whispers to Ada as she leaves the store. "If I'd had the upper hand, we'd be going on to Fort Hall with the Minks and the Radfords."

"Why didn't you speak up then, back when I said the same? You told me, 'Hush.'"

"Can't argue with Patrick Breen."

"I still got my doubts," Ada says. "For whatever that's worth."

Ada wonders if Ma Breen noticed about the tobacco. If she did—or if she cared—she's silent on the matter.

In a crowded pen outside the dispensary, men dicker over new pack animals. Jacob Donner haggles with Vasquez over a pair of oxen and William Eddy eyes a new horse. Ada tarries by the pen. Should she sell the mules here? It's a fair question. She's prodded them halfway across the continent. But for what? She doesn't know what she'll do with them in California. *I'll ask Dolan what he'd do.*

George Donner's picked up a new teamster, a short Frenchman named Trudeau to replace Hiram Miller who left with Edwin Bryant. While Donner is introducing Trudeau to the others, a lanky man approaches.

"Looking to hitch on with a new party," the stranger says.

Donner looks him over. "Look a little gaunt. Everything all right with you?"

"Bit of the lung fever, but I'm feeling stronger." Ada recognizes an Irish brogue, not unlike Dolan's. "Rested up here a few weeks, and am right ready to go now," the Irishman says. "Looking forward to the good California air. Got a horse, too. Not too many effects. Willing to pay my way for taking me on. Name's Luke Halloran."

Halloran is thin and coughs into a handkerchief. Ada is alarmed. *Is that blood?*

"Welcome," Tamsen Donner says. "The more men the better at this point."

Ada walks briskly toward Green River and stuffs her purchases in Bert's side pack, not before swiping a small piece of snuff with her teeth and lips. A meandering creek empties into the Green River at the western boundary of the field. Simon and Peter Breen splash in the shallow water. Ada hides behind a tree and tosses a rock in their direction.

"Hey!" Simon yells.

She tosses another rock. Simon rushes at the tree and finds Ada there, laughing.

"You'll get what's coming to you, Miss Ada," Simon says.

She tousles his hair. "We'll see about that, mister."

Dolan enters the clearing toting his old Hawken. "Miss Ada! How about that shooting lesson?" He's lean and tall, his grimed vest over a blousy shirt Ada recognizes as Augustus's. His trousers hide his form above stout boots. He stands a full three inches above Ada, who's five-eleven in stocking feet. "I've got a few spare minutes."

Ada takes the smooth bore flintlock from Dolan.

"Heavy isn't it?" he asks.

Ada follows Dolan to the far edge of the field overlooking the Green River. Sparrows flit in and out of the cottonwoods.

"Got everything you'll need here. May want to pick up more powder, if you've got script," he says. "But there's one thing I might mention. I've seen you carrying the rifle upside down. Here's how you carry it."

He repositions it on her shoulder, butt end up. She looks down, smiles.

"Well, I weren't a shootin' girl."

Dolan smiles, takes the Hawken and stands it upright, muzzle up, pointing away.

"After today you will be. A shooting girl, that is. First thing, make sure you're not primed."

"Primed?"

"No powder in the pan. Now look here," Dolan says.

Ada peers into the mechanism at the center of the rifle.

"Best to shoot it clean, like this." Dolan tips the rifle over and pulls the brass trigger. A muffled ping exhales from the end of the rifle. "Here's how you load it." Dolan pours black powder from a horn and measures with its cap. He funnels the powder into the muzzle. "Then you take a wad—a lubricated cloth is all, but you can use most anything. Place the ball inside the cloth and load it."

Ada watches closely. Dolan removes the ramrod from the base of the rifle and shoves the ball deep into the barrel. "Now cock the hammer and ready the cap. But be sure you're ready to shoot." He balances the rifle, aims for a distant tree, and pulls the trigger. The rifle explodes with a loud pop. "Now it's your turn."

His hand brushes hers as she takes the rifle. "I think I've got it." Ada carefully repeats Dolan's instructions. She shoots, reloads.

"Mighty fine, Miss Ada."

"Thanks for your trouble, Mr. Dolan. I'll keep practicin'."

"I'll be back to camp now. Shoeing oxen today, nasty job. Told Breen I wouldn't be more than a half hour. Good thing you're a fast learner, Miss Ada. Might have made a liar of me."

"Before you go, Mr. Dolan, I've got a question. I'm thinkin' of sellin' Bert. You got any opinions on that?"

"Just Bert?"

"Yes, not Rosie."

"Won't get two nickels for him here," Dolan says. "They buy low and sell high. Better to run him to California. Better market there."

"If you say so," Ada says. "It's just that he's beginnin' to be a bother."

"Life's full of bother, miss. Best get used to it."

Ada's shoulder is sore, and she's only gotten off a half dozen rounds. She'll have to spend some of her saved-up coin on powder, and if she's not selling Bert here, she'll have to ration what's left. She walks toward the creek, places the rifle in the tall grass beside her, and lies down. *Did he mean to brush my elbow?* She pictures Dolan's long fingers and imagines them running through her hair.

"What in all creation!" she yelps. Ada slaps at biting flies: first her shoulder, then her elbow, then her neck again. Even her ankles. There are mosquitoes, too, and gnats. She'll have to ask around for pennyroyal—it doesn't seem to grow wild here, like in Indiana. Ada gets up, grabs the rifle. She waves her arms but cannot dodge the cloud of insects. She runs to the edge of the field and crashes into camp.

"What's got into you?" Ma Breen asks.

Ada shakes her head, splats a mosquito on her arm. She licks her finger and wipes the blood smear away.

"Can't get away from these gallnippers," she says.

"Hmph," Ma Breen says. "Can't get away from all this." She sweeps her hand around the camp to the yellowish-brown hills beyond.

Ada follows Ma Breen's gaze. Another mosquito attacks Ada's neck. "Dumb it!" She sets the Dutch oven over the fire, adds salt pork, and sets the plank table. Her neck is covered with red welts. Even when Breen picks up the fiddle after supper, Ada can't get her mind off the itching. She tries not to scratch.

10

August 3, 1846
Into the Wasatch

Three days out of Bridger's Fort, it isn't evident which route Hastings has taken, although he's a week ahead with sixty wagons. *Where are the ruts?* East is west and west is east. The travelers argue at every turn. It's this way, man. No, it ain't. You blind? It's this way, dammit. Shut yer trap. Shut yer own. Pull it, boys. Easy, now.

Trail to nowhere, Ada thinks. Wagons roam in and out of arid hills and ravines rimmed with red dirt cliffs and sparse vegetation. The wind weaves and whines and wails, churning up even more dust. Ada covers her mouth with Augustus's stained hanky. The dull rumble of wagon wheels drowns out trail chatter, as wheels scratch and scrape over sand and gravel, one slow revolution at a time. Yesterday, the small McCutcheon family—William, Amanda, and baby Harriet— joined the group, their wagon left behind near Bridger's because of an irreparable axletree. They're walking, their horse trailing behind them carrying sparse supplies.

"Tolerable rough road," Reed says, as he rides past Breen.

Tolerable? Ada thinks. *Not too tolerable.* When they stop for the nooning, Ada decides to catch a quick nap. As she beds down, she hears a loud, piercing scream.

"Ada! Come quick!" Ma Breen runs toward Ada. "Edward's had a bad fall."

Ada comes out from under the wagon. "What's happened?"

"Was off riding with Virginia Reed, and met with a badger hole. Sent Mr. Breen back to Bridger's to see if a doctor's available."

Ada sits by the boy and waits for Patrick Breen to arrive. When Breen rides back into camp, a whiskered mountain man accompanies him. The stranger examines the boy's leg and grunts. "It'll have to come off," he says, as he removes a large knife from a leather sheath. Edward's eyes grow wide as saucers.

"No," Ada interrupts. Her voice is shrill. "Give it three days. Time for the swellin' to go down. Time enough to, well," she pats the boy and looks Patrick Breen in the eye. "Time enough to see what needs doin'."

Where is Edwin Bryant when they need him? *Probably almost to California by now.*

"Wait and see?" Breen says.

"Shouldn't go rushin' this," Ada says. "Boy's in a fix, all right, but he's got time. I've seen plenty of broken bones in the undertakin' trade, but that's rarely what killed them." She winds a clean cloth around Edward's leg and turns toward the Breens. "My pappa was forced to break limbs"—*even saw some off,* she thinks—"to fit all shapes of bodies into coffins." She recalls the German undertaker, Earl Grundinger, and how she and Augustus squeezed nearly three hundred pounds of flesh into a spare, wooden coffin. Augustus had to saw off the butcher's arms to make room. As he stuffed the severed arms between the dead man's legs, he laughed. "Von't be having any competition now." Then he nailed the cover shut.

But maybe this isn't a good time to be thinkin'—or talkin'—about coffins.

Ada motions to Mr. and Mrs. Breen, and takes them aside. "Don't want Eddie maimed for the rest of his God-given life," Ada whispers.

She can't get the image of Earl Grundinger out of her head and swallows bile. "Missin' limbs act in strange ways. Phantom pain all the time. Better to wait and see."

"I think it's for the best, Father. To wait," Ma Breen says.

"I rode all that way back to Bridger's, and now I'm henpecked?" Patrick Breen says.

"I said I think it's for the best," she answers.

Breen hands the rider five dollars. "Thanks for your trouble, but we'll be waiting to see how he fares before, you know."

The mountain man grumbles. Ma Breen looks at Ada pleadingly, and Edward even more so, his pupils now constricted to the size of a needle. Ma Breen bends over her son and wipes his sweaty brow with a damp cloth. "See you're not wrong, Ada."

Wrong? There's so much goin' wrong. The list is lengthy: exhaustion, spats, accidents. Eddie's break unnerves her. What use is a boy with a missing leg?

Ada's aware of all she's missing—not just companionship or camaraderie. There's plenty of that on the trail. It's something else, something she hasn't felt since her ma died in the fire, and really, even before, back before her ma sank into depths of despair. It's been a long time since she's felt it or known it, that hazy, ethereal thing that falls between want and need. That's the something she's missing more than all the foodstuffs or china or books stuffed into wagons.

What to do about it? she thinks. *Somethin'. Anythin'.*

That night, Dolan stops Ada on her way to get water for washing up.

"I got to congratulate you. Not too many people speak up against Breen."

"I wasn't speakin' up against Breen," Ada says. "I was speakin' up for Eddie."

As wagons snake in and out of slot canyons, Ada is awed by massive, marbled cliffs that bank steeply on both sides of the rough trail. Edward's injuries are so severe he's forced to ride inside the wagon, cramped between pork barrels and flour sacks. It's a bone-jarring ride. Ada mixes up ground chokecherry and mush and spoons it to Edward at the nooning. But that's all the time she—or any of the travelers—rest. The wagons creak and roll and lurch over uneven terrain thick with prickly sagebrush and half-buried boulders. Ada battles between looking up and watching her feet. She can't afford a broken ankle. But she knows what Edwin Bryant would do. He'd look up. To miss the grandeur of this canyon would be a sin.

Ada's concept of sin is vague. One is born with it (or so she was taught), and however valiantly one tries to adhere to the Commandments, invariably, one sinks into it. Ada's record on a couple of the biblical admonishments—honor your father and mother or do not kill, for example—will never be in doubt. She admits she's guilty of taking the Lord's name in vain. And stealing. And, try as she might, she is an abject failure at the ninth commandment: do not covet your neighbor's ox or ass or wife. Ada's always been jealous—of people's appearance, wealth, family. She's not pretty (*and too tall*). She's not dirt poor, but she has little more than two nickels to rub together. It's the word, *family*. That's where Ada takes a plunge into a jealousy so thick a butcher's knife can't puncture the rind, and nothing, not prayer or self-deprecation or guilt, can rid her of the sentiment. She has no family and she's *jealous as hell* of those who do.

Ada hears a low moan from deep inside the Breen wagon. She pokes her head inside the waxed canvas folds. "How's our patient?"

"Poorly, Miss Ada," Edward answers.

"Let me have another look at that leg, young sir." Ada watches the wagon wheels as she climbs up into the wagon box. She tries to keep her balance as she takes his injured leg in her hands and unravels the bandage. The wagon pitches back and forth and it's difficult to keep her hands steady. The boy's splint is still intact but the swelling concerns her. She masks her apprehension and refastens the bandage. Are those fleabites all over his legs? For the boy's sake, let alone her own, she wishes she had pennyroyal. Her welts are now scabs, and it's a losing battle between her will and her weakness as she picks at them.

"You'll be up in no time, chasin' around like before," Ada says.

"Thanks, Miss Ada. Can you tell Ma I'm awful hungry?"

"Well, that's a good sign. I'll tell her straight away." Ada wonders how long it will be until Eddie is up again. She isn't sure he ever will be. And if he's done for, then what? Who's next? She times her jump out of the wagon and lands on her feet.

Edward Breen isn't the only one riding in a wagon. Luke Halloran's horse trails behind one of George Donner's wagons. So far, Halloran hasn't left the confines of the Donner's wagon box. Ada hears his rattling cough when she passes the Donner's camp on her way to do her business. "Anythin' I can do to help?"

Tamsen Donner shakes her head. "Just a matter of time, I'm afraid."

Wagons lumber on through the day, making slow progress. The riverbed is narrow and strewn with jagged rocks, the canyon obstructed with willow and cottonwood and serviceberry. There's animal scat along the trail: wolf, sheep, mountain lion.

"A poor place to put any confidence in," Breen says. He goads the oxen over rough boulders and across the creek.

It's difficult to find level ground in the ravine, so the wagons land in whatever spot they can, some bunched together and others set apart. The Breens set up camp at a large *V* in the canyon along an unnamed creek. Ada goes to sleep with a nagging ache in her stomach. Even though they've replenished supplies at Bridger's, Ma Breen is already rationing food.

And it isn't just Ma Breen who's cross—all the women are testier than usual. Even the otherwise sweet-tempered Eleanor Eddy is sullen. The baby is colicky, and Eleanor can't get a good night's sleep. It's already been three months of drudgery: walking, cooking, washing, tending babies. Day in, day out, day in. It leaves little time for gossip now, and all of it centers around Halloran this and Halloran that, as if talking about him will make him better.

There hasn't been a death since Ada's parents on the Big Blue at the end of May and Tommy Radford's on the high plains. The thought of death unnerves Ada in this desolate wilderness. If Halloran were to die here, his burial would be unceremonious, his grave shallow and unmarked. *"As for man, his days are as grass,"* Ada thinks, remembering Psalm 103. *"For the wind passeth over it, and it is gone."* Ada shivers at the thought. *We're all just passin' through.*

Ada can't remember the last time she washed her hair. Was it at the Little Sandy River? Certainly it hasn't been longer? Days on the trail drown into weeks until Ada can't remember one day from the next, except when the wagons pass landmarks or a significant event happens, like a wedding or a calamity. She'd like to see another wedding: hers. But that takes two, and one of the twosome isn't showing much interest. Her mind wanders. She wonders if Amelia Mink and Luke Radford are married yet. Or have a baby.

The next morning, Ada hears the familiar: "Chain up, boys! Come ha!" Last night she was kept awake by coyotes, one so brave as to approach the wagon and slink around the campfire after dark. She watched the coyote's darting yellow eyes, once catching her own. The animal froze. Ada shouted, and the skittish coyote slunk back into the dark. Within the hour, they'll be on the move again inching their way on this ass-headed road through the canyon. No time to wash her hair.

Ada ties Rosie and Bert to their familiar spot at the rear of the Breen wagon. The mules stink of sour breath. Rosie turns her head toward Ada. Ada takes the mule's face between her hands and rubs her face close to Rosie's. "What was I thinkin' about sellin' you? I won't never do that, girl." She gives Bert the stink eye. "About you, buster, I'm not so sure." He looks away.

Ada swipes her greasy hair away from her eyes. She hurries to catch up with Dolan. She's shouldering the rifle the way he taught her. He's preoccupied with the oxen, but tips his hat. The wagon train lurches into formation. The sun slants through the canyon as the wagons travel in and out of sunlight and warmth to shadow and chill. Bouncing bonnets list as wagons navigate over cavernous rocks and fallen trees in deep ravines. The shrill *twitter-twit-twit-twit-twit-twit* of a junco pierces the clear air. Ada wishes she could fly.

11

August 7, 1846
Weber Canyon, Wasatch Mountains

Wagons inch along the rugged path, iron tires striking gravel. Each night Ada repairs her boots with twine she purchased at Bridger's. She's going through the twine like melted butter. By the end of each day, her open toes meet the rocky trail and scabs pulse open with fresh blood. Soon there will be no sole left at all. Between rotten boots, prickly cacti, and rough gravel, Ada's feet haven't been without blemish since May.

Errant cottonwood branches and serviceberry brambles scratch her arms and legs as she walks. The narrow path through the canyon is clogged with straggly alder and scrub pine; it makes for tedious travel. Flies buzz around her ears, and Ada spends most of her waking hours dodging biting flies and mosquitoes. Her armpits itch. She longs for a long, cool soak in a mountain stream, the water washing over her body and taking with it all the tailings of dirt and drudgery and desolation.

That night, James Reed calls for a halt. "I'll ride ahead—see what's in front of us," he says. "Maybe catch up with Hastings. Who's with me?"

Charles Stanton and William Pike volunteer.

"Anyone willing to offer a horse?"

"You can take one of my mules," Ada says. "The john, not the molly."

"That's mighty generous of you, Miss Weeks," Charles Stanton says. "Anything we should know about—"

"Bert, his name's Bert. Stubborn son of a jack, but shouldn't give you much trouble, if you scratch him right here." She rubs Bert in front of the ears. "And he's partial to sugar." She pats the mule on the rear. "Don't go gettin' Mr. Pike and Mr. Stanton in any scrapes, you hear?" She removes her bedroll and blanket, Inger's jerky, and tobacco from Bert's pack and stuffs it all into Rosie's pack. "Be seein' you in a few days, you old sourpuss."

The next day, the wicked sun bears down on the camp. After the noon meal, Tamsen Donner gathers the children. Even in the wilds of the Wasatch, school is in session. She holds aloft Samuel Kirkham's heavy tome of the English language.

"Today, we will learn the letters d, e, and f," Mrs. Donner says. Children squirm: one boy elbows another, girls whisper. "D has one uniform sound; as in death, bandage." Mrs. Donner enunciates the "d" sound. "Do you hear that? 'Duh' as in death. Can you think of any other words that begin with the letter d?"

Ada perches on a ledge at the outskirts of the circle, swatting at flies. *Death? Why not doll or dog or doughnut?* She brushes off her skirt and slinks away from the group to tend to Rosie. The mule raises a lazy eye to Ada as she approaches. *I say we dispense with Mr. Kirkham altogether,* Ada thinks, *and get on with learnin' our own way.*

"What do you say, Rosie?" she says. "I say D is for dog. Dogged. Dog-tired. Dog-eared. Dog-gone-it."

Mrs. Donner continues. "E has a long sound; as in scheme, severe; a short sound, as in men, tent; and sometimes the sound of a flat a, as in sergeant. F has one unvaried sound, as in fancy, muffin . . ."

Her voice fades from Ada's earshot. Ada washes her clothes in the stream and spreads them on a waist-high brittlebush to dry. That mornings and evenings can be so cold and days in between so blistering hot makes it difficult to get comfortable. Cloak on, cloak off. Shawl on, shawl off. Ada's shirtsleeves are rolled up today.

Ada finds Ma Breen dozing in the shade beside the wagon, her chin low on her chest. Bella squirms in her cradle under the jockey box. Ada plucks Bella up and leaves Ma Breen to her napping. She finds a shaded spot between two small boulders near the stream and checks for snakes before she wedges between warm rocks. Maybe she can get a short nap in, too. She rolls her skirt up above her knees and stretches her long legs.

Simon saunters by. "Hey, Miss Ada."

Ada quickly smooths her skirt down to her ankles. "Gettin' away from your lessons again?"

"Please don't go telling my da. No one can cross him. Learned that back at home. My backside used to be raw from the switching."

"Get along, before anyone sees you. I won't spill your secret."

Bella shifts and settles into sleep. A junco flits above Ada's head and darts up into the cloudless sky. Ada gazes up through the canyon and squints at the sun. If she were the sun, she could see everything. What she would most like to see is how to get through this choked canyon.

None of the men dare to voice second thoughts on taking the short cut, but Ada knows by now what everyone's thinking: *We're long behind schedule.* Winter is in the air. Children are the only ones oblivious to the emigrants' dilemma. In the afternoons—once Tamsen Donner frees them from their lessons, that is—they play tag and hide-and-seek. Girls set out simple tea parties for their ragdolls. Boys run and roughhouse. The sun courses through the sky and disappears much earlier than on the plains. Darkness comes on faster in the canyons, and, with it, a chill.

All at once, she bounces back to attention. Has the baby stopped breathing? Ada shakes the infant gently. Bella takes a long, deep breath, and then settles into a comfortable position to continue her nap. Ada focuses on each of Bella's breaths: in, out, in, out. Ada shakes her own leg, which has fallen asleep. The baby wakes, but doesn't cry.

A few days later, Reed returns alone. "Caught up with Hastings. They've run into some trouble. He rode partway back with me and pointed us in that direction." Reed waves his arms southwest. "But there's no road and no sign of any wagon ever going that way. We'll have to clear it ourselves."

"Damn Hastings," one of the German teamsters says.

"Bastard," another German yells. He mimics wringing a man's neck. "Vouldn't hear much from him after dat."

All the men grumble. If Lansford Hastings rode into camp right now, there'd be no judge and jury.

"Where's Mr. Pike?" Harriet Pike asks. "And Mr. Stanton?"

Reed shakes his head.

Harriet Pike blanches.

"Not what you're thinking, ma'am. We got separated, is all."

"Separated?" William Eddy yells. "I vote we mount a search, and straight away."

"They're good riders. Give them a day or two," Reed answers. "I've blazed trees along the way."

"But we'll be moving on by then!" Harriet Pike interrupts.

"Maybe, maybe not. Depends on how long it takes us to clear a trail wide enough for the wagons," Reed says. "We'll leave fires burning all night, whether we're here or a few miles down the canyon. Give them credit, ma'am. They'll find their way."

"Bert will get them through," Ada says to Harriet. "He's ornery enough."

"Thanks, Miss Ada, but I'd rather see William. He's ornery enough on his own."

Ada pats Harriet's arm. "They'll be comin' in, you'll see."

At dawn, all able-bodied men shoulder pickaxes, spades, hatchets, hunting knives, and chains—whatever they have to clear the impasse—and strike out to hack away at thick brush, blazing a pathway barely wide enough for the emigrant wagons to navigate the Wasatch. One day. Three. Then five. At the end of each day, the men return, haggard, bloodied, and blistered. A mile at a time, they bushwhack a crude road around wheel-sized boulders and through a never-ending thicket of aspen, box elder, and brush. Bridger's word that the road is level and fit for a wagon is a flat out lie. Talk is cheap.

Even the younger boys are pressed into service. Any boy over twelve is by now out with the brush party whacking trees, moving rocks, and clearing brush.

"Take me," Simon says.

"Enough. You stay and help your ma," Breen says.

"Hey, Simon," Ada says. "I've got a riddle for you." She dries her hands on her apron and sits on a campstool.

Simon shuffles his bare feet in the dirt. He looks after his father and older brothers as they move out with the work party.

"Okay, mister, here you go. Tell me when you've figured it out: what would have been yesterday and will be tomorrow?" Ada asks.

Simon puzzles his brow. "Maybe today?"

"Yessir, Simon Breen. For all your skippin' out of Miz Donner's classwork, you're sharp as a razor. I'll have to come up with more riddles for you."

Ada pats Simon's backside as he scampers off. He picks up a branch and swats at gnats.

Today, a new family overtakes the entourage—Franklin and Elizabeth Graves, their nine children, *and a right surly teamster,* Ada thinks. She assesses a young woman about her age. As far as Ada can see from the lack of a wedding ring, the young woman must be single. She mentally tabulates the girl's features: a prominent masculine face, a small chest. Soon she berates herself for being petty. She could use a friend.

"Mary Graves, is it?"

"Yes, and you're . . .?

"Ada Weeks. From Indiana."

"I've never been to Indiana. Can't say as I'll ever go there now. Do you work for the Breens?"

"No, no. They took me in when my parents died, back in Indian Country."

"Oh, I'm terrible sorry for your loss. I don't know what I'd do without my ma. What do you aim to do, then, once we reach California?"

That's the question that's nagged on Ada for weeks, first burbling under the surface, and then creeping up into her daily thoughts. Now it's been spoken aloud.

"Haven't given it much thought," she lies. "You?"

"Can you keep a secret, Miss Ada?"

Ada nods.

"I'm promised to Mr. Snyder, our teamster, only my pa don't know. My ma knows, but hasn't said as much. We've been stepping out for some time now."

Ada can't fathom what Mary sees in John Snyder, a gruff teamster with a permanent sneer. But it subtracts Mary from Dolan's affections, and, anyway, people see all kinds of things in others that Ada doesn't see. *Like what Ma Breen sees in Patrick Breen. Or what Philippine Keseberg sees in that rat, her husband, Lewis.*

When the sun dips below the hills, Ada estimates the men will be back within two to three hours. It's near dark when the men drag into camp, sweaty and ravenous. Her heart quickens when she sees Dolan. And Ada doesn't have to worry—Mary isn't a threat to her designs on him. If and when she and Dolan ever get together, she'll figure out what "stepping out" means.

Calendar days fall behind them as wagons thunder over rough and rugged roads. With the addition of the Graves family, the overlanders in the Donner-Reed Party now number eighty-eight people in twenty-three wagons as they rumble through the Wasatch.

A loud hurrah emanates from the back of the train as Stanton and Pike emerge from the hills a few days later. Stanton is on his borrowed horse, but Pike is walking. Ada falls back. She glances behind the men, who are being hugged and congratulated.

"Where's Bert?"

William Pike looks at her blankly.

"My mule?"

"Stupid son of bitch, you mean? Didn't make it," Pike answers.

Ada stares at him, speechless.

"He was bad-tempered all right. A day ago, big ravine, he wouldn't go another step. I whipped him sore and he bellowed, still didn't move. So I told him right there, 'You move, you goddamned mule, or I'll shoot you.'"

Ada's eyes grow wide.

Pike continues, "He stood his ground, and I kept my word."

"You didn't!" Ada cries.

"I did, and I'll pay you for your troubles. We were mighty hungry by then, three days with no food, so we . . ."

"Stop." Ada looks away.

"I'm good on my word, miss. I'll be paying half of what you'd get at market."

"Half?"

"Well, he didn't finish the job he set out to do now, did he?"

"A mule won't go any further than he thinks safe. He were tellin' you somethin'. Not to go that route."

"You saying I should have listened to a damn mule?"

"They know more than we do, most times. You should have listened."

"If we'd listened, as you say, we'd still be up on that ridge trying to talk sense into that damn animal."

Ada turns her back on Pike. *Half! For my troubles?* She finds Dolan and pours out the story. "I'd rather have sold him at Bridger's for half than have it come to this. I didn't mean for Mr. Pike to kill him." She takes Rosie's face and nuzzles in. "Sorry about your brother, Rosie." She squeezes her eyes shut and breathes in Rosie's coat. No, she won't cry. Not here. Not in front of Dolan.

One day, they only make a mile. At an impasse, the wagon train comes to a standstill, the ravine so narrow and clogged with trees and brush that it's an effort to make ten yards without stopping to remove branches and boulders from the path. Reed returns to the ravine after scouting high on the ridgeline. "It's maybe six miles until we reach Great Salt Lake," he says. "But we aren't going to make the best time here in the ravine. I say we take the hill."

"Can't get these wagons over that steep of slope," Eddy says. "What do you think, Donner?"

George Donner eyes the tree-strewn canyon and then the ridge. "I'll side with Reed on this one."

The weary emigrants know what's ahead: unloading the wagons yet again. Scrubby sagebrush scuffs Ada's ankles as she skirts the wagon. Eddie is sitting up and reading now. He doesn't groan except when Ada unravels his bandage and pokes at the wound. It's healing now, a purplish-yellow ring around the once gaping hole where the bone protruded from his thigh. She's relieved. Except for the summer complaint, he's doing well.

"Can you roll over onto your side? Looks like we need to do a little cleanin' here, Eddie."

"I'd rather Ma do it," Eddie says.

"Well, your ma isn't available right now. Turn over, now. Let me help."

The boy grunts and turns on his side. Ada removes his underdrawers and mops up the mess from the ticking. "Sorry about this, Eddie. You've got enough troubles with your leg." She wipes both his legs and backside with another cloth and recovers him with the sheet, which is only lightly soiled. "I'll dig around for a new set of underdrawers. Maybe you can manage to get them on yourself."

"Am I going to live, Miss Ada?"

"Of course you are."

"I'm not so much afraid of dying as I am losing my leg," Eddie says. "It hurts awful bad, Miss Ada."

"I'll see to it if I can't get you somethin'. It's goin' to be a rough ride ahead, up and over this hill." Before she leaves, Ada gives her charge a large spoonful of castor oil and a hug. "Won't last forever, Eddie. I'll be back after supper and we can play cards, okay?"

She wraps his soiled garments in a burlap sack and hangs the sack on the outside of the wagon. The stench is overwhelming, and she fights bile rising in her throat. Flies buzz around the sack like it's filled with cattle dung. When they get to Great Salt Lake, she'll offer to help with the washing.

Here, at the base of the steepest slope they've encountered so far on the journey, wagons are offloaded again, item by item. Only Edward Breen, Philippine Keseberg, and Luke Halloran ride inside wagons. Mrs. Keseberg's time is imminent, and she's been bedridden for a week. Ada wonders when the baby will be born. Today? Tomorrow? She catches up with Mary as they plod up and over the hill, arms laden with clothing and hats.

"Wouldn't want to be Mrs. Keseberg today," Mary says.

"Wouldn't want to be Mrs. Keseberg any day," Ada answers.

They kick at sagebrush and move left to avoid the teams, twelve yoke of oxen for each wagon as men and animals labor to pull to the summit. For the Breen and Keseberg wagons especially, the men take extra care on the ascent and descent. By the time all the wagons reach the far side, it's been twelve hours of pulling and grunting and—at least once—narrowly escaping tragedy when an axletree split and one of the Reed's wagons began to roll downhill. If it weren't for the quick thinking of Milt Elliott, one of Reed's teamsters, the unthinkable might have happened as the wagon slipped and began a lurching descent. Elliott grabbed the tongue and yanked with the full force of his shoulder so the front wheels of the wagon turned off course and the wagon ran into a tree. He stood there, panting. Ada had watched, mouth agape, thinking Elliott must be counting his lucky stars that a tree was the only thing standing between him and disaster.

"What day is it, Mary?" Ada asks. "I've lost track."

"It's been eighteen days to make thirty-some miles, my pa said," Mary answers. "So I guess it's the first day we're out of these mountains."

Ahead, Great Salt Lake offers little in the way of rejuvenation. It's briny and tepid, not good for drinking or washing or bathing. And, it's poisonous to cattle.

So the travelers don't stop. August 22 turns to 23 turns to 24, as if days peeled off like the skin of an onion and smelled as sour. Mrs. Keseberg hasn't had her baby yet, and moans inside her wagon. Eddie's feeling much better, and Ada's glad the summer complaint has passed. On the twenty-fifth, a buzz of news speeds up and down the camp: Death has come for Halloran. Amid a sea of grim faces, Ada closes her eyes. She turns away from Ma Breen and continues drying breakfast dishes. Ma Breen touches Ada's shoulder.

"Best you go help Mrs. Donner."

Ada puts down her drying rag and nods. At such times, Ada thinks the world slows to a crawl. Everything associated with the everyday—washing up, chaining up, trudging across mile after mile of scrubby desert; the arguments, the sweating, the swearing—it all comes to sudden halt at death. It's what no one says: This, too, will come for you.

Ada pulls back the yellowed, waxed folds of the canvas and climbs into the Donner wagon. It's outfitted much like the other wagons, four feet wide, ten feet long, and two feet deep. Tamsen's low bed is tucked onto the left side of the wagon where barrels of salt pork would have been in any other outfit. Tamsen Donner refuses to sleep out of doors. She agreed to the journey, but she didn't agree to give up every comfort, like a feather bed and roof—albeit waxed canvas—over her head.

Halloran's lanky legs hang over the edge of the Tamsen's cot; he's a foot taller than Mrs. Donner and looks like a giant in child's bed. For all the bodies Ada's prepared for burial before in Augustus's undertaking trade, she's never dressed a body in a wagon.

"Thank you for coming, Ada."

Tamsen folds Halloran's extra clothes and sets them in a pile. He'll wear his best clothes for the burial; the rest will be divided by lot between the men. Ada stares at Halloran's peaceful face. She sits next to him and places her hand on his cool forehead. After a minute, Ada lowers her head to his quiet chest. She thinks of his mother, wherever she is in the world, but not here when her son needs her most.

"*Gud velsigne deg*, God be with you," she whispers.

Ada wrings out vinegar-soaked cloths and works the cloths down Halloran's emaciated body, first his slack face, and then his dirt-grimed neck. She takes care to cleanse all the folds and crevices. At the cleft above his collarbone, Ada worries the cloths across Halloran's sunken chest. She rinses the cloths in a barrel and resumes her work, washing his bruised torso before descending to his concave pelvis. She's seen many men naked before, and they've all been dead. She notices one of Halloran's testicles is much smaller than the other as she washes his privates and then she moves on, making long strokes on his pale, almost hairless legs. As she peels off Halloran's boots, she assesses the size. *Perfect.* She can't believe her luck. As she washes his putrid feet, she's careful to bathe between each toe. *Can't go meetin' your Maker with dirty feet.*

"Finished, ma'am."

Ada assists Donner in dressing Halloran. She makes a long slit down the back of Halloran's trousers and tucks the fabric around his thin corpse. She does the same with Halloran's shirt. Tamsen buttons the shirt to the collar. She looks through his clothes.

"No tie."

"I'll see if I can rustle one up," Ada says.

"This will do." Tamsen plucks a thin piece of leather from a jumble of discarded cords and twine in a nearby box. She knots the strip into a thin tie.

Ada combs Halloran's hair, and slicks his cowlick back with a dab of grease. She powders his face and sits back. She had never spoken to Halloran directly, and rues she had not. "Goodbye, Halloran." Ada turns to Tamsen Donner. "I was wonderin', Miz Donner, if could I have Mr. Halloran's boots." She holds her breath. Maybe one of the Donners could use them as much as she could.

Mrs. Donner nudges the boots toward Ada. *Is this God's way of answerin' my question?* Ada wonders. *That death's not random, after all?* Ada takes the boots, her hands shaking.

"Much obliged, Miz Donner. I could use them, that's a certain." Ada unlaces her battered boots and slides her bare feet into Halloran's, turning her face to evade the smell. She could cry, she's so thankful. But she hasn't cried since the fire.

Ada makes her way back to the Breen's, scuffing at the dust. Another life, another death. A piercing scream comes from the Keseberg wagon as she passes their wagon.

"Ve're needing help here!" Lewis Keseberg shouts.

Ada dashes back to the Donner's wagon. "Miz Donner, it's Miz Keseberg. I think it's her time."

The women race to the Keseberg's wagon and climb up. Eleanor Eddy is there already, along with Doris Wolfinger, who is holding tight to Philippine Keseberg's hand. The young woman's face is contorted and tears stream from her eyes.

"Is vorse dan last time," she cries. "Don't know as I can bear it."

Tamsen Donner takes charge. "Ada, get some water on to boil. Mrs. Eddy, fetch as many clean rags as you can. Mrs. Wolfinger, you stay here with Mrs. Keseberg. I'll be right back."

Donner rushes to her wagon to get herbs. She's back in less than two minutes.

"It's a bit crowded in here. Mrs. Wolfinger and I should be fine," Donner says, as she re-enters the wagon.

Eleanor and Ada tend to the boiling pot and rinse bloodied rags. Lewis Keseberg paces, scowls. Not an hour later, Eleanor and Ada lock eyes. The faint mewl of a newborn carries through the wagon cover.

"My granny used to say that a baby brings its own hope into the world," Eleanor says.

"We could be usin' some hope right about now," Ada answers.

It's onward the next day, scrub brush, juniper, and sage crushed beneath wagon wheels on the crude road. Halloran isn't dead twenty-four hours, and the Keseberg baby is less than twenty-four hours old. Water is now scant and miserable for both human and beast. Rather than walking next to the Breen wagon, Ada falls back to walk with Mary Graves. The Graves wagon is last in today's march after assuming the lead yesterday; it's just done that way, the lead wagon falling to the rear the next day like geese in flight, letting another take the lead for the day and moving back up through the train until it's time to lead again. With twenty-three wagons, it's a slow slog up the train to the lead again. The constant thrashing over rough, rocky terrain and dry desert air takes its toll on wagon wheels. They shrink and crack, causing frequent breakdowns. Wheels are soaked in riverbeds at night and repaired along the way. Too slow, you're left behind.

Ada swats at a mosquito. Since Bridger's Fort, any exposed portion of her torso or arms or ankles or neck have been covered with small red welts. And still no pennyroyal.

"Ma swears by peppermint," Mary says. "She packed enough peppermint for the whole train, and two trains more."

"Peppermint? Heard it used for colic or rhinitis. Sour breath, too. I use it for, you know. Used to read my pappa's medical tracts—he was an undertaker, you see."

"That's what my ma said. Why you helped with the burial."

Ada nods.

"Does it bother you, seeing all those dead bodies?" Mary asks.

"You get used to it."

"But what about when it's your parents? How does a body get used to that?"

"I don't think on it much. We got enough to think about most days, Mary. I just push it out of my mind. I'll grieve when I get there, I guess. Wherever it is that we're goin'."

"You seen the baby yet?" Mary asks.

"No, have you?"

Mary shakes her head. "I see you got some new boots."

Ada starts to speak, stops. She pictures Halloran's slack face, the peace that passes all understanding. "From Luke Halloran."

"You aim to be an undertaker?" Mary asks.

"Ever seen a lady undertaker?"

"Can't say as I have. Sometimes I long to be a sight more than a wife and a mother," Mary says. "Although I won't say it too loudly."

"I do, too. But it's not possible now anyway, way things are goin'. What is it you've got a hankerin' to do, Mary?"

"Own my own shop, a millinery. Fancy hats. I used to make the finest creations from scraps of lace and ribbon. Beads, too. Even feathers. You should have seen them, Miss Ada. Anything but these awful bonnets. What about you?"

Ada has never said it aloud, except to Augustus. "A proper midwife. There's a handful of colleges in the States acceptin' females now, but none for medicine. There's one in Germany takin' female students, though. My pappa was savin' up so as I could go."

Mary looks quizzically at Ada. "Germany? Well, we ain't headed that direction, are we?"

"'Fraid not," Ada says. "Pappa said I've got the mind for it, but, well, he's gone now. No use chasin' rabbits down the wrong hole." Ada wriggles her walking stick on the grassy slope ahead. "Speakin' of holes, watch your step, Mary—that hole there could be a rattler." She bends down and gathers a handful of gravel. She tosses the gravel over the mound, but there's no rattling sound. "We're lucky this time. Best to scare 'em up afore they scare you up."

"How d'ya know so much 'bout snakes?"

"Don't really. But if you're bit and you've no medicines, it's a race for time. I've read about it. You tie a string above the bite, lance it, and suck out the poison. Best to have hartshorn handy, and apply it freely. Or dilute it and drink it."

"You thirsty, Miss Ada?"

"Always." Ada slugs from Mary's canteen and spits it out. "That's the most wretched water I've ever tasted. You'd think we'd have plenty of water, plenty of grass, plenty of wood. But no. I think we've been hoodwinked, Mary. There's no good comin' of this journey."

12

August 28, 1846
Great Salt Desert

If Ada hears another profanity, she'll have to stop up her ears with cotton. Patrick Breen stomps and swears, sweat dripping off his bearded, rugged face.

Simon mimics his father. *For chrissakes!*

His mother boxes his ear. "Mind your tongue, young man. There'll be none of that coming from you, dammit."

At the edge of the Great Salt Desert, all hopes of finding direction from the scoundrel Lansford Hastings are shredded. Only the tattered remains of what was once a scrawled note are found scattered at the foot of a message post. Tamsen Donner ferrets around the base of the post collecting paper scraps. Ada is on her knees now, crawling through matted grasses and dirt, scooping up stray, ragged bits of paper. Tamsen takes the vestiges of Hastings's note and lays them out on the buckboard. She pieces together snippets of letters and words like a ragged puzzle, wrinkling her brow as she arranges and rearranges the slips of paper. A crowd circles her, silent. Finally, she looks up. "It reads: *2 days—2 nights—hard driving—cross desert—reach water.*"

Jacob Wolfinger cusses so loud his prim wife blanches. James Reed kicks at sand. Patrick Breen slaps his grimy hat against his thigh. Pat

Dolan, usually so good-natured, scowls. He leads the Breen's oxen to a shaded spot to graze. He does not linger.

Everyone strikes a silent agreement; it is not a time for words. There are knives to hone, guns to clean, wheels to grease, and the list goes on so long there's nary time to catch a full breath. Children bind grass for livestock, gather kindling, fill containers with potable water. Men check choke chains, re-shoe oxen, repair canvases. Women begin the dreaded task of unburdening loads. With a loud grunt, Ma Breen dumps her iron stove off the back of the wagon. It falls, making a sizeable indentation in the soft ground. She does not try to hide it or move it from where it falls. Others scout for suitable spots to cache extra furniture, dishware, bedding, and household supplies—wagons, even. What seemed a necessity in Iowa or Illinois or Missouri is just extra weight now.

At supper, the Breens eat heartily, after dispatching the last of the extra oxen. What little they have left they will parse out on the desert trek. Late that night, Ma Breen continues to divest non-essential items in the wagon: a washtub, the sack of flour just bought at Bridger's Fort, piles of clothing. Ada salvages a few rags and stuffs them into her now full apron pocket. She feels like a pack rat nosing into the Breen's discarded pile of rubbish. But she can't carry a whit more without compromising her own strength.

Patrick Breen throws an auger, plane, and chisel into a pile. "A hammer and a saw will have to get us through," he says. "See to it we don't take any more than necessary." He faces his harried wife. "And that includes your mother's china."

"Not the china!" Ma Breen shrieks.

"You heard me, woman. If you don't unload it yourself, I'll be doing it."

Ma Breen turns, her shoulders hunched and head low. Three minutes later Ada hears a muffled cry as a large box crashes out of the wagon.

Wagons roll out at twilight to take advantage of cool desert temperatures. Pilot Peak is but an apparition in the far-off distance, at least forty miles away. It soon becomes evident that each family is in a race of their own against the ravages of heat and cold in this tedious pull across salt-covered mud flats. The Breen's oxen are shoed with hide cut and fashioned from the carcasses of dead cattle, worn flesh side out. Patrick Breen hedges that these rough, comic-looking shoes might save his oxen's feet as they trudge over blistering sand. The animals are well watered but it will be difficult to steer them away from fatal alkali ponds. Oh, there's a home remedy to save cattle after they've gorged themselves in alkali—rub lard and syrup and vinegar and shove it down their swollen throats. Best to keep them away from it.

The Eddys and Graveses gain time and distance, leaving other wagons behind. Ada walks briskly alongside the Breen wagon. The ashy, hard salt flats color her new boots a dusty white, like dry snow. The only sounds are iron wheels crunching on salt, a steady *criiiick criiiick* as the emigrants hurry west. Other than that, the desert is dead quiet, naked except for shifting salt mounds. The moon is sliced neatly in half, the far side only just visible. Just ahead, a huge sun-bleached skeleton glows in the fierce moonlight, its once robust head shrunken and hollow, its bones contorted and legs severed.

"Ox?" Simon asks.

"Yes," Ada answers. "Watch your step, there. Don't want you trippin' over bones or skulls."

"There's another one," he says.

"Your da will see it. Now mind to your own business." Ada swats Simon on the rear. She clambers over a broken yoke, its chains buried in white sludge.

Ada licks her chapped, cracked lips. *When do we next have water?* She warms up some by walking, and keeps her shawl and her blanket wrapped tightly around her shoulders to ward off the night air. Silent stars above give off light but no heat.

Patrick Breen offers sips of water once every two hours. As for food, Ma Breen doles out thin beef strips and sugar lumps. Ada swirls sugar in her mouth for as long as she can savor it. When there is no more left, she swallows in small, sweet gulps, prolonging the taste until her saliva runs dry. Then she licks her lips again. They sting.

From across the barren salt flat, Ada hears muffled voices and cries. The Reed's dogs bark incessantly, and she's glad the Breens have put distance between their wagons and the others. Muzzles keeps up with Ada as best he can on short, wiry legs. "C'mon pup," she says. "Just a little longer. We can't none of us stop now."

But the purported forty miles of desert is clearly twice the distance. The Breens zigzag across the desert in silence as miles evaporate under Ada's boots. There are no more wet towels to soak the oxen's mouths; their tongues hang like disused appendages from their wide, foaming jaws. Dolan moves from one animal to the next and whispers.

Hours give way to dawn as the Breens plow on, the rising sun's heat mounting with rapidity. Blood drips from Ada's nose and she plugs her nostrils with a rag. Her eyes, dry and dryer, sting from salt pricks. The Breens have run out of water.

Ada steals glances at Dolan. He's a few steps ahead of her, prodding the oxen. No one—man or beast—can afford to rest. If they stop, they are done for. The animals sink to their bellies in ashy salt. So far, Dolan has not resorted to the whip. His grunts and shouts are merely to guide the exhausted animals toward promise of water. Ada falls in beside him as they plod through crusted salt.

"How're you faring, miss?" Dolan asks.

"A little dizzy. Mighty thirsty, too. You?"

"Mighty thirsty myself. Here, take a swig."

Ada takes a full draught from Dolan's canteen. It's not water.

For a sleepless night and a full, scorching day, Ada continues to plod west across the salt flats. Dunes alternate with long, low, level stretches of fine salt, which is littered with the mundane: feather beds, patched quilts, pillows.

"Leave it, child!" Ada hears. Then sobs. Echoes of a thousand arguments dissipate in the clear desert air as oxen and wagons and overlanders labor across dry, baked earth. Mile after mile, specters rise from the wasteland. As Ada passes the latest load of discarded items, the eyes of a rag doll stare lifelessly up at the stars. She circumvents castoff casks, trunks, and cook stoves. She eyes a lone spinning wheel, an oil lamp, a tin washtub. *Mrs. Wolfinger's piano?*

Into another night, she walks hunched to the cold. Near midnight of the second day, dry, crusty salt gives way to a mushy sludge. The emigrants have been traversing the salt desert for more than thirty hours straight. Each step is like walking through wet concrete as wagon wheels mire in slurry. To rid caking salt from iron rims, the Breen boys walk next to the wagons pressing towels against turning wheel rims. The younger boys stumble, trying to keep up with the older boys. Ada cannot keep from yawning. Her eyes, like slits, are raw from sand crystals stinging her face. It is too terrible. Oxen strain to move forward, crazed with thirst. They sink to their knees and grunt. To stave off dehydration and malnutrition, Breen gives the oxen a ration of grass at regular intervals. Ada is so hungry and so thirsty she begins to resent the animals. She yearns to eat grass.

The wagon overtakes the old Belgian, Wilhelm Hardkoop, who is lagging behind the forward wagons, struggling to keep up.

"Not long now, Mr. Hardkoop," Ada whispers.

He nods, his face taut.

Ada pulls at Rosie's halter line as they slog through sludge. "That's it, girl. We're halfway across now. Good girl." The mule shakes her huge head and whinnies. "What's that you're sayin', girl? I know, I'm thirsty, too. Come on, now." Suddenly, the molly stops in her tracks. "Rosie! Don't quit on me here." Ada tugs on the halter line. "Rosie!"

"What the devil?" Dolan asks. His beard and his trousers are covered in white powder. He looks like a ghoul. Dolan takes the line from Ada and yanks. The mule stands her ground, mournful, salt-rimmed eyes downcast. "She's not going a foot farther, miss. You know as well as anyone that mules will do that. Overworked, over-tired, overheated, they'll just quit."

"But she can't quit now! I already lost Bert due to his stubbornness."

The Breen wagon overtakes them.

"You can try to talk some sense into her," Dolan says.

"Dolan!" Patrick Breen yells.

"Got to attend to the oxen, miss. They're crazed. Breen isn't going to stop for anything now. Certainly not a mule." Dolan plods to catch up with the wagon, which is slogging through mire.

Ada reaches for Rosie and puts her face up against the mule's warm flesh. "Don't do this, Rosie. We got a while more to go. And then there'll be water. And sugar. And maybe an apple somewhere."

"Miss Weeks! Hurry it up!" Breen shouts across the barren salt flats. The wagon is now a hundred yards ahead moving slowly toward Pilot Peak, its silhouette clear in the night sky.

Rosie continues to look down, her hooves planted in salty mush.

"You aren't goin' to move, are you, girl?" Ada drops the line and slowly removes the halter and bit from Rosie's mouth. "I wish I had somethin' for you . . ." Ada throws her arms around Rosie's neck. "You come when you're ready, girl. I'll be waitin'."

"Miss Weeks!"

Ada pats Rosie again and trudges through sludge. She looks back every ten paces, but the mule doesn't move. "Come on, girl," Ada whispers.

At dawn, Ada sees a shimmering ripple just steps in front of her. But the closer she gets to the ribbon of water, the farther it retreats. *It is a cruel trick,* she thinks. *Am I seein' things? Or goin' blind?* In the constant wind, fine white salt pricks her ruddy face. Her eyes sting angrily. She does not even have enough saliva now to wipe her eyes free of flying granules. Only her eye slits squint out of the kerchief wrapped around her face. As the sun glares off the salt, she takes turns shielding her eyes. When one arm becomes numb, she lowers it and raises the other. Her exhaustion is eclipsed by survival. There is nothing ahead except the mirage of safety.

Will I live? Die? Ever see Rosie again? Ever see California? Ada's clothes are crusted white. It's not worth the effort to try to shake free of accumulated salt. She works to put one foot in front of the other. If she could wish herself away, anywhere, she would.

On the third day, the Breens stumble into the shadow of Pilot Peak at the far end of the Great Salt Desert. Ada collapses under a tree and trembles involuntarily.

"Ada!" Eleanor Eddy's bucket sloshes as she sets it down. Eleanor gives Ada a warm hug and hands her the dipper. Ada's eyes are moist. She has never known such heat, such cold, such hunger, such thirst. And now, this kindness. Her hand is unsteady as she scoops a dipperful and lifts the large spoon to her parched lips. She closes her eyes as cool water streams down her throat. A few droplets escape and fall onto her chest. She reaches for the drops and nods at Eleanor in silent thanks. Any words that bubble under the surface are curbed by exhaustion.

"Where's Rosie?" Eleanor says.

Ada stifles a sob. "She plumb quit, right in the middle of the desert."

Eleanor pats Ada's shoulder. "Everybody's come into camp now, and for that we should be thankful."

"Even old Hardkoop?"

"Yes, everyone. But Mr. Donner's lost a wagon. Mr. Keseberg, too."

"I'm sure as salt I passed one of Mr. Reed's wagons on the flats," Ada says.

"Yes. Had to leave two of his wagons behind. And lost all of his oxen, he did. Bolted. Nothing to stop them. It looks like the high-and-mighty Reeds are down to one wagon, one ox, and a horse."

"What's to become of us?" Ada moans. "Is anyone goin' out after the wagons? Or the animals?"

Eleanor squeezes Ada's arm.

"I haven't given up hope of findin' Rosie, Miz Eddy. She's a smart one, will be comin' in soon for water. How much longer, do you think?" Ada asks.

"Until what, Ada? The next desert? The next mountain range? The next spring?"

"The next spring, I guess."

"Your guess is as good as mine. They say maybe sixteen miles."

Men, boys, teamsters, and drovers backtrack to the desert with freshly watered animals in hopes of retrieving valuables—heirlooms and documents and keepsakes and gold—but much is still left behind in the flats. Next year, westering folk will find the desert strewn with furniture and clothing and tintypes and gear and wonder what led overlanders traveling before them to part with so much after traveling so far, littering the desert with precious items like pearls cast before swine. But by next year, will it all be covered over? The detritus of their lives?

I won't never get to Germany now, Ada thinks. *Or be a midwife. A midwife? What about a wife? At this rate, I'll probably never be one or the other.*

Ada's dead to the world for six days as the entourage pauses at the foot of Pilot Peak. Each morning and evening, Eleanor Eddy brings Ada water and sits with her. Ma Breen checks on Ada, too, but never stays long. She brings scraps of meals and weak coffee. "A little something for you, Ada. Come now, eat up."

Even Patrick Breen offers words as he passes by. "Be up soon, miss, you hear me?"

Eddie brings a blanket. "Thought you might need it, miss."

Dolan tips his hat. "You'll be a-right, Miss Ada, won't you?"

It's all fuzzy. Days have no rhythm; men and women and children mill around camp like wraiths, eyes dulled. There is little work or play. The desert has sapped all of their energy, like a great cloud of despair from which they cannot escape. Ada feels life draining out of her, one drop of perspiration at a time. When she has the energy, she shields her eyes and looks east for Rosie. She wills the molly to saunter into camp and shove her soft muzzle into her face. But every day, her hopes come up empty, and all she is left with is a halter and no mule.

On the seventh day, Ada is strong enough to rouse herself. She gets up weakly. A group is gathered by the lone Reed wagon.

"We'll be needing an accurate account of provisions and stock," James Reed says. "What's one's is all's now. We'll evaluate the situation tonight." He looks at Lewis Keseberg. "And see to it there's no deceit."

As Ma Breen takes stock of supplies, Ada sits and records numbers on a scrap of paper: two pounds coffee, ten pounds sugar. It's all she can do to keep awake. Patrick Breen and Dolan join men to count remaining cattle and horses. *Still no Rosie.*

That night, the overlanders hear Reed's calculations. "I've seen to the numbers, folks," Reed says. "It's plain as day we don't have enough to go on. We're coming up far short to feed the entire group before we reach California, even if it's but six weeks away."

Ada crosses her arms and shakes her head. *Can't make it six more weeks.*

"I've been thinking," Charles Stanton says. "A man on a horse can make quick work of the mountains. I'm willing to ride ahead to Sutter's for supplies. You can continue on, and I'll meet you on the trail. The way I figure it, it's two—maybe three—weeks' time from here to Sutter's and back. That should put you on the eastern slope of the Sierras by then."

"Bullshit," John Snyder says. Mary Graves blushes at her intended's word. "You've no reason to return—no wife, no children. Who's to say you won't ride off and abandon us?"

"You've got my word is what you've got," Stanton answers. "Might be short, but my words live large."

"I'll accompany you." William McCutcheon unravels himself from a campstool and steps into the circle where Stanton holds court. McCutcheon stands over six and a half feet tall, a stark contrast to the small man beside him. He pats Stanton on the back and addresses the crowd. "I've got every reason to return. Wife and child. And two of us going for supplies means twice as much coming back."

The deal is set. Within an hour, a stash of food, blankets, and ammunition piles in camp. The men will take a horse and a borrowed mule. Ada thinks of Bert. *I can't even offer Rosie now.* Letters directed to John Sutter, proprietor of Sutter's Fort, cram into the men's saddlebags, along with provisions for their journey.

Hope was what used to fill our cup, Ada thinks. *Now we are down to dregs.* Supper is a paltry half-cup of beans and one slice of johnnycake. Ada can't ignore the hollow pit in her stomach. She prays the gods of the mountains will protect the men, although she can't remember any of their names. *The Ourea?* She used to be so good with poems and speeches; more than once she won a medal for recitations. Now her mind is scrambled with uncertainty and blunted with confusion. Questions skulk in her brain, and she has trouble putting coherent thoughts together. *Is this what starvation can do to a body?*

"Will we really see Stanton or McCutcheon again?" Ada asks Ma Breen. No one knows the answer with certainty. It is already the second week in September and snow is threatening. But it is survival over sentiments, survival over speculation. Despite the low odds, Ada hopes against hope and banks on their return.

Summer is rapidly giving way to fall. By Augustus's calculations, the overlanders should be in California by now.

Ada leans against a straggly tree, eyes unfocused. Someone comes up from behind and stands next to her. She sees dirty trousers, worn boots, and large hands fiddling a hat before she knows for sure who's addressing her. *Dolan?* He kicks at the dirt. Ada looks up.

"I'm sorry about the mule," he says.

Ada nods. "Me, too. I loved that Rosie. I'm goin' to be mighty lonely now."

"I know about lonely," he says. "A fella can get mighty lonely, too, if he has no one to call family."

"Don't have any family t'all, either, 'less you count the Breens."

"Like family to me, too, miss. Took me on before we even left Illinois. But it's not like being with real family, is it?"

"No. But there's no goin' back to what was before, that's a certain. Best to keep goin' forward."

"Would you consider a fella like me, going forward?"

Ada's heart races. She wants to say, "About time." Instead, she looks at Dolan, nods.

Dolan grabs Ada's rough hand in his own. "I thought we'd lost you there. Didn't realize how much I thought of you 'til I saw you lying there. I knew right then, it was time to ask you. For your hand, that is. May I?"

Dolan bends to kiss Ada's cheek. A shiver runs through her body.

"I'm a poor excuse for a suitor, I'm the first to admit. But you've made me a happy fella, Miss Ada Weeks," Dolan says.

"Does that mean we're engaged?" Ada asks.

Dolan slaps his thigh. "I suppose we are." He lets out a loud howl, like a wolf. "Though we'd best wait to reach Sutter's—have a proper marriage ceremony there."

"I've been watchin' you, Mr. Dolan," Ada says. "And I don't mean like a sister. We don't need to wait 'til Sutter's. If you find the right time, and the right place, I'll be willin'. I'll be more than willin', Mr. Dolan, sir."

13

September 10, 1846
Alta California

The man walks briskly, his gait sure and quick. The weather is pleasant for early fall, sixty degrees, if he were a betting man. His mouth waters. Tonight, Salina promises her famous cornbread, dripping with thick butter and honey. He's a regular at Salina's. Every Thursday. He always brings her something—matches, usually, or extra coffee if he has enough. He's got two new figurines whittled for her two boys to add to their collection. Keeps his hands busy nights, sloughing off bark to conjure wooden soldiers or pirates.

He scratches the three-legged cat before he leaves. "Watch over everything, Boy. I'll be back. Don't let Old One peck your eyes out." He whistles toward the raven. "Mind your manners while I'm gone."

The creek is low, barely a riffle at the bend. The man heads upstream, wading through damp grass on the creek bank. Beyond the curve, he follows a deer trail away from the water for a quarter-mile through bramble thickets and scrub oak. He meets up with the creek at what he calls "Fishtown" and gauges where he'll build a weir to trap migrating salmon. The weir will be constructed with rocks and will funnel salmon through a small opening where unsuspecting fish will tumble into an open-topped willow basket. Much easier than standing on the edge of the creek with a pole and spearing them, like the Paiute.

The sun is gone from the foothills, although there's hours of daylight yet. He remembers the wide plains where the sky arced from horizon to horizon, sometimes bluer than he thought possible. Once, before he got to California, somewhere in Ute territory, he stood on the high plains as the sun dove toward the edge of the earth. He howled it down. As the sun neared the charcoal abyss, it answered back, and mightily, a split-second flash of green before its golden halo seared the sky orange before fading to peach to apricot to melon. The sky was cleansed then from the rigors of another day, bedded down on a cushion of the faintest mother-of-pearl. Colors lingered until they could not hold onto the horizon any longer and then slithered from sight, as he set up camp alone on the prairie. The man was surrounded by inky black then, as if the sun had never been there at all.

The boys rush the man when he enters the clearing. He scoops them up, one at a time, and flings them around above his shoulders. Salina stands in the doorway, dark hands on hips. Her lusty laugh rings through cottonwoods. He's never seen breasts as large, and he's seen plenty, white and black and brown. Her dusky skin disappears in the crevice of her blouse. Ordinarily, he'd dwell on the thought of disappearing in the folds of her blouse himself, but he leaves those thoughts for later that evening.

Before supper (the baby girl is asleep by now), the boys scamper up the porch.

"Riddle! Do you have a riddle?"

"I do." The boys crowd him, and he ruffles their hair. He begins: "Geese fly, one ahead and one behind, one behind and two ahead, one between two, and three in a row. Now tell me, how many geese altogether?"

The boys squirm with laughter. "How do we figure that one?"

"Grab a stick and do the sums. I'll be waiting right here." He tips back on the chair, smoking.

The boys bend their heads. They scratch in the dirt. "Nine?"

"Try again."

"Six! It's six!" the younger boy answers.

"No, not six. Try again."

The boys look at him quizzically. "Tell us!"

"It's three, three in a row."

"But how?"

The man jumps down from the porch and draws figures in the dirt. "See, one ahead and one behind, one behind and two ahead, one between two, and three in a row. It's three, plain and simple. 'Three in a row' was your clue."

"More riddles!"

The man starts in again. "If you have nine apples, and take two away, then add four more, and times it by two . . ."

Salina says, "Enough of that, now. Supper's on. Go wash your hands now."

She touches him on the shoulder. A ripple descends through his arm down to his fingertips. As he approaches the table, he observes Salina's wide hips as she sways back and forth between the table and the stove. Salina plops loaded plates on the rough table: venison, beets, and the promised cornbread. They sit then, all of them, and eat. Whatever manners the man was taught have long since vanished. He takes the venison in his hand, slices the end off with his knife, and spears it into his mouth.

After supper, the boys do what boys do—run and yelp into the woods until their dark skin dissolves into the burgeoning dusk. Salina drags chairs to the porch and they sit and smoke in silence. He wants to reach for her, just brush the tips of his fingers lightly on the front of her blouse, but he cannot, for reasons obvious and not.

Eventually, the boys tire and sit on the floorboards of the porch, their heads lolling into sleep. Salina carries them inside and returns outside.

"Been talking to the wind?"

He grunts. "Wish I had boys like yours, is what I said."

"Well, you better find yourself a lady friend."

When evening collapses into blue-blackness, the man says his goodbyes and follows the well-worn trail downstream, away from boys and breasts and taboos. He'll be home soon enough, thinking of honey dripping slowly from Salina's cornbread and smothering gasps with his pillow. He'll lick his fingers and cry.

14

September 13, 1846

Mad Woman Camp

(150 miles west of Great Salt Lake)

Six long miles into the winding canyons of the Pequop Range, the emigrants meet the first snow of the season. It's not a tranquil snowfall that blankets the earth with a breath of calm, the kind where men take pause and hurry home to their armchairs in fire-lit parlors. This storm starts out innocuously enough, in small spits and starts, but the snow's intensity, along with piercing wind, increases as the day wears on. By supper, there's no denying winter's onslaught has begun, and it's only September.

The troupe makes camp at dusk. The low-ceilinged sky continues its assault; foot-high drifts swell at the edge of camp. Ada rifles through the Breen's winter wear and winds a long, brown muffler around her bare neck and up over her ears. There are no extra mittens, no parlors to rush home to, no cozy armchairs or coverlets or cocoa or cats.

Under an awning stretched from the wagon, Ada helps with washing up. Ma Breen's up to her elbows in dirty dishwater, hardly warm enough to comfort her cold hands. Ada helps with drying, first tin plates, then tin cups. She brushes blown snow off the tea towel, reaches for the last of the worn and dented utensils. Ma Breen leans into Ada. "Heard you've got yourself a sweetheart."

"Suppose I do," Ada says. She wants to say, "Mind your own business," but reins in her tongue. Everything is everyone's business by this time. No one can fart without someone else noticing. Ada has grown inured to petty quarrels, marital arguing, spousal violence even, let alone screams of childbirth.

"I'm tired of ashes in my coffee," Patrick Breen complains.

He throws his coffee grounds in the mud and flings his cup into the dirty dishpan. A splash of cold, greasy water hits Margaret Breen in the chest. She kicks at her husband as he walks by.

"Get your hide out of my way, man!" she says. "Think we don't have enough to do already?"

"Who's talking about enough to do, woman? Try walking in my shoes. Can't take a mite more of your guff," Breen grumbles as he walks off. He yells over his shoulder, "I'm not the only one calling this 'Mad Woman Camp.'"

Ada hangs her soiled dishrag on a nail protruding from the wagon bed. It'll probably freeze stiff as a board in minutes. She grabs her blanket and wedges in next to Dolan, who's sitting on a downed tree near the fire. She pulls her blanket over her knees and midsection and settles into the crook of his arm, the warmth of his body soothing. Muzzles scampers over and plops into Ada's lap. Ada whispers into Dolan's ear. He smiles, blushes a deep red, clears his throat.

"Got an announcement," Dolan says. "Me and Miss Weeks here are, um, you might say we're engaged. I hope you'll offer us some privacy."

"About time, Dolan," one of the teamsters quips. "Why, you ain't been with a woman since the Fourth of . . ."

"Shut your trap, Williams."

"She was something, wasn't she?" Williams uses his hands to

mimic the shape of a woman's body. "Could use me some of that Carlisle girl right about now . . ."

Edna Carlisle? Who Dolan was dancin' with on the Fourth of July?

"I said, shut your trap." Dolan glares at Williams.

Dolan helps Ada up. A chorus of whistles follows them as they disappear behind the Breen wagon. "Git what's comin' to ya," Williams laughs.

"Don't mind him," Dolan whispers to Ada. "He's been in his cups tonight."

He presses Ada up against the wagon box and kisses her roughly. A strange desire bolts though Ada's groin. She puts Edna Carlisle out of her mind. Simon peeks his head around the wagon and scampers around them. Dolan swats him away. The wagon lurches as Ma Breen climbs up and in with Bella. Patrick Breen shuffles to his tent. The Breen boys sweep snow from beneath the wagon and nestle together in bedrolls. Simon peeks again from his spot under the wagon.

"Dammit, boy," Dolan says. "Give a man his space."

Ada's mind races. If she had acted on her own desires, she might have approached Dolan as early as Beaver Creek. *Before Edna.* Didn't Bryant admonish her to be bold? But boldness crept up like a sloth; the intervening days have all been wasted time, like biblical plagues of frogs and flies and locusts. *This whole journey has been filled with missteps,* she thinks. *And no blame way to get any of the lost steps back.*

Wind tears through the canyon, right through Ada's clothes and down to her bones. She and Dolan linger, shivering, catching kiss after kiss until Ada tears herself away. "It's time, Mr. Dolan." But not time for them to consummate any engagement. Tonight she'll sleep in her clothes and wrap her blanket tight around her.

She wriggles into her sodden bedroll and wedges into a depression near the rear wheel of the wagon. She watches through dying firelight as Dolan puts up a snow shield near the front wheel and burrows into his bedroll. He looks over to where Ada's scrunched into her sleeping spot. He places his hand over his chest and thumps it. She offers a shy smile, although she's not sure he can see her in the backlight. She wishes they were wrapped in each other's embrace, but they're separated by four feet, six boys, and a thousand missed moments.

By the next morning, a foot of snow envelops the camp. Ada shakes involuntarily and looks across lumpy sleeping bodies to where Dolan slept. His bedroll is empty. She shakes off snow, crawls out from beneath the wagon, stands, and stomps her feet. Her hands are raw and chapped. Why hadn't she thought to buy salve at Bridger's? She clenches and unclenches her fists, shaking her hands to get blood flowing. If only she had gloves. She berates herself for not thinking ahead. She'd bought powder and twine and licorice and snuff at Bridger's, but forgot camphor in her haste to purchase tobacco. At least, she has sturdy boots, thanks to poor dead Luke Halloran.

Many of the tents have collapsed over night, including the Breen's. Patrick Breen and the boys try to lift the soggy canvas to shake it loose of accumulated snow. There is no chance the tent will dry today.

Oxen snort, their thick bursts of breath puffs of white. Dolan is nowhere to be seen. Ada walks a short distance and hides behind a rock to pass water. A small yellow trace splatters on the blanket of white. She shivers as she eliminates and hurries back to assist Ma Breen with coffee. Thankfully, they are out of beans. Ada turns slowly in front of the campfire, toasting one quarter of her body at a time in the waning heat. Embers dance in the air, flickering and fizzling.

"Been but two seasons since Independence," Ada says. "Summer and winter. Nothin' in between."

Ma Breen grunts. "Don't you start complaining, too, Ada Weeks. I hear enough of it as it is." She whips her apron from the fire, its edges singed and black. "For chrissakes! Is there no end to misfortune?"

There's much to complain about, not the least that the travelers have diverted up a box canyon in the snows of the night before and are forced to retrace their path. It's downright rough country. Every ascent is steep and every descent steeper still, and another lost day to add to a string of lost days that finds them here in the Pequops so late in the season.

Ada begins to fear the worst. The overlanders could be lost in this maze of unforgiving mountains right here for the winter, starving and clawing for life in one narrow snow-clogged canyon or another. One wrong turn. Another mislaid day. *Can't count on tomorrow.* Ada tries to quell these thoughts as the party wends its way back to the known trail. The men are of singular mind: Get to California, and get there fast. There is no turning back, either to Bridger's or to the States. California will be home, and it's straight ahead, goddammit.

In the distance, the Ruby Range looms larger than anything they've encountered, mountaintops draped in snow. They're two hundred and eighty miles from Bridger's, but still six hundred miles from Sutter's. It's rumored soon they'll reach Marys River and meet up with the original trail to California. *The trail we should've taken.*

The emigrants stray through low, snow-covered passes and skirt the edges of ancient mountain chains. If they're lucky, by tomorrow the train will make Mineral Valley, sixteen or eighteen long miles from here, where they're promised wells of fresh spring water. No one can argue that home—any home—would be more pleasant than this.

Mid pleasures and palaces though we may roam . . . Ada shakes her head as she thinks of the familiar camp song. *What pleasures?* Mares disappear at night. Water is brackish, undrinkable at some camps. Wheels and axles crack and split in the rocky terrain. Overlanders are testy, avoiding other families except at nightfall. There are no more sing-alongs. *And what palaces?* The only home Ada knows now is a bedroll under an emigrant wagon that rolls through drifts of snow toward *where is it, anyway?* As for any home she has left behind, one was burned to the ground when she was eleven and Vik's

Furniture and Undertaking Parlor in Noblesville, Indiana, belongs to someone else.

There are snippets of pleasure, though. Her nightly rendezvous with Dolan offers an escape from the day's drudgery of walking through dense sagebrush, squatting to pass water, minding rough-and-tumble boys, avoiding snakes, gathering scant kindling, and burning fingers. She and Dolan have taken to retreating to the far side of the Keseberg's wagon after supper to avoid the eyes of the Breen boys or snide comments from coarse teamsters. Keseberg grunted when he saw them there the other night but didn't wave them away. Each night, their wanderings over each other's bodies have become more brazen.

Tonight, Dolan's hands wander up and under her blouse. "Oh, sweet Ada," he whispers. Ada shivers, closes her eyes, and leans back against the wagon. He rubs her nipples and wetness spreads between her legs. Ada moves Dolan's hand to touch her there. His breathing is ragged as he presses against her. "Can't wait much longer."

15

October 5, 1846
Pauta Pass
(345 miles west of Great Salt Lake)

The great hurrah that rumbled through the wagon train when the emigrants met up with Marys River and regained the established trail to California is a distant memory. The proven trail has woes of its own. Bad water. No timber. Not enough undergrowth to shade a fly. *Juncture to hell,* Ada thinks.

"Trail meeting tonight," George Donner says, as he walks from wagon to wagon.

After supper, the travelers gather at the Donner wagons, shuffling feet and avoiding eye contact. The last time Donner called for a camp meeting was back at Independence Rock when he suggested a parting of the ways.

"There's enough evidence—and I don't need to go into any detail; it's plain as day," Donner says. "We're too big a group to continue on together."

What? Splittin' up again? After everythin' we've been through?

"Jacob and I will go on ahead with our families," Donner continues. "This way, each of us can move along at our own pace."

It's like a braid, Ada thinks, all coming undone. Their entourage was all a-straight and neat enough for Sunday (like her ma used to say) when they left Independence, but by now it's come apart and the ends are flying *every which-a-way* and there's no putting it back together for any man or woman or reason under the sun.

The next morning, the Donners—brothers George and Jacob with wives Tamsen and Elizabeth, twelve children between them, and a handful of teamsters—leave camp soon after dawn. Reed walks from camp to camp, the new *defacto* leader.

"Best be off within an hour. Two at most. We'll let George and Jacob get a head start on the day. No doubt we'll reconvene with them most nights, depending on our progress. No crying, Margaret." He turns to his wife. "We're nigh to California now."

At the base of the steep, scrubby trail at Pauta Pass, the wagons halt. It is only the third time the party has had to double chain oxen and proceed one wagon at a time up a long, sharp incline. It's all hands to work as wagons are unloaded and goods hauled over the pass. The last time they were forced to double yoke was a month ago before reaching Great Salt Lake.

The morning is moist with melting frost; a palpable nip pricks the air. From beneath the low, grey ceiling of sky, an orb of yellow pierces through. Ada winds her shawl around her shoulders and layers her cloak over the shawl. Within a few hours, when the sun bursts through the cloud layer to scorch the earth, she'll shed first the outer layer, and then the remaining layers. She fumbles with her bun and pins up defiant wisps of hair. This morning, she begged eye balm from Ma Breen, but there was none to spare. Her eyes hurt from the sun's glare off white, sun-dried mud and her limp bonnet does little to ward off the sun's harsh, slanted rays. Her bonnet hangs down her back now as dirt pricks her face. She can almost see the wind.

Now that the party's split in two distinct groups, the Reeds, Eddys, Graveses, Murphys, Breens, and Kesebergs travel at least a day behind the Donners. Already this morning, two of the three Graves's wagons have summited the pass successfully, both with double teams. The last of the Graves's wagons is next in line, commandeered by Mary's beloved, John Snyder. His single team of oxen strains under the whip.

"Move it, boys," Snyder shouts, as he approaches the hill.

As the remaining wagons wait their turn to crest the pass, a scurry of women and children offloads pots and sacks and chests. Ada is on her second trip up the pass with an armload of loose clothing. Desert broom and sagebrush prick at her skirts. She joins a snaking caravan up and over the steep hill, dogs yapping at her heels. She sidesteps prickly pear and animal scat, brushes away mosquitoes. Back and forth she goes, along with so many others, up and over and back again, struggling to keep her footing on shifting scree until all goods are ferried across the sharp, treeless gap. Now Ada's headed back down to the wagon to claim the last of the Breen's supplies for a third run, and then she'll wait on the far side of the hill to watch Dolan and Breen navigate the downward slope. There are just two wagons ahead of the Breen's now, the last of the Graves's and the Reed's. The rest of them wait behind.

Amid shouting and huffing animals, Ada moves to the side to avoid the teamster John Snyder as he starts up the hill. His face is grim and contorted as he wrestles with oxen. He cracks his whip and drives the hulking animals forward. The oxen labor, heads down and shoulders low, as they strain against their yokes.

Patrick Breen sprints past Reed's wagon. "Hold up, Snyder. Foolhardy to attempt this alone. Got wagons waiting behind you. Chain up, like the rest of us. Let me help."

Behind Snyder, Milt Elliott, the Reed's teamster, is double-yoked and ready for the climb. Ada nods to Elliott as she passes the Reed's wagon on the way to the Breen's.

"Miss Weeks." He tips his hat, and then resumes the reins. It is unusual for the teamsters to drive oxen from inside the wagon; they usually walk beside the beasts. Because of the sharp incline here at Pauta Pass, coupled with the chance of losing footing, teamsters are threading the pass from the front of the creaking wagons.

"Step up, boys," Elliott bellows. He goads his team past Snyder's stalled wagon. A shuffle of heavy oxen feet and audible snorts accompany the oxen as they overtake Snyder.

"Bastard!" Snyder yells, a pernicious sneer pasted on his pockmarked face. He strikes his team repeatedly with the butt end of the whip. His oxen bellow under the burden. "You have no business here, Elliott. This is my place."

"Drive on!" Elliott yells.

Reed reins Glaucus in just feet from the melee. "Whoa there, Snyder. Let Elliott pass! You'll be next. I'll see to it. You've got to double up, like the rest of us."

Snyder and Elliott ignore Reed's entreaty and begin a shouting match. Furious, Snyder doubles down on his oxen. Within seconds, the yokes of the Graves's and Reed's teams entangle. Mary appears at Ada's side and stands shoulder to shoulder with her. Ada instinctively puts her hand on Mary's arm, swollen with an angry welt.

"Blasted! Now see what you've done," Elliott shouts. He leans forward to extricate tangled lines.

"Wait your bloody turn, Elliott," Snyder retorts. He thrashes his frightened oxen again. "Move it, boys!"

"We'll settle this, John, when we get up the hill," Reed shouts.

"No, Reed. We'll settle it now." Snyder rises on the wagon seat and slashes Reed with the whip.

Ada grows clammy with fright. She digs her fingernails into Mary's arm. It has not yet come to blows between the members of their party. And now this.

Reed reels, his face a mass of blood. His horse whinnies and sidesteps. But Snyder is a man unfettered. He strikes Reed again, despite Elliott's cries.

"John! Stop!" Mary shouts. Ada grasps Mary's arm tighter as the imbroglio unfolds before them. Animals paw wildly and rear their heads as they disentangle from the lines.

Margaret Reed races between John Snyder and her husband. "James!"

Then the unthinkable happens. Snyder raises his whip and slings the butt end squarely at Mrs. Reed. She falls back with the blow, her face laced red.

"What the devil!" Reed, bleeding profusely, bounds off Glaucus and charges Snyder. "Bastard! You've crossed the line now." Reed climbs up onto the wagon seat and brandishes a knife.

"Coming at me, are you?" Snyder rips his shirt open and taunts Reed.

With a desperate lunge, Reed thrusts the blade into Snyder's ribs.

In tandem, Ada and Mary turn their heads away.

"My God!" someone yells. "John!"

Snyder continues his barrage on Reed. He unleashes two more heavy blows with the butt end of the whip before crumpling to the ground. Billy Graves attends Snyder as Reed swipes blood from his eyes. Within seconds, Snyder is bathed in red and gurgling.

"Give us some room here," Breen yells. Dolan rushes to Snyder's side and cradles the dying man's head.

Ada shields Mary from the sight of blood. Mary buries her head into Ada's shoulder and shakes. Ada trains her eye on Reed, who, stumbling as a man drunk, flings his knife away. Patrick Breen kneels beside Snyder and puts his head close to the young teamster's.

"God forgive you," Breen whispers, his voice at once urgent and condemning.

Snyder stares at the sky, his eyes stilled.

Ada has dealt with many dead bodies in the past, but has never seen someone die in front of her. Augustus Vik had fourteen deaths in three days during one spring cold snap the year before in Indiana. Ada helped Augustus with the new practice of embalming, holding vials as he drained blood and injected arsenic to preserve bodies for viewing. She didn't shy away from the unpleasant task. Before this newfangled practice, Vik had used cooling boards beneath cadavers to preserve bodies before burial. It was a messy affair, melting ice mixing with bodily fluids. Embalming was an improvement from the standpoint of tidiness. It also mitigated the stench of decaying flesh.

While Ada helped Augustus in Noblesville, Inger Vik did what she did best: comfort the bereaved. "*Sam har vært ute en vinternatt sjøl.*" "I have been out in a winter night myself alone."

"Before Augustus, I had my Claus," Inger would say. "At first, you vill be lost. You vill feel like you are all alone vit nothing. But soon, you vill be looking at da brighter side of life." *Cluck cluck cluck* (if Ada had a nickel for every time she heard Inger say this, she would own a bank). Then Inger would serve up her delectable Norwegian kransekakes. It *just wasn't fair* that her adoptive parents had been two of the first to perish. Augustus could have used his skills with this burying. Inger, quiet as she was industrious, could have fed them all cake.

Ada watches as the life drains out of John Snyder. He had been a mouthy teamster. Today, his impatience killed him. And here they are, the Donner-Reed Party, months out of Independence in the middle of an unforgiving continent, with a man dead. There is no undertaker, no arsenic, no ice to be had for hundreds—if not thousands—of miles.

Keseberg reaches out to grab Reed by the collar. "String him up," he yells. "Ve've a murderer in our midst."

"Get your hands off of me," Reed explodes.

A divided camp faces each other. Mary Graves sobs openly. Ada releases Mary's arm as the young woman stumbles toward her mother.

"One man's death doesn't warrant another," William Eddy fumes.

Milt Elliott concurs. "Whoa there, Keseberg. Put down that wagon tongue. There'll be no lynching here today."

Franklin Graves stands his ground, his face grim and his voice measured. "If I don't see you strung up, I'll see your ass heading out of camp, Reed. And I mean today. Now. Consider yourself a lucky man I've given you another chance."

Voices mutter agreement.

Margaret Reed, still trembling from Snyder's assault, weeps into her handkerchief. Mary Graves is crumpled on the ground, wailing, "John! John!" Her mother leans over her. "Shhh now, Mary."

Reed mounts Glaucus, his head now swathed in a crude bandage. "I'll ride ahead. Take just enough for the ride to Sutter's. I'll see you there, Margaret. The rest of you, too."

"You'll take nothing," Graves sputters, his voice imbued with hatred.

"Are you heartless? Send a man to his certain death for protecting his wife and family?" Reed implores.

"Nothing," Graves repeats. "You'll take nothing." He trains his pistol on Reed. "Off that horse. Now."

Reed dismounts, his hands in the air. "I'll be all right, Margaret. Been up a stump before, and I can do it again. You must take care of yourself and the children."

"No, James. You cannot . . . I cannot go on alone."

"Shush, now." Reed bends to kiss his wife. "Soon. We will be together again soon." He marches out of camp, his back stiff and straight. The last Ada sees of him, he disappears over the pass without food, blanket, or supplies.

"What will we do without Reed?" Ada asks Dolan. "And how will he survive?"

"It's none of our concern," Dolan answers. His hands are spotted with Snyder's blood. He wipes his hands on his filthy trousers. "We've got enough concerns of our own. Now see to it you don't slip. Move on, Ada."

Move on. *That's the answer to everythin'*, she thinks. After deaths. After snowstorms. After rivers. *Move on, move on, move on.*

Ada takes the last of the Breen's flour and the heavy Dutch oven from the now empty wagon. There's a small hole at the corner of the flour sack so she folds the corner over so she doesn't lose any flour as she walks. There's a small heap of flour in the wagon bed and a few loose trinkets: nails, buttons, a lone wooden stake. She cannot carry any more. Ada hefts the limp flour sack, careful not to leave a trail of flour behind her. It's difficult to manage the Dutch oven and the flour, so she kneels next to a prickly pear and dumps the remaining flour into the cast iron pot. She discards the sack, which catches on the short, fanned cactus nearby. She carries the oven in front of her like an offering and gauges each step as she pants up the incline. Drips of sweat pour down her face, but she cannot reach up to wipe her brow. By the time she reaches the far side, Reed is gone. *What have we come to, that we banish a man to a certain death? Are we no more than mere animals?*

When she reaches the far side of the pass, Ada sits on the iron pot and scratches her ankles. Wilhelm Hardkoop shuffles past, his right leg dragging behind his left.

"How you gettin' along?" Ada asks.

"Vell as can be expected, miss, thanks for asking. Glad to see you've got yourself a fella."

Ada colors. If Hardkoop has noticed, it must be evident to all that she and Dolan have been "stepping out." She vows to be more circumspect. That night, she avoids Dolan. She unrolls her bedding under the Breen's wagon and turns in early. Dolan reaches across to pat her shoulder. She shrugs him away. The next morning, Ada again shuns Dolan's advances and bundles her cloak tighter as she joins the column walking west, her sturdy new boots shuffling through sagebrush and cacti. Thin white puffs of breath disappear into the brisk fall air. She marches on, despite everything: deaths, turbid water, unpalatable food, fights, indiscretions, a lumpy bedroll, no clear wagon master. Her skin itches from heat and grime and insect bites. Her stomach rumbles and her armpits reek. But there is no way except forward, counting out steps.

Five hundred miles to go.

16

October 8, 1846
On Marys River

Ada rues it every day, the choice she made to follow the Donners and Reeds instead of the Radfords and Minks when they parted ways near Bridger's Fort. If she'd hitched onto the caravan going north to Fort Hall on the established route, she may well be to California by now *and eating grapes.* But here she is, fate sealed, confined to a moving prison of eighty-three souls. There's not much trail chatter. Ada concentrates on other sounds: moaning wind, rustling sagebrush, jangling harnesses, snorting oxen. She can't get away from the ever-present groan of splintered wagon wheels—chewing and spitting out warm, pink sand on each slow, tortuous revolution. If it weren't for the rusted iron tires circling the wooden wheels, they'd likely splinter like toothpicks by now in this arid heat.

But of course, if she had followed the others, she would not be with Dolan, unless he had also left the party. One decision had begat another and another and another. The decision to follow the Hastings Cutoff had been the worst mistake. Hastings promised his route would cut hundreds of miles from the original route, but it's unmistakable that the opposite is true: the option to take the short-cut has added more than a hundred miles—and much lost time—to the journey. Now that the emigrants have reclaimed the established trail to California, they've lost more than a month.

With every dawn, there is nothing but more heartache, more dissention. There's no stopping on the Sabbath anymore. "No rest for man or beast," Ma Breen complains. Mrs. Reed, plagued by more headaches, abandons her last wagon and transfers her supplies to the Graves's and Breen's wagons. There are only fifteen wagons left, pulled by gaunt teams of mixed oxen and cows, eyes dulled and half starved. Three hundred miles of discarded cargo is behind them. By now, California is but an illusion. *We won't never get there.*

Ada scuffs fire-red dirt with each step. Clouds of vermillion balloon around her ankles. Her calves are covered with welts from brushing up against sage. She's seen scorpions and spiders as big as California itself. And plenty of snakes. She spies another rattlesnake hole. She throws a handful of stones in the direction of the mound. This time she hears the distinct hollow *rrruhhh* of rattles. She sidesteps the hole and keeps her eyes trained on the ground. Nothing much scares Ada. She's faced coyotes at eye level under the wagon. She's sliced her hand and avoided gangrene. She's seen death and more death, bellies distended and discolored. Death itself isn't the enemy, this she knows. It's a certainty one can dread or accept (or even welcome), when bloody spittle chokes a throat closed or a gunshot wound splays an abdomen wide open. *Death's a blessin' then.*

She counts blessings, one per footfall: food, companionship, coffee. When she runs out of blessings, she counts curses: illnesses, accidents, weather. She lopes to catch up with Dolan, takes his free hand. *Help me to see the blessin's, Lord. 'Cause the curses are takin' care of them damn selves.*

Four days after Pauta Pass, the rear group overtakes the Donners, who are behind now with wagon troubles. When the forward party reaches a second dry drive, Ada is at her wits' end. No one has anticipated this, a long, hot pull across forty more miles of wheel-wrenching scrub and deep, loose sand. They thought the desert was behind them, once and for all. And here is another one. They begin the trek in late afternoon and slog on through the night. There is no place to pee, so Ada lets urine run down her legs as she walks. It evaporates as soon as it hits the sand.

"Dammit," Breen yells. "You worthless creatures!" He beats his remaining oxen on the head.

"And what are you doing, Mr. Breen?" Ma Breen screams at her husband. "Without them oxen, we'd be up a dry creek."

"Nag," he mutters.

"Don't you go walking away from me, Mr. Breen. Who're you calling names? I've got a few for you."

The travelers reach the far side of the drive demoralized and exhausted. Ada's feet are blistered, and her legs smell soured. The desert sun continues to beat mercilessly, and then, like a thief, scorching heat disappears and cool night temperatures crowd in to mock the travelers. One day there are no events worth noting, the next day a murder; one day merciless cold, the next day hotter than Hades; one day plenty of water, the next day none.

At the sink of Marys River, the scene screams desolation: not enough timber for fuel or vegetation for feed, and nothing but alkaline water, deadly to cattle and undrinkable to man. At the first sign of stomach distention or raspy cough, teamsters force a large dose of grease down stricken oxen's throats. If they don't catch it in time, the oxen's abdomens swell—a death sentence, most times, and no time to slaughter.

Ma Breen disappears multiple times a day into the yellowish-red brush. Ada suspects it's mountain fever. "Bad humours," Ma Breen calls it.

A piercing scream comes from the direction where Ma Breen has gone to do her business again. Ada rushes in Ma Breen's direction, her boots thundering on red soil. There, not seven feet from where Ma

Breen sits on her haunches, a tremendous rattlesnake coils. Without thinking, Ada grasps Ma Breen and jerks her away from the snake. A bite could prove deadly, but her mess could be cleaned. When they are out of the snake's reach, Ada tears her handkerchief from her neck and mops up Ma Breen's legs, splat with diarrhea.

"Wait here," Ada says. "Be back in a minute." She sprints up to the wagon, grabs a handful of rags from the ragbag hanging on the side of the wagon box, and runs back to Ma Breen. "Let me help you. Don't want to get too far behind."

"No, Ada, I'll manage. You catch up, see to the boys."

With little to sustain them, the divided group winds toward Truckee River. During nighttime raids, mixed Indian bands of Shoshones and Paiutes pierce eighteen of the emigrants' oxen with poisoned arrows. Men frantically make chase into the woods, firing at the perpetrators and swearing. The Indians have long vanished. Rather than leaving cattle behind to die, they are slain. When the travelers have taken all they can, they leave the rest, carcasses rotting in the autumn sun. Fly-crusted strips of beef hang from the sides of battered wagons as wheels roll through dry brush. Men grumble. Women grouse. If children complain, they're boxed on the ears or swatted with a switch. The dogs don't fare much better, but by now, few dogs are left, and even fewer horses and mules.

The emigrants have gotten sloppy in their corralling. At the beginning of the journey, the wagons would cluster in neat formations, the two front wagons parallel to each other and the next set of wagons pulling up on either side of the anchor wagons so their rear wheels touched the front wheels of the first wagons, and so on, turning out, until the circle was wide enough to house all the animals. Then the following wagons turned in to complete the circle, leaving a twenty-yard opening for the animals to pass through and closed off with heavy ropes for the night.

Now they are lucky to have wagons at all. Once well-packed

wagons—loaded four feet high on both sides with a narrow passageway through crates and boxes and family memorabilia—are now mere skeletons of wood and battered covers. Each day, another wagon is abandoned.

"Where's Hardkoop?" Patrick Breen asks after supper.

Keseberg glares at Breen. "Couldn't keep up."

"What do you mean, 'couldn't keep up'? You mean you left him behind?" Breen explodes with anger. "You're nothing but filth of the earth, Keseberg," he spits.

"What's the commotion?" Milt Elliott asks.

"Keseberg here thought it best to leave poor Hardkoop behind," Breen says.

"Eddy, come along with me," Elliott says. "We'll show you what right Christians do. We'll be back before nightfall."

"Wretch, that's what you are, Keseberg," Eddy sneers. "You, and the rest of you Germans."

Eddy and Elliott ride out of camp to retrace today's route, Eddy on a borrowed horse. When the duo rides into camp late evening with Hardkoop, Ada binds the old man's bloodied feet.

"Like da Good Samaritan today," Hardkoop says in broken English.

The next morning, Hardkoop's feet are no better. "I beg you, Keseberg, yust a day or two on your vagon. I can't find my spectacles so I'm like one valking blind today."

Keseberg doesn't budge. "I told you yesterday, I tell you today. Ve're all of us valking. You can't valk, ve leave you behind. It's valk or die."

"Breen?" Hardkoop asks. His eyes are rheumy.

Ada holds her breath. She stares at Hardkoop's grizzled face and oozing feet.

Breen doesn't answer. He whips the oxen and the wagon rolls forward.

"Breen!" Hardkoop entreats. "I vill repay you!"

"With what?" Breen mutters. He doesn't look back.

"Vat about you, Graves?" Hardkoop asks. He leans against his walking stick, breathing heavily.

"You heard it from Keseberg, old man. It's walk or die. Walk on!" Graves shouts to his oxen.

Hardkoop sinks to the ground, his head hung low.

"It's time, Ada," Ma Breen says.

Ada turns her head every few steps to see if the old Belgian is hobbling behind. Soon, she cannot see him at all. *Keep up, keep up,* she wills him. If only he could shuffle in behind the wagons, do his best to cover the miles. But all she can see is dust. Still she looks. *It's madness,* she knows, *but what's left if we don't have hope?* After a few hours have passed, she knows the hard truth: Hardkoop will not be coming into camp. And tonight, no one will go back to retrieve him.

Ada brims with anger toward Patrick Breen and the other wagon owners. What would George and Jacob Donner have done? It's hard to say, as they are now ahead again. She cannot reconcile leaving a member of the party behind. She sucks in a hard breath, remembering the day after Augustus and Inger drowned. What if the wagon master had said to her, "There's no room for you, young lady. Walk or die."

D is for die. Die die die.

A few nights later, Indian arrows wound twenty-one head of cattle. Men and boys butcher dying animals on the spot. It makes for a temporary feast. Ada's stomach bulges. Without full teams to pull their loads, the Eddys and Wolfingers are forced to cache their wagons the next day. Hopes to return to this spot at a later date ring hollow. Everyone knows, but no one says aloud, the obvious fact that no one will be returning for anything, not wagons or china or coins.

The ragged entourage continues on toward California. They've left the sink of Marys River and are now winding through the Sierra Nevada foothills. It's hard going, from crumbly to crusted sand to vast plains of dense scrub brush to narrow ravines choked with pine. Ada is continually thirsty. She hears the rumor: the California border is a stone's throw over the Sierra Divide. Why, she can't throw a stone more than fifty feet. But she knows what it means. One more push. One more mountain range. One more stone to throw.

One morning, as autumn spins uncontrollably toward winter's cold solstice, Jacob Wolfinger lingers near his wagon as the other wagons roll on. "Ve'll be along," Wolfinger says to his wife, Doris. "You go ahead. C'mon Spitzer. You, too, Reinhardt, come help." All the Germans, save Keseberg, stay behind.

What's the worth of cachin' anythin' at this point? Ada thinks. *The only currency needed now is courage and fortitude. Coins are worthless.*

None of the men have returned by dark. During the night, Patrick Breen orders fires kept burning to guide the Germans into camp. Breen and Dolan roast red willow bark over a low flame late into the night. There's no tobacco left, and the fine, pulverized powder of the inner willow bark serves as a substitute. Ada's glad she's got a little bit of snuff left. She's used to chewing it, not smoking it, so she'll have to ration it even more carefully. Ma Breen knits, her needles clicking in the firelight. The boys have bedded down, and the camp settles in for another night.

When the drovers ride into camp the next day, Wolfinger is not among them. In a spattering of German and English, Spitzer blames a lone Paiute for slaughtering their companion.

When? And why? Did the Indian see them secreting the wagon or sneak up on them afterward? Where is Wolfinger's body?

The men are peppered with questions. Their responses are guarded. Doris Wolfinger collapses. If Inger were there, she'd be the first to comfort the widow. But Ada doesn't know how to do that. By now,

she is not sure she believes what she purports to believe: that there is
a life after this wretched one. *D is for devil,* Ada thinks ruefully. *No
use bargainin' with God anymore. It's a bargain with the devil from
here on out.*

"Don't come another inch closer," Patrick Breen warns.

"I beg you, Breen. I've got a wife, two children. All I'm asking for is
a cup of water," William Eddy says.

"I said, not another inch." Breen trains his rifle on Eddy.

William Eddy stares at Breen and advances on the wagon.

"I've warned you," Breen says.

Eddy raises his rifle and sets a bead on Breen. "I'll have a cup of
water, even if it means killing you for it." He walks slowly, his eyes
focused on his fellow traveler. When Eddy reaches the wagon, he
lowers his rifle and fills his cup.

Breen drops his rifle and mumbles. "Damn if I'll kill a man over
a cup of water." He retreats to the far end of the wagon and sits on a
campstool, glowering.

Ada is distracted by a deep, orange glow in the morning sky. It
can't be the sunrise; it's too late for that. *A fire?* She squints. It's
definitely flames. Last night's lightning storm lit up the sky with
fiery zigzags, and Ada worried then about the possibility of fire. Her
fears are realized this morning; the dry tinder of the Sierra foothills
sparked overnight. Flames lick a hillside roughly a half-mile from
camp, a ribbon of sizzling golds and ambers and reds that devours
everything in its path. Trees look naked, their branches stripped of
leaves and bark. Only the topmost leaves left on distant trees point
their tips upward, like fingernails etching the sky, trying in vain to
escape heat's offensive.

Breen follows Ada's gaze. "Wind's in our favor," he says. "Wouldn't be concerned just yet." He kicks dirt on the embers of their morning fire.

As the day wears on, Ada keeps one eye on the trail and the other on the wildfire. The speed at which the blaze moves surprises her, crackling and popping and whooshing, sometimes as close as a quarter-mile away. She can smell destruction, an acrid, hot stink that singes her nostrils.

"There'll be no fires tonight," Breen announces, when the travelers stop for the night. "We'll have to drink the last of the coffee cold."

The emigrants bed down warily. If they have to move hastily to avoid the forest fire, more wagons will have to be abandoned. And there is so little left.

By morning, the fire has turned south, leaving behind an angry sun that glares blood red through the hazy sky. The path west is clear. Wagons creak through growths of uncharred pine and cedar. Ada breathes in the scent of the forest. *We are almost to California.*

Reaching the Truckee River is the first sign of hope Ada has had in weeks, months even. She gulps handfuls of cold mountain water, closing her eyes as it slides down her parched throat. She washes her face, her neck, her wrists. Rivulets of river water stream down her dirty blouse. *Enough water! Enough grass! Enough wood!* She dunks her head in the river and shakes the excess off, like a dog.

The party continues to travel in two distinct groups, crossing and re-crossing the Truckee River, and, by Edward Breen's count, forty-nine times in eighty miles over a matter of days. Patrick Breen is anxious to keep moving. The moon, sliced perfectly in half, gambols in and out of high clouds. After supper, Dolan motions Ada to the edge of a stand of scrub pines.

"I've got a plan," he breathes into her ear. "It's low ground, over there, behind the trees. We can sneak away tonight. After dark. I've got plenty of bedding."

Ada sighs, looks down. "It's just that, well, I've got my monthlies . . ."

"Nothing to be concerned about."

"Won't that make for an awful mess?"

"The only mess is what Reed and Donner have gotten us all into."

His face presses close to hers. "I need you, Ada. Please."

Ada calculates the risk. Yes, they could probably disappear without much notice. Yes, she could bring extra rags to clean herself. She is nervous, but she trusts Dolan to be gentle with her this first time.

"Ada?"

"Yes, Pat. Yes."

"I'll be counting the minutes."

"You won't be the only one countin'," she says.

17

October 23, 1846
Alta California

The man curries his horse with slow, deliberate strokes. He's off to Yerba Buena today, will stay three nights, two at Hedrin's Boardinghouse and the last with Fay. At least, with Fay, he can get Salina out of his mind. Why is it then all his waking hours are consumed with Salina? And (*here's the rub,* he thinks), he can't have her. Never could, never will. It's as impossible as snow in July.

Seeing Salina makes it worse, instead of better, like placing your hand over an open flame and leaving it there to char. It's so visceral, so deep; he pounds his fists on the rustic table until his hands sting.

She's got to know how much I want her. Then again, she probably doesn't. He's never said anything to her about his lust for her. And she's so busy with the children and the cooking and the laundry and visiting her people she must see him as only a neighbor, a friend. She's never—not once—given him any indication she has feelings for him. And didn't she tell him lately he needed to find himself a lady friend? When he can't stand it anymore, he tears off his grimy clothes and crashes naked through the clearing, plunging into the cold mountain creek to get back to his senses.

The best and surest way to rule his senses is routine. Up at dawn.

Make coffee. Feed horse. Set traps. Cook breakfast. Clean gun. Shine boots. Check weir. Hunt for supper. Stack wood. Any or all of these things, the ways a man cements himself to place and calls it his own. Laced through his days, a niggling question gnaws at the edge of his consciousness: *Why here?* Is there someone else—maybe someone he hasn't met yet, someone in Yerba Buena or coming over by emigrant train or back in Wisconsin—who will take his battered heart and mend it, one crooked stitch at a time?

He pets Boy, calls to the raven. He's headed out of the woods and into the city. His horse nickers as he mounts. *Screw it all,* he thinks. By nightfall, he'll be with Fay. Why does he kid himself? Say he'll stay at the boardinghouse? He never stays there anyway. At Fay's, he can lose himself or just fall asleep. She lets him decide. It's two bits either way, enfolded by mounds of warm, perfumed flesh.

He doesn't know Fay's story, probably better that way. Maybe she was taken advantage of by her father or uncle or brother. Maybe her mother kicked her out of the house. Maybe she had a wild streak. Maybe none of the above. He's got more questions than answers these days.

He spurs his horse and heads out of the clearing. There's a nip in the air, and he picks up his pace.

18

October 24, 1846
Truckee Meadows (1,800 miles west of Independence, Missouri)

Ada awakes to blistering cold. Snow whorls around the camp and makes a silent coverlet over the tents. She's bundled in a corner of one of the two Breen tents underneath a buffalo hide she's borrowed from Dolan. It's rimed with hoarfrost and stiff to the touch. Ada shivers. For all of her five foot eleven frame, she must now weigh less than one hundred ten pounds. Her hipbones project from her sides like the shoulder blades of dying cattle.

There are six in her tent: Ada, Ma Breen, and the younger children: Simon, James, Peter, and Bella. In the adjacent tent, Patrick Breen beds down with the older boys: John, Edward, and Patrick, Jr. There's no room for Dolan, so he goes off to sleep with a couple of other teamsters at the far edge of camp. Ada longs for Dolan and lets herself down into sleep thinking of his rough, needy lovemaking. At first, she hadn't known how much she would enjoy the coupling (most women object to it). But for Ada, it takes her to a place she didn't know existed. She craves the stolen moments she and Dolan can slip away unnoticed and doesn't consider the consequences; if she isn't mindful, she might find herself with child. *It's enough to keep Bella alive. Can't be thinkin' of another baby now.*

Ada hasn't seen snow this unrelenting since last March, when Indiana froze for two weeks straight. *Weather doesn't wait for the dead,* Ada thinks. She and Augustus had six bodies to ready for burial during that cold snap, and a whopping ten afterwards. Yes, snow dusted the mountaintops over the past month and the emigrants were caught unaware in an ominous snowfall west of Great Salt Lake, but today it's more like a mid-winter blizzard—not what anyone would expect in late fall. Since crossing the Great Divide, it's been cold in the mountains, scorching hot in the desert, and cold again here in the high meadows.

Six months ago Ada left Independence on the way to the Promised Land. In the intervening months, so much has happened she can hardly remember details of the lively conversation she shared with Edwin Bryant the night before the Fourth of July. And it seems like years since the laborious day she spent scratching her name onto the backside of Independence Rock or shared intimacies with Mary Graves.

Why, she can't even recollect a conversation she had with her friend the other day. What had she promised to tell Mary? There have been so many miles, with troubles layered on top of them all. Yesterday, there was more trouble. In an instant, another bride became a widow, this time Harriet Pike, her husband William killed accidentally by his brother-in-law William Foster as he readied firearms. Ada didn't shed a tear for Pike. He killed Bert, after all. But there is no stopping the group now, not even—or in spite of—death. Harriet nestles her baby Catherine as they amble around the clearing at Truckee Meadows. Harriet's older daughter, Naomi, trails behind her mother. "Where is Papa? Where is Papa?" she wails.

Breen and Dolan slaughter spare cattle, crunching bloodied snow beneath steaming carcasses. Tripe and sweetbreads, kidneys and liver, these are all cooked up first. John and Edward assist, quartering and packing the renderings. What they can't use or carry is left for wolves or Indians.

Time, that race from sunup to sundown, brings fewer light-filled hours and more dark-filled ones. Ma Breen barks at the boys. Ada snatches Bella and walks as far from the wagons as she deems prudent with hostiles about. What they would do to a single woman and a baby is beyond speculation. Dolan winks at her as she leaves camp. As she squats to pee, she remembers what Mary asked her: "Have you lain with Dolan yet?" Ada wonders if she'll feign ignorance or tell Mary every chapter and verse. But the Graves family is bedded down in another camp several miles away tonight. She doesn't know when she'll see Mary next. *Tomorrow? The next day? Ever?*

Ahead, the towering, snow-capped Sierra Nevada Mountains are the last barrier between the emigrants and California. Even though Sutter's is estimated to be only ninety miles away, Ada doubts her energy for this last leg of the trip. Her world has winnowed down to the confines of the Breen tent, or, more specifically, to her bedroll. Tonight is no different from last night. She is exhausted, bitterly cold, despondent. A halo circles the moon, signaling an imminent storm. She wavers between wanting to fly like a hawk over the mountain pass to reach Sutter's Fort as fast as she can and closing her eyes forever right here.

Wind picks up around midnight, letting loose a fierce howl around the battered tents. Every inch of Ada's frail body quakes with tremors. She coughs, using her filthy sleeve as a handkerchief. It's an effort to sleep with cold nagging inch by inch over her torso and limbs. Ada grasps her shoulders with her arms crossed to conserve any heat. She must have dozed off, so she isn't sure if voices she hears are dream-locked or from the awakened world. She shakes her head to clear the scrim of sleep. Indeed, the loud voices *are* real, coming from outside the tent. Ada throws her hair into a bun and opens the tent flap. A blast of frigid air stabs her face. She squints to see who is yelling for anyone to answer.

Can it be? Stanton?

With the sun's glare, Ada cannot see his face, but she knows that voice. She squints and runs toward him. "Mr. Stanton!"

True to his word, Charles Stanton has returned, trailed by seven pack mules and two young *vaqueros.*

Ada clusters with other members of the party to hear what Stanton is saying. As she joins the group, Margaret Reed weeps openly.

"Yes, ma'am, you heard me right. Your husband made it safely," Stanton says. "As we speak, Mr. Reed's mounting a rescue party. He aims to be here within a fortnight."

Voices and questions punctuate the air. How long did it take to reach Sutter's? And how was the route? Is it passable for wagons? Where is McCutcheon? Give us bread!

Stanton answers questions as he hands out provisions. Yes, the route was fairly clear. How long? Two weeks and a day to Sutter's. We battled one blizzard. No Indians. These men? No, not hostile. Not at all. Miwoks. Christians, in fact. Names are Luis and Salvador. Sutter? Gracious hospitality. Generous, too. Wait 'til you see what he's sent along, beans and flour. Jerked beef, too. No, McCutcheon's fine; he's just fallen ill and stayed behind to recuperate, not to worry, Mrs. McCutcheon, ma'am.

"It should come as no surprise we are the last to cross the Sierras this year," Stanton continues. "We've got to attempt the summit, and soon. Next two or three days. Not a day longer. It won't be easy with all these little ones. My advice? Take only what's necessary. Be prepared to leave your wagons behind. At the very least, unload them— take only what is absolutely necessary."

"For the sake of Mary," Ma Breen grouses as she unloads clumps of extra clothes. "What do we mean to wear once we get to Yerba Buena? These old rags?"

Tamsen Donner and Samuel Shoemaker pass the Breen camp. Tamsen nods. "Care to help, Ada?"

"I'd be obliged."

Mrs. Donner walks to a natural swale between two pines in a dense stand of trees east of camp. "We'll bury the crates there."

"Your books?" Ada asks.

"Yes, botanizing books, school books, Bibles. Meant to utilize them in my schoolroom once we reached California. But I've marked this spot. I'll be back for them."

Tamsen Donner bends to clear away limbs and underbrush. Ada joins her.

"Might've been better to leave them Bibles back at Bridger's Fort," Shoemaker says. "I know more'n a few men who might've had a use for them. Most likely to wipe their—"

"Watch your language, Mr. Shoemaker," Donner says.

"Excuse me, Miz Donner. But when you're outta newspaper, you gotta use what you can."

"Well, you won't be touching these."

Shoemaker hefts the crates into the deep indentation in the soft ground. "Will that be all, ma'am?"

"Yes, thank you. Check with Mr. Donner. He's hurt his hand and might need help dispatching inventory."

On the way back to camp, Ada observes women divesting supplies and clothing. Elizabeth Donner's stash could fill a small dry goods store. Eleanor Eddy pulls blouses and skirts out of her pack and examines them before dropping them to the ground.

"Soon, you'll have nothin' left, Miz Eddy."

"We're down to the clothes on our backs, I'm sorry to say," she answers. "If we leave anything else, I'm afraid we'll be"—she lowers her voice to no more than a whisper—"naked."

Ada snickers. "Can't be goin' about like Adam or Eve."

"At least, they had fig leaves," Eleanor says.

"More than we'll have, if everyone keeps tossin' garments away like trash." Ada looks longingly at the pile of Mrs. Wolfinger's slips and bloomers, but she has no way to carry them. When she reaches the Breen wagon, Ma Breen is unloading trousers and blousy shirts and holey socks.

Wagons rasp on the next morning. Ada takes her place to the left of the Breen wagon, toting Bella. Not five miles from last night's camp, the entourage passes an abandoned hut on the shores of a small lake. No one is about. Ada trembles at the thought that any emigrants— ones that came before or ones to come behind, *or us*—could be so close to California and then be stopped by weather or sickness or exhaustion and forced to spend a winter in this small cabin. It is less than two weeks to Sutter's now. She wraps Bella tighter. Each step is closer to the illusion that has danced before their eyes since leaving Independence. She can almost touch California. *Are there really grapes there?*

None of the Donners make camp that night. Speculations abound. Might've broken an axle. Or been hampered by Indians. Jacob Donner's looking poorly, don't you think? Heard George Donner sliced his hand open, nasty business.

The Breens, Eddys, and Kesebergs are gladdened to see Charles Stanton, Mrs. Reed and her children, the Murphys, and the Graves family straggle into camp. The next morning, there is still no sign of the Donners. Cold rain pelts the travelers as the great wall of Sierra Nevadas looms directly in front of them. "We've got to make a run for it," Stanton says. "Today."

"But what about the Donners?" Eddy asks.

"We've got an opening today, and we've got to take it," Stanton says. "They will have to take their chances when they get here."

Wagons lumber through three-foot snowdrifts, winding upward in the wooded foothills. The oxen are exhausted, their mournful bellows pitiful. *They've had less to eat than we have, and they're doin' most of the work,* Ada thinks. Men employ crowbars to move boulders and, when gargantuan rocks prove unmovable, they block wheels with drags, heaving lines and sweating profusely beneath heavy clothing as wagons lurch up and over them.

"It's no use," Stanton says. "We've got to leave the wagons."

"Ve'll hear nothing of dat," Keseberg says. He strikes his oxen forward.

"You're a fool," Breen says. "Listen to the man. He's traveled this way just this week. If he says we've got to leave the wagons, we've got to leave the wagons."

"Take only what you need," Stanton says. "Blankets, ammunition, food. Leave the rest. Mules and horses can go on."

The Breen wagon grinds to a halt. Ma Breen shakes her head. "Damn if I've traveled across this whole country and have to leave it all here." She paws through the wagon and extracts a small box. "This I am taking," she says. She opens the box and caresses a small pink cameo.

"Leave the rest," Patrick Breen says. "All of it."

Mrs. Reed removes a quilt from her last chest. "Was my mother's." She folds it into a neat rectangle and stuffs it under her arm. "You can take one thing each," she says to her children. "Just one. Your father is waiting for us, or already on his way for us. We'll get anything else we need on the other side."

Mrs. Keseberg argues with her husband over a rocker; Mrs. Murphy laments about her china. Ada wants to stop up her ears. She assists Ma Breen stuffing food and woolens into knapsacks. The remainder of their effects will be abandoned: wagon and animals included. Breen doesn't even unhitch his oxen. Ada thinks it cruel. She urges Muzzles on.

Earth's calendar has turned its icy fingers toward November as the travelers continue up the steep incline, clawing for breath. Men and women scratch their way through thigh-high snowdrifts and coax their children on. A few miles shy of the summit, the emigrants stop, too weary to plod on.

"It's but three miles until we're clear," Stanton thunders. "If we break here, we risk not making it through. Looks to me that we're in for a big storm. Breen! Graves! Eddy! All of you, up. We haven't time to waste."

Breen shakes his head. After twelve hours wrestling with snow-drifts, numbing cold, and hunger, the travelers can't muster the energy to go on, even a scant three miles more. Stanton shuffles and leans against a tall pine. He puffs his pipe, shakes his head. "I feel it in my bones, we've got to keep moving. Don't a one of you have any sense?"

"We stop here," Breen says. For once, Ada agrees with him. What makes the most sense right now is to sit down and conserve any shred of warmth and stamina to push ahead in the morning. There is no supper. Ada unrolls her bedding next to Dolan's on the snow. She doesn't care about propriety. Dolan covers them both with his buffalo robe and whistles for Muzzles.

Other travelers moan and cry. It is pitch dark and numbingly cold. Ada's teeth chatter. As the night unfolds, she can't feel her toes. She can only imagine life half-hour by half-hour. It will be a miracle to make another day. She burrows herself against Dolan and struggles to sleep.

At dawn, Ada awakes from a fitful sleep to a living nightmare. Last night's snowstorm has obliterated the camp. She bolts upright, sprays of snow shooting from her upstretched arms. "Dolan!" She looks around and does not see him. She is frantic.

Dolan reaches up through a dense blanket of snow and pulls Ada down again.

"Shush, now, Ada." He rises, stretches, and disappears behind a tree. Other men gather in clumps. Women and children shake off the snow mantle that has covered every animate and inanimate object.

Stanton plods into camp from uphill, his short, stocky body encased in snow. "It's no use," he says. "We can't make it more than a quarter-mile. There's no way we can clear the summit today."

"What do you mean, Stanton? I can almost spit that far," Breen says. "Let's push on."

"It's no use," Stanton says.

"We'll see about that!" Breen explodes. "Mother! Dolan! Miss Ada! Boys! Now!" Ma Breen bundles the younger children and rubs their hands. Breen and Dolan take the lead, blazing a snow trail. Step by step, the emigrants push on toward California, single file through the snow. They walk for two hours, teeth chattering and extremities blue.

"This is fool-hardy," Breen says. "Stanton was right. We're better off going back to the lake camp for a day or two. Wait for a break in the weather." Grumbles pass down the ranks like a chain.

"You can go back, but I'm going on," Keseberg says.

"Me, too," William Eddy says.

Eleanor Eddy stifles a gasp. Ada reaches for Eleanor's arm.

"The baby, she's so cold," Eleanor pleads with her husband. "I'm afraid for her if we don't turn back."

Ada peels away the blanket and sees Baby Margaret's blue lips, a faint wheeze emanating from her tiny mouth.

"Please, William!" Eleanor entreats. "If I don't warm her soon she'll be gone."

"Let me take her," Ada says. "You go on ahead with Mr. Eddy and Jimmy. We'll be back to the camp by nightfall, make a fire, follow you in a few days." She lifts the near-lifeless baby into her arms and rubs her vigorously. A weak breath escapes the infant's lips.

Eleanor's hollow eyes bore into Ada's. "That I could never do."

Men shake their heads, mumble.

"There'll be no mutiny here," Breen roars. "Today we retreat. We should have pressed on when we had the chance."

"No good talking about what we should've or shouldn't have done," Stanton says. "Listen to Breen. All of you. We'll try again tomorrow or the next day. It's all of us or none of us."

Keseberg glowers. Eddy sets his mouth into a grimace. "I guess a day or two won't make a difference," Eddy says.

With sluggish resignation, the travelers turn around and descend the slope they struggled to attain the day before. They regain their wagons and oxen. Miraculously, none of the abandoned animals has perished overnight. Breen urges his family ahead. "Step lively. Simon, Peter, quickly now." By nightfall, they are back at Truckee Lake. Small fires dot the clearing.

Ada knows now why Patrick Breen moved expeditiously on the descent: their survival was at stake. He reached the camp first and commandeered the little cabin they had passed earlier at the edge of the lakefront. Patrick Breen barked orders as the boys stripped the wagon bare. Within an hour, he ushered his family into the austere cabin, squeezed tightly as eggs in a basket, and just as fragile.

The musty shanty measures no more than twelve by fourteen feet with a jumble of hides, branches, tents, and wagon canvases covering gaps in the leaking roof. A rough hide serves as a front door. Crowded and dark, the windowless structure stinks like a bear's den. Only the sweet smell of Patrick Breen's pipe tobacco staves off body odors, wet wool, and malodorous buffalo hides.

Before bedding down, Ada goes out to pass water. In the burgeoning dark, she gathers armfuls of pine boughs to cushion her bedroll. A callous, November moon hangs overhead, indifferent to her—or anyone's—plight. She shuffles back to the shanty and lines pine boughs under her bedding. As she burrows in for the night, she is overcome with tears.

Ada cannot remember the last time she cried. Not since before the fire, when she was eleven, this she knows for certain. The fire had stripped her of all emotion and forged her into a walking shell of a girl, almost without soul. For eight years she did not shed a tear, not when her cat was smashed by a drover, not when her parents died. Is weeping a sign she is slowly returning to herself? Or is it sheer desperation, an undeniable unraveling of everything she is, down to the core?

It has been three months since leaving Bridger's Fort, where James Bridger proclaimed Sutter's Fort was a mere seven weeks (*seven weeks!*) away by an easy road. Here, by the shores of a frigid mountain lake, the emigrants are hardly closer to their goal than they had been ninety days before.

A miss is as good as a mile. Bryant's words have never been more prophetic than now, with a wall of impenetrable mountains standing between here and Sutter's Fort and winter closing in like a fist. Instead of feasting at Sutter's, Ada is holed up in a dark cabin with ten others, like pack rats in a damp, windowless den.

Ada closes her eyes. *We're never goin' to get to California. Hastings be damned, damned, hell and be damned.* She shuts out Dolan and the Breen boys and Ma Breen's bickering. She cannot feel her extremities. The air is thin and icy, and her breaths are shallow.

Once there had been much to go on, and later, little to go on. Tonight, there is nothing to go on. It is not worth the effort to move, or to breathe. Ada folds in on herself and makes to die right here, in a dank, vagrant cabin miles from anywhere.

Dyin's not the hardest part, Ada thinks. *We've been livin' that.* She swipes at bloodshot eyes and wills tears to stop. *When we leave, we go alone, one breath away from meetin' our maker. Or slippin' into the void.*

She worms deeper into the bedroll and crosses her arms over her chest, like Augustus used to do when dressing cadavers.

No, dyin's not the hardest part.

Part Two

THE MOUNTAINS

19

November 29, 1846
Truckee Lake

Here, on the ledge of winter, Ada's stomach gnaws with hunger. She's survived another day, although food is scarce, and dwindling. The emigrants take any chance—a short break in the weather, a new route—to brave the summit. It is not the full contingent, however. It's a man or two here, a woman or three there, blended families, whoever is strong enough that day. The latest attempt by fifteen people on rough-and-ready snowshoes fails; the group is battered back by insurmountable snowdrifts and wailing winds.

Truckee Lake—a mere three miles long and less than a mile wide—is now solid ice. All endeavors to fish come up short. There's no game, no fowl, nothing. Patrick Breen and Dolan butcher the last of the cattle and stack it chest high outside the cabin. Every day, snow obscures the cache inch by inch, first ankle high, then knee high, then thigh high. There are no more live oxen, mules, or horses. Ada pulls Muzzles closer, his thin, mangy body wracked with shivers.

"Get your lazy ass up and out there, Mr. Breen!" Ma Breen barks. "Do you think trees cut themselves down? And the water bucket's empty again. Now, boys!"

"I'll go out by and by," Breen says.

Ada's certain he won't budge, hasn't budged for days. That means no more wood or water today unless she or one of the older boys goes out. And what's the matter with Dolan? It's like he's retreated into a shell. He slumps in the cabin's far corner and stares at the ceiling. Ada swears he talks to himself.

"What's become of Mr. Dolan? And Mr. Breen?" Ada whispers to Ma Breen. She pulls in another fold on her skirt at the waistline and secures her rope belt with a square knot, *right over left, left over right, cinch it tight.*

"They've given up," Ma Breen answers. "It's up to us, now."

Ada rocks Bella back and forth. The baby barely murmurs. Ada wonders how many days Bella has left. None of the other children have much vitality. Even Edward, who by this time has made a full recovery from his broken leg, sits and stares at the meager fire as if staring at it will coax the flames to burn bigger and brighter. Peter and James whimper; there is little to comfort them. Even if they're prone to sniveling, John, Edward, Patrick, Jr.—and Simon, at nine years old now—do not stoop to such childish behavior.

Ma Breen doles out thin beef strips, which quiets everyone for several minutes.

Then moans begin again. I'm so cold, Ma. Quit your complaining. But, Ma! Quiet, I tell you, or else.

Keseberg, ever unsavory and sour tempered, pounds out a lean-to against one of Breen's cabin walls.

"Damn German," Breen mutters. "Never knew a more disagreeable fellow."

Ma Breen rolls her eyes toward heaven. "What did he do now?"

"After he chased me with a hammer? Sent the rest of the Germans packing to Donner's. Six or seven miles from here, or so Eddy says."

Ada counts off the Donner contingent: George and Tamsen Donner, Jacob and Elizabeth Donner, children, teamsters, helpers, and unaccompanied men . . . *maybe twenty? Twenty-two at the Alder Creek camp?*

Tallying in her head, she counts emigrants at the lake camp: *Mr. and Miz Graves, Mary and her siblings . . . Miz Murphy's brood . . . Miz Reed, Virginia, and the three little ones . . . dear Miz Eddy and her family . . . poor Miz Wolfinger and Miz McCutcheon, and then all of us . . . Sixty? Sixty-two?*

A loud *whoomph* travels through thin cabin walls. Then a wail. Philippine Keseberg sobs. Margaret and Patrick Breen shake their heads. Ada moves toward the door.

"No, Ada. There's not room," Ma Breen says. "Not that I don't want to, you understand."

Ada goes out anyway, but steers clear of the Kesebergs' door. If it hasn't already been patently obvious that it's every family for itself, *it's sure as snot now.* She wades through dirtied snow past the Murphy's cabin, built against the side of a huge boulder two hundred yards south. How all those Fosters and Pikes and Eddys and Murphys can squeeze into the crude structure they're building is a mystery. *They'll be sleepin' one on top of another.* A slight quarter-mile further, Ada hears Franklin Graves as he yells orders. She finds Mary Graves in a dense clump of fir trees.

"Are you makin' do?" Ada asks.

"Not fast enough," Mary says. "And it's not only us—we've got Mrs. McCutcheon and Mrs. Reed with us, as well, you probably heard. Pa's lobbying for a double cabin, so families can have some privacy. I should let you in on a secret, us being friends and all. There's been some not-so-kind words spoken about Mr. Breen appropriating that cabin you're in."

Ada knows this all too well, although she's unsure what appropriating means. It's as if the Breen clan has smallpox the way everyone avoids them. "We're eleven," Ada says. "Not an inch of space to breathe." Not that anyone has come over to look in on them. Ada can understand why the others are hotheaded. Of the sixty-plus at the lake camp, only the Breens have adequate shelter and remnants of real food, which, by all accounts, they are not sharing.

Fistfuls of snow fall into the cabin and muddy the floors when Ada returns from her visit with Mary. All of the Breens have claimed a corner or a wall or spot by the fizzling fire. To conserve the meager supply of cut wood, a fire is lit only at night with thin sticks of green kindling and dead ends of pine branches. The air fills with a sickly-sweet aroma, more smoke than heat. It's hardly enough to see, let alone emit warmth. In near darkness, Simon and Patrick, Jr. hold lighted pine sticks aloft, lit from embers. They pretend they are writing their names in sooty air. That, or they spar like pirates.

"Shush your cavorting, boys," Ma Breen says. "Baby's sleeping."

"She's always sleeping, Ma," Simon says. "We're not at a library."

"You talking back to your Ma?" Patrick Breen counters.

"No, sir, just . . ."

Patrick Breen raises his hand. "Be quiet now, mind your ma."

Ada hears faint scratching on the chimney. Whether it's coyotes or mountain lions is anyone's guess. It's not mice. She crosses the cabin and shakes Dolan.

"You awake?" she asks.

Dolan stirs. His eyes flutter open.

"I'm wonderin' if you can teach me more about bein' Catholic," Ada says.

"Mary, Mother of God, that would take a year." He yawns.

"We got nothin' but time here. I heard tell Catholics have saints for every day and every trouble," Ada says. "Who's the saint protectin' us here?"

Dolan shakes his head awake and blinks his eyes. "That'd be St. Christopher."

"That's a good name. For a baby, I mean."

"You aren't saying . . ." Dolan sits up, his eyes wide now.

"Don't know, exactly," Ada says. "There's been no bleedin' for a while, but I don't feel any stirrin's. But it's got me thinkin'. Tell me the names of your brothers and sisters. Will help pass the time."

Dolan fans his fingers, one at a time. "Mary Claire, then me, then Michael, then Mary Agnes—she's my favorite."

"Four of you?"

"No, three more. Joseph, Francis, and the baby, Donagh."

"Seven?"

"Five boys and two girls."

Ada thinks of all the little coffins that stole her brothers and sisters away. Not all of them lived long enough to be named. Two of them bore the same name, as if trying again would save them. It did not.

"Your mother?" she asks.

"Mary Ellen Dolan, goes by Lelly. Her brother couldn't say her name proper." He draws Ada in closer, and she nestles her head on his bony shoulder. "Before long, you'll be Ada Dolan."

"I've had my share of names." *Stick girl.*

"We'll have a big house," Dolan continues, his voice gaining strength. "Rooms for every day of the week. Oil lamps, quilts . . ."

"Don't need much, Pat."

"If I could wish all this different, I would." He gestures around the dark cabin.

The fire has smoldered and all Ada can make out is the bare outline of Dolan's face. "I know you would. For now, we have to rest, save our strength."

Ada wakes the next morning to an overwhelming smell of feces. One of the boys has shat indoors. She bursts out into the snow and gasps mouthfuls of fresh mountain air. There's been no sun for days and another bank of clouds threatens. If she wants to talk to Mary, she'll have to go to the Graves's cabin because, according to Mary, her mother won't let her come over to Ada's anytime soon.

When Ada arrives, cabin walls are up and the roof is covered with hides and old blankets. Mary meets Ada at the doorway, but makes no effort to step outside or invite Ada in. "Yes, Miss Ada?"

"I was just wonderin' how you and your family are gettin' along today . . ." She is repulsed by the smell there, too: soiled babies, boiling hides, unwashed bodies.

"Not as good as yours, according to my ma." Mary changes the subject. "How's Mr. Dolan? I haven't seen him outside lately."

"Poorly, I'm afraid." Ada rubs her hands together to keep warm and reaches for Mary's hand. "We've been talkin' about after . . ." She trails off, remembering that Mary's intended is cold as stone underground. "I'll look in again, Mary," she says. "I can't sit in that cabin all day, even if it's colder than an icebox."

Ada wants to ask Mary if she had been intimate with John Snyder before his death. Unlikely, with her stern father around. But maybe she had. Who knows what "stepping out" really means anyway. Maybe it means holding hands. Maybe it means rutting behind wagons when no one's looking.

Ada shuffles back toward the Breen's along the dirty snow corridor. She hopes to see Eleanor outside the Murphy's cabin, but only William Foster is out. He hacks at the tip of a young sapling with half strength, nods at Ada, resumes his work. She continues on.

When she opens the hide door of the Breen cabin, only the boys look up. Her eyes adjust to near darkness again. A small candle burns on the single table where Patrick Breen sits, his shoulders hunched. He scribbles in his journal with ink-stained fingers. Ma Breen has her back to the door as she stokes the paltry fire.

"That you, Ada?" she asks.

"Yes, ma'am. Been to Mary's."

"How are they getting on?"

"Can't say as they're doin' too well."

Ma Breen harrumphs and turns her attention to the boys. "John! Get yourself outside. You too, Edward. We'll be needing more firewood."

"Oh, Ma," Edward says. "My leg's sore."

"I've heard plumb enough about that leg of yours. Get yourself outside. Now."

Ada sidles up to Patrick Breen. "What you writin', sir?"

Breen grunts.

Ada reads over his shoulder: *Snowing fast wind W about 4 or 5 deep, no drifts. . . no liveing thing without wings can get about.*

"Recording the days," Breen answers.

Ada notices his misspelling, but holds her tongue. The sentiment is accurate, misspelled or not. *No livin' thing without wings can get about, that's a certain.*

"Can you spare any paper?" Ada asks. "I'd like to . . . well, anythin'. Do my own recordin' of the days. Maybe sketch. Make lists."

"Ask me tomorrow," Breen grunts.

Ada contemplates stealing paper and pen from Breen after he falls asleep, but discounts that thought as fast as ink spills on a clean sheet of parchment. No, she can't take paper and pen in plain sight. Who is she fooling? Other small items, yes, a nail, maybe, or a piece of string. Even a stringy piece of beef when Ma Breen's back is turned. But not paper and pen.

There's only a cold bite tonight, two thin strips of tough beef. Ada wonders what's on the fare at other shanties (certainly not the princely supper the Breens are relishing). No wonder the others complain about the Breens. She's surprised there hasn't been any pilfering. Or has there been? Is that what the night sounds are, *scratch scratch scratch*, on the chimney pipe?

Ada chews and chews and chews until she's biting her tongue. She sees that Dolan hasn't yet touched his supper.

"Here." She nudges the beef toward Dolan.

Dolan looks blankly at Ada. "Not hungry."

Ada creases her eyebrows.

"Or maybe I'm so hungry I don't know the difference," he says. "Come closer, keep me warm."

Ada wedges in next to Dolan and rocks back and forth.

Although the Breen's beef stores are cached right outside the cabin, the boys can't locate any of it now that all the frozen meat is buried under twelve feet of snow. John and Patrick, Jr. prod the ground around the hut with long sticks, to no avail. Holes the diameter of a broom poke the snowy surface, but to date, not one of the thrusts has found purchase. *It's like lookin' for a needle in a haystack.* So the women cut strips of rawhide into smaller pieces and boil the tougher ends. The residual water is now bone broth, tomorrow's breakfast. The tenderer ends of rawhide they char over the smoky fire until the hair singes off, and, as they gnaw on hairless bits, they hope that just maybe the next day the boys will strike the mother lode.

Edward picks at the cabin walls, peeling strips of pine from exposed logs. He tosses the shreds to the floor and digs in again, his knife gauging deep into soft wood. Simon picks up pine scraps and flings them into a basket by the fireplace.

"Git yourself outside!" Ma Breen yells. "Lazy as an ox, all of you. There's a forest out there, and you're tearing down this shack for firewood?"

All of a sudden, Simon drops to his knees and lunges. "Got one!" He spears a rodent with a fork.

"Think that one rat's going to feed us all?" Ma Breen continues her rant. "John! Patrick! Go find us some beef. If you don't, we'll be eating shoe leather. Do you like the sound of that?"

Edward and Simon stare at their mother. No one's going outside. Ada sympathizes with the boys; they're trying to help. But at this rate, there won't be a cabin by springtime. Simon deposits the rat by the fireplace and Ma Breen scoops it up.

Peter starts at the beginning of the alphabet—*A, B, C*—for the third time in as many minutes.

"Not again!" Simon says. He pinches Peter on the arm.

"Ma! Simon pinched me!" Peter starts to bawl.

"Sakes alive!" Ma Breen says. "Quit your blubbering, child!"

Simon taunts Peter.

"Watch your step, Simon," Ma Breen says.

Peter wails louder, and then Bella begins to cry.

"Heaven help us!" Patrick Breen begins to pray, his voice drowning out every other voice in the cabin.

Ada can't hear herself think. It's as loud as a circus, without the fun or the popcorn.

Ada covers her ears. "T-H-O-M-A-S." She enunciates each letter, one by one. "What do you think of the name Thomas?" she yells to Dolan.

Dolan nods.

"Or Belinda?" She spells again, this time louder. "B-E-L-I-N-D-A."

He nods again. "Whatever you want, Ada."

"Whatever I want?" Ada explodes. "Do I have any say in this matter, or any matter?"

Dolan hangs his head. "I'm sorry—"

"You should be! It's you men—you and Mr. Breen and Mr. Reed and Mr. Donner, all of you—got us into this trouble. If you'd listened to any sense—"

"Pray, Ada. Only thing we can do."

She sucks the insides of her mouth and shakes her head.

"Do you think anyone's listenin'? St. Christopher or any of those dead saints? Really, Pat? Do you?"

Ada looks around the cabin. No one meets her eye. "*Sam har vært ute en vinternatt sjøl.*" Ada recalls Inger's words and, for the first time since her death, Ada is glad her mamma didn't live to experience this nightmare of veritably living out in a winter's night alone.

Ada has been thinking about her real ma lately and has resorted to talking to her just for *someone* to talk to, because there's no one to have a conversation with at the cabin, unless you count raving and yelling and crying as conversation, but Ada doesn't, so she carries on an ongoing imaginary dialogue with her mother, even though her mother's long dead.

Try each day to get to evenin', Ma. Then try each night to get to mornin'. I am all alone, Ma. A-L-O-N-E. Five little letters. Alone. Like panic and venom and ditch. Whine and joker and smite. Paper, fever, stink. Stink! We all stink!

Ada pulls her blanket over her mouth and screams. No one bothers to look, not even Dolan. He looks ghoulish, eyes sunken and face nothing but angles and bones.

I think he's dyin', Ma.

Ada tries to picture heaven, where her ma supposedly resides. All she sees is smoke and flames coming from her pa's barn that fateful night eight years ago.

What if there's no pearly gates, no angels, no streets paved with gold? Maybe we're all goin' to hell, down, down, down. No redemption. No everlastin' life. Just darkness and gnashin' of teeth.

She fumbles with the blanket, her fingers cold as ice.

I think we're all goin' down, Ma. One by one by stinkin' everlastin' one.

20

December 5, 1846
Truckee Lake

Bitter cold, but sunny. Spent day with Mary. No coffee left.
—from Ada Weeks' diary

In contrast to their dim hovel, the bright, early winter sun stabs Ada's eyes as she emerges from the snow tunnel. Virgin snow sparkles with flecks of silver and gold as she conjures words to describe the wintry scene: alabaster, ivory, eggshell, bone. *Or brilliant.* After nine days of snow, Ada welcomes the sun's return like the prodigal son. For a few minutes, she forgets about hunger.

Snowdrifts reach rooftops now; by Ada's estimate, banks of snow stand ten or twelve feet high. Only treetops shoot up like daggers through the vast sea of white. Fifteen-year-old John Breen spends the day carving a snow staircase from the cabin's threshold through thick drifts. Chunk by chunk he shovels snow and ice and slush and pounds it down into useable steps. Now, when Ada needs to clear her head or lungs or bladder, she'll trudge up snow stairs to the world beyond darkness and stink of soiled bedding. But today is glorious. Almost all the emigrants spend time outside today, milling about, sharing stories, gazing west.

"It's like the balm of Gilead," Mary says.

Ada pats Mary's arm. "I don't know about that, but I'm ever so heartened to see the sun."

Mary drops her voice to a whisper. "What's it like in your cabin? I mean, is it *vile?*"

Ada nods.

"It's bad in ours, too, Miss Ada." Mary shakes her head. "Sometimes I wonder what it is we've done wrong to deserve this."

"We haven't done anythin' wrong, Mary. Expect maybe do what everyone tells us to do."

When she can stand it no longer, Ada takes a snow corridor toward a stand of pines poking up through the world of white and hides behind a forked treetop. She lifts her fouled skirt, and squats. Some of the women have sewn their skirts together like trousers. Ada has not. Not because she doesn't think it useful. No, it's because she no longer has needle and thread, and doubts anyone else has any to spare. Cold drafts run up her unstockinged legs and bite at her thighs.

She finishes and hurries back to find Mary Graves. They huddle and whisper, rubbing chapped hands over and over again, Mary repeating the same words over and over again, too, until all Ada can do is nod: In all God's creation, has there ever been a lovelier day? Don't you think so, Miss Ada? You must agree? Don't you?

Nightfall comes earlier as December unspools, although inside the cabin, by day or by night, it's always dark. Ada works alongside Ma Breen, stoking the fire, emptying slop buckets. Patrick Breen is gaunt, his eyes hollow. He complains of the gravel, a disease of the kidneys.

Before bedding down, Ada begs four sheets of paper from Breen. He's too weak to protest. She folds the paper in half to make a chapbook eight pages thick. If she writes small, and uses both sides of the paper, she'll be able to cram more words onto sixteen half-sized pages: weather, lists, a few rough sketches.

There is only one pen, so Ada writes by firelight while Breen sleeps. She peeks into his diary to read today's entry: *Fine clear day beautiful sunshine thawing a little, looks delightful after the long snow storm.*

Yes, it had been the finest day in ages. The last day that evoked such a sense of calm was way back at Beaver Creek, on the Fourth of July. Ada thinks longingly of Edwin Bryant and revels in the thought of standing beneath the arch of the natural bridge, back when the sun generated warmth, not just light.

When Ada's fingers cramp, she tries to warm herself until shiver after shiver runs up her spine. Ma Breen lights the fire and, one by one, each person takes his or her turn before weak flames. Ada goes last, when the fire dies to embers.

The next morning, Ada breaks the skin of ice on the water bucket and scoops a cupful of icy water. Her teeth chatter. She wishes it were coffee or hot tea or—here she closes her eyes to remember—*cocoa.* Anything to warm her throat, her hands, her body. The last of the coffee is gone now, and it's been months since tea ran out. As for cocoa, well, that's a dream from bygone days.

Ada's joints ache. She goes back to her corner and wraps her blanket around her head, neck, and shoulders, leaving the lower half of her body exposed. The dirt floor is frozen and hard. Minutes later, she unwinds the blanket to cover her shaking legs, leaving her head and upper body uncovered. She clenches and unclenches her fingers to keep blood circulating and shoves her hands under her bony bottom for a vestige of warmth. Her face is dry and scaly, with deep indentations in her cheekbones. Even though the day before had been *the loveliest day* by Mary Graves's estimation (and, Ada agrees, it had been a respite), Ada knows that winter is closing in. It's not the advent of summer. She knows she shouldn't succumb to melancholy, but it's in her blood. She's ill-tempered, like everyone else. And, wouldn't you know it, tobacco is long gone, too.

21

December 12, 1846
Alta California

Winter has set in earlier than usual. On record, winters on the west side of the Sierra Nevada Mountains receive scant traces of snow, an inch or two at most. This year, it's different. Already, there have been two significant snowfalls, and it's only December. The man coaxes his horse over the wet ground, his cabin in sight. It spit snow last night, but by mid-morning, the icy slush turns a muddy brown. The sky is threatening, roiling balloons of dark grey. He's glad to be back from Sutter's with a month's worth of supplies, not the least of which is a stash of snuff. He puts his goods down on the table, cuts a small piece from the long plug, and tamps tobacco deep into the bowl of his pipe. Lights a match off the heel of his boot. Inhales again. A thin wisp of smoke curls from the end of the pipe. He goes outside and sits on a stump in front of his cabin.

"C'mon up, Boy." He scoops the dirty cat onto his lap. Shame the poor bugger lost his leg last year in one of the man's own traps. He puffs on the pipe and strokes the cat's head.

Old One cackles from the pine. "Do you never take a break?" the man yells. "Give a man a damned headache, all your screeching."

"*Barrrrh,*" the raven replies.

The cat bounds out of his lap and chases a field mouse behind the cabin. The man picks up his project, a toy he's whittling for one of Salina's boys for Christmas. He shaves the sides of the sling handle until it's smooth. It keeps his hands busy while his mind wanders.

He's got a decision to make, and it weighs on his mind. He's not used to thinking beyond the next day, better that way. Wake up, make a fire, brew coffee, hunt. There's fox and rabbit and deer; geese and sage hen and grouse. Last year, a grizzly. His slim rifle makes a good companion, does its job, doesn't require conversation or explanation. But he'd trade his rifle, his horse, his cabin, everything, if he could have Bet back. But that's like spitting in the wind. It gets you nowhere.

This is as long as he's spent in one place since he started west. And now he's considering the offer. There's a call to arms, he heard about it at Sutter's. At war with the bloody Mexicans. For what? *The Republic,* they said. *The Republic of California.*

He shifts his weight. He's fought before, at school and hand-to-hand with thieving trappers and against Paiutes. He's killed three men, two Indian, and one not. He's not a fighting man at heart, but he'll do it again, without hesitation, if the stakes are high enough.

The man puts down his whittling, and goes inside. "C'mon, Boy. Got a treat for you." He unpacks provisions: potatoes, onion, flour, rice, honey. He cuts a strip of dried venison and fries it with potatoes and onions in a worn cast iron skillet. A savory smell fills the cabin. He hums an old French tune, one that Bet taught him. He blows on the fat to cool it and lowers the pan for the cat. When he sits at the table, he imagines Bet. She's clouded in his memory now, like a wraith. Had she been real? Or a figment? No, she had been very real, so real it hurts.

Maybe poets are right. Love is better lost than never experienced. He chews the last of the venison, swallows, takes a swig from his canteen. Or maybe it's just too painful to think about at all. He dims the light, lies down, and stares at the ceiling. He lets his mind spool back to his childhood.

"Catch me if you can," Henri had called. Henri and Jean-Claude (and Robert when his family lived in town) taunted him from a paced-off distance. His eyes were closed as he leaned up against a black spruce. "*Trois . . . quatre . . . cinq*" (at eight, he knew how to swear and count in French; the rest—the love words—he learned later from Bet). And then they were off, playing tag and climbing trees and throwing rocks in the Iowa River. Fighting with sticks, playing soldier, running races in bare feet.

There were never enough hours in a Wisconsin day for all the games, all the mishaps, all the daring someone to do something that resulted in mountains of laughter and a thousand skinned knees. Making forts. Building rafts. Swimming in summer, skating in winter. Tossing rocks. Jumping over logs. Skinning hares. Fishing for crappie or walleye or pike (they never caught a muskie, although Henri claimed he had). And the once, that time they taunted a mother moose grazing with her calf with stones no larger than a small boy's fist, and then the grunt and the thundering and the chase through the Wisconsin woods that left them breathless, not knowing whether to shit their pants or laugh uproariously.

In the remembering of it, the man laughs. Yes, he had been happy then.

22

December 16, 1846
Truckee Lake

Blowed terrible again last night and froze hard, wind SE.
Snowshoe party leaves today.

—from Ada Weeks' diary

"I'll stay," Ada says.

"Come where I'm going, won't you, Ada?" Dolan implores. "I'm not going over that pass without you."

Ada hangs her head. She is more than tempted by Dolan's offer, but no, she won't consider trekking across a vast wall of snow-bound mountains in the dead of winter with what's left of her skimpy clothing, inadequate supplies, and no sense of direction. Darn if she couldn't have used Breen's compass now. She'd finally returned it to the wagon, but now the wagon's been battered down to nothing more than sticks. Plus, her big toe is twice the size of normal since she stubbed it on a stray nail on the cabin's dirt floor. Her toe hasn't completely healed from the walk west—first from lack of boots, then from kicking a prickly pear, and now re-injur-ing it on a rusted nail. Teach her not to walk barefoot, *ever,* even for three steps to the chamber pot. Maybe better get used to sleeping with her boots on. For now, she can't wedge her throbbing foot into her boot at all.

When it comes right down to it, she thinks the snowshoe party is no more than a death march, and that's why she lets reason reign today. Augustus would be proud of her. What is it beyond the camp, except a vast, white unknown anyway? Someone is sure to come rescue them soon.

"Can't say I'm not tempted," Ada says. "But look around. Ma Breen needs my help. Plus I got a naggin' toe. Can't be long afore proper help comes. But I know when you've made up your mind to do somethin', you'll do it. So I won't try to sway you."

"I've made up my mind on one thing," Dolan says. His eyes bore through her.

"That's it, is it?"

"I haven't been much good these last few weeks, and I'm sorry for it. I lost my way, but I've found it again. You mark my words, Miss Ada Weeks. I'll provide you with everything you want. That warm home, food on the table. I beg you to come along."

Ada catches on the words, "warm" and "food." She can hardly remember what being warm feels like. And food . . .

"There'll be fifteen of us." Dolan counts on his fingers. "Me and Eddy, Stanton and Graves, the Fosdick's, and your friend Miss Mary . . ."

Mary Graves, Ada's friend. This is almost enough to sway her. She and Mary can escape to safety together. Ada's jealous of Sarah and Jay Fosdick, newlyweds on this journey. If only she and Dolan were married already . . . that might make the difference in her decision, toe or no toe.

"And there's Mrs. McCutcheon and two of the Murphy boys, can't remember their names," Dolan continues. "Mr. and Mrs. Foster, Miss Harriet, a handful of us wagon men, and the Miwoks. Won't have to live on old bones or glue once we reach Sutter's."

"What about the McCutcheon baby?"

"Staying."

Ada stands immobile. Did she hear correctly? What in heaven's precious name could possess Amanda McCutcheon to leave her only child behind? Ma Breen would never leave Bella. Truth be told, neither would she. And she knows Mrs. Eddy would never leave Margaret.

Dolan flings his arms around Ada. Ada has never been embraced in public (has she ever been embraced by anyone other than Dolan?) Startled, she doesn't know what to do with her arms. They hang at her sides. She pushes Dolan away. "Go on, Pat; I won't be long behind. Wait for me there, at Sutter's, you hear? Now I got to find Mary, say my goodbyes."

Ada bundles up. She sees Mary huddled amidst a group of emigrants taking flight of the lake. "Take care of yourself, Mary."

"Won't you please come along?" Mary's eyes plead from beneath a crude scarf wound around her head. Her hands are encased in mittens. Thick, woolen socks cover her boots. Mary shivers, stamps her feet, blows warm breath onto her mittened hands, as if she could warm them, but no, no one has been warm since soon after the Great Salt Desert, and that memory is as hazy as an illusion. "We could help one another along," Mary says.

"Not that I'm not tempted, Mary," Ada answers. "I'll be along shortly. There's bound to be another rescue soon. 'Cause of this naggin' toe, I couldn't keep up with you today anyway. Look for me in a week's time, maybe two."

"Think of us, Miss Ada. Can't say as I'm not scared as a cat." Mary pauses, grabs Ada's hand. "If it's not too much trouble . . . "

"What, Mary?"

"It's not an easy thing to ask, especially since you're not family—"

Family.

"—but could you please look in on my mother? I would appreciate it so." Mary drops her voice to a whisper, her eyes darting left and right to be sure no one is eavesdropping. "She just don't seem right in the head."

Ada thinks of her own ma. *Not right in the head.* That's what her pa said. She shudders. Having children sets so many *not right. Like Miz McCutcheon. She can't be right in the head, leavin' her baby behind.* But then she thinks of Tamsen Donner, who doesn't seem worse for wear after two husbands and a passel of children. *Maybe it's only some women? How does one know? Is it worth the chance?* Ada feels a stirring in her abdomen. Or is it hunger?

Dolan comes up beside her. "Don't know if I can forgive myself for not taking care of you, especially now. I'm of a mind to stay."

"Hogwash," Ada says. "You're well enough. I can survive another week. Let's not make this our goodbye."

Dolan leans over and kisses Ada's scaly cheek. "All right then, Ada Weeks, no goodbyes."

Ada holds Dolan's hand for as long as she's able and then lets his fingers slip from her hand. She watches as the travelers plod toward the far end of the lake and battles with herself. *Shall I at least try?* Her toe throbs. *No. No, no, no, no.*

For a few minutes, she can distinguish Dolan and Mary from the sea of heads bobbing away from the lake camp. She reaches her hand out, as if to touch them. As they near the curve of the lake they disappear, swallowed by a low-lying fog spun to mist spun to silence. And then they vanish. Ada wraps her blanket closer around her shoulders and hobbles back to the cabin. She hesitates before she descends into the dankness and then helps Ma Breen with a tragic apology for supper. Before she eats, Ada breaks the crust of ice on the bucket and mixes up a thin gruel made of snow water and a pinch of flour for the baby's sugar-tit.

After supper, Ada returns to her corner. It's too dark to see. She cancels out sounds (sniveling and cross words, the standard) and smells (farting and sour body odor, also typical). She thinks fondly of her dear friend, Mary. A piece of Ada's heart walks close to her friend—*as close as a lover,* she thinks—or as much of a lover as one girl can be to another. She hopes against hope that Mary's safe tonight and tomorrow night and the night after that. She will surely look in on Mary's mother, as Mary asked.

When Ada recalls Dolan's face, it is as if a great winged thing climbs out of her breast and finds its slick feathers pumping in the thick grey air. It beats a laggardly *thwump thwump* until its tortured body gains on itself and rises, first with uncertainty, and then with what can only be called a stuttered, halting rhythm before it gains purchase in the air. It then bears west without glancing back.

Ada curls up, spent and shivering. All she sees is blackness. All she feels is her pounding toe (if you discount hunger and fright and desolation). *If I fall asleep,* she thinks, *I might never wake up.* And so she stays awake, quaking in the frigid air. In the silence of her despair, coiled like a fetus, all she hears is the slow, hollow thudding of her weak and shattered heart.

It's walk or die, Mary. Walk or die, Dolan. It's walk, walk, walk. Walk or die.

23

December 24, 1846
Alta California

The man wades through a half-foot of snow the short distance to Salina's place. Not usual to have this much snow in the foothills. He glances to the east, socked in with thick, dark clouds. *Must be a blizzard up there,* he thinks. He's got a present for each of the boys and the baby girl, too. He doesn't feel it's right to give Salina a gift, although he'd like to give her one of his mother's handkerchiefs or a spool of red thread he saw at Sutter's. No, under the circumstances, that wouldn't be right.

For Buddy, he's crafted a slingshot. For Benjy, the younger boy, a toy gun. He didn't know what to make for the baby, so he wrapped some sugar in one of his mother's handkerchiefs and hopes she likes it. Before Christmas dinner, he gives the children their gifts. The baby accepts the sugar-tit with smiling gums. Benjy races around the cabin pointing his gun and everyone in the room. "Bang, bang, you're dead," he whoops.

"Git outside with that thing," Salina orders.

"Come on, boys, we'll get out of your mother's way," the man says.

The boys stumble off the porch into the snow. Benjy runs, falls, laughs. He gets up, points the toy gun at each tree. "Bang, bang," he says.

"Let me show you how to use that slingshot, young man."

Buddy hands the slingshot over. The man bends down and rifles through the snow to find a rock. He places a rounded stone inside the leather pouch that stretches across the crotch of the *V.* He pulls back the rubber strips, aims for a cottonwood at the near side of the creek, and lets go with a zing. The rock hits its target with a sharp plink.

"My turn," Buddy says.

"Got to be patient with a slingshot. When you narrow onto your target, that's when you take your chance, Buddy. Not before."

The boy nods. "Have you ever killed a rabbit with a slingshot?"

"Sure have, but it's best for birds. Catch them unaware."

"Supper's on," Salina calls from the door.

The man corrals the boys inside and stops on the porch for a minute. He closes his eyes and breathes in the tantalizing smells emanating from inside. Grouse with oily gravy. Roasted turnips. And poor man's pie, his favorite, thick crust topped with sugar and a sprinkling of precious nuts and currants.

After supper, they sing all the Christmas carols they remember, humming when they forget the words. *Fol-de-rol-de-rol* fills in the blanks (there is a lot of *fol-de-rol-de-rol*-ing). Salina has a gift for him: tobacco. He is sorry now he didn't bring anything for her.

Later, at home, he sits on the porch balancing on the two rear legs of the chair, his back against the cabin. He's beyond full. Tomorrow it's back to bacon and grits. He wishes he could write. If he could, he'd write to Salina and thank her for the Christmas meal and her thoughtful gift. He'd tell her how pretty she looked with her hair swept up.

He's beginning to miss female company. Not just the coupling part, he can get that at Fay's if he wants. It's not even the talking part, it's the comfortable silences between people as they get about their days, having someone to go home to, and someone looking forward to you coming home to them.

But the pickings are slim in the foothills of the Sierra Nevadas. He wrestles with himself. Would he really settle for a Spanish woman or an Indian, like Salina? For the first time in a long time, he thinks he might pull up stakes here, go back to Wisconsin Territory. Confront his ghosts. Find another woman like Bet. Settle down.

But first he'll go to Yerba Buena. "They're calling it San Francisco now," his neighbor said. See about signing up for the militia. After they've quelled the Mexicans (and there is no doubt in his mind they will), then he'll consider heading back East. The sun's about to go down on another year, and he's not getting any younger. He's got a horse and some money and borrowed time.

Maybe, come spring, he'll say his goodbyes to Fay, and to Salina, although he'll have to rip himself away from her. It's the only way he'll keep himself from doing something he'll regret (and he's thought about it plenty, even tonight). Of course, he can't take Boy with him, and he can't entertain leaving the poor thing alone to take care of itself. He'll drop the three-legged cat off with Salina, a small reminder of him after he's gone. It's high time he lets go of inner demons, forgets about Salina, gets on with his life.

He lights another pipe, hums a few bars of *Silent Night*. He settles in, listens to the night sounds. Old One *thwumps* his wings as he rearranges himself in his nest high in the pine. The Missus still hasn't returned. It smells like more snow. The man remembers that last Christmas he had with Bet, and the pleasure she radiated as he clasped the small gold cross at the cleft of her neck. Her face had turned to him. In the firelight, he had never seen anyone as lovely.

24

December 25, 1846
Truckee Lake

Christmas Day. Rained terrible last night, torrents more today.
—from Ada Weeks' diary

Dolan's group has not returned. Of their fate, Ada can only assume the worst, although she holds to a glimmer of hope. It's Christmas, after all. She forms unfamiliar words: *beseeching you, O Lord; if it be thy will; hear my earnest plea;* all ending with the foreign *Hail Mary, full of grace* . . . If she is to become a Catholic, she must learn to pray more earnestly and more often. And what is the name of the saint who watches over travelers? The one Dolan told her about? *St. Christopher.* She implores St. Christopher to watch over Dolan and Mary and keep them safe from the elements, from wild animals, from Indians, from death.

Here at the lake camp, there are husbands without wives, children without mothers. Within a week, three more teamsters have died, all on the same day: James Smith, Joseph Reinhardt, and Samuel Shoemaker, the one who helped Tamsen Donner and Ada cache books and Bibles. All of the Reeds have by this time come to live in the Breen cabin. There isn't a square inch of space between unwashed bodies.

Early Christmas morning, a man's voice *halloos* through the hide door.

"Trudeau? What brings you here from Alder Creek?" Patrick Breen asks.

"Miz Tamsen sent me. It's Mr. Donner—Mr. Jacob Donner. He's left us."

"Left us? As in . . ."

"Yes, a couple of nights ago. And Miz Elizabeth is in a bad way, too. Miz Tamsen said if there's anyone here who can come to help with Miz Elizabeth, she'd be right, what is the word? 'Ap-pre-ci-a-tive,' I think she said." He stumbles over the English word. "Uncle George Donner, is poorly, too," Trudeau says. "His arm is useless."

Breen eyes Ada. "Miss Ada here will go."

Ada closes her eyes. She can't fathom leaving Bella.

"Ada?" Breen asks.

"No, sir. I'm fixed to stay right here."

"It would be one less mouth to feed," he says.

"No," Ma Breen answers. "We need Ada here."

Trudeau shrugs, and exits the cabin.

Ada quivers. *I'm not goin' to Alder Creek, unless they drag me there.* She offers a quick prayer of thanksgiving for Ma Breen interceding on her behalf. Her breath forms icy clouds with each exhale. She rearranges her cloak so her shoulders relax, and then shoves the garment down to cover her near-frozen feet. She wiggles her toes to make sure they are still attached. Her toenails need clipping, and she pulls on a corner of a nail to shorten it. She yanks so hard she draws blood, which she stanches with her sock. She hasn't washed her socks in so long she's grown immune to the stench. She makes a fist, first with her right hand, counts to ten, and releases. Then she repeats with her left. Her stomach rumbles with hunger. She holds her midsection to ease the pain. Her head aches. As she rubs her head, a clump of hair comes out into her hand.

Margaret Reed prepares a feast for her children: dried apples, beans, tripe, and bacon. "I saved it for today. For the children," she says.

Ma Breen glares at Mrs. Reed.

"Just your children?"

"I'm afraid so."

Ma Breen resumes her task, moving about the cabin in slow deliberation, as if she needs winding, like a clock. Patrick Breen invokes the Thirty Days Prayer; his mouth moves in silent entreaty: *Ever Glorious and Blessed Virgin Mary, Queen of Virgins, Mother of Mercy, help and comfort of dejected and desolate souls . . .*

"Tell us again about Mr. Boone, won't you, Virginia?" Ada says, to mask Breen's ranting prayer.

"Are you sure, Miss Ada?"

It's got to be the nineteenth or thirty-first or fifty-seventh time Ada has heard Boone's story recounted on the overland trail, but it passes the hours.

"Yes, Virginia. You have a good, strong voice."

Virginia offers a weak smile. She picks up her well-worn copy of *The Life and Times of Daniel Boone* that she squirreled away when everything was left behind in the Great Salt Desert.

"Talk like a book, you do," Ada continues. "Like Mrs. Donner."

Everyone listens as Virginia reads aloud, her voice thin and nasally, not at all strong, as Ada stated minutes before. Ada decides then and there to encourage Virginia more, seeing as Virginia's recently joined the ranks of womanhood, one month's bleeding at a time.

Ada wonders where Mary Graves is today, she and Dolan and the rest of the forlorn party that left the lake camp. But Ada can't ask Mary anything—anything at all—because Mary's gone to Sutter's and freedom and pie.

There are no other books in the cabin. At least, the children are no longer being drilled in lessons from Samuel Kirkham's *English*

Grammar in Familiar Lectures. Ada wonders of what use Kirkham would be in this desperate situation. Would knowing the indicative mood of a verb from the subjunctive mood benefit anyone in the near future?

I'm starvin'. We're all starvin'. That's all. Not 'if I were starvin', I'd eat a loaf of bread' or 'if we were starvin', we'd go a-huntin' today.' Just starvin', Mr. Kirkham. S-T-A-R-V-I-N-G. I'll tell you what else the letter D stands for. Death, yes, you nailed that one square on the head. And I've got a few more for you: D is for depravity. D is for despair. D is for delirium. Shall I go on?

Ada laughs aloud.

Ma Breen eyes Ada suspiciously.

Ada ignores Ma Breen. "Up, up, all of you," she says. "Come on, Eddie. You, too, Simon. Come on, boys, up, up! You, too, Virginia. It's Christmas. Time for games."

Ada gets to her feet. Virginia drops her book and stands behind Ada. The Breen boys eye one another and then unfold themselves to stand. Ada walks around the cabin singing and swinging her arms. The children follow her aimlessly, like the Pied Piper of Hamelin. As Ada marches, she hums a little tune. Soon the cabin is filled with discordant voices. Mrs. Reed nods her head and joins in. A thin film of spittle covers her lips.

Today, Ada would relish the taste of a rat, or a mouse, or any other rodent; she would not lure them over a cliff as in the fairy tale. No, she'd snatch them one by one and twist their little necks and roast them whole. Maybe eat them raw. The Breen boys have caught a few rats, but they've offered little sustenance. One great bear and several deer have been the only exception, thanks to William Eddy (earlier in the winter, before he left with the Sutter-bound entourage). Since then, all attempts at hunting have come back void: no game, no fowl, no fish. Now the Breens live on boiled hides and shoe leather. If only they could find the stash of beef hidden under mammoth drifts outside the cabin, they might have energy to do more than breathe. Weak broth—albeit warm—is the staple of their diet, along with bones pulverized and chewed like tobacco.

Tobacco! Now that would be a treat. There hasn't been any since the last assault on the summit. Now there's only melted snow. Ada assumes the fare at other cabins is the same or worse. That is, if no one's hiding any food.

Ada has been waiting for Christmas to break out Inger's jerky. *But later, when no one's lookin'.* After the silly march around the cabin, Ada sits with James and Simon and deals out worn playing cards, seven each. The boys reach for the cards, their movements sluggish, as if their brains are dulled. They play in silence until James whispers, "Rummy!"

Ada pulls him close and rubs his arms. "You beat me, fair and square. Here, I have somethin' for you, somethin' I have been savin' for today." Ada's eyes well up. She reaches into her apron pocket and unwraps dried meat. Has it only been seven months since they left Noblesville, all their hopes ahead? Ada catches a sob in her throat. *Seems like a year.*

Would anyone depart for Lansford Hastings's California if they knew they would be confronted with starvation? Would it not be better to sit and crochet on a porch in Noblesville or Independence or, for that matter, any farm porch in Illinois or Indiana or Missouri and cluck one's tongue at fools heading west? It was said that if one did not try, one would never succeed. But in between the lines, one might read an opposite meaning: who guarantees success? Is not failure an equal partner in the grand bargain of chance?

A loud wail emanates from Keseberg's lean-to. Ma Breen shrugs.

Ada breaks her piece of hoarded jerky into five strips, one for each of the Breen children except for John and the baby Isabella. She saves one for herself. Maybe she should share it with the German teamster who now languishes in the Keseberg's lean-to next door. There are so many who might need it more than she does.

"This is our secret, understand?" Ada hands the jerked meat to James and Simon. The boys grab the sticks and gnaw on them. Simon's eyes grow wide as saucers as he chews. Ada offers skimpy pieces to each of the boys when their parents aren't looking. That's simple enough. Patrick Breen sleeps most the day. Ada feels guilty not sharing her bounty with Ma Breen (or the Reeds, or the Kesebergs, or Eleanor). But her heart beats with certainty that if she does not do all she can do—including sharing her precious bounty with the children in her care—she will surely rot in hell. Muzzles pleads with Ada, and she breaks off a hunk of her share. He wolfs it down and pants for more from behind clouded and shrunken eyes. She chews the last of the jerky and drools. Has she ever tasted anything so good?

Behind closed eyes, she pictures a Christmas table heavy laden: turkey with trimmings, roast duck and new potatoes, lamb chops with gravy. Her mouth waters at the thought. Spare ribs with sausage and creamy mash, stewed chicken with carrots. All the delights of Christmas dinner: crabapple preserves, rhubarb pie, plum pudding. Today, there isn't a present or a decorated tree in sight, no paper stars or popcorn strings. There will be no visit from Saint Nick.

With the jerky gone, an even bigger hole cramps Ada's stomach. She fantasizes about bread. She does not dare to dream of butter or jam or honey.

What is that Scripture verse? The one about man not livin' on bread alone? Ada knows now that every word of Scripture is not true. *Bread alone would be sufficient for me,* she thinks. She would give any-thing—her clothes, her virtue, her soul, even—for a crust of it. She is certain she could live on it. She eyes her boots. With deft slashes, she could filet Halloran's boots into strips and stack them under her skirt. Eat them when no one's looking. She stumbles to the table and grabs a knife. It's dull. She hacks at her boots, but doesn't make much prog-ress. With zigzag motions, she's able to saw off the looped bootstrap. It's a sloppy attempt and she gives up for today. Maybe better to gnaw on the cover of a book or the edge of a blanket. Ada bundles her scarf around her head and layers her cloak over her filthy shirtwaist. "Am goin' out awhile."

Snow mounds in drifts outside the cabin. Ada sees whipped cream, steamed milk, and meringue in place of snow. Her mind plays cruel tricks on her. She reaches for handfuls of it, expecting it to taste like mashed potatoes or cream pie. But, in the end, it is just snow, thin and pure as frigid water. She walks to the Murphy cabin and announces herself. Levinah Murphy answers the door, her hair wild and frizzled. Her apron, once white and crisp, is stained and full of holes. She peers out from a wizened face, no teeth and rheumy eyes.

"Wishin' you and your family a Merry Christmas," Ada says.

"And what's merry about it?" Levinah sneers.

"Nothin' much," Ada says. "But it's the sayin' of it makes the difference."

"Come in, Ada," Eleanor Eddy says. "You are a sight for sore eyes."

Ada sits by Eleanor on the cold ground. "How's the baby?"

Eleanor's cheeks are hollowed and grey. She looks cadaverous. "See for yourself."

Ada lifts the blanket to see Margaret, still and bluish, but breathing. She quickly re-covers the child and reaches beneath her cloak. *Not long now, for this little one.*

"Brought you a little somethin'," Ada says. She pulls out the strip of leather she sawed off Halloran's boots. "It's not much, but it's somethin'. Somethin' to chew on, anyway."

Eleanor snatches the piece of leather and stows it in the pocket of her filthy skirt.

"Go on, eat it," Ada says.

"Later, after prying eyes aren't leering at me."

Ada looks around. Empty eyes stare back at her. "What, you too proud to eat your own shoes?" she asks.

Eleanor smiles weakly. "Someday, we will laugh at this."

"Maybe," Ada says. "Though that day can't come soon enough. Next Christmas, we'll be eatin' roast and potatoes and . . ."

"Cake," Eleanor says, her voice hardly above a whisper. "I love a pound cake, don't you?"

Ada squeezes Eleanor's arm. "I do, more than almost anythin'. I'll be back in a few days, ma'am. Bring you some more shoe leather. All I've got for now."

Ada plods back to the cabin, descends the snow steps, and sheds her snowy cloak. She holds her hands out to the weak flame. Ma Breen moves over so Ada can have a share of warmth.

"Done with your visiting?" Ma Breen asks.

"For today, yes."

Ada focuses on the embers, turns her hands over. Eleanor doesn't look well. Neither does Margaret. Who is next? And when? If a relief party does not come soon, what will they find?

We're just dyin' a little bit more every day, Ada thinks. But if she is to die here, Ada wants to be found as if she is living, with her head up and her eyes looking forward, ever west, toward Dolan, toward Mary, toward California, *toward grapes.* She prepares for another night, propped in the dim corner of the cabin. She leans back against the rough cabin walls, draws the blanket over her drawn-up knees, closes her eyes, and hums, tapping her frigid toes to a familiar Christmas hymn.

"O come, all ye faithful, joyful and triumphant . . . "

She remembers all the words.

25

February 7, 1847
Truckee Lake

Worst snow yet this winter, all shantys covered. Miz McC's and Miz Eddy's babes gone now.

—from Ada Weeks' diary

Ada cradles Eleanor Eddy's head. Eleanor has not come up from the well of grief so deep she's urinated on her bedroll. "It is all my fault, Ada," Eleanor whispers. "I didn't have the milk."

"Shh, now Miz Eddy. We need to get you well now. For Jimmy and Mr. Eddy."

Eleanor spills tears, disconsolate. "I don't know if I have the strength anymore. I couldn't—even—keep—my baby—alive." She turns her head to the side. Her shoulders shake.

"Jimmy, can you get another blanket for your mama? That's a good boy."

Philippine Keseberg has just lost her baby boy. The McCutcheon's Harriet has also died. Ada will not share this news with Eleanor today. Ada rocks Eleanor gently, like a child. If there were ever a day Ada despised more than this one, she'd have to go back to the day of the fire when she was eleven. And that day has been pushed into the farthest closets of her mind. "Can I get you some water?"

Eleanor shakes her head. There is nothing to do, nothing to say, as Eleanor wills herself away. Minutes pass in silence, and then a moan. Eleanor drifts in and out of consciousness, her eyes wild and sunken.

"Please, Miz Eddy. Don't leave us."

Ada strokes Eleanor's hair. She hums any hymn she can remember: "Guide Me, O Thou Great Jehovah"; "God Our Help in Ages Past"; "On Jordan's Stormy Banks I Stand." Others in the cabin have shied away, but Ada sits with the dying woman through the afternoon and into the evening, long after the last breath passes her lips.

D is for death, Tamsen Donner had instructed children back in the Wasatch. *And there's been altogether too much of it,* Ada thinks. She listens for any more breath, but there is none. Ada stifles sobs as she caresses her friend's slack face. "Not you, Miz Eddy. Not you, too." She closes her eyes to hold back tears, and begins to sing, her voice low and warbled: "Gabriel's message does away, Satan's curse and Satan's sway . . ."

She stares down at her beautiful friend, whose soul has flown.

". . . out of darkness brings our day: So, behold, All the gates of heaven unfold!"

Ada sings Eleanor home, keeping a slow, somber beat with her fingers on Eleanor's chest, as if drumming could bring her back to life.

"Art by art shall be assailed; to the cross shall Life be nailed; from the grave shall hope be hailed: So, behold, all the gates of heaven unfold!"

When she finishes singing, Ada looks around. "Go get John, will you?" she asks one of the Murphy boys.

A few minutes later, John Breen appears at the Murphy's door. "Miss Ada?"

"I'll be needin' your help again, John." She places her hands over Eleanor's breast. "We'll bury her up next to Margaret. Get Eddie and

Patrick, Jr. if need be. It'll be dark before long. Go on, now, gather up some quilts and some help."

Ada smoothes Eleanor's hair and shutters her eyes. Eleanor Priscilla Eddy, aged twenty-five, loving wife of William Eddy, mother of James, three, and Margaret, one (now deceased), lately of Belleville, Illinois, is dead to the world forever. Ada runs her hands down the length of her friend's bodice and tucks Eleanor's once-clean blouse into her soiled skirt. She repositions the corpse like Augustus would have done, the dead woman's hands crossed on her chest, her head propped on a small pillow. Ada removes Eleanor's boots. Her friend won't have much use for them where she's going; someone else will have much more use for them here. Ada lowers her head onto Eleanor's chest. Once there had been a heartbeat. Now her chest is silent, and cool.

"Goodbye, Miz Eddy. God be with you."

John, Edward, and Patrick, Jr. peek into the cabin.

"Come in, boys," Ada says.

They move hesitantly toward the woman, eternally at rest.

"Careful now," Ada says. "Be as gentle as you can. She's light as a bird."

26

February 19, 1847
Truckee Lake

Froze hard last night, thawing now, clear, wind light, SE. Everyone weak.

—*from Ada Weeks' diary*

"HALLOOOOO! Is anyone here?"

A booming voice ricochets around the clearing. At first, Ada chides herself. Now she's hearing voices. But then she thinks better of it, rouses herself, and opens the drafty hide door of the cabin to check. By now the snow is more than twenty feet high and precludes her seeing anything beyond the opening except the filthy snow staircase.

Again she hears the voice, so she scrambles up the snow steps to see who has come to visit, or if she is, in fact, imagining it. It wouldn't be the first time. When she reaches the top of the snow bank, others have emerged from their snow tombs, ghost-like, grim, and frail.

Dolan?

Ada rubs her eyes to see that they do not deceive her. Time slows. It is to her like a snow mirage, similar to one of the frosted glass paperweights Inger Vik kept in her hutch in the parlor in Noblesville. *Can it be? A rescue party?*

A group of men staggers into the clearing.

"Are you from California, or are you from heaven?" one of the women cries.

Ada runs, stumbles, cries, gets up, falls again. *I will lift up mine eyes unto the hills, from whence cometh my help.* She lopes toward the strangers. But it is not Pat Dolan.

"Mr. Eddy!" Ada exclaims. The cold knocks the wind out of her lungs. With Eddy's arrival she knows those who fled the lake camp have made it through to Sutter's Fort.

"Relief! Thank God! Relief!" Patrick Breen lifts his hands to heaven. "Mother, boys, up now," he shouts down the icy staircase. "All of you! There's help come."

One by one, the Breens climb up the stairs into the clearing. Their withered bodies shiver in frigid air. Eddy is swarmed with questions. Shouts. Even laughter mixed with tears.

"Where is Eleanor?" Eddy cries.

Ada cringes, clenches her eyes shut. *He's twelve days late.*

When Eddy left in December, there were no mounds that masked the dead strewn between the cabins. Even if the ground were willing since then, no one had the strength to bury anyone. The living did their best, wrapping bodies in quilts, and praying that animals wouldn't defile the dead as snow mounds over their frozen bodies.

Seven more died at camp since the outgoing party left, including Louis Keseberg, Jr., born along the Oregon-California Trail. At the death of her only son, Mrs. Keseberg was inconsolable. Ada had no food to offer the grieving mother, or cards, or flowers, or any other form of sympathy. Even words failed her. With every death, their numbers dwindle, and dwindle again. The emigrants are down to two choices: prayer or profanity as they cloister in huts, under lean-tos, in ragged tents.

Not a minute later, a piercing shriek echoes through the clearing. Patrick Breen clasps Eddy in a bear hug and holds the grieving man, his shoulders shaking and face streaming tears. "No, no, no," he cries. "God Almighty, say it isn't true . . ."

Ada joins the emigrants huddled around the relief party. She can't stomach watching Eddy grieve.

"Aquila Glover, here." A large, rough-looking man addresses emigrants as he dismounts. He motions to the man next to him, already off his horse. "And this is Reason Tucker."

Tucker addresses the group. "Word's out about your party all up and down California. We came as soon as we could. There's every reason to think we can make it back across the pass before the weather turns on us."

Ada can't meet the eye of the stranger who offers her bread. It is too much intimacy. She puts her hands out in supplication, murmurs, "Thank you." *Like Catholics,* she thinks, *they eat the sacrament of Christ's body.* Where Ada might have scoffed at that notion before, she's convinced now the stranger offers the very body of Christ to those huddled around. She will make a good Catholic.

Simon Breen runs at one of the men and pounds his fist against the man's leg. "More!"

"There's more, boy. But you got to wait," Glover says. "If you gorge yourself, it will bring on nausea, or worse. Your bodies ain't used to this fare."

Ada chews the hard crust with relish. Forget the jerky, she has never tasted anything so good, not even meringue.

Over the next two days, the rescuers go shanty to shanty to assess who is strong enough to depart with them for California. Ada is cleared to go, along with Margaret Reed and her four children. Philippine Keseberg and her daughter Ada will go, too, and Doris Wolfinger. Also selected are the Reed's hired girl, Eliza Williams, and John Denton and Noah James, two remaining teamsters who are still alive. Joining them are several of the Graves and Murphy and Donner children, nineteen in all.

"I'll be leavin' in the mornin', Ma," Ada says.

"Not us, I'm afraid. Father's not up to it—his gravel is back and he's doing poorly," Ma Breen answers. "The next rescue party will arrive soon. Father should be better by then."

"I hate to leave all of you," Ada says.

"You hurry on. See to Mr. Dolan. We'll see you on the other side of the mountains."

Ada spends a sleepless night. Her toe, almost healed, still drains pus. She feels her heartbeat in her toe, dabs at the drainage. Her new sock is soaked through with discharge.

This can't stop me, she thinks. *Not after everythin'.* When she pulls on the remnants of Halloran's boots, the pain in her foot is excruciating. It's a chore to hobble in the cabin, let alone walk sixty or ninety more miles. *Dumb it! Not again!* Ada sits in the corner, eyes welling.

"Your toe again?" Ma Breen asks.

Ada nods. "Dolan will have to wait."

"Edward, Simon, now," Patrick Breen says. "Get your things. It's best you go ahead. Take Miss Ada's place."

Ma Breen turns on her husband. "Mr. Breen! We pledged to stay together!"

"I make the decisions in this family," Breen says.

Ma Breen rushes to put a bundle together. Edward and Simon scramble up the snow stairs. Ada follows, dragging her foot.

"Ready?" Glover says to Ada.

"Stayin' behind with the Breens," she says. She doesn't mention her foot.

"Don't know as I agree with your thinking. But others will be here shortly," Glover says.

Shortly. Ada mouths the word over and over. *Shortly, shortly.* Soon she'll be reunited with Dolan and their lives can go on as planned, without regard for hunger or thirst or cold.

"Eddie! Simon! And you, too, Virginia! Be good!" Ada waves and waves until the Breen and Reed children round the end of the lake. The cabin will be almost empty now. And she'll follow. *Shortly.*

Ada wends her way to the shanty, descends the snow staircase, and burrows into her corner. Her vision is crowded with zigzags. In addition to bad eyesight, her hearing is muffled. She only passes water once a day (there are no more clumps).

News from the neighboring cabins is grim: the baby Catherine Pike and young James Eddy are wasting away. In the Breen household, Bella is weak, pale, and listless, but still nursing the meager milk Ma Breen provides.

Late that night, Ada hears a faint cry.

"Miz Breen! Miss Ada!"

Ada climbs up the ice stairs to see the outline of two children staggering into the lake camp.

"Patty! Tommy! What ever has happened? What of your mother and Virginia?"

"We couldn't keep up, Miss Ada. Ma sent us back to you. Between Ma and Virginia, they can only handle the baby."

Ada bundles the middle Reed children to her side and descends the steps. Ma Breen stands at the entrance, her arms crossed. "Make way," Ada says.

Margaret Breen scowls at Ada and moves aside.

"What in heaven?" Patrick Breen explodes. "We don't have room enough, or food enough for two more."

"Shame on you, Patrick Breen!" Ada says. "We can't turn these children away. Look at them!"

Breen turns his back. Ada shuffles the children to a spot near the fire and quickly undresses them. Tommy and Patty Reed shiver violently under coarse blankets while Ada strings their clothing up to dry. She kneels between the two and rubs their shoulders. Patty starts to cry.

"Won't be long now," Ada says. "We're sure to see another group soon, now that people know of our troubles. But soon enough, we'll be sittin' at a table eatin' pies."

"And cakes?" Patty asks. She licks her cracked, chapped lips.

Ada thinks of Eleanor Eddy. *"I love a pound cake, don't you?"*

The next day, only a day after two of his own sons walked west, Patrick Breen hobbles to the hide door. His gravel has been acute, and he has trouble walking. Ada thinks it odd that he's going outside, especially in today's foul weather.

"C'mon, Muzzles. Good boy." Breen rouses the skinny dog and exits the cabin.

Ada changes Bella's diaper, singing a quiet lullaby to the baby. A minute later, Ada hears a single gunshot and her eyes fly open. *Muzzles?* She bolts to the cabin door. Breen descends the staircase with the lifeless dog in his arms.

"My God, what have you done?" Ada yells. She rushes Breen and pounds on his shoulders.

"Get out of my way, Miss Ada. What would you have me do, see my family starve? And now two more mouths to feed? You're the one who welcomed them in."

"So this is my fault?" She turns away.

Ada cannot bear to look as Ma Breen skins and dismembers the faithful dog. She feels ill. Muzzles had been her quiet and loyal companion. *He didn't deserve to die that way.*

Later, when Ada's offered a crisped morsel, she shakes her head, *no.*

"Take it," Ma Breen says. She drops a piece of burnt dog flesh in front of Ada.

Ada turns her head to avoid Ma Breen. *If we eat our dogs, what's next? Each other?* Ada mumbles a hasty prayer. *I beseech thee, Lord, to rescue us. If you do, I will never—I say, never—complain again.* Ada realizes she is speaking aloud. She raises her voice. "When I say never, I mean never."

Patrick Breen shoots her a puzzled look from his writing desk. Ma Breen wrings her hands. By now, everyone in the shanty is staring at her.

Ada raises her voice even louder, her words vibrating off dull, chinked walls. "Hell and blasted never, ever again!"

Breen scowls. "You'll watch your words, Ada."

She glares at Breen, pauses. Her face hardens, her eyes narrow. "Hell and blasted never again, I say!" It might be heard a mile away, her voice is so loud and shrill.

Breen moves toward Ada. He raises his hand. She does not back down.

"In the name of the Father, and the Son, and the Holy Ghost," she says.

Breen lowers his hand.

Ada takes a long, slow inhale, and, without breaking eye contact, tacks on another word. "Amen."

The evening passes silently with no candlelight. Later, after Patrick Breen drowns into snores and Mrs. Breen finally beds down after doing this and that (she is always doing this and that, with nothing to show for it), and all the children lie still, their shallow breathing sending white puffs into the thin night air, Ada stares at the piece of dog meat at her feet. She wills herself not to touch it.

Sometime in the dead of night, Ada reaches with a shaking, blue-tinged hand and curls the dog meat in her fist. Her teeth chatter as she takes a bite.

27

February 25, 1847
Truckee Lake

Froze hard again, wind brisk, SE. Losing so many now.
—from Ada Weeks' diary

"**S**he says she's going to commence on Milt, and eat him."

Patrick Breen enters the cabin, his voice low. Ma Breen stops her hands in mid-air. Ada turns, eyes wide.

"You can't mean . . ." Ma Breen says.

"Yes, I do mean it. That Murphy woman, she's not right in the head. And Trudeau was just here. Saw him outside. Says the Donners are set to do the same over at the Alder camp," Breen replies.

"Holy Mother of God," Margaret Breen says.

Ada tightens her blanket and presses her eyes shut again in her corner of the fetid cabin. From beneath her eyelids, she sees the egregious scene. Just yesterday it had happened, the unthinkable, the worst of human nature become manifest, worse than torture, or maybe even war. Mrs. Murphy had warned them all, but no one, not Patrick Breen, not Margaret Breen, not Ada, *not a one,* had thought Mrs. Murphy so depraved, so *unright,* that she could do what she had done, slice into a man she once called a compatriot, a fellow traveler

on this road to glory (*or perdition,* Ada thinks) and, with cold, calculating hands, carve him into edible bits. *This is the stuff of cannibals,*
Ada thinks. *Pygmies or desperate sailors marooned at sea, maybe they
resort to cannibalism to survive? But here?*

That a man—a teamster so revered and admired by the Donners—
was now flayed and parceled out, pits Ada at a crossroads of faith and
despair. Whatever faith she has in human decency is now fileted as
sure as Elliott's forearm and thigh. As for despair, it's heaped as high
as meringue on her ma's Christmas pie, the thought of which causes
Ada's hands to clench involuntarily. The Breens are down to glue
from boiled hides, shoelaces, edges of blankets, and leather covers
of books cut into strips and roasted. She wonders what human flesh
tastes like. *Chicken? Veal?* She pushes out the abhorrent thought. It's
gruesome enough to have eaten dog meat.

Remind me, Ada thinks. *Remind me, Ma, what your voice sounds
like when you're singin' me to sleep, or when you're peggin' out laundry,
or when you're fixin' up supper.*

It's Ada's way of disappearing from her thoughts. She's eight again,
and her ma is still well.

Remind me, Ma, she thinks, *what your cool fingers feel like as they
lather my hair. That soothin' song you sing as you pick at knots and
tangles.*

Ada smooths her matted hair, remembering.

*I'm so alone, Ma. There's wrong in every right and right in every
wrong and I don't know how I'm goin' to go on this way.*

Ada goes out into the bleak clearing to do her business. Flakes as
fat as moths swirl in the clearing. She sees Levinah Murphy hauling
an ax and an extra piece of sheeting to the far side of the Murphy
cabin. Her son is with her. *What are they doin'?* Ada sneaks to the
corner of the Murphy cabin and peers around. By this time, John
Breen is standing next to Ada.

"Shhhh," Ada says. They watch as Levinah Murphy hacks at a

corpse half-buried in snow. Ada reaches for John's arm and squeezes. It's three-quarters of an hour before Ada and John return to the cabin. John shuffles to the wall and sits, eyes dulled.

"What is it?" Patrick Breen demands.

Ada stares at her feet.

"Answer me, dammit."

"We've seen them. The Murphys," Ada says.

"And?"

John looks up. "She, Mrs. Murphy, sir, she—defiled one of the dead. Right there in the open."

"No!" Ma Breen covers Peter's ears and hugs the boy to her breast.

"Might've been a leg, can't be sure. Wrapped it in a parcel and took it inside. I know I shouldn't have looked, God forgive me, Ma."

Ada breaks in. "I looked, too. Weren't right, I know it. But I couldn't help myself either, had to see for myself if what we heard was true. They mean to eat it." She looks away. Later, when Ma Breen offers her a weak broth, she takes three small sips. A shooting pain stabs her midsection and she doubles over.

I'm fadin', Ma. I can't eat, can't sleep. And it's so cold. Can you rub my head again? Yes, like that. That's so nice. Your fingers are so soft. You're the only one can take this pain away. Can you do that, Ma? Take all of it? Make it all just go away? Please, Ma? Please?

28

February 26, 1847
San Francisco, California

The man gathers a few supplies and loads them into saddlebags. The raven squawks from its nest as the wind slithers through the tops of the branches. Time he left this place behind.

"Goodbye to you, too, Old One," he says. "Hope you find your Missus."

It's dawn, with a full day's ride ahead. He delivers the cat to Salina's, and is glad no one's up. He hates goodbyes.

The man lopes down the creek. The sun weaves in and out of cottonwoods and oak as he follows the trail. Water rushes downstream, clear and cold. At the junction of the American River, he stops, unbuttons his jacket, takes off his hat, and wipes his sweaty brow. A slight breeze ruffles his shirt and warmth coils around his neck. He closes his eyes.

There's nowhere like California, he thinks—not Wisconsin, or the vast prairies of the Mandan or the Sioux, or the great Rocky Mountains, or the arid deserts of the West. No, California has everything a man could ever want. And it's big and wide and free. He spurs his horse and replaces his hat. Yes, all the guidebooks are true. California can hold all the joys a man could ever wish for. Maybe it's time he put yesterday behind and started dreaming as big and wide and free as California itself—look to the future, not the past. *But where?*

He points his horse southwest and rides all day. He crests the hill into San Francisco late in the day. It's balmy, with a breeze. He coaxes his horse past several groceries, an apothecary, a bakery, a butcher, and a newspaper office, its block letters white against a rough board. He recognizes just one of the letters in the three-word name. The city teems with activity. Shanties have replaced adobe. A city of muddied tents sits at the base of the hill and tall-masted ships rest at anchor hundreds of yards off the city's long, wooden wharves.

In 1845, when he first arrived in Yerba Buena, the city was sleepy, peopled with Mexicans and sailors and Indians and priests and drifters, almost all men. Now there are white women and children, likely arrived from New York via Cape Horn or by wagon across the wide plains. So much change, maybe five hundred people now, and called San Francisco.

He bypasses Fay's for now and registers at Hedrin's for one night's stay. The first order of business is a bath. Man had better be clean to sign up for the militia—and before he sees his lady. He peels his stiff clothes off. Tomorrow, he'll likely have new clothes, if the militia will take him.

After the bath, he re-dresses in his grimy clothes and walks three blocks to the Red Dog Saloon. "A pint," he says, and swigs the beer. Of the fifteen or so men in the establishment, a tall stranger at the bar talks louder than most. The man listens in, might as well hear the news. Been awhile.

"You've read it in the *California Star*," the tall stranger says.

"Can you write something for me?" the man asks the bartender.

"What's your pleasure?" the bartender answers.

"California Star."

"Name of the newspaper? Here you go." He writes out in block letters:

C-A-L-I-F-O-R-N-I-A S-T-A-R.

"That's an *a,* isn't it?" the man asks. He points to the second letter of the word, California.

"Sure is. And here, at the end of the word, too. Another one in the word, star. S-T-A-R."

The man traces the letters. He knows the rhyme about the abc's, but doesn't know a *c* from an *f* from a *y.* Because he can't read, the only use for the *California Star* he has now is to use it for a fire starter or to wipe mud from his boots. He pockets the piece of paper. Later, he'll ask Fay to read it to him, to teach him the name of each letter. Of course, he'll see Fay. Tonight.

"Where do I sign up? For the militia?" the man asks the bartender.

"Too late, buster. Treaty's been signed. California belongs to the United States of America."

"When?"

"Few weeks ago."

The man slugs his beer, orders another. *What to do now?*

It's impossible to ignore the tall man at the far end of the bar. By now, the stranger has commanded the attention of everyone in the establishment.

"There's families, some with children—*my children, I might add*—left stranded on the east side of the Sierras," he says. "I'm aiming to mount a relief party. Could use help, any of you."

The man has heard of stranded emigrants before. Every year, always some poor clod or sad group of westering folk stuck in the Sierras—people who have no business traveling over mountains in any season, let alone winter. They're farmers mostly, not mountain men, putting all their belongings in overloaded wagons and pulling up stakes only to be killed by Indians or die from dysentery or find themselves stranded on the east side of the Sierras in a howling blizzard. *Stupes.*

The man considers it. He is heading out anyway. "How much?" he asks.

"Enough," the tall man answers. "You interested?"

"Might be," the man answers. "I'm between places. But if the money's good . . ."

"You a woodsman?"

"Been a trapper in the North Country most of my life."

"It's a deal, then. We've got the backing of most of the city, and a hefty loan from John Sutter himself. And we've got ten good men. Time's a-wasting so we'll leave tomorrow, early. James Reed's the name. Yours?"

29

March 3, 1847
Truckee Lake

Clear and cold. Wind light, SE. Ten men arrived from Sutter's yesterday.

—from Ada Weeks' diary

Ada layers her shawl over her stained shirtwaist and secures her grimy wool skirt. There is so little of propriety she now undresses without regard to leering eyes. There is so little of hope that when another day dawns, Ada thinks it like one of the seven days of creation—a miracle that *just one more day* can be eked out of immeasurable void.

She's been confined to the cabin now for a hundred and twenty-four days. More than twenty of her compatriots are dead, and who knows how many more at the Donner camp. At least, Reed swears all those ahead have made it to safety. And now it's her turn. She wraps her feet in rags and pulls on Halloran's boots. It'll be but days until she sees Mary Graves and Dolan again.

Ada's eyes, now accustomed to semi-darkness all day, wander over rubbish scattered around the Breen's dank hovel: bits of glassware, beads, bolts, square-headed nails, shards of a clay pipe, a fishing hook, darning needle, the heel of a shoe, a lone button. She grabs for the button. In her haste, she nicks her palm on a jagged piece of porcelain jutting from the dirt floor. She picks out a sliver of blue china from her hand and stems the trickle of blood with a dirty rag. Ada winds the rag as tight as she reasons prudent and wishes for axle grease—or a shot of Dolan's whiskey.

Today, all the thoughts and feelings that have crisscrossed her mind over the past ten months gather in the growing knot in her stomach. But it is not hunger that turns her insides out. Today is the day Ada has only allowed herself to dream about, the day she will shoulder her few belongings on her bony back and walk up the narrow snow staircase for the last time, her feet bound in rags beneath the remnants of Luke Halloran's boots. With eyes glued to the jagged ridgeline, she'll join thirty-one walking skeletons trudging toward the summit, the last barrier that separates the lake camp from the Promised Land. Where she is going exactly—paradox that it is—little of that matters. What matters is she is leaving the lake camp behind: its trials, its heartaches, its misery. She will never again descend ice steps to spend another night in a stinking pit burrowed beneath layers of bloodied snow, her dungeon home for the past four months.

Ada pushes past the hide door and counts the stairs for the last time—*sixteen, seventeen, eighteen*—and moves into daylight. The snow is well over twenty feet deep now. She uses her rifle as a walking stick. There are no cabins, no roofs visible anymore. Only the Breen's chimney sprouts from the snow like a mushroom. The other cabins don't have the luxury of chimneys, and snow holes that top their enclosures are ringed with soot.

Ada stamps her feet as she waits for instruction. Her hand throbs. At least, her toe is better. She is now at the mercy of the rescue party and capricious weather as the emigrants confront the indomitable wall of the Sierra Nevada Mountains. Over the past four months, Ada has memorized the rise of the Sierras, every crag and dip and spire. Nothing will stop her. She is like a moth diving into flame now.

The emigrants move slowly through snow, single file, following James Reed.

James Reed, you say? Exiled back in October after killing John Snyder? Sent over Pauta Pass without a rifle, or a horse, or food enough for a day? Thought lost to all eternity because of guilt or shame, weather or hostile attack? Yes, the very one. Just yesterday, Reed appeared as if out of thin air with a band of men in tow, one of them as old as time itself. It was as improbable as a dream.

"Reed! McCutcheon?!" Breen yells as he envelops his old friends. "Praise Mary and Joseph! Tell us, man, how many have made it to safety?"

"All, thanks be to God," Reed answers. Reed's youngest, more wraiths than children, stumble to his side. "Patty! Tommy!" Reed turns his head, wipes his eyes. "I've seen your mother. Near the pass. We'll be back together in a few days."

"Virginia, too?" Patty asks.

"Yes, child. Virginia, too. And little James."

Reed faces haggard and sunken wisps of people who left Independence hearty and hale the year before. "We'll take as many of you as can make it. Snow doesn't show any sign of letting up. Could be stranded here until June. So tomorrow we'll roll out.

"This here's Caleb Greenwood," Reed continues. He motions to an octogenarian clad in mountain gear. "Knows these mountains better than God himself. And his son, Brit."

A wily teen nods to the crowd.

"Is that you, Hiram? Hiram Miller?" Breen asks. Breen clasps Miller. "Haven't seen hide nor hair of you since you rode out with Edwin Bryant on the Fourth of July. How've you been, man?"

Ada thinks she recognizes Miller, but can't be sure. There have been so many teamsters in and out of camps along the dusty trail through Indian Territory and beyond, and so many are gone now. Ada's curious what became of the newspaperman Bryant. *"Watch your g's, Miss Weeks."*

"And this is John Turner."

Reed ushers an unkempt giant to the front of the entourage. Ada has never seen a man as tall.

"Cady, Clark, Stone, front and center," Reed continues.

Three young men emerge from the pack of rescuers and move toward Reed.

"These men will stay with any of you not strong enough to travel. There's another rescue behind us, and those not traveling with us tomorrow will be coming over just behind us."

"Up front, Riddle. You, too, Dofar and Gendreau." Reed introduces the last of the relief party to the stranded overlanders.

Ada takes a piece of stale bread from one of the stout French-Canadians. He looks like he could whip his weight in wildcats. She murmurs her thanks and sucks on the crust. One of the other frontiersmen hands Ada a pair of oversized woolen socks. She puts them on her hands.

"We tried to reach you last fall," Reed says. Mrs. Graves moans. "But we were beaten back," he continues. "After the first emigrant party made it through to Sutter's, we gathered as many men and supplies as we could to come for the rest of you."

"Tell us of the emigrant party," Ada says. "Where are they now?"

"We'll tell you after we dole out provisions." He directs the mountaineers to distribute rations. "Sorry we don't have more for you, but when we saw the break in the weather, we couldn't delay another day, even if it meant leaving behind the bulk of the goods."

"What do you mean?" Breen asks. "What goods?" He leans on a large branch to keep his balance.

"Plans gone awry. We were set to meet a boat northeast of Sutter's. Had on it pork, flour, coffee, the like."

Ada's eyes water. *Coffee.*

"What about blankets and boots?" Ma Breen says. "We're woefully short of them."

"Yes," Reed says. "Had those items and more. Hides, axes, tobacco."

Tobacco!

"But weather couldn't wait," Reed says. "We've got enough here to see you through. And we've cached supplies along the route. Be ready to leave in the morning." Reed hoists Tommy onto his shoulders and squeezes Patty.

Ada is one of four adults chosen to go from the lake camp, in addition to Patrick and Margaret Breen and Elizabeth Graves. The others, Lewis Keseberg and Levinah Murphy, will stay behind. Keseberg's foot is swollen to twice its normal size, and Murphy is clearly unwell.

Over at the Alder Creek camp, teamster Jean-Baptiste Trudeau argues to leave, but Reed tasks him with the care of Tamsen and Elizabeth Donner after Tamsen Donner refuses to leave her ailing husband and failing sister-in-law.

Eighteen children need rescuing, all of them under fourteen. In the end, three of the Donner girls remain with their mother, Tamsen. Reed cannot be burdened with the rest of the children, so those too small or too weak to walk on their own must stay.

Ada pleads to take James Eddy along; it's the least she can do to get her friend's son to safety.

"No," Reed says. "He'll come over on the next relief."

Ada prays that day is soon so James can be reunited with his father, now on the west side of the mountains. It is sorrow enough his wife and daughter have not survived. *Can't count on tomorrow.*

This morning, the entourage sets out on its perilous trek, ineffable joy or ineffable sorrow their reward. Ada is mid-pack, behind one of the woodsmen, trying to keep up. She's forced to lift her skirts to her knees, and snow sifts down into her boots. She no longer has bloomers. *How am I goin' to walk ninety miles? God help me, or I'm goin' to be meetin' you right soon.* She slogs through crusty snow, inserting her feet into the deep footsteps of those in front of her. Her rifle bobs at her side and hits her below the hip. She bruises easily now. Sol Hook is behind her, and gaining, so there is no time to stop to take a breath or sweep snow from inside her boots. Her toes are frozen.

Walking. Walking. Walking. Ada enunciates the last letter of the word. *Mr. Bryant would be proud of me.*

Bitter cold gnaws deep into Ada's body and psyche. Her lungs hurt as she gasps frigid air. She has not exerted herself this much for months. The farthest she has walked in the past few months has been to the Graves's cabin to visit Mary. She never went as far as Alder Creek to see the Donners. After Mary left and Eleanor died, Ada's visits to other cabins all but ceased. She's down to a skeleton: no fat, no muscle. Carrying Bella is added weight she can't afford. She could put the baby down, right here in the snow, and no one would notice. She gasps, thinks there must be ten feet of wind ahead of her, not just ten feet of snow. The wind punches her face, her hands, her legs. When her nose runs, it's an effort to raise her gloved hand to wipe away mucus. After a while, it becomes too much an effort, and mucus drips in a frozen slurry into her mouth. Hoarfrost coats her eyelids, and snow bites her cheeks. Time is of the utmost concern; although the calendar is sliding toward spring, winter still holds fast in the Sierras.

Ada carries Bella close to her chest. When she stumbles over a snow hole, she grasps the young child tight as she falls. Her landing is soft; she regains herself and rearranges the baby's wrap. She keeps her eyes focused on the ground in front of her feet to avoid another mishap. A red stain seeps through the rag on her hand. When she reaches down to scoop a mouthful of snow, she leaves a mark.

A full day's trek equals a mere two-mile gain. The mountain party camps at the far side of the lake. Ada is bone-tired, flat, battling lethargy. She swallows a small cup of broth and chews a piece of hardtack.

She squirms into a comfortable position under her cloak and blanket and dares not move. Inertia invites warmth. Breen brings his fiddle to his chin (it hasn't left its case in months). Ada thinks of Dolan. By this time next year, she might have a child of her own. Ada's lulled into a dreamless sleep. In what seems like only minutes, she hears a shout.

"Up and about," Reed commands.

Walking. Walking. Walking. Two by two and three by three, they plod single-file behind the rescuers. Reed and McCutcheon's reasons for leading the expedition—like Eddy's in the first relief—eschew explanation. They came back for family and friends. Ada's unconditionally thankful for the efforts of the frontiersmen—even though she's sure they've been paid a hefty sum to risk their lives to save those stranded. Greenwood, Turner, the French-Canadians. A couple more. And the quiet one, the one with the scar down the side of his face. He moves with the grace of a deer and the strength of a bear, and does not allow merciless cold to stop him. He lugs children, hefts logs, breathes life into damp kindling. Ada is not quick to judge appearances; after all, she is plain. *Beggars can't be choosers.* So she follows this giant of a man and does not complain, at times falling uphill it's so steep. He could be a charlatan. He could be a savior. She has no choice but to hope for the latter. Every step is a step closer to California. Every step is a step closer to Mary and Dolan.

When the group pauses for a meager meal, Reed and McCutcheon trade stories with Breen. The frontiersmen chew tobacco, spit, share stories out of earshot, guffaw. Haloes of breath exit their mouths and dissipate in the frosty air. The three women are left with the care of the children. Ada is thankful for the new wool socks the rescuers brought with them. Even though they are damp, they keep out the biting cold. By now, she has rolled them over Halloran's battered boots, like Mary Graves had done.

By day's end, Ada is raw from exertion. There are no jigs tonight, just another twelve hours to endure until sun up. Ma Breen collapses in the snow and moans. Except for their clothing, there are only a few blankets or hides for any vestige of warmth. Ada is fortunate to have a blanket. She does not share. Elizabeth Graves tosses and turns, talks to herself or God or no one. Ada blocks out cries and murmurings. If she is to survive this last leg of the journey, she needs her wits—and every last ounce of fortitude her wasted frame will allow.

Where she once uttered prayers or whistled hymns, she cannot put two words together. Her brain has slowed to match her breathing: shallow, sacrificial, silent. Ada counts her breaths, in, out, in, out. She won't make it to morning without a fight.

30

March 7, 1847
To the Summit

A nother foot of snow blankets the camp overnight. *Will there be no end to it?*

"Faster, all of you," Reed urges.

Ada is beyond fatigued. Moving one foot in front of the other is all her near-lifeless body can manage. The sky threatens more snow and rations are dangerously low. She plods on—one foot, then the other. She sees spots in front of her eyes like black, blinking stars. The octogenarian Greenwood and his son Brit have already gone ahead in hopes of meeting others to assist the travelers to Johnson's Ranch, the emigrants' first stop before reaching Sutter's Fort.

"Turner, Gendreau. You, too, Dofar," Reed summons. "Looks to be a bad storm coming in. Go on ahead. Try to locate our cache before nightfall, then backtrack. We're counting on you."

The three men trudge off ahead of the rescue party to salvage supplies hung in trees some five miles west. Ada wants to run after them, every step closer to her goal. But her feet move like they're encased in cement.

Within minutes, the steel-grey sky opens with a deluge of driving sleet. The wind, at first fierce, now howls. Elizabeth Graves's eyes grow wild with terror. She fumbles with her skirts and lets out raw, animal sounds. At one point, she darts away from the trail into a clump of snowbound trees. Before Reed can stop her, Graves turns and steals down the route they've come.

"Mrs. Graves!" Reed's shouts go unheeded. "All of you! Keep ahead!"

Reed races down the trail and disappears around a bend. Ada tramps behind Turner, who by now is carrying two of the Breen boys, one piggy-back and another straddling his waist from the front. She worries after Elizabeth Graves. Mary had said her mother wasn't "quite right."

I'd say she's raving mad.

Twenty minutes later, Reed gains on the travelers with Mrs. Graves in tow. He walks ahead of her, leading her by a rope bound to her wrists. Reed glances over his shoulder to see she does not try to flee again. His eyes are streaked with red.

It is all Ada can do to concentrate on each step. To focus, she begins counting: . . . *three hundred eleven, three hundred twelve, three hundred thirteen*; later, *six hundred thirty-six, six hundred thirty-seven, six hundred thirty-eight.* She is so focused on her task she is unaware the stragglers have crested the summit until Reed sends up a *hurrah* through the ranks. The man with the funny name touches her elbow as he counts off the party.

So this is California?

There is no laurel wreath of victory to mark their arrival to the Promised Land, only a silent, snow-filled alpine meadow that stretches ahead for miles. *Where is Johnson's Ranch?* Ada hankers to ask how far they are from Johnson's now, but reins in her question. Whether it's ten miles or forty miles is of no consequence. Tonight— another day hedged against death—they will camp again in the snow.

By dusk, Reed signals a suitable spot for the travelers to stop for the night. He leans against a gnarly pine and puffs on a pipe. He keeps his eye trained on the wandering Mrs. Graves.

Ada brushes snow from atop a boulder and sits. Her backside is sore from walking and the bare, cold, granite does nothing to comfort her. "Do you know the date?" Ada asks the mountaineer with the jagged scar.

"Can't say I do, miss. Middle of March, I'd reckon."

Ada counts the months on her fingers. *Ten months since we left Independence! And today—March the tenth? The fifteenth?—I have finally reached California.* She thought it would have been more of a celebration.

Within minutes, Reed gives orders. McCutcheon, Miller, and a handful of others begin to build a platform from downed logs. Other mountaineers erect a windscreen, like a fort. Ada stumbles around the boundaries of the camp to collect boughs for bedding. If she doesn't keep moving, if she doesn't find shelter from the cold, she'll likely freeze to death.

There's little kindling, so McCutcheon and Miller set two downed trees in a crosshatch on the platform and coax a fire at the center of the X. Between the logs, Ada spreads pine branches for warmth and comfort. Soon a roaring fire emanates from a hole cut into the center of the platform. Ada edges in to warm her backside. She rotates to warm her front and hunches over the flame.

Snow clouds bank up against the east side of the mountains, wind rasps through the treetops, and temperatures plunge toward zero. Ada hears a guttural moan. Elizabeth Graves is even more unstable than earlier in the day; she rocks back and forth hugging herself, her skirt frozen to the snow. Ada sits close to the fire and hugs her own knees. Ice crystals sting her face, and her lips chatter involuntarily.

"Closer, boys," Ma Breen whispers. The family huddles together as they bed down, ringing the fire that pops and crackles in the center of the platform. Ada is sandwiched between John and Patrick, Jr. The dim warmth of other bodies brings with it a rush of emotion. She longs for Dolan. Meager warmth seeps into her body and she dozes.

Long after midnight, a piercing scream floods the meadow. Ada awakes to an inferno. The log platform has tilted downward into a raging fire. Memories flood Ada's mind. *Her ma. Her pa. The barn.*

"John!" Ma Breen screams as she lunges after her oldest son. John has slipped into the fire pit, a gaping hole six feet deep in the center of the log platform. In a flurry of shouts, McCutcheon and the tall mountain man grasp John under his armpits and haul him back onto the steaming platform. His leg is badly burned; Ma Breen peels charred leggings from John's singed flesh. The mountaineer bends over and runs his hands along the edges of the burns. Ada moves closer to John. She scoops a handful of snow to rub on his burns.

"Don't know if that's the best treatment, miss," the mountaineer says.

"Well, we don't have grease, do we? Here, John, we're just trying to help."

John groans. "Thanks, Miss Ada."

The rescuer tips his hat. Ada wonders how he became so disfigured, a scar slicing his face from his eye to where it disappears under a black bushy beard.

"J. R. Riddle, miss."

"Ada Weeks. Now, if you please, can you help me here?" She moves to McCutcheon. His skin is scorched black and raw. "Sorry we don't have grease for you," she says. "Snow should help some."

As if in a trance, everyone moves away from the fiery ring and its diminishing warmth; there will be no more sleep for tonight. Ada trembles. She is soaked through to the skin. By morning, her skirt will be frozen stiff as coffin boards.

Buckets of snow continue to dump on the weary travelers the next morning. "Best to muster our strength," Reed says. "It's less than four days now to Sutter's. Rest while you can."

He rubs his red-rimmed eyes and turns to Bill McCutcheon. "I'm seeing double, Bill. Need the rest myself. See to it that everyone's fed." Reed retreats to his buffalo robe and burrows beneath it.

McCutcheon distributes steaming cups of broth to the group. Ada takes short sips and swirls the tasteless soup before swallowing. It's hot. She makes sure Peter and James gulp their share, and then watches the other Breen boys. John is listless; Ma Breen drips broth into his mouth. Then she dribbles the soup into Bella's bird-like mouth. Bella's faint mewls rip Ada's heart in two. After the scant meal, Ada silently takes Bella from Ma Breen's arms and cradles the baby close to her own breast. She wishes she had milk to offer. With Bella asleep in her arms, Ada stands and stamps her feet. She walks to a nearby tree and rubs up against the tree to scratch her back.

While she stands there, a flurry of men rushes toward Reed. "Miller! Riddle! Step to it! I think we may have lost Reed," McCutcheon yells. Reed lies unconscious as men bunch around his lifeless body. Miller and Riddle take turns rubbing Reed's arms and legs vigorously.

"Faster, man," Riddle says.

Reed, the paragon of leadership and governance and order and duty, does not respond, his mouth slack. Patty Reed shivers as she watches the men attend to her father. Tommy stands as if dumb. Ada pulls Bella into a makeshift sling made out of her cloak and puts one arm around Patty and the other around Tommy.

"'Hail Mary, full of grace,'" Ada begins. "'Our Lord is with thee . . .'"

"There's a pulse, but it's weak," Miller says. "We haven't lost him yet."

Ma Breen stands beside Ada and murmurs. "'Blessed art thou among women, and blessed is the fruit of thy womb, Jesus.'"

"Pa!" Patty cries. "Don't leave me, Pa."

Ada raises her voice. "'Holy Mary, Mother of God, pray for us sinners, now and at the hour of our death.'"

Patty whimpers. Tommy is still as stone.

After what seems like an hour, Reed murmurs. He tries to sit up, his eyes glazed. Patty and Tommy haste to their father. "What the devil?" Reed asks.

"We thought we lost you, captain," McCutcheon answers. "Pulse was as weak as a bird's. Good thinking on Riddle's part."

"Obliged," Reed says.

Riddle nods. "You would have done it for me, sir."

Ada sighs relief and mimics the rescuers' actions by rubbing Bella's soft body. She is aware of Bella's shallow breathing; she breathes in and out with the baby. *Please, God, not Bella.*

That night, Ada listens for familiar sounds: the hoot of an owl, the howl of a coyote. She hears nothing except muffled sobs, ardent prayers. Then silence. It is so complete—no fire crackling, no voices, nothing—that Ada wonders if she is, in fact, still alive. She checks her own measured breathing by placing a frigid finger on the weak pulse in her neck. Silence alone might kill if cold and hunger and thirst don't get to her first.

Mrs. Graves whimpers and twitches. But death does not grab her right away. Instead, death's icy fingers pry the life out of young Isaac Donner, who slips away so peacefully no one notices until first call the next day. Ada suppresses her tears. It is no use grieving the dead. There have been so many deaths now she is inured to it. Besides, tears freeze on contact with her red and scaly skin. She winds her blanket around her neck and up and over her head like a hood.

Reed is still too weak to travel so McCutcheon calls for a second day of rest. Ada is anxious to get underway. This is how Edwin Bryant must have felt about the slow progress of the wagon train when he and a handful of others ditched their wagons and rode ahead on mules back in Indian Country.

Should I forge on alone? No, that would be madness.

There is no breakfast, and Ada does not pass water all day. *Where are the other rescuers?*

Several men from the relief party bury Isaac Donner in the snow. His sister Mary Donner wails. Ada sits by Mary Donner but does not talk. She takes the girl's mittened hand and rubs it.

"Here, Mary, have some." Ada shovels snow with her bare hand and gives a small snowball to Mary. Then she reaches for a handful of snow and eats it herself.

J. R. Riddle approaches Ada. "Better to boil it first."

"You got a kettle?"

"No, miss, but there's the one pot of McCutcheon's." He jerks his head to where Bill McCutcheon bends over a small flame. Three or four children surround him.

"Seems he's got a line up," Ada says. She bites into another handful of snow and stares at Riddle's face. "You ever have that mole looked at? It looks nasty to me."

Riddle puts his hand to his face, just beneath the scar that disfigures his cheek. "It's nothing."

"I seen worse. But it don't look good. If you'll let me, I can lance it."

"As if we don't have a heap enough of trouble, and you're spouting off about a mole? We've got bigger problems here, miss."

On the morning of the third day, the trekkers wake to a break in the weather. Reed stands. "We'd best be moving out." He beckons the rescuers and emigrants to press on.

It is none too soon for Ada, she is but days from Dolan and safety and food. Ada bundles in her blanket and tosses her small pack and rifle over her shoulder. "C'mon, now, Mary. Time to go," Ada says.

Mary Donner shakes her head. "Can't leave my brother."

"You've got to come along," Ada implores. "It'll be you next if you don't rouse yourself. 'The Lord helps those who help themselves.'"

Mary plows her frostbitten feet directly into the snow. "No, Miss Ada."

Ada moves on the Breen boys and signals to Patrick, Jr. "Up, sir. We're almost there. You, too, James, Peter. Here, let me help you with that hat."

"No, boys," Patrick Breen says.

The boys look at their father, then toward their mother.

"Can't walk another mile," Breen utters. "The pain is worse than before, damn this gravel. Better to die here than risk dying on the trail." Breen hunches over and holds his abdomen.

"What are you saying, Breen? If you stay here, you might as well sign your own death warrant," Reed says. "Up now, all of you. We'll be to Johnson's Ranch in two days, and then on to Sutter's soon after that. We are nearer than you think." He gestures west. "I implore you, Breen. Your family is counting on you."

"We'll wait," Breen says. He bows his head in prayer.

Ada can't believe her ears.

"I'm sorry, Ma Breen, Mr. Breen, sir. I have to go. I have to find Dolan. Won't you please reconsider? Or let me take the baby?"

"You go on, Ada," Ma Breen says.

"Let me take the little ones," Ada says. "You sent Eddie and Simon ahead with the last party. I'll be sure to get the boys to safety."

Ma Breen shakes her head. "Better that the family attends their da, especially in his last days. Can't leave Father here alone."

"But . . .?" Ada says.

Margaret Breen shakes her head.

"I won't be arguing with you, then," Ada says. "I'm mighty grateful to you both." It's the closest Ada can come to expressing her gratitude. She chokes up and pecks the younger boys on the cheek. She won't embarrass the older boys.

The Breens are not the only ones sitting immobile. Solomon Hook begs his stepsister Mary Donner to accompany the group to Sutter's, but she sits stock-still, her naked feet buried into a snowdrift.

"Miller, McCutcheon. You too, Riddle. You're my witnesses here," Reed says. "I won't have the blood of these fools on my hands. Above my bend to figure the reasoning for staying behind." Reed faces Breen. "Send the boys on, Breen! Less of a burden to us than to you."

"Not a chance," Breen whispers.

"Well, you're at the mercy of the wolves now," Reed says. "God help you."

The group moves out single file across the meadow. Ada doesn't have much time. She turns to John Breen. "Take care of your ma and pa. And see to it that Bella . . ." Ada can't finish her sentence. She wipes her eyes and turns to follow Reed, who, by this time, has vanished into the woods at the far end of the clearing. She had vowed not to leave Bella, and now she is walking away.

A new gush of snow spills from the heavy, leaden sky, its jagged rim bruised purple. It comes on fast, first as fine powder and soon thicker, a torrent of fringed cotton. Snow fills all crevices in the landscape; Ada knows the march will be far more difficult than it looks if she can't see footfalls in front of her. She's got wind colic, and it's hard to move. She plods through drifts, her breath shallow, her eyes focused ahead. She muffles a sob.

Ada picks up her pace, her arms swinging. She wonders why she still carries the rifle. She hasn't shot it in months. Her breath catches in sub-zero temperatures as she marches defiantly toward twilight.

If one could look down on the scene, like a puppeteer, he would see a tall, disheveled marionette, arms and legs pumping, cloak flailing behind her as if alive. She lopes across the barren meadow, tripping every other step in thigh-high snow. Her moans are muffled; one cannot make out what she says. So otherworldly she looks, one might mistake her for a wild, demented ghost racing offstage until nothing is left onstage but deep, dark footsteps. The wind howls, but no one—not human nor beast—howls back.

31

March 11, 1847
In the Wild

"One step. There. Now another. That's it, Miss Weeks," Riddle says.

One foot, now the other. I can do it, Ma. I have walked from Independence. I have walked to California. Walking. Walking. Walking.

There are now nine in the party as they trek across Bear Meadow on the windward side of the Sierras. James Reed commands three grimy rescuers: fellow emigrant, husband, and father William McCutcheon, former Donner teamster Hiram Miller, and the Californian homesteader, J. R. Riddle. Their charges from the lake camp number four: Patty and Tommy Reed, Sol Hook, and Ada. The rest of the people they started out with from the lake camp—those who have survived, that is—are now abandoned at the snow camp because of Patrick Breen's stubbornness and the infirmities of several others. *It's madness,* Ada thinks.

Miller has gone ahead to scout for a campsite. The Reed children take turns walking and then being carried by Reed and McCutcheon. Sol Hook trudges behind them. Ada lags behind.

"Watch your step there," Riddle says.

One foot, two, one foot, two. Still she falls farther behind.

"Faster now!" Reed bellows. "We've got one—maybe two—hours of daylight left. And dammit, Riddle, help Miss Weeks along."

D is for dammit. And doctor. And doldrums: D-O-L . . . Dolan! D is for Dolan. I am coming, Dolan, fast as I can.

"We're almost to the river," Riddle says. "What river? The Bear. Two days until Johnson's Ranch from there. Yes, just two days. No, I am not lying to you."

We're almost there, Ma. Follow, follow, one, two, three. Three rhymes with free rhymes with tree. Oh! Do you see, Ma? The branches are so heavy with snow. Like they cannot carry another flake. Or they will break! Rhymes with cake!

Ada scowls.

Gosh darn it, Ma! March the first has come and gone. Come. And. Gone. Maybe I do not like remembering birthdays? Because every birthday reminds me of . . . oh, how I would have loved a sister, Ma.

"A little bit more, and we will rest. No, not here. A little bit more, Miss Weeks. Wait, where are your gloves?"

Gloves? I do not need gloves.

"What are you saying, Miss Weeks?"

Hot, hot, I am so very hot.

"Reed!" Riddle yells. "May I have a moment? Stay here, Miss Weeks."

Stay here. Do this; do that. Get up; sit down. Here, eat. And there is nothing to eat but snow! Snow, blow, flow, go. Go, go, go.

Reed pauses and waits for Ada and Riddle to catch up. "Miss Weeks, here, put these on," Reed says. He peels off his own gloves and offers them to Ada.

Ada pushes Reed's hand aside. *No, no gloves, I don't need your gloves! Has anyone ever said what they think of you? That you are so tiresome, Mr. Almighty James Frazier Reed?*

"I believe you may have snow fever, Miss Weeks. Here, this is the last of the blankets. Please, take it. Riddle, stay with her, don't let her stop now. We'll be to camp in three-quarters of an hour if we hoof it here." He lopes ahead and scoops Tommy from a snow hole.

Take it away, I say! I am burning. Burning, burning, the barn is burning. Where are you, Ma? I have looked for you everywhere: in the kitchen, the bedroom, the cellar. Did you go to the barn? I can hear it, the fire. It's crackling and popping, there goes the door! The rafters are crashing in! My pony! Pa! And where are you, Ma? Ma!

Ada throws her rifle into the snow and rips off her shawl.

"Miss Weeks, please, no," Riddle says.

Ada fumbles with her shirt and squirms out of it. She is not wearing a chemise. Her breasts, shoulders, and arms are bared to the cold. She laughs and spins, trampling her clothes.

"Miss Weeks!" Riddle lunges at Ada. He throws the blanket over her torso and fumbles to secure the ends at her waist. "Please, let me help." When he has covered her, he reaches down for Ada's blouse and crunches it into a ball. He drops his knapsack, opens the flap, and shoves Ada's blouse inside. "We'll dry your clothes later. Keep that blanket tight now. It's a cruel trick, but it's just a figment of your imagination. You are not burning. I understand, more than you might know. I've spent many winter nights in the wilderness."

No, he does not understand, Ma. He does not understand everything I have seen: skies and rivers and mountains and deserts and high plains and low plains. And everywhere I go, I am chasing the sun. Look at the sun, Ma! Like a kaleidoscope! Oranges and yellows and blues all spinning and twirling and oh! Not again. D is for dominos, down down down.

"Up, Miss Weeks. I know it's not easy. That's it. Those boots of yours look like two Sundays ago."

Riddle picks up Ada's rifle and hoists it over his shoulder. Ada stares at Riddle. She falls in the snow again, but this time, she doesn't get up.

"Reed!" Riddle yells.

Reed backtracks to where Ada is splayed in the snow, her blanket again askew. "I hate to do this, Miss Weeks. But we cannot stop here," Reed says. "We've come a long way today, and we're almost to camp." Reed retrieves a long piece of rope from his waist.

Leave me alone! Get your hands off me! Ma! Help me! Not my hands! No!

"We'll free you as soon as we make camp," Reed says. He faces Riddle and hands him the rope. "Take this, will you? Not too tight. I have my hands full with Tommy. And Patty . . . she's stopped talking. It looks grim."

Ada stumbles. Her tethered hands break her fall. She lies on the snow, half-laughing, half-crying, her head addled. *I cannot see straight. I cannot think straight. And now you have tied me up, like a prisoner. How dare you! Let me go, I tell you.*

"Just another mile until we make camp," Riddle says. "I know the spot well, been there before. Maybe snare a big, fat rabbit. How's that sound, Miss Weeks?" He goads Ada along, talking her through each step. "Miller's up ahead, he'll have a fire going. We'll camp there, then another day, maybe two, 'til we reach Johnson's. When we get there, you can eat whatever you like."

"I don't believe you!"

"Found your tongue, I see. If you don't believe me, that's your prerogative. But what I say is God's gospel truth, miss. You thirsty?"

Ada nods. She sips icy water from Riddle's canteen. She tries to rub her head. Her wrists move in tandem. She stares at Riddle. "Unbind my hands."

"Do you promise to act like a lady?"

"A lady? No, I can't never promise that. But I won't run off, if that's what you're after."

"Well, I've been known to spit at convention myself," Riddle says. He loosens the rope binding Ada's wrists. She shakes her arms out. Already there is a red circle imprinted on both forearms.

"Come along now, Miss Weeks. Another fifteen minutes, that's all."

"What time is it, do you think?" Ada asks.

Riddle stares at Ada. "What time is it?" He thinks it an inane question; it's obviously dusk and coming on quicker than an arrow. "Why, I'd say it's five thirty-eight." A hint of a smile borders his mouth. "Maybe five thirty-nine, give or take. We'll be to camp by . . ."

Ada sprints across the meadow, her blanket flapping and her breasts bobbing up and down.

"Six!" she yells.

Riddle lunges through snowdrifts and reaches Ada's side. He grabs her arm. "You said you wouldn't run off."

Ada slows and looks into Riddle's deep-set brown eyes. "I'm not running off."

"Then what in tarnation are you doing?" Riddle reaches for the blanket but Ada pulls away, her eyes boring into his. Riddle raises his hand in defeat. "I don't aim to hurt you, miss. It's just that—" He doesn't break eye contact as he slowly moves his hands toward Ada's waist to secure the blanket again. "—we can't have you running around without a stitch on."

Ada struggles to be free of his grasp and sprints ahead again.

"Miss Weeks!"

"Don't you smell it, Mr. Riddle?" she yells over her shoulder. "The rabbit?"

32

March 13, 1847
Johnson's Ranch, Alta California

Is it an illusion? Smoke curling from the crooked chimney of that squat adobe? Ada falls to her knees in the mud. She cries out, her voice ringing through the clearing. She long ago stopped caring what others think. Mud oozes through her fingers. When she swipes at her eyes, she leaves a dark smudge on her cheek. She is laughing now, then crying, then laughing again.

D is for deliverance! And Dolan!

She squints. One by one, faces materialize. Dolan is not among them. Along with the rest of the stragglers, Ada is shepherded into a warm room and set in front of a meal that could only come from her imagination: cold mutton with gravy, potatoes, and bread. She has so many questions. They will have to wait.

Ada shovels food into her mouth and swallows without tasting. When gravy starts to congeal at the side of her plate, she mops it up with the last of her crust. Her stomach swells. Not ten minutes later, cramping begins. Her gut is on fire and bile erupts in her throat. She dashes outside. Afterward, she stands with her back against the mess hall and holds her stomach. She trembles.

"Miss? Come with me, *por favor.*"

A short, mixed-breed woman reaches for Ada's arm. Ada flinches. "Please, miss. I have for you a bath."

A bath?

The *Californio* leads Ada to a small closet where an old tin wash-tub brims with scalding water. The room is steamed and warm. Ada peels matted socks off her feet as the matron assists her in undressing. Ada strips her blanket and skirt from her bony body. Ada drops her tattered clothing onto the floor. She has never been naked and alone with a woman before, at least since puberty. But she is too weary to care.

The woman scoops up Ada's used clothing and leaves. Ada feels the searing water with her toe and steps over the lip of the tin tub. She kneels in the water and cups handfuls over her shoulders. A shiver runs up her back. As she melts into the bath, a thousand hideous images wash away. She soaps her body again and again and again from shoulders to feet and drenches her limp hair. She lathers and rinses twice until her hair squeaks. As she lingers in the now-tepid water, Ada looks at her naked body, all bones and sagging flesh. She pictures Dolan's naked body in her mind. *Where is he?* He must have heard by now that new parties of emigrants are arriving at Johnson's Ranch with regularity, hadn't he?

But what if? Perhaps he has left the area? Abandoned her? *No, not a chance.* Ada shuts down that train of thought like the lid on a canning jar, sealed and snug. *Tomorrow we'll find ourselves a preacher.*

Ada steps out of the tub and pulls the plug. Muddy water drains through the floorboards as she towels off. Ada peeks out the door of the bathing closet. Her filthy rags have disappeared. In their place, the Mexican-Indian woman has left a skirt, blouse, stockings, bloomers, belt, and shawl. And boots. Ada gasps.

Tears mark her cheeks as she maneuvers the light woolen hose over her legs. When was the last time she had clean stockings? Noblesville? She noses her toes into the new boots and stamps them on the floor. They do not pinch her toes. The flannel skirt is shy of her ankles, but Ada does not care. No matter how she repositions her breasts, they are crushed under the starched fabric of the snug white blouse. Ada pins and re-pins the front of the blouse from neck to waist until she covers herself without a gap in the fabric. She cinches the belt around her waist and ties up her wet hair. It's been almost a year since she's been this clean. She remembers the morning she left Noblesville with Augustus and Inger Vik, hopes and dreams in large supply. She glances at the glazed looking glass. A gaunt face stares out at her, all angles and not a shred of fat. She moves closer and reaches toward the mirror, as if to touch who she was before. She stares at the mirror, and then slowly wraps the shawl tightly around her shoulders.

I am in the Promised Land, Mamma and Pappa.

Ada sits on the side of the cot in the spare room and bounces up and down. There's a faint knock on the door, and Ada springs from the bed.

"*Senorita,* you are *buena?* Well?"

"Yes, thank you. Perhaps you can tell me? The other travelers? Ones from the mountains?"

"They have all gone to Mr. Sutter's. You must sleep now. It is *viaje largo,* long ride tomorrow."

The next morning, a cadre of horses snorts and snuffles as they band in a circle. Two Indian guides have raced ahead to bring the news to Sutter's Fort that new emigrants will arrive late this afternoon. Ada's stomach churns. She declines all food offered except a slice of bread and weak tea. Her stomach is still tender.

James Reed mounts a borrowed horse and hoists Patty and Tommy to ride with him. Tommy has not spoken since they left the snow camp. Patty, usually so emotive, is also subdued. They cling to their father. McCutcheon motions to Ada, and helps her up onto his horse. Then he swings his lanky leg over the flank in front of her. She arranges her skirts to ride like a man and places her hands on McCutcheon's waist for stability. Riddle and Solomon Hook ride behind.

Reed leads the group through a tangle of woods. Late morning, they stop by a creek and eat standing up. McCutcheon coaxes a small fire to brew weak coffee. Ada chews another slice of bread and swallows in small bites. She sloshes down some camp coffee and remounts behind McCutcheon. At least, she can keep bread and coffee down. A feeble afternoon sun slants through the pines and oaks. They cannot get to Sutter's Fort fast enough.

"Mary? Mary Graves?!"

"Oh, Miss Ada. Look at you. I have not been so happy to see anyone in ever so long."

The young women embrace for a full minute. Ada shakes. "You made it through! Tell me, what of the others? Where is Mr. Dolan?"

"There is so much to tell you. I don't where to begin," Mary says.

"Dolan! Begin with Dolan. Where is he, do you know? I expected him here."

Mary lowers her eyes. "Oh, Miss Ada, I don't know how to tell you."

"Tell me what? What, Mary?"

"Mr. Dolan did not—he did not survive . . ."

Ada stares at Mary. "What do you mean, did not survive? You must be mistaken." She shakes Mary's shoulders. "Tell me you are mistaken, Mary Graves. Mr. Reed told us that everyone—*everyone*—survived. Who is telling the truth here, you or Mr. Reed? I choose to believe Mr. Reed this once."

"It was best that you did not know," Mary says. "At least not then. Many of our group did not make it out of the mountains alive."

With grim reality as her counterpane, Ada fights every urge to scream. Of the fifteen who set out for Sutter's Fort in December in Dolan's party, only seven arrived: William Eddy and William Foster, the two Sarahs—Fosdick and Foster, Amanda McCutcheon, Harriet Pike, and Mary Graves. The others perished in the mountains: Pat Dolan, Jay Fosdick, Franklin Graves, Lemuel Murphy, and the teamster Antonio. And the story didn't end there.

James Reed had lied; all of the emigrants had not survived. Reed protected those at the lake camp from knowing the grisly details, in order to spur them on to potential safety. Ada hates him for it. But would it have changed anything, really? Wouldn't she have risked everything to leave the lake camp? Wouldn't she have raced for safety at the first mention of food, or warmth, or a future? Whether everyone had made it safely or not?

"I must know, Mary." Ada leads Mary to a rough wooden bench outside the mess hall. They sit. "Now, tell me. Tell me everything."

"Are you sure, Miss Ada? Everything?"

"Everything."

"There are few people I can talk to regarding our ordeal. You would think we are lepers the way everyone looks at us. 'Dirty cannibals,' they call us."

Ada squeezes Mary's hand. "I am listening."

"Those are thirty-two days I would rather forget for all eternity." Mary's eyes well with tears. "We were barely over the summit when— you remember my father? Tough as nails? Well, he just faded away. That night, we lost two others, including Mr. Dolan. I cannot be sure, but I think it was Christmas Day."

Christmas Day! The same day Ada sat at the Breen cabin and prayed for Dolan's safety . . .

Mary is crying freely now. Ada grates her palms together and wills herself not to cry. "More. Tell me more."

"There was . . ." Mary falters. She lowers her voice. ". . . partaking of . . ."

Her voice drops to little more than a whisper. "It was only out of necessity, Miss Ada. You must believe that. But we had to do it. Eat."

Ada hangs her head, clenches her eyes shut. She pictures Mrs. Murphy's ax striking a cadaver, and the deranged woman carrying severed limbs inside.

"Is it not the worst sign of depravity?" Mary asks.

Ada's mouth is set in a grim line.

"I am loath to speak of it, Miss Ada. But I feel I owe it to you to be frank. You were promised to Mr. Dolan."

His rough kisses, arms and legs wrapped around me, skin to skin.

Mary whispers now. "I could not partake of my own father's flesh, Miss Ada. But of course, as you know, Mr. Dolan had no kin . . ."

Ada blanches, feels a sourness rising in her throat. "What of Mr. Stanton?"

"Couldn't keep up. On account of his feet. Of course, no one was going to murder him, even if he was going to die there in the Sierras. He never caught up to us, and hasn't come in since. His Indian guides, though, well, I can only say that they—the Miwoks, I mean—you might say they saved us." Mary retracts her hands from Ada's and looks away. "Once you put the notion out of your mind you're eating human flesh, it's not any different than eating chicken, or . . ."

Ada stifles nausea. "That's enough, Mary."

"But you said you wanted to hear everything."

Ada nods. "Go on."

"It's a miracle that even seven of us found our way to the fort, Miss Ada. It was more difficult than you can imagine." Mary looks beyond Ada into a space only she can see. "We were lost many times, had to retrace our steps. Just when we thought we were on the right trail again, we would take another wrong turn. Probably added more than a week to our journey. If we hadn't lost our way . . ." Mary breaks down into sobs.

Ada pulls Mary closer and strokes her hair. "There, there, Mary.

You did what you needed to do. Now tell me. About the next group."
She thinks of Edward and Simon Breen.

Mary sniffles and sits up. "The next group? You mean the one led
by Mr. Glover?"

Ada nods.

"I think it was seventeen—no, eighteen—came in with their
group. But not all survived Mr. Glover's rescue. You remember Mrs.
Keseberg? She lost her little Ada, but Mrs. Keseberg, she survived."

Ada cringes. *And Mr. Keseberg left behind at the lake camp.*

"And others died, as well," Mary continues. "You remember George
Foster? William Hook?"

Memories of the departed flood Ada's mind. Boys running and
playing and making mischief. She takes a deep breath before asking,
"What of the Breen boys?"

"Yes, they came through. They are with Mrs. Reed near the city."

Ada exhales.

"Now, please, Miss Ada, what news do you have of my family? I
long to see my own dear mother again. Until we have news of all our
family and friends, I cannot leave this place. I have had three offers
of marriage already, can you imagine?"

Ada's eyes widen.

"Of course, I refused all of them. I am doing what I can to help in
the kitchen, waiting . . ." Mary wipes her nose on the sleeve of her
blouse. "Tell me, why are not Mr. and Mrs. George Donner with you?"

Ada turns away and shakes her head. "I don't know, Mary. I don't
know why."

Mary touches Ada's arm. "I am sorry to bring you this most
dreadful news. There's not a one of us left unscathed."

Ada does not know what "unscathed" means. Does it mean no
one has endured the journey unharmed? Or unhurt? Or undamaged?

Ada has held in her emotions just long enough. She races to her
room, falls to her knees, jerks the slop bucket from under the bed,

and retches into the pail. She kneels there, spent, dry heaves wracking her body. After while, Ada hauls herself onto the cot and clutches the coverlet. She squeezes the blanket so hard her knuckles hurt.

More memories creep in. The elder Mr. Graves and the young Mr. Fosdick. Gangly Lemuel Murphy. Simon Hook. The quiet Miwoks. Dear Mr. Stanton. Ada recalls glances, smiles, insignificant details, every day exchanges.

And Dolan. Ada's heart thuds with a sharp pang. There is nothing—not a cry or a prayer or an incantation to a dead saint—that can bring him back. She lies on her back, face up, and gazes out the uncurtained window. She remains there all day, staring at the clouds. She skips supper. Day curls into evening, and Ada stares at the great pin-dotted sky, Venus winking from its perch above the horizon. She is heartbroken and enraged and shocked and helpless, all at once.

She pounds the bed, thrashes the blankets. All the while, her mind spins, filled with reminiscences of Dolan: breathing raggedly behind the Keseberg wagon; walking, stride by stride into Truckee Meadows, their future within reach; whispering about saints and oil lamps and names; tentatively, so tentatively, cradling each other's hearts. Ada digs her fingernails into her thighs until she draws blood. She lies there, moaning.

Sometime after midnight, Ada rises, walks to the window, and parts the curtain. The dark moon slants into the muddy courtyard, and she barely makes out two horses tethered to a hitching post. The stars have not yet risen, and she squints to make out a form in the center of the square. *A dead body?* As her eyes adjust, she realizes it is merely abandoned tack atop smashed crates covered loosely with a blanket. She shudders.

Ada stands at the window and wills the stars to peek from behind their dark drapery. She is patient. One by three by twenty they appear from the void. She feels as if her heart is like the sky, pin-dotted with grief. She searches the heavens for a sign, a comet or a falling star.

The wishing of it doesn't mean it will happen. But it doesn't stop her from trying. She stands there through the night, waiting. Her body shakes. She watches the night sky until every last star closes up shop and goes home. There is no sign. At dawn, she sinks into her bed and sobs.

⌐୨

Ada awakes to birdsong. Its euphony is so foreign it startles her. In that fleeting moment between sleep and waking, she remembers her conversation with Mary Graves yesterday and it pains her all over again.

Memories will have to sustain her: Dolan's winks, Eddie's recovery, Bella's smiles, John's escape from near death in the campfire. And dear Simon. Even Ma Breen and Patrick Breen's constant bickering.

The Breens have yet to come into Sutter's. Should she wait for their arrival? *No,* she chides herself. *I've got to find work in Yerba Buena. And fast.*

What is she thinking? She has less than ten dollars to her name now. She can't support herself for three days in the city on that amount. Unless she resorts to, *no,* she tells herself, *no.* And now—to add insult to injury—according to Mary, the entire Donner-Reed entourage is tainted with shame and disgrace and humiliation. She cannot go to Yerba Buena, unless she does not reveal how she arrived there. That would entail lies, and more lies.

Or maybe I should find me a husband. Mary has already had three offers of marriage. *But who?*

No, Ada thinks. *I don't need a man. I got here on my own two feet, men be damned. I've got to make it here on my own.*

33

March 17, 1847
Sutter's Fort, Alta California

Ada rubs her hands. The pads of her thumbs are raw from chafing. She approaches Sutter's adobe house and raps loudly.

A scowling man opens the massive wooden door.

"Mr. Sutter?"

"I am not."

"Is Mr. Sutter in, sir?"

"He is not."

"Do you know when he plans to return?"

"If I did, I wouldn't be disclosing the information to a stranger. You *have* heard that we have been at war with the Mexicans?"

No, Ada says, she doesn't know. She knows little of what has happened since she left Noblesville except for what occurred to her—and around her—for the last ten months.

"Mr. Sutter is a very busy man. He hasn't time for petty concerns." The manservant begins to close the heavy wooden door.

"I beg your pardon, sir. I have just come from Truckee Lake . . . you have heard of George and Tamsen Donner? James and Margaret Reed?"

The surly man spits at Ada's feet and shuts the door.

She turns and sees Riddle across the yard. She walks toward him. Riddle tips his grimed hat. "Miss Weeks."

Ada stands up straight. She almost meets him eye to eye. "I've got to find myself a place." She tries to hide the panic in her voice.

"A place? Where? Alone?"

"Well, whatever are my choices, Mr. Riddle? I hear we've been at war so I can't go to Yerba Buena, or San Francisco, whatever they call it now. I don't have any family or a husband. And it seems that any connection to the Donner-Reed Party is, how should I say it? Unpalatable?"

Riddle colors. "I see your dilemma, miss. Perhaps you can stay here, at the fort."

"And do what?" Ada says. "Seems like there's enough women here, cooks and maids . . ."

Riddle coughs, covers his mouth. "Yes, there are enough maids. What do you have in the way of other skills, Miss Weeks?"

Ada pictures her boisterous lovemaking with Dolan. "Skills? I assisted my father—my adoptive father, that is—in the undertaking trade back in Indiana. I could find a position with an undertaker if I were to go to the city. But the war . . ."

"War's over now, miss," Riddle says. "Ended earlier this spring." He shuffles his feet, fingers his hat. "Have you considered asking Mr. Reed to take you in?"

Not in a thousand years.

"Or wait here for the Breens to come in?"

No, they've taken me on long enough.

"Surely the rest of your party will be here soon," Riddle says.

Ada shakes her head. "How can you be sure? What I need now—" Ada takes a step toward Riddle.

He backs away.

"To be frank with you, Mr. Riddle, I don't have anyone else to ask." *Damn you, Dolan. Why did you have to go and die on me?* "I've existed on next to nothing for so long, I can't see why I can't make something for myself. And I'm plumb sick of everyone I've traveled with. Help me find a place, and you'll be rid of me."

Riddle whistles through his teeth. "Suit yourself, young lady. I'm not your father or your brother or your husband, so I've got nothing to say to dissuade you. Except that I think you're plumb crazy." Riddle squirms. "Don't mean to be rude, miss. Be here in an hour, and I'll see if I can't get you settled in to my old—with some old neighbors up the American River."

Ada packs two changes of donated clothes, some rags, and a heavy shawl into a knapsack. She swipes a Bible—one gone missing won't be noticed. She shoulders her rifle and meets Riddle outside. Ada looks for Mary Graves, but can't find her. She scrawls a hasty note and gives it to the *Californio*. "For Miss Graves."

Dear Mary—

I say my goodbyes for now. You might think me hasty in departing, but I cannot live another day weighted with all the news. When I left Independence, I thought I would be living in this land of plenty with my parents. Then I planned a life with Mr. Dolan. Little did I think I would arrive alone.

I have decided to strike out and see what this California has in store for me. I will look for you again on my return, and wish you all the best &c. My dearest hope is that you are able to see your poor mother again.

Your friend, Ada Weeks

"And this, for you," the mixed-blood woman says. "For your journey." Ada accepts a lumpy package and nods her thanks.

"There you are, Miss Weeks," Riddle says. He leads his horse to the center of the square. "Ready?"

Ada sloughs off light rain that dampens her shawl. She mounts the slumped-back horse behind Riddle and tentatively puts her left arm around Riddle's waist. He coaxes the animal into a trot as Sutter's Fort disappears behind them. Her only regret is she has no news yet about the fate of the Breens.

"It's a full day's ride," Riddle says. "Best get comfortable."

Riddle and Ada traverse the hilly terrain and fall into a steady rhythm. They ride across large meadows and dip in and out of stands of oak. *How much faster we can get along riding.* By midday, they reach the American River. Another two hours upstream, the horse turns abruptly to the left and follows a well-worn path on the banks of a smaller, cottonwood-lined creek.

"This here's called Answer Creek," Riddle says.

Fifteen minutes later, through a tangle of brush, Ada spies a small cabin twenty yards from the water in a stand of oak and pine. Riddle dismounts and helps Ada slide off his horse. "And this here's my old place. We'll stop here for a bite and then be on our way again."

A mangy cat peeks out from behind a woodpile. "Well, what do you know. Found your way back here, did you? Come here, Boy."

The cat lopes over on three legs, skirting Ada and sidling up to Riddle's trousers.

"Poor thing," she says. "How'd he lose his leg?"

"One bad step, you might say."

Riddle's cabin is sturdy, maybe sixteen by twenty, with a chimney butting out the shingled roof. She reads the sign over the door. "Answer? For the creek?"

"Why not? Mighty good place for a fella named Riddle."

Ada smiles. "Very clever, Mr. Riddle."

"Knew I was meant to end up here, after . . . well, never mind about that."

Ada's of one mind to put her new plan on hold and revert to last night's plan. Why, she could march into the cabin, take off her clothes, and will Riddle to have her this afternoon. That would save a lot of worry and work. But he said he was leaving soon. And she doesn't want to give in to convenience, not after enduring so much. She will make it on her own, without anyone's help, let alone a grizzled bachelor. She digs the toe of her boot into the ground. "I'll stay out here, if you don't mind. Stretch my legs a bit."

Ada wanders to the creek while Riddle disappears into the cabin, Boy on his tail. Riddle emerges with a hunk of stale bread and a link of old sausage. He sits on a stump at the water's edge.

"Like some?" He holds out his hand.

Ada shakes her head. If Riddle had appeared at Truckee Lake a month earlier, she would have grabbed the bread from his hands and devoured it whole. The sausage, too. Ada opens the package the *Californio* gave her and eats a hunk of yellowed cheese. They eat in silence, the sound of the rippling creek murmuring in the background.

A loud "*barrrrh*" echoes in the clearing.

"That's Old One, nuisance of a thing, but you get used to him. Like Whipple. Prickly son-of-a-bitch, if you'll excuse my language. Best shot you'll ever see. I think you'll like his wife. I do. Makes the best cornbread this side of a cornfield."

Ada and Riddle remount and make for Whipple's place, two miles upstream. Upon entering the small clearing, there's no noise that accompanies people at home, no shrieks of children, cracks of an ax striking wood, or chatter. And the sure sign: no smoke spiraling from the shanty's chimney.

"Don't seem to be anyone home," Riddle says. "Mule and wagon gone as well. I'll stay with you, if you like, until Whipple and his lady return."

"Tell me about Whipple and—"

"Salina's her name. Native. A real beauty. Whipple, Rufous Whipple, he's a free black. From back East somewheres. Virginia, I think. They're a right handsome couple, them and their kids. Best neighbors a fella could ask for. Out here, a mile or two or four or even ten amounts to nothing between neighbors."

"I'm sure I can manage on my own," Ada says. "But what happens when they—Rufous and Salina, is it?—return to find someone squatting at their place?"

Riddle lets out a belly laugh. "They shoot vigilantes, but a squatter, no, they won't be surprised. It's as natural as breathing, finding a wayfarer in your bed, or in your clothes. They'll likely say howdy-hey, ask where you've come from, and where you be going. They'll be mighty surprised to hear you're staying on at the creek. We don't have many neighbors up here. With you, me, Rufous, and Salina, that's four. With their three young'uns, that makes seven. A right city, if you ask me."

Part Three

THE CREEK

34

April 25, 1847
Answer Creek, Alta California

Ada ambles through rough underbrush on the winding pathway bordering the creek. A half-mile upstream from Rufous's place, she enters a flat and sparsely wooded plot, gently shaded from slanting spring sun. To the east, the creek curves around a bend and disappears toward its source in the Upper Sierras. From this angle, it's a straight shot downstream to Rufous's cabin, a requirement she measures carefully. She doesn't want to be taken unaware by vigilantes, even with a firearm and a new knife. Ada ponders if it would be better to stake a claim between Rufous and Riddle to not be upstream alone. It's a tempting thought. As she sits on a downed log at the edge of the creek to argue with herself over the merits of one spot over another, a pale ray of sunlight pools at her feet. *A sign?*

Answer Creek rushes in front of her. It ripples and riffles over rocks as it flows swiftly toward the American River. Golden flecks of mica glisten in the sun on dry boulders. She tosses a stone into the stream and hears it plop in the rushing water. A mockingbird rasps and trills above her. The sun slants between pine and oak and cottonwoods. She turns her face to the spring warmth and closes her eyes.

Two thousand miles she's come, over high prairies and rugged foothills, salty deserts and foreboding mountains. *And a hundred rivers.* She's walked every step of the way, besting weather and strife and hunger—especially hunger. She's clawed her way through mosquitoes and brush and grime so thick she could spread it with a knife. She's held her tongue when she felt like bursting and lusted so achingly her groin was on fire. She's loved and lost and sunk into despair so profound she felt swallowed by quicksand. And now she's here, with less than ten dollars, two sets of clothes, a few supplies, a rifle, and a knife. Noblesville is a long, long way away. She's not going back.

Ada settles into Rufous's and Salina's shed.

"I hate to put Molly out," Ada says, as she puts her nose into Molly's face and inhales the familiar scent of a mule.

"It's spring, she'll do just fine outside, won't you, girl?" Rufous says.

Salina brings an extra blanket and a hay-stuffed pillow to the shed and plumps up the straw ticking. Rufous sticks his head in. "It's not much, Miss Weeks, but soon you'll have a place of your own. In the meantime, you can take meals with us. Privy's out back." He cocks his head to the edge of the property. "Riddle and I can help with a cabin, now that you've found a spot. Might not be none too pretty, building it with scrub pine like we have around here."

"I aim to help," Ada says. "You might say I'm a bit tougher than I was a year ago."

"That I can imagine." Rufous readies Molly. "Step up, girl, that's it."

Ada pats Molly on the flank. "I had two mules on the westward journey. Rosie and Bert. They were good mules, for the most part."

"I won't be asking what happened to them."

"That's best."

Rufous finishes harnessing the mule and tugs on the traces.

"Between Riddle and me, we've got the tools and Molly here can haul logs for us. You'll be needing some tin sheeting for the roof . . ."

"Don't know as I can afford tin sheeting."

"Credit's good with me."

Riddle enters the clearing. "Overheard you, Whipple. Credit's good with me, too, miss."

"Be along in a minute," Rufous says. He runs for the privy. Riddle walks ahead with Ada.

"Make a list, credit or no credit. We go to Sutter's at least once a month, Rufous and me. Don't ask for trouble, him being colored and all. And no one's going to bother us on account of his size."

They step over a log that blocks the pathway. Riddle offers his hand to Ada.

"Got a proposition for you, miss. I'll float you the roof for your cabin if you promise to make me a pie."

"One pie for a whole roof?"

"Well, make that two pies." Riddle smiles. "I don't get pies regular, Miss Weeks. A pie's like a sack of gold to me." They enter Ada's clearing just as the sun angles into the property. Riddle shades his eyes and surveys the plot. "Nice spot, Miss Weeks. Flat and on a bit of high ground so it won't get muddy. And plenty far from the creek—it's known to rise in the spring and again in early winter. And you'll want the door to face into the afternoon sun. Want one window or two?"

He doesn't stop for an answer.

"Since we gotta haul the logs a ways, it would be best if the cabin's no bigger than ten by, say, fourteen feet. That's about as long as we can get a straight log out of these scrub pine anyway. Hope you don't mind a dirt floor. For now, at least."

Ada's mind flashes back to when she rooted around the Breen cabin's filthy dirt floor the morning she left Truckee Lake. *A piece of china. A square nail. A button.* She has a scar on her hand as a reminder.

"I don't mind a dirt floor for now," Ada says. It's the slightest of worries, like lace for the windows. Or a dresser. *Or a bed, for that matter.*

"And there's the matter of an outhouse . . ." Riddle looks away.

Rufous barrels into the clearing leading Molly. "Good spot, Miss Weeks. We can keep a watch over you here."

"I'm not asking you to watch over me," Ada says.

"Is what neighbors do," Rufous answers.

Riddle's using his arms to measure. "I figure it'll take maybe forty wall logs and a ridge log, and about half that for the rafters. You agree, Rufous?"

The two men pace the clearing.

"I've got maybe half the wall logs down and stacked behind my place already," Rufous answers. "Think there's one long and stout enough that'll work for the ridge pole. Let's see how many logs we need before we go cutting more."

"But first things first," Riddle says. "Miss Weeks, your job is to haul river rocks. For the foundation. Start your pile right here." He points to the near side of the clearing. "In the meantime, Rufous and I will get busy hauling logs." He turns to his friend. "You in, Whipple?"

Rufous nods. "When you want to get started?"

Can't count on tomorrow, Ada thinks.

"Soon as yesterday," Riddle says.

Ada begins the slow process of dragging and carting rocks from the creek. Large stones she rolls uphill. For smaller rocks, she fills a bucket, three or four stones at a time. When she dumps them on the ground, they displace dirt and splatter her bare legs with mud. When she has collected enough rocks, she lays them side-by-side and one atop the other to form the foundation's perimeter.

There is no hurry here, unlike the emigrants at Truckee Lake who hastily constructed crude huts against incoming weather. It's springtime in the Sierra Nevadas, and with it, balmy temperatures and long, languid evenings as the sun curves toward the western horizon. Evenings linger deep into the night, still two months until summer's zenith. Ada relishes warmth, and when she sweats, she doesn't begrudge the smell. She's growing strong, and—this is the most important revelation to her—she's not in want of food. The woodlands are full of rabbit and squirrel and deer and enough fowl to keep her: goose, duck, grouse, chukar.

The fields surrounding the cabin are rife with wild blackberries and currants and wild onions and watercress. Oh, there are mosquitoes, yes. But she can pull up mint and rub it all over her skin so abundantly she smells like the plant itself, woody and pungent.

Ada's spent each night and tucks in right after supper in the Whipple's shed. Sunup comes early, and she hears Molly, collared up and ready to work at dawn. Riddle and Rufous labor beside Ada, ten, sometimes twelve, hours a day in cabin building. *Do they have nothing else to do?*

Today, Rufous and Riddle work two logs around at a time until they're parallel. Rufous ropes the butt ends of the logs to a wooden skid plate and calls to the mule. "Hee-aw," he yells. Molly bolts forward and pulls tight on the traces. After a couple of hard tugs, Molly gets the logs moving and skids them through the meadow and down a gentle slope to the cabin site. The threesome repeats the exercise until all the logs are in.

Riddle's tall and broad, with long, dark hair sprouting from beneath his grimy hat. His feet are as big as any Ada's ever seen. *Must have boots made for him. Nobody's got feet that big.* His deep-set ice-blue eyes penetrate from his leathery, bearded face, and he bares his teeth when he laughs. Rufous is a brick of a man, wide and muscular, without an inch of fat on his lean black torso. He's an inch or two taller than Riddle, who's taller even than Ada. They work without conversation and few breaks.

Rufous attacks the biggest log, using a broad ax to cut small limbs away from the trunk. Riddle straddles the log behind Rufous and grabs the drawknife. Riddle grasps both handles and pulls the blade of the drawknife toward him. Wood tendrils curl and fall to the side as bark peels away. One by one, the men finish each log and move on to the next.

Ada rubs Molly's nose. "Wish you knew my Rosie. She were a good girl, like you." She stokes the fire and puts on Riddle's coffee pot. Sap pops in the flames. She reaches for the handle and burns her fingertips. *Dumb it.*

"What about a fireplace?" Ada asks Riddle, when he stops for coffee.

"A stove makes more sense," Riddle says.

And who's going to pay for that? I can't make that many pies. Or be that beholden to any man.

Rufous's sons burst into the clearing.

"Lemme help," Buddy says.

"Maybe when you're as tall as Miss Weeks, I'll give you your own hammer," Rufous says. "Now get on and play."

The boy stands straight, a half-foot shorter than Ada. "Almost as tall," he says.

Ada pats his head. "Keep on eating like you do and you'll be as tall as me in no time."

Buddy runs off with his brother, disappearing through the woods. Ada clears the wood shavings from peeled logs and makes a huge pile at the edge of the clearing. *Will make good kindling.* Soon, the sun surrenders behind trees and leaves a purplish afterglow in the clearing.

"Quittin' time," Riddle says. "I can smell Salina's cornbread from here."

It's Thursday, the night Salina cooks her weekly meal for Riddle. "Is what neighbors are for," Rufous says again.

Ada's sweaty and exhausted. She pops into the shed at the edge of Rufous's and Salina's property and strips off her blouse. Taking a damp cloth, she swabs her face and underarms and changes into her spare blouse. Ada's face is filling out and her hipbones have receded from the surface of her skin. She feels as strong as when she left Noblesville sixteen months ago.

Ada's aware of a slight trickling between her legs. *Is it?* She's relieved to see fresh blood. For all their sloppy lovemaking, she is not with Dolan's child. She pins a rag to her bloomers, fixes her hair up into a bun, pinches her cheeks, and bounds up the steps to Salina's. "How can I help?" she asks.

"Take the baby."

Ada bounces Bea on her lap. "A lady goes a pace, a pace, a pace; a gentleman goes a trot, a trot, a trot; a beggar man goes a gallop, a gallop, a gallop. And where does Bea go? A-boom!" Bea's eyes crinkle. *I wonder what's become of Bella . . .*

"You're from where?" Salina asks.

Ada snaps back to attention. "Far from here. Noblesville, Indiana."

"A city?"

"No, nothing like a city," Ada answers. "Not that I have much in way of comparison, except it's nothing like Independence, Missouri, the place we left from. I lived in Noblesville after . . . well, after my adoptive parents took me in. Lived above an undertaking parlor, next to a newspaper office. You?"

"Paiute. Some call us Diggers, but we call ourselves *cawu h nyyhmy.*" Salina's voice gravels in her throat.

"How did you and Rufous . . . ?" Ada asks.

Salina colors. "Trade."

"Trade?"

"For a rifle and tobacco."

Ada stares at Salina. "Did you have any choice in the matter?"

"Rufous is a good man."

Over the next few days, Rufous and Riddle peel and notch logs, some greater than the size of Ada's waist. Log by log by log, they lift and place them, notch down, to fit snugly over the curved log below. Ada chinks and daubs the lower logs with mud and sticks as the walls rise to the level of her knees, and then her waist, and then her shoulders. Soon Rufous and Riddle are struggling to place the last of the logs, two feet above Ada's head. It's been three weeks of felling and hauling, peeling and notching, and now the walls are up. Riddle cuts a doorway. "We'll start on the roof tomorrow."

The next morning, Rufous and Riddle lash a tall spar pole at either end of the cabin. They've rigged ropes and pulleys to raise the heavy ridgepole and rafters into place. Lines crisscross the empty space.

"Go, girl," Ada says, as she urges Molly forward.

Straining against her harness, Molly struggles to lift the ridgepole to the roofline.

"Got it," Rufous yells, as he and Riddle grunt and maneuver the pole into position to secure it. The men clamber up to the roofline to await rafters.

Ada strains to loop a double half hitch onto the end of each log. "Up, girl." She pats Molly on the rear.

One by one, Molly pulls the rafters up. After a whole afternoon of sweating, the trio stops for water.

"Headin' back," Rufous says. "Plumb tuckered out."

"Me, too," Ada says. "Coming along, Mr. Riddle?"

"Not going to quit yet," he answers. He climbs up to the roof again and begins to nail tin sheeting to the rafters. "Got yourself a cabin, Miss Weeks," he yells down. "Just need to finish the door and windows. We'll see about getting you some glass right quick. For now, you'll have to use a blanket."

Ada only has one blanket. And tomorrow she'll have to tear it up to cover her window. She follows Rufous back to the homestead to spend one last night in the shed. "Hey, Molly girl." She pats the mule and pushes into the lean-to. She's so exhausted, she doesn't go in for supper. She doesn't even take her clothes off. She pulls the blanket up to her chest and falls asleep within minutes.

The next morning dawns bright and clear, sky as blue as a robin's egg and still, except for lazy clouds creeping across the morning. Ada stops in to Salina's to say goodbye.

"From us," Salina says. She hands Ada a loaf of cornbread covered with a faded tea towel. "And here's some necessities—you'll be needing them. Don't be a stranger now."

"Many thanks, Salina." Ada tucks the plate and utensils under her arm and pats Molly before she heads upstream. *Home.*

Riddle is at the cabin before Ada. As Ada enters the doorway, he is sitting on a chair nailing the last of three legs to a rough table. "Hope you don't mind I spent the night here," he says. "By the time I was finished with the bedstead I got to working on the chair, and by then, it was long past midnight. So I thought, well, as long as I'm here, I might as well finish."

"You slept here?"

"No, didn't sleep. Wanted it all nice for you when you got here. And I just finished off your privy." He tilts his head in the direction of the outhouse.

"May I?" Ada asks. She strides to the outhouse and opens the door, which sports a rough-hewn crescent moon. Inside, there's a level platform with a single hole.

If Ada could have thrown a party, she would have. Of course it would just be for Riddle and the squirrels. But she doesn't have any fixings for a party, no sarsaparilla or cakes. Instead, she asks Riddle for a plug of tobacco.

He eyes her curiously, and breaks off a piece. She gnaws off a corner of the plug and puts the rest in her dress pocket. "What, you've never seen a woman dipping snuff before?"

Riddle shrugs and bites off a corner for himself. "I'm not judging you, Miss Weeks. You surprise me sometimes."

"Can I beg you for a tin cup next time you're up the creek? Salina gave me a plate and utensils." She fingers the bent spoon.

"Sure as I can oblige," he answers. "But for now, I'm going to go get me some shut-eye."

After Riddle departs, Ada walks around the outside of the rustic structure, inspecting every log. She is filled with equal parts pride and panic. Thoughts of the Breen cabin flood her mind, but this is nothing like the Breen cabin. It's airy, with a window facing the creek. And it's got a solid door (with metal hinges!) that swings out so bears can't barge in. She's got a snug cabin and three wonderful neighbors. What more does she need? Maybe a simple garden? Carrots and beets? Potatoes?

Ada tacks a torn piece of blanket over the open window and tosses her mangled coverlet on the bedframe. There's a crude shelf on the far side of the cabin for an eventual washstand. Beneath the window facing the creek, Riddle built a single shelf. But without a fireplace, she'll have to cook outside. *Maybe someday,* she thinks, *I'll be able to afford an iron Oberlin stove.* To do that, she'll have to secure rabbit pelts or collect duck down or tan deer hides for money. *Because for now, I can't afford anything.*

Her mind wanders. *Maybe someday . . .* She crinkles her forehead. *Maybe put all these 'maybes' behind me and do what needs doing here.* She takes her shawl off the single hook on the back of the door and stands on the threshold. *Home.*

Before dark, Ada scours the property for boughs. She lines her stiff bed with them. But when she settles into bed, she can't get comfortable. She tries lying on her back and then her side. She pulls the half a blanket up around her chin and settles into the hard platform, wedging between pine boughs.

Every twig snap, every wind prowl, every sound is magnified (she won't hear mountain lion—they're too stealthy). For the first time in her life, she is alone—no family, no adoptive family, no overland family. *Can't get too close to people,* she thinks. *They all disappear.*

As she sinks into sleep, an owl hoots in a nearby scrub pine. Its haunting *whoooo* delves straight into her bones.

Riddle appears the next day, early. He hands Ada a large Dutch oven. "Cup you asked for is inside. And a good knife." He returns to his horse and gathers an awkward-looking package from a large pouch. "It's a lamp. Filled with enough oil to keep you for quite some time."

An oil lamp! Ada thinks.

Riddle says, "I got to thinking last night that you were in the dark. I almost came back, but I didn't want to scare you."

"Or get shot, you mean?"

Riddle smiles.

"There's nothing I've got here to thank you with," Ada says. "If you come around day after tomorrow, maybe I can scrape up a supper for you. As a thank-you for all this." She raises her arms and spreads them wide.

"Sounds mighty good. I'll be seeing you then, Miss Weeks."

"How 'bout you call me Ada," she says.

Riddle tips his hat. "All right then, Ada—Miss Ada—it is."

He lopes out of the clearing and disappears in the straggly cottonwoods. Her back aches; her fingers are raw. She closes her eyes and sighs.

Later in the day, when she enters the cabin, it is nearly dark. *Dash it! What I'd do for a match!* She scours the clearing and finds two short sticks. She peels the bark and rubs the sticks together, Indian fashion, to procure a flame. The sticks warm to the touch, but no matter how hard or fast she rubs the sticks together, she is far from producing fire.

Just as she starts to complain again, she remembers her solemn vow on Christmas Eve that if the Lord, *in his infinite mercy,* spared her, she would never whine again. There are certainly things to whine about, but Ada is a woman of her word. So every time she starts to utter a nasty word, she bites her tongue. By this time, her tongue is scarred.

35

May 16, 1847
Answer Creek, Alta California

Riddle appears stealthily as a fox through the thicket to collect the supper he's been promised. Ada is caught off guard and puts her hand to her throat.

"Scared me, there," she says. "Maybe make a noise so I know you're coming."

"Sorry, Miss Weeks—Miss Ada. Will do, next time."

"Here, see what I caught." She leads Riddle to the shallows near a clutch of reeds. A large cutthroat trout nestles in two inches of clear mountain water. She had thought about taking a stab at fileting it, but left it for Riddle. She also has to admit she'd forgotten to ask for a match.

"You mean, you've been living in the dark for two days and nights? And no fire neither?"

Ada nods. "I've got a lot of learning to do. Been like a cow on skates these last couple of days."

"Now that's one I haven't heard before, and I thought I'd heard it all."

"Spare me a match, and I'll get a fire going."

She lays the fire carefully, the way Ma Breen taught her, using a stick to dredge a small trench and layering small sticks and dry leaves as kindling. She strikes the match and ignites the tinder. With slow, careful breaths, she coaxes the fire to life. She adds larger sticks and soon has a steady fire.

Riddle cleans the trout. Ada watches from the corner of her eye. When he finishes, Riddle threads the fileted fish on a green willow branch and brings it to Ada. "Like the Indians do it," he says.

Ada holds the stick about eight inches from the fire and turns the stick slowly. A slight wind picks up, and she moves to set her body between the gusts. Tonight, she doesn't want dirt mixed in with the meal. "We'll be having wild onions, too, and the last of Salina's corn-bread. I'm sorry it isn't grander."

"I don't eat grand, Miss Ada. We were spoiled at Fort Sutter for a few days, and don't think I wasn't grateful. It's been so long since I've eaten that much that when I did, I wasn't a-right the next day. Not saying I couldn't get used to it. Like going to Salina's. I take an invite there anytime it's offered. Don't happen to have any honey, do you?"

Ada shakes her head.

"Reckon I'm pretty well set for the rest of the spring," Riddle says. "Got my share of deer meat hung, but I've been known to eat rabbit if I'm desperate. This time of year, I count on early salmon and this here trout." Riddle bites into the fleshy, charred fish. "I'm curious how you snared this one."

"Used my hands. Didn't have anything in the way of a fishing pole or line. I'm sure you would have had quite the laugh if you'd seen me thrashing about after that trout. Especially when I landed on my backside."

Riddle shakes his head. "I would've given a week's wages to see that. You're really something, Miss Ada. Really something."

"Thought you said you were heading out of here," Ada says. "Wasn't that what you said?" She doesn't know how she'll react to his answer.

"Thought so, too, until yesterday. Here, look at this." Riddle pulls out a handkerchief. He unwraps it with care. Inside is a rough nugget, streaked with gold.

"Is that . . .?"

"Sure of it. Found it right in front of my place. Haven't told anyone yet, not even Rufous. Might be staying on after all. Our secret?"

At first, there are excuses for Riddle's visits: How is she doing and does she need anything? And look here, see what else I've found. You should be looking, too, Miss Ada. I've an inkling these creeks are plumb full of it.

After a few weeks, excuses are no longer needed. Ada enjoys Riddle's company, rough as he might be. There's a tender side emerging, and for that, she's grateful. Riddle makes a habit of always bringing her something: more matches or a second tin mug, so he can beg a cup of coffee when he's here.

Ada pries for information. Where had he been born and raised? What about his parents? Siblings? Had he had any formal schooling? Northern Wisconsin Territory, he says. Been a miner, a trapper, an Indian scout. No, never attended school. Whatever formal schooling he lacks, he makes up for in ingenuity and industriousness. There is nothing the man cannot do.

Well, maybe except read.

Ada makes a mental list of questions she needs to ask him. It is a slow process, this homesteading. Riddle teaches Ada how to trap squirrels and rabbits, track deer, and read the weather. He places his rough hands over hers as he instructs her how to use a saw.

Ada picks up the saw and resumes the task she began the day before, hewing logs for the lean-to. Ada has grand plans for the addition. She'll buy a couple of pigs, a goat, and a brood of chickens. She has already fashioned a coop in her mind, and has become so proficient with the saw she won't have to ask for Riddle's help to complete that project.

What would Augustus and Inger think if they could see me now? Ada shakes her head. Inger would surely cluck—she could worry about a single raindrop, let alone imagining a life alone in the woods. But Augustus would be proud of her thrift and ingenuity. "Vy, you're a proper Norvegian," he'd belly laugh.

When she goes to Sutter's for supplies, she'll have to beg for credit, but she'll be good on her word. Old Sutter will get his return in bacon or furs or pies. She is also anxious for news of any of the emigrants. When did the Breens arrive? And Mr. and Mrs. Donner? And what has become of her friend, Mary Graves? Virginia Reed? And little James Eddy? It's as if the whole journey west is a blur of getting up and getting moving and getting supper and getting to bed, without a lot of loving squeezed in. *Did I do everything I could have? Show Simon enough affection when he hurt his leg? Or Eddie, when he broke his? Or Miz Donner, for all she did for everyone on the train? Or help enough with Miz Eddy? Or Ma Breen? Or did I walk through the days without feeling? Just getting on?*

Her mind wanders. *Ouch!* The saw nicks her thumb, and she winces. She drops the saw and brings her thumb up to her mouth. Blood dribbles from the wound. The cut is not deep, but smarts. Ada hurries to the creek and lets the cool stream water run over the wound until she can't see any more blood. Cottonwood snow drifts through the clearing and settles on every surface, an echo of winter. Ada returns to the cabin and wraps her thumb in strips of cloth. There will be no more sawing today.

Instead, Ada sets about to bake a pie. She measures flour and cuts in lard and uses her good hand to roll out a ragged crust. She dumps the remainder of yesterday's first blueberries into the pie shell and crimps the corners of the crust. Riddle says blackberries and boysenberries and raspberries follow blueberries. "As sure as day comes after night," he said. She will never want for pie.

While the pie bakes in the Dutch oven, Ada lies in the grass and daydreams. She dozes off, and wakes to the smell of burning food. "Dash it all!" *You can put boots in the oven but it don't make 'em biscuits.* It's not even noon, and her day is a bust. Well, she didn't promise God not to swear.

Ada takes a plug of tobacco out of her precious stash, and even though it isn't a Saturday, she pops it into her mouth. Tobacco juice spills from the corners of her mouth and drips onto the front of her dress. She spits into a tin cup. She needs a new apron, but doesn't have fabric. She adds fabric to her long list of supplies. All afternoon, Ada watches for Riddle, but he doesn't come.

Before dark, Ada goes outside to gather up enough wood for the morning. It takes her longer than usual. Her hand stings from the wound and makes lugging wood more of a chore. She uses her good hand to pick up three logs and uses her bum hand to steady the pieces against her chest. She sidles up the porch and drops the load under the eaves to keep it dry. She nudges the door open with her elbow and hip.

Day surrenders into night. Ada picks at the middle of burned pie and calls it supper. She doesn't bother to get undressed or light the lamp. As she climbs under the blanket, she listens for the night sounds to begin. The screech owl. The rustle of wind in the treetops. The distant howl of a coyote or yelp of its prey.

Why did I survive? Ada has suppressed her thoughts since arriving at the creek. Pieces of memory flitter through her jumbled mind. She cannot think in any linear fashion. Bits and pieces of delight and horror swirl together in a phantasmagoria of memory. *I've got to be kind to myself,* she thinks. *I've got guilt enough for making it through.*

36

July 21, 1847
Answer Creek, Alta California

July blazes (Ada can't remember being cold). Ada's arms are strong and sunburned. Her long, dark hair has lightened in the summer sun. She doesn't wear a bonnet anymore. Days and nights hover at the same temperature, warmer than an oven.

Ada takes her hunting knife and a small knapsack and heads downstream. The cottonwoods have filled out, their green finery listing in the slight breeze. She walks around mushrooms on the worn path and waves to Salina and Bea as she passes the Whipple place. Rufous and the boys have gone off with Riddle for a few days in the Upper Sierras to hunt. They're not due back for another day.

Another two miles downstream along Answer Creek and she's at Riddle's place. Ada looks for Boy, but either he's hiding or out mousing. The raven isn't around either. It's as quiet as she's ever heard it in these woods. She opens her knapsack and dumps three rags on Riddle's table. She takes a bucket, fills it with creek water, and lugs it back to the cabin. It's the least she can do, clean Riddle's place, after everything he's done for her. If she'd asked, he would've put her off. "Don't need it," he would have said. She can't have him knowing she was here so she makes a mental note of where he left his knife on the sideboard, how various hats and coats hang on hooks, the disarray of bedding.

Ada starts at one end of the cabin and rinses soiled rags fifty times or more as she cleans. She wipes down cobwebbed walls, rough shelving, the solid table, three chairs. She cleans crumbs from crevices and rubs chair backs until they're clean. Whether Riddle notices or not is in question, but Ada banks on the side he doesn't. He would never suspect anyone would do such a thing.

Near noon, she stops and sits on the front stoop. Boy stretches and yawns from his spot on the corner of the porch. He won't tell her secret. She nibbles on a rind of cheese and gnaws on a piece of stale cornbread. Hadn't she seen a honey pot on the counter? She bounds up, picks up the knife, and reaches for the honey. The slick container slips from her hands and crashes on the planked floor. The crockery explodes in slivers. Honey oozes out along pine boards and flows into cracks between the planks.

Confound it! Ada drops to her knees. She mops up the honey and picks up the broken honey pot. Bundling pieces of crockery in her skirt, Ada races outside and tosses the load into the creek, pottery shards flying airborne before plunking into the gurgling water. Her skirt is sticky, so she whips it off and soaks it in the creek. Down to her bloomers, she gathers the dripping skirt under her arm, drags a chair outside, and hangs the wet mess over the chair back to dry. Then she refills the bucket and scrubs the floor in her bloomers and shirtwaist. The floor is so clean she could eat off of it.

When she's through, Ada sits on the edge of Riddle's bed and falls backward into the blankets. In the mussed bedding, she inhales Riddle's sweat and musk. She closes her eyes and slowly loosens her clammy blouse. The air tingles her skin. She reclines on the cot and wills Riddle to walk in the door.

On the way back to her cabin, Ada meets Salina at the edge of the creek in front of the Whipple's. She's weeping.

"Salina?"

Salina looks up from where she's crouched. Blood eddies around the hem of her damp dress.

"Oh, Salina. Is it . . . ?"

Salina nods. "Don't tell Rufous. He wants another so bad."

Ada moves tentatively toward Salina and squats next to her. She puts an arm around Salina and lets her cry into her shoulder. "You're a lucky woman, Salina. Three already."

Salina nods. "I know. It's just that . . . Rufous . . ." She sinks into more sobs.

Ada helps Salina up, guides her toward the cabin. Ada shimmies Salina out of her wet dress. She puts the kettle on to boil and makes tea. They sit in silence until the baby awakes.

"May I?" Ada asks.

Salina nods.

Ada straps Bea to her waist with a sling. "Time for you to rest now," she says to Salina.

Salina sits on the porch as Ada washes the woman's dress in cold creek water. A river of red flows downstream as she wrings the hem.

Buddy bursts into the clearing. "Ma! Ma!"

Salina offers her son the alms of a huge smile.

"I got a deer! Shot it myself!" Buddy yells.

Rufous, Riddle, and Benjy come into sight. Rufous shoulders the dead deer.

"We wondered where you were when we came by your place," Riddle says to Ada.

"Was paying Salina a visit," she lies.

"Right neighborly of you," Rufous says. "Now, Salina, why don't we put on an extra two plates for our guests?"

Ada interrupts. "Not necessary, Rufous. I'm headed home."

"I'm plumb tuckered, too," Riddle says. "I'd take a piece of your cornbread, though, if you've got any, Salina."

Ada catches her breath. If he takes cornbread, he'll be sure to notice the honey is gone. She interrupts. "Why don't you come to my place? I want to show you something I found. I think you'll be surprised."

He looks at her quizzically. "Okay, then, until next time, Rufous, Salina." Riddle tips his hat.

Riddle and Ada walk companionably toward Ada's. They pass a large clutch of blackberry bushes. "Reach for it, Miss Ada." Riddle holds the thorny branch down with his gloved hands. Plumped blackberries drip from thin stalks, gushing juice as soon as her fingers touch the nubby fruit. She gobbles two berries for every two she plinks in her bucket. "You'll never have enough to make a pie if you eat as many as you save."

"I'll be the judge of that." *Ow,* Ada yelps. She hits her neck. A large welt forms, red and hot to the touch. "A bee?"

Riddle nods and touches the back of her neck. "Careful," he says. He picks the exposed stinger from her flesh. "Now, wait here." He lopes to the creek bed and cups a small handful of mud. He plasters it on Ada's neck. "Should be a sight better now."

"A sight better? Looks like I've been in a mud fight."

Riddle smears the rest of the mud on her hands. "Well, then, have at me."

Ada smudges mud on Riddle's face and neck. "There." Inadvertently, she fingers the mole on his cheek. He doesn't pull away.

Ada's pail brims with berries, her muddied hands stained wine-purple. She eats a handful more, her tongue scored with deep, dark ridges.

"Here, let me," Riddle says. His hand brushes hers.

"If you insist."

They walk in silence to Ada's, the creek for company. A warm, earthy smell emanates from the path as they crunch over decaying leaves, pine needles, and small curls of cottonwood bark. When they reach the cabin, Ada washes her hands in the creek.

"To get you started," she says. She puts out a half loaf of cornbread. "Sorry I don't have honey." She recalls the mess she made at Riddle's cabin a few hours before.

"But I do have a razor and some vinegar. For that mole."

Riddle's hand flies to his cheek. "I told you . . ."

"I know what you told me. But I know more about doctoring than you might think. And undertaking. I didn't want to tell you before, but a mole like that will lead to more troubles. After all you've done for me, I'm not going to let you die over a little mole."

"What is it you propose to do?"

"I've got to lance it."

"Are you sure about this?"

"Sure as I've ever been."

Riddle sits stoically on the rustic chair. He glances at Ada. "Don't know why I'm agreeing to this."

"You're not agreeing."

Taking the razor blade in her hand, Ada deftly undercuts the mole and dabs the wound with vinegar. Riddle clenches his mouth, but doesn't speak. Ada covers the wound with a large rag and applies pressure. "Now that wasn't so bad, was it?"

Riddle shakes his head. "I've hurt worse."

Ada starts supper, squirrel sautéed with wild onions, cornbread without honey. To take his mind off the injury, Ada says, "I've got a riddle for you. Thought with a name like Riddle you'd be good at them." She stands in the center of the cabin and uses her long arms to punctuate her words.

> *I'm captain of a party small,*
> *Whose number is but five.*

She splays five fingers in the air.

But yet do great exploits, for all,
And every man alive.

Riddle creases his brow.

With Adam, I am seen to live,
Ere he knew what was evil;
But no connection have I with Eve,
The serpent, or the devil.

"You'll definitely have to help me on this one," Riddle says. "Don't know much about the Bible."

"Shush! Certainly you've heard of Adam and Eve!" She continues, her arms waving as she talks.

Matthew and Mark, both, me have got;
But lo! To prevent vexation,
Luke and John possess me not,
Though I'm found in any nation.

Riddle shakes his head "Matthew and Mark? Luke and John? The apostles? I believe you've stumped, me, Miss Ada. Tell me, what's the answer?"

Ada wipes her hands on her skirt. She leans against the counter. "Think of it: captain of a party of five—meaning the vowels. Found in Adam, not Eve; found in Matthew and Mark, not Luke or John.

"It's the letter *A*, Mr. Riddle. Captain of the vowels: A, as in A-E-I-O-U."

She remembers then that he cannot read. "Or for Ada," she says quickly. "A-D-A. That's how you spell Ada. Three little letters, two of them the same, one on each end. It's also the first letter of the sign above your door."

"Ah," he says. "A is for answer."

She bites her lip, thinks to kiss him, turns away.

"What is it you wanted to show me?" Riddle asks.

"Nothing, really. Used it as an excuse."

"Excuse for what?"

Ada colors. "Want to tell me about that scar?" she asks.

"Rather not. I killed a man over it."

"He must've been deserving of it."

"Can't say that he was. But it was me or him. I've agonized over it plenty. And I'd rather not talk about it again, if you don't mind."

"I don't mind, Mr. Riddle. I've had an ocean of troubles I don't want to talk about myself. Maybe tell me about Boy. How you came to have him. I could use a cat around here if you come across another."

Day crumbles into night, one conversation turning to another, from cats to commodities to Christmas. Ada boils water for tea.

"What was your favorite gift you ever received for Christmas?" Ada asks.

"My father made me a sled once," Riddle answers. "Got years of fun out of it. And you?"

"A little box my pa made. I put treasures in it. Rocks and feathers. But I lost it, in the fire."

"The fire?"

"I guess that's one of those stories I'd rather not tell."

"A miss is as good as a mile, I guess."

"That's what Mr. Bryant said. Have I ever told you about Mr. Bryant? The famous newspaperman?"

Riddle shakes his head.

"No, why would I? He traveled with our westering party until he got the notion to go on ahead. Thinking on it, he was the smartest one of all. To keep moving, that is. He was fond of that saying. But he twisted the meaning. Said if we don't take advantage of a situation, we'll miss out on the best parts."

"I can see his reckoning." Riddle rises, stretches.

"Won't you stay?" Ada asks.

Riddle shoots her a puzzled look. "Are you sure of that, Miss A-is-for-Ada? I don't mean to take advantage of your hospitality."

"I'm sure of it. I've got some playing cards here somewhere." Ada gets up from the table and rummages in her satchel. Her hand comes up triumphant. "Do you know seven-card rummy? I bet I can beat your britches off."

37

August 1, 1847
Answer Creek, Alta California

Ada records passing days on a crude calendar she's fashioned from plain paper and a charcoal pencil. She notes phases of the moon and keeps track of her monthlies, which have resumed like clockwork. A small star indicates the days Riddle visits, twenty-two of thirty-one days in the previous month. Riddle's visits accentuate Ada's days, but do not define them. She is satisfied with her own company.

If what Riddle says is true, she'll often have unexpected visitors and news from the outside world. And she can walk to Sutter's Fort in two days, although she has yet to do so. When the war is officially over, she might go to San Francisco, look up the Breens and maybe the Reeds. Find Mr. Eddy. See if Edwin Bryant has stayed in the West or ventured home again. Until that time, she won't have to dress for town, or spend time on her hair; she's now a Californian and doesn't care a whit about her dress or her toilette. *But it's too soon,* she thinks. *Too soon to face the outside world.*

Evenings, she reads the Bible. It's the only book she has. Maybe there are others at Sutter's she can beg, barter, or borrow. Or maybe she can send for books from San Francisco. But in the whole compendium of the world's library, Ada never hopes to see the three books that resurfaced over the course of her long journey on the Oregon and California trails: Lansford W. Hastings's *The Emigrant's Guide to Oregon and California*; Virginia Reed's well-worn copy of *The Life and Times of Daniel Boone*; and Samuel Kirkham's *English Grammar in Familiar Lectures*, Tamsen Donner's reference book she used to teach children on the trail.

Ada snorts. *What I would like to say to you, Mr. Hastings, would make a ruffian run for his life. Mr. Boone, not so much, but I know your tale by heart and am not anxious to read it yet again. As for you, Mr. English Grammar Yourself? D is for Dull. I don't ever want to see your ridiculous book again.*

Ada hasn't seen Riddle for four days since he rode to Sutter's. *Should've been back by now.* She sent a list of supplies for him to pick up and money enough to cover the cost of flour, sugar, coffee, and bacon.

When Riddle returns, he plops her goods on the table. "Good news, Miss Ada. Your Breens, they've all been rescued."

Ada notices a hole in the knee of Riddle's trousers. She wishes she had a clean rag for a patch. "All?" Ada catches her breath.

"Yes, all."

Ada sits, fumbles with her hands. *Bella!*

"They're in San Juan Batista, not far from San Francisco. But there's also somber news. I'm afraid the Donners didn't come through."

"No!" Ada says, her voice shrill. *George Donner, the reluctant wagon master. Tamsen Donner, the determined schoolteacher.* "Please, God, no!"

"And there've been some unsavory reports, Miss Ada. About many who you traveled with."

Riddle hands Ada a battered copy of the *California Star*. She scans the first page and puts it aside.

"Do you mean to spare me news about what I already know?"

"What would you know of . . .?"

"More than you would like to know, Mr. Riddle." It dawns on Ada she doesn't know Riddle's Christian name. *James? Joseph? John?*

Riddle stares at Ada. "Are you saying . . ."

"No, not what you think. I didn't partake, nor did the Breens. We were the lucky ones—still had boiled hides." *And a dog*, she thinks. "But there was feeding off human flesh in other cabins before our rescue. May you never know such desperation, Mr. Riddle. Don't say as I blame them, though. A family needs to eat."

She looks away, thinks of Dolan, consumed by acquaintances on the trail. *"But of course, as you know, Mr. Dolan had no kin . . ."*

"So, no, Mr. Riddle. No newspaper article will shock me on that account."

Riddle goes out to make a fire, and Ada turns to unpacking. All that keeps her from spilling over into tears is the wonderful news that Bella is alive. Bella would be walking by now, pulling herself up onto Ma Breen's skirts, and saying her first words: *mama, dada, doggie, ball*. She would be running soon, and playing with rag dolls.

Ada exhales, closes her eyes. She imagines the toddler's mass of dark curls, her button nose. The way her arms curled up around Ada's neck. Her gurgling and babbling. Ada is filled with buoyancy. *Bella is the luckiest of all*, Ada thinks. *She'll have no memory—none—of our ordeal*. Ada and the others are the ones left with memories, many too disturbing, too unsettling, *too beastly*, to ever dredge up again, tales of tribulation and woe and revulsion and despair that leeched into all of their lives in that horrific year that Isabella Breen spent napping.

Ada's hands shake as she picks up the newspaper.

A more shocking scene cannot be imagined, than that witnessed by the party of men who went to the relief of the unfortunate emigrants in the California Mountains . . .

Ada slams the paper down. She's of half a mind not to finish the article, but she can't help herself.

> *The bones of those who died and been devoured by the miserable ones that still survived were lying around their tents and cabins . . .*

"No!" Ada says. "This is all wrong!" She tosses the newspaper to the ground and stomps on it. She fumes, stomping around the cabin. After her fit, she picks it up again. *I must force myself to read every word.*

> *Calculations were coldly made, as they sat gloomily around their campfires, for next and succeeding meals. Various expedients were devised to prevent the dreadful crime of murder, but they finally resolved to kill those who had the least claims to longer existence . . .*

"Lies, all of it lies!" Ada screams.

Riddle appears at the door of the cabin, hands charred black.

"What is it, Miss Ada?"

Her hands shake. "This account, it says we devised ways to dispatch one another. Dined on babies! Ate raw flesh! How can they say such a thing?"

"I'm afraid that's not all, Miss Ada. The most distressing news is about a lone German . . ."

"What German?"

"The last one to be rescued."

"Keseberg?"

"I think that's it."

"I hated him. He mistreated his wife, and that's not all . . ."

"No, not all, indeed. I didn't want to tell you."

"Tell me what?"

"There's speculation he killed two children, and perhaps Mrs. Donner herself."

Ada turns white. "Mrs. Donner? And what children?"

"If I remember correctly, it was the sons of two men on the last relief. Men in your party who returned for family."

Ada thinks back to who was left at the lake camp when she started for the Sierra Divide and who would have come back to rescue family members. "Mr. Foster? Mr. Eddy?"

"Could have been their names."

"Oh, God," Ada gasps. "Not Jimmy!" She turns away, wipes her eyes.

Riddle moves closer. "I'm sorry I've brought you this news, Miss Ada."

Ada's brows furrow, and she blinks back tears. "I should have taken Jimmy! I blame myself for this! Why Jimmy? Why not me?"

Ada takes an empty mug from the counter and throws it against the cabin wall. It bounces off with a ping and lands by her feet. She bends to pick it up and sinks to her knees. Dry sobs wrack her body.

"Miss Ada." Riddle squats and puts his arm around her shaking shoulders. "You cannot blame yourself."

Ada moans. "But I can! I had the chance to bring Jimmy out, and I was overruled. I should have insisted. His mother was my friend, and she died in my lap. And she had already lost her daughter two days before. Now Mr. Eddy has no one—no one at all—to call family."

Riddle bounces on his haunches. "Shh, now, Miss Ada. There's nothing to be done."

They remain silent.

"But, wait," he says. "Maybe there is something you can do."

"Whatever could that be?" Ada looks up, her eyes rheumy. "I can't bring Miz Eddy back, or the babies."

"No. But you were there, Miss Ada. An eyewitness. It's up to you— you and the others—to set the record straight about your troubles. The news is by now out of hand." Riddle bites his lower lip.

"Lies, I tell you. Damn lies, all of them," Ada snuffles. A full minute passes before Ada raises her eyes to meet Riddle's. "Maybe I can do what Miz Donner did—write my own account of the journey. Miz Donner was always writing stories to send back East somewhere." Ada wipes her nose again on her sleeve. "Do you think I should write . . .?"

"Yes, Miss Ada. I think that best," Riddle says. "Set the record straight."

"I'll do it, and straightaway."

But Ada puts it off, and puts it off again. Days go by. She is plagued by unsavory details. *How to write it all? Where to even begin?*

She's standing near Eleanor Eddy at Independence Rock when George Donner announces the decision to take the Hastings Cutoff. She's slogging across Great Salt Desert and gulping water from Eleanor's bucket at Pilot Peak. She's cradling Eleanor's face slack as she dies in Ada's lap. Every time she thinks of Eleanor or Margaret or James Eddy, her eyes tear up. One day as she's rinsing out her tin cup in the creek, she hears Eleanor Eddy's voice. *Can't count on tomorrow.*

> *Little Western Courier, Noblesville, Indiana*
> *To Whom It Does Concern:*
> *I have, through direct experience in these matters, come across the vast plains with the George Donner and James Reed party and have arrived at the coast of the Pacific after an arduous journey spanning almost a year. There have been many accounts of our travails and perils, all expounded at great expense to the men and women who traveled with our party, many of whom did not survive.*

Ada puts down her pen. The Donners. Mr. Stanton. Dolan. Eleanor and Margaret and Jimmy. She counts them, more than forty in all, plus the two Miwoks who came in with Stanton.

When men and women put their hopes and dreams to a notion, we must respect their reasons.

Ada crosses out the last sentence. *Can't be sentimental. Just the facts.* She bends her head over the blotted paper.

Our expedition took us across the vast Unorganized Territory and through the Wasatch Mountains southwest of Bridger's Fort, where we took an alternate route.

Ada rubs her eyes. *Damn you, Lansford Hastings,* she thinks. She resumes writing.

Not long after we departed from the established route, we encountered the Great Salt Desert and every woe known to man or beast. The chain of failures that followed belies description.

Our wintering over at the foot of the Sierra Mountains begs explanation and consideration, not sensationalized accounts that some think make for salacious reading. Here is what I will tell you. Some people did what they needed to do to survive. Others survived by the grace of God or sheer luck. Ask yourselves what you would have done.

You might say it would have been better to stay in Noblesville. My answer to you is this: yes and no. Yes, we would have been spared the rigors ~~and horrors~~ *of the overland journey. No, if we had not risked at all, we would not now be here in the land of plenty* ~~eating grapes.~~

Sincerely,
Miss Ada Vik (now Weeks)
Near Sutter's Fort, Alta California

P. S. You may also enter the following obituary:

Departed this life on May 31, 1846, in Indian Country enroute to California, Mr and Mrs Augustus Vik, ages 51 and 49, formerly of Alesund, Norway, and Noblesville, Indiana, lately owners and operators of Vik's Undertaking Parlor (corner of Logan and Anderson streets) from 1841 until their demise. ~~Let those who read this notice bear with humble submission to the Will of God as it relates to their untimely end.~~

Ada re-copies the letter without mistakes and lets it dry. Before she folds it, she adds one more sentence.

P. P. S. Here is one dollar to cover costs associated with placing this announcement, &c.

AW

She is down to two dollars in coin.

38

August 23, 1847
Answer Creek, Alta California

It's noon before Ada ventures outside. A constant cold drizzle fights with her moods. Fall is descending early on the Sierras. This time last year, the emigrant train had just departed Bridger's Fort. Ada again rues Donner and Reed's decision to take Hastings Cutoff. It had been their undoing. The thought of their ordeal in the Wasatch Mountains clouds her mind. She blocks out all memories from Truckee Lake as too gruesome to remember. Now, when nasty weather restrains Ada's day-to-day movements, she forces herself to go out. Her survival depends on it; she has two dollars to her name.

Ada set a trap the day before; she hopes for rabbit. It will be a welcome change from her diet of chukar and quail. She ambles up Answer Creek about a quarter mile from her cabin. A pile of dead-wood chokes the creek at the bend. She kicks at the mound to dislodge it and continues upstream.

Aha! A nice rabbit! Ada untangles the mangled hare from the trap. She unsheathes her knife from her waistband and squats in the shallows of the creek. Tiny minnows scurry from her feet and dead leaves flow around her on their way downstream. Uneven stones line the creek bed so she digs her feet into a comfortable position. She skins the scrawny creature and wades out to her knees to rinse it, letting its entrails shiver down the creek. She's careful not to lose the organs. Then she wraps the meat in cloth and packs it into her pouch.

As Ada turns toward the bank, her boot slips sideways on a slick rock underfoot. Her foot becomes pinned there between the rock and a larger boulder. She tries to wriggle her boot free, but it's lodged tight. In the process of trying to dislodge her foot, she falls backward, landing on her rear in the middle of the stream. Her pouch slips from her hands as she flails to break her fall. The package bobs down the stream until it's out of sight.

Ada maneuvers to a sitting position with her foot angled sideways. *Now this is a fix.*

Rain patters on the surface of the creek as afternoon declines into evening. Ada shivers. She works against her better instincts and tries and tries again to dislodge her foot. It's fruitless. "Is anyone there?" Ada hollers. She yells and yells again. Hers is the only voice she hears echoing in the thicket. Soon she is hoarse.

Water wicks up her dress until she is completely soaked. After an hour, she no longer feels her feet or legs. She starts to shake—one moment conscious, and then sliding into black. *I've got to stay awake.* Her eyes focus and blur. Two cottonwoods at the creek's edge lean together like a couple of old drunks. *I'm seeing things now.* As the wind picks up, every tree, every branch, every leaf is animate, dipping and swaying and bending and groaning. *Now they're laughing. They're laughing at me.* She blinks in and out of reality.

Maybe it is funny, she thinks, *to come all this way only to die here in Answer Creek. Seems God is determined to have me freeze to death one way or another.*

"Miss Ada, wake up!"

Is this heaven? 'Cause it's too cold to be hell.

Ada climbs through a scrim of fog and disorientation. Rufous is standing above her, his hands outstretched. He kneels half under water, his shoulder against the boulder, his arms wrapped around it and his cheek pressed against it, water up to his ear. He lets out a deep guttural grunt as his powerful shoulders and arms tighten, veins bulging from his thick neck. Ada feels a slight relief of pressure on her foot. Rufous pushes again and utters a shriek that reverberates up the creek bed. The boulder moves just enough for Ada to pull her foot away.

"R-r-r-r-ufous?"

"Shush now, Miss Ada." Rufous heaves Ada's soaked body from the stream and bolts toward her cabin, crushing leaves and twigs and pinecones as he runs. His breath is ragged and short. Ada can't see beyond Rufous's shoulder. Her teeth chatter and her body spasms. When they get to the cabin, Rufous bursts through the heavy door and sets Ada on a chair.

"Your clothes. Take them off." Rufous turns away.

Ada sits numbly. She can't think or move.

"If you don't do it, I will." Rufous spins and fumbles with Ada's shirtwaist and all but rips it off her near-blue body. He peels off her chemise, turns her around, and roughly rubs her shoulders and back. He pulls at her belt and her skirt falls to the floor.

"Your bloomers, too, miss." He averts his gaze as Ada shimmies out of her underclothes. With a swift motion, Rufous lifts Ada's naked body and bundles her into her cot. Within moments, he has stripped down, leaving his ragged clothes in a heap by the bed. He clambers into the narrow cot stark naked and envelops her.

Rufous winds his long, black arms around Ada and brings her close to his chest. Ada smells the familiar scent of a man and feels his hairy legs and body prickle next to hers. She still doesn't know if she's dreaming or awake. Slowly, very slowly, warmth returns to her near-frozen limbs, and she relaxes into his body. Rufous is a great bear of a man, hair and all. She feels his manhood stirring and thinks of Dolan. She burrows her backside into his crotch. She still cannot form words, but no words are needed. She sleeps then, full and deep, as still as death, but breathing.

Ada wakes the next morning alone in her bed. She smells coffee. She opens her eyes and scans the cabin. Riddle sits at the rough table, fully dressed. His eyes are riveted on her. Ada realizes she is naked under the blanket. Her mind races to the night before, and she can't put one coherent thought to the next.

Answer Creek. Delirium. Rufous.

"I saw Rufous coming out of your place this morning. Just wanted to see if you was all-a-setting," Riddle says. He grabs his hat, nods, and leaves. Ada has not spoken a word, no "Wait," or "What the hell?"

Ada cries tears of relief and remorse—she can't decide which. A wan ray of sun shines on the dirt floor from through the opened doorway. Of all the feelings that engulf her, she is most embarrassed not that she has lain with a black man, but that she has been naked with someone she wasn't promised to. Ada hobbles into underclothes and dry clothes. She pulls on woolen socks and wraps her blanket around her. *Certainly, Rufous did not take advantage of me? Or did he?* She checks her vulva. It is dry.

Ada shoves her feet into her boots but does not lace them, and rushes out of the cabin.

"Riddle!"

But Riddle is nowhere to be seen, not near the cabin, nor anywhere along Answer Creek. She looks upstream and down, but he's disappeared, silent as a deer in surrounding cottonwoods.

"Riddle!" she shouts again. Her words return empty. She starts down the stream, kicking at stones and swearing aloud. *No, I won't go begging. Damn him anyway, leaving like that.*

The creek whispers by, unrepentant of its near claim on her life.

Ada hates the creek. And she hates everything about her life: the knowing and the unknowing and the weather and the poor excuse for her home and her bed. She hates that her mamma and pappa died along with so many others on the long trek west. She hates that Rufous has seen her naked; she hates that Riddle didn't wait for an explanation. But most of all, she hates that life has tumbled and scraped and squeezed and wrung her dry and landed her here with nothing more than a patch of dirt to call her own and no future to speak of except this, that, and more of the same.

Now, no one can call Ada emotional. Her mother was the only one who had ever seen her cry. Not Inger, not Ma Breen. Certainly never a man. If she's hurting, she stuffs it all inside. On the days she can't contain it any longer, she goes off on her own and it all comes out in a rush so full it's like the Big Blue all over again, debris crashing home in spring after a winter logjam, taking everything in its path.

She thrashes around the homestead, kicking at stumps until her foot throbs. She unleashes a flurry of swear words and screams until her voice grates against the darkening sky. Soon, she dissolves into wracking sobs, and lies spent on the hard ground. Her hair is matted, her clothes awry. And she's shivering again.

I'd be better off dead, she thinks. *"For dust thou art, and unto dust shalt thou return."*

39

September 14, 1847
Answer Creek, Alta California

Riddle avoids Ada for three weeks. He doesn't know what to think, what to say. And she doesn't come knocking on his door, either. Riddle sets his mind toward another winter, now that he's found gold. Won't be going to Wisconsin until spring, at least, so got to get in enough wood and food.

Now that Buddy's eleven, he comes more regularly to Riddle's. He can navigate the woods on his own in daylight. Riddle enjoys the boy's visits. He loved being eleven; he remembers trapping in the deep woods behind his parents' cabin. His neighbor taught him how to skin muskrat. His father was gone for long stretches with the Hudson's Bay Company, and when he came home the following year, he slapped the boy on the back. "All grown now." His mother made him a muskrat coat that year. He was never so proud. It kept him warm by day, and again at night when the temperatures plummeted. Life was simple then: eating, trapping, pumping his cock at night beneath the thick, wooly coat.

Today, Buddy bursts into the clearing. "Look what I've got, Riddle! Caught it myself, coming into your place. Sitting there waiting for me."

Buddy holds out his hands. *Old One.* The lifeless raven is splayed on its side without a mark, its turbid eyes open and still.

"Oh, no, no, no, Buddy. *Nooooooo.*"

The boy's face puzzles into a grimace. "I did what you told me to. Took my chance."

Riddle closes his eyes, and exhales. He takes the limp raven from the boy and sits on the stump. He shoos the cat away. "Yes, I told you that. It's just, well, this old bird was a friend of mine."

Buddy looks down, kicks the dirt. "I didn't know . . ."

"Of course, how could you?"

The boy's lip trembles.

"Buck up, boy. Nothing to do about it now." Riddle gets up and places Old One on the stump. "See that shovel there, behind the woodpile? Grab it. We've got some burying to do."

Later, after the burial (and awkwardly wiping Buddy's tears dry), Riddle sits against the raven's pine, his back straight. He's not one for crying much, but he feels a well of something rising up his throat. He hangs his head and sits there with his back plumb up against the tree until his rump is soaked through to the skin. Dusk tarries and then steals away as day tapers into night. Darkness descends on Answer Creek, dead quiet and pitch dark, a dark so deep that the man can't see his own hands. *It's black as sin,* he thinks. *Or charcoal. Or*—he catches a sob in his throat—*jet black, like Bet's hair.*

The fingers of night surround him like raven feathers, mounding softly and silently as blackened snow, covering first his legs and then, inch by inch, his torso. When it reaches his chin, he jumps to his feet, lashes out at the blackness, rants at the void. He stomps in the clearing and pounds the trunk of the pine with his fists. He bangs his head on the lichen-crusted bark until his head bleeds. His fingernails are crusted with slime and he digs them deeper into the gnarled bark. Tears spill from the corners of his eyes. *Why, Bet? Why?*

Riddle shakes the pine violently, all his strength focused on the task. In a cascade of twigs, the nest crashes down on his head. It is heavier than he imagined a nest would be, even for a sizeable bird. He bends to examine what Old One has squirreled away in his aerie: a mass of string, dried leaves, fur, and bones. In the detritus, Riddle sees the outline of a skull. *Is it? Old One's mate? The Missus?*

He sinks to his knees and his head falls onto the pillowy ground. *No, no, nooooooo. Not The Missus!*

He sobs like a child, first shoulders, then torso, then body, curled tight like in the womb. He lies there all night, willing dawn not to come.

40

September 29, 1847
Answer Creek, Alta California

Riddle perches on the edge of the chair in Ada's cabin. He chews a piece of grass and pumps his knee. Ada busies herself with mundane tasks and tries to ignore what Augustus would have called *elefant i rommet*, the elephant in the room.

Riddle clears his throat. "It's been a tough time, these last few weeks."

Ada nods yes. "There's something I've been meaning to tell you."

"You don't owe me any explanation, Miss Ada."

Ada looks puzzled. "I thought—"

"Whipple told me what happened," Riddle interrupts. "And I aim to believe him. I might have done the same, if I had found his Salina in a bad way. Of course, I'd probably be a dead man if I'd been caught in bed with his missus. Rufous Whipple is a crack shot."

Ada pours coffee into two mugs and sits across from Riddle. "I got to say my piece. There weren't no shenanigans."

"If I thought there were, I wouldn't be here."

"Well, that's that, then." Ada gulps coffee.

Riddle has not touched his mug. "What I come to say, Miss Ada, is my mother told me to find me a Proverbs woman. God-fearing woman, my mother was."

"I thought you said you weren't too keen on the Bible," Ada says.

"Maybe I would've been more keen on it if I could read."

Ada colors. "I'm sorry, I didn't mean—"

"Don't bother me any, Miss Ada. I can't read, but I know a good woman when I find one. I found one once, and I think I've found another."

He found one once? And what does he mean, another?

"Maybe should have told you before. I was married once. Long ago."

Ada stares at Riddle, her face taut.

"We were married four years—four years, two months, eight days, to be exact. She died a most horrible death. Brain fever. Nothing I could do to save her. That's when I started west."

Ada doesn't have much time to wrestle with details.

"Never thought I'd love another woman again. Been with others, of course, I'm shamed to say. But after the *incident* . . . Miss Ada, this is what I've come to tell you. Might not be a man of many words, but there's something about you. Can't quite put my finger on it. But I saw it when you came blustering out of the house the morning after Whipple left."

"You were there?"

"Of course, I was there. I watched you fume and stomp. Same spark as when we marched over the summit. But you mightn't remember much of that journey."

"Oh, I remember plenty. You bound my hands. I hated you."

"Yes, you did. And I loved you for fighting it. I saw that spark again when you asked me to take you upriver. What woman would ever think she could survive on her own? That nailed it, sure as the last nail into a coffin. And then you built this cabin and made it"—he sweeps his arms around the interior—"into a home. So I'm here to ask you. If you'll marry me. There. I said it."

Ada has much to ask, and to say, but she has lost her tongue. She doesn't know what to make of Riddle's declaration. She had one proposal before this one, for all the good that does her now. Ada walks across the cabin and removes her shawl from the single peg behind the door. She reaches for the latch. Her face burns with shame. She has lain naked with another man not her husband—again—and Riddle knows about one of them (he'll never know about Dolan).

Ada wonders how she can ever look Rufous in the eye again. He has seen her naked. *Naked!* It will be impossible to avoid him for long; they are neighbors, after all. This will take some getting used to, knowing Rufous has seen her—and felt her—without a stitch of clothing. Has he told Salina? Or are some things better left unsaid? And in spite of all of this, the word, "marry."

Riddle clears his throat. "There's a question on the table."

Ada turns toward Riddle. First she makes a quarter turn, keeps her eyes lowered. Slowly, she turns fully toward him and raises her eyes. She stares at him and does not break eye contact. She bites her lip.

"You know, I don't even know your full name."

"Julian. Julian Rogers Riddle."

"Well, Mr. Julian Rogers Riddle. You'll get your answer. You'll get your answer by and by."

41

October 17, 1847
Answer Creek, Alta California

A da wakes, her breath barely starting to coalesce in the crisp, fall air. Early mornings, Ada says what could be construed as prayer, if one has a liberal view of what prayer looks or sounds like. She's thankful, that's it. Not just because each day represents new beginnings. It's something deeper, more visceral, like the earth groaning around on its axis and coming up for air.

Ada wraps in her shawl, steps off the crude porch, and coaxes a slow fire. Autumn fog blankets cottonwoods on the far side of the rushing creek. The creek's burbling seems more urgent than yesterday. Dew drips from branches overhanging the creek. The subtle color changes in autumn leaves are nuanced by weak sunlight that filters in through a tangle of limbs. Within the hour, the sky blues into a deep cerulean. It's another gorgeous autumn day in the foothills of the Sierras with no hint of winter prowling around the corner.

A year earlier, on this very day, Ada saw the Truckee River for the first time. It seems like eons ago, that day and all the vile days that followed stranded on the eastern slope of the Sierras. She's buried it all in a vault of memory so deep, so unfathomable, she wonders if any key will open it again.

Ada has a pattern to her days: dress, set a fire, make breakfast. Chop wood, haul water, skin rabbits. If she's ambitious, make a pie (she is certain not to burn it). A mantle of discontent still lingers. Is it because she's been uprooted not once, but twice, in her life? Or because last year the wagons never stopped for more than a few days' rest as they traveled the wide and desolate continent? Or is it something deeper, a dissatisfaction that stems from somewhere intangible?

Whatever it is, Ada berates herself. She's got shelter and food, the latter not a necessity, but a luxury, now that she's known starvation. And she has an offer of marriage.

But is this all there is to life? A wagging *no* twitches at the edge of her mind. *Or,* she reframes her own question, *all that I need in life? Am I relying on long-ago dreams as a crutch? Hoping for something I can't have when something I want more than breath is right in front of me?*

Ada knows it won't be more than four days before Riddle is back at her door. It's a day to Sutter's and a day back. He will have all the items on her list plus any news. Ada pours coffee, opens to Proverbs 31. She knows the verses well:

> *Who can find a virtuous woman? For her price is far above rubies.*
> *She will do him good and not evil all the days of her life.*

Riddle says he didn't know the Bible well. She aims to teach him how to read.

Ada reads the next portion aloud:

> *Strength and honor are her clothing; and she shall rejoice in*
>   *time to come.*
> *She openeth her mouth with wisdom; and in her tongue is the*
>   *law of kindness.*
> *She looketh well to the ways of her household,*
> *and eateth not the bread of idleness.*

Ada shuts the Bible and closes her eyes. After a while, she rises and rinses her dishes in the creek. A rivulet of grease meanders downstream. She follows the grease trail as it speeds around small boulders and debris. A glint of gold catches her eye. *Can it be?* She tosses the tin plate to the bank and wades into the creek. She hitches her skirt up above her waist and tucks it into her waistband. She squats and reaches down into the flowing water to extricate the mottled rock. She jimmies it free and turns it over in her hand. A large vein of gold streaks the rock. She kneels, paws at the creek bed. In the shallows of Answer Creek, she pulls out one rock, then another. Many of them are marbled with gold.

Inside the cabin, Ada lines the rocks in order of size. As they dry, she outlines the gold veins. *Can it really be?*

Four days later, Ada begins to worry. There is no sign of Riddle. Has he come to harm? Or worse? She busies herself by necessity. It dawns on her she's become accustomed to him. Maybe he won't return. *A miss is as good as a mile.* Winter is near, and with it the possibility of being shut in her cabin for days or weeks at a time. It can't be as dire as last year, can it? *No, no, no,* she tells herself. *No.*

Ada estimates she'll need five cords of wood to make it through December and January and February. She'll also need to parse out the coming supplies. *Lists—I need to make lists.*

Ada wills Riddle back. *Where is he?* If he doesn't mind standing down the ladder of stubbornness, she'll start on reading lessons as soon as he's back. She'll start with the Bible and subscribe to newspapers if they ever settle in town. And then, she'll bring in books. She pictures him reading to children, if ever they are blessed with any. He will be a good father. Without consciously thinking of her answer to his unexpected proposal, Ada knows what she'll say and how she'll say it.

But what if he doesn't return, like Dolan? What then? I haven't asked much of you, Lord. But then again, I haven't offered you much in return. We had a bargain once, and we both kept our word. Is there one more bargain left?

Ada sweeps the porch, stokes the fire, puts water on to boil. She sits on a stump near the edge of Answer Creek but soon pops up; she is too restless to sit. She has enough energy to skin a buffalo, so she returns to her woodpile. There is a familiar rhythm to the chore, and she works her arms until they throb. She wipes beads of perspiration from her forehead with the sleeve of her blouse. A rivulet of moisture courses down her back, and she reaches around to scratch. She can't quite reach, so she shimmies up against fraying bark of a nearby cottonwood to rub her back, like a bear. Her clothing stinks of sweat and smoke.

When the water boils, Ada ladles water to her mug and adds tea. She is out of sugar. The tea burns the tip of her tongue so she swirls the tea to let it cool. She sits again on the stump and savors it, a slow slurp at a time.

So much to do here. She wonders where to begin. Wood beetles scurry across the ledge of the stump and she brushes them away. She drains the last of the tea, sets the mug on the porch, and returns to the woodpile.

By mid-afternoon, Ada stops mid-chop and wipes droplets with her sleeve again. Her blouse feels clammy. She drops the ax and peels down to her chemise and bloomers. *That's better.* She gathers soap and a towel and heads to the creek. After toeing in, Ada sits on a boulder near the bank and lathers her legs. Cool creek water eases suds downstream. Ada peels off her underclothing and tosses them up the bank. As she loosens her hair, she throws her combs near her discarded clothing. She wades to the middle of Answer Creek and sinks into a deeper pool. There, Ada stands naked, facing downstream, water up to her breasts. She soaps her face, neck, and shoulders, wringing the cloth over and again, and then bends back to drench her long, dark hair. Using her fingertips, she kneads her scalp until it tingles, then rinses her hair by submerging her head fully under water. She pops up and shakes her head like a dog. Tip-toeing gingerly, she picks her way to the shallows, careful not to stumble. Her skin prickles.

How she had loved Beaver Creek, where she discovered the natural bridge with Edwin Bryant the night before the Fourth of July. Near Independence Rock, the Sweetwater had been a tonic after brutal, dry days of mid-July.

Along the Little Sandy, Ada wondered if she'd ever reach California, and at the sight of Marys River, she bathed in icy water and swore never to take water for granted again. After the Truckee, well, there Ada stops and catches her breath. Just the word, Truckee, gives her shivers.

Ada cups her hand and drinks a mouthful of creek water. *Do I dare think of those dear people with whom I traveled?*

Ada steps out of Answer Creek and towels off. She rinses and wrings her clothing and sets them out to dry over a bramble bush. Inside the cabin, she dresses, and then sits on the porch. Using her tortoise-shell comb, Ada makes fluid sweeps through her hair and leaves it loose to dry. She's done with chores for the day and reaches for the Bible. She turns to Proverbs 31 again and reads it through for the thousandth time. When she gets to the twenty-first verse, she stops cold.

She is not afraid of snow for her household . . .

The word *snow* conjures a flood of memories, long buried: Baby Bella, her lips blued with the cold. Strips of bark and boot leather, fringed with teeth marks. Footprints, stamped with blood. Eleanor Eddy, eyes dulled and laid out cold. Mrs. Murphy's ax.

There Ada shuts the door on memory. She will not think of Mrs. Murphy's ax again. She turns her attention to Riddle's question. He had been so earnest in the asking: *"There's a question on the table."* Of course, she will say yes.

Long after the sun has arced and begins its descent, Ada hears a crunch of footfalls. Riddle comes into view on the narrow trail that borders the creek. He has a large sack strapped on his shoulders. Ada watches as he walks, his stride long and sure. He walks with authority. Ada thinks him eye-catching, *if you overlook the rough edges,* like the deep scar on his face, the grime beneath his fingernails, the long, stringy, dark hair, the slightly yellowed teeth. *He's a good man,* she thinks. *More than that. He's a good man for me.*

Riddle drops the bundle with a thump on the bare ground and places his rucksack next to the stump. He wipes his mouth with the back of his hand and grins.

Ada doesn't drop her gaze. Riddle moves toward her, his hands holding a package wrapped in burlap and twine. She can smell him as he approaches: must, blood, sweat, grime. Before he reaches her, he stops short.

"Ada."

Riddle hands Ada the bundle. She unties the twine and peeks inside. *Honey.* She puts the jar down and wipes her hands on her skirt.

"Got something else for you."

Ada cocks her head. Riddle hands her a letter, addressed to her in a man's large hand. Ada doesn't recognize the ornate handwriting.

"You'll never guess who I met in town. Mr. Edwin Bryant. Thought he'd crack a nut when I told him you were homesteading. 'Hoo-ey,' he said. And slapped his thigh."

The hint of a smile, leathery and slow, creeps up from the corners of Ada's mouth. "'Hoo-ey,' yourself." She stuffs the letter in her pocket and steps off the stoop. "Had me biting nails, you were gone so long."

Riddle attempts to hide a smile. "Miss me?"

"Hmph." Ada moves closer. "Got something to show you, too." She reaches into her pocket and pulls out a gold nugget the size of a child's fist.

Riddle whistles through his teeth. "Well 'hoo-ey,' to you, too, Ada Weeks. I do believe you're rich."

"Pshaw. It's just a rock." She moves closer to Riddle and grabs his collar. He places his hands on her waist and pulls her in. "Not so quick, Mr. Julian Rogers Riddle. Come inside, I'll get coffee on. You look like you need it."

Riddle bends to kiss Ada's ear.

She shakes him off and swats at his chest. "Before you get all sweet on me, you've got a heap of explaining to do. Where is it you've been since I seen you last? To hell and back?"

42

Present day
Grass Valley, California

"Hey, Jimbo, come look at this. I'm onto something." Emma pops a grape into her mouth and motions to her brother.

Jim pushes his glasses up his nose and shuffles through ankle-deep debris strewn across the living room floor. They had buried their mother just this morning; boxes of family memorabilia are dumped all over his sister Emma's living room floor: diaries, photos, yellowed scraps of loose papers, folded newspaper clippings, receipts. And they haven't even opened the strong box yet.

"What's up?"

Emma hands her brother a fragile parchment. "Read this."

Ada Weeks Riddle
b. February 28,1827
d. December 24, 1909
Aged 82

Julian Rogers Riddle
b. July 8, 1810
d. July 21, 1861
Aged 51

Christian Rogers Riddle
b. March 31, 1848
d. February 4, 1849
Aged 10 months, four days

Margaret Eleanor Riddle
b. August 1, 1851
d. November 10, 1859
Aged 8 years, three months, ten days

Grace-Anne Riddle Clark
b. September 29, 1855
d. September 29, 1942
Aged 89

Julian Rogers Riddle, Jr.
b. July 21, 1857
d. October 8, 1955
Aged 98

"Look here," she continues. "I mean, we know Ada was with the Donners and ended up with Riddle near Nevada City. Also that he died young. But wait: Christian and Margaret? Two other children before Great Grandma Gracie?"

"What the hell?" Jim crinkles his nose as he studies the parchment.

Emma loves when he does that. It makes him look ten again instead of nearing seventy.

"Hmmm," Jim says. "Two older kids? Let me do the math." He looks at the ceiling, his mouth silently calculating. "Great Grandma Gracie would have been what—four, then?—when her older sister— what's her name?"

"Margaret."

"—when Margaret—died. And her brother would've been a toddler.

Chances are they didn't remember, or even know. That, or they were told not to talk about it. That's more likely."

Emma reads aloud. "'Christian Rogers Riddle, ten months, four days. Margaret Eleanor Riddle, eight years, three months, ten days.' I can't imagine burying a baby and a child."

Jim bristles.

"I'm so sorry, Jimbo. I didn't mean . . ."

"It's okay. Forget about it." He lowers himself to the floor next to his sister. He reclines against the ottoman and removes his smudged glasses. He rubs the bridge of his nose. It crinkles again.

"Let's burn it," he says.

"What?"

"Burn it. All of this mess." He sweeps his hand in Emma's direction. "I'm afraid I'm not up to knowing any more details. Too many skeletons in the family closet already. And what about Ada? A cannibal? Nothing I want to think about.

"Really, Em. Don't you think we've got enough baggage already in this family? I don't care to know a whit more. We're a screwed up family. Admit it. No one can hold onto a marriage. Let alone a job. Our brother? Now there's a disaster. Not to mention Jim, Jr. Back at Sunbright Treatment Center, as of yesterday."

"Again? I'm so sorry, Jimbo."

"What makes you want to dig around and find out more about people and places better left buried?"

"Fascinated with our family story, I guess. Fill in some of the blanks."

"Who's got time for that? You're finally retired. Go to France or Italy. Volunteer at the soup kitchen. Take up pottery. Or painting. Anything. But please don't dredge up prickly family business." He sighs, unfolds his lanky limbs, and yawns. "I'm tuckered." He pecks his younger sister on the head. "'Night, Em. We've got the strongbox to tackle tomorrow. Not to mention the basement."

Emma murmurs a response. Again she mouths the names: *Christian, Margaret, Grace-Anne, Julian.* She goes to the kitchen, pours herself another coffee, and lugs the strongbox to the couch. She fiddles with the lock. It won't budge. After retrieving a screwdriver from the junk drawer, she pries open the lock.

Musty deeds, documents, and envelopes are jammed in the oblong, metal container. Emma takes them out, one by one. She paws through the documents, drains another coffee. Fueled by caffeine, she goes to the basement door, flips on the single bulb hanging over the steep wooden stairwell, and descends to the cellar.

She moved the majority of her mother's belongings to her own house after her mom had that nasty fall. *Beginning of the end,* she thought, and correctly. A broken hip, rehab, the nursing home. There, her mother descended into dementia, one coherent thought out of ten. By the end, she didn't even know Emma's name.

Emma peruses the boxes, thirty-nine in all, scrawled on the side to mark them: "Family Photos," "Scrapbooks," "Letters," "Quilts," "Memorabilia." She slits the memorabilia box open and sits on an old chair, the carton by her side. She reaches in. Beneath wads of crumpled newspaper, she lifts out the first shoebox. There had been so many shoeboxes filled with papers under her mother's bed, she first thought to dump them all when she packed up her mother's house. Now she's glad she didn't. But this will take some time.

In a box labeled "Nevada City," Emma reads old deeds, marriage and death certificates, assay documents. She unfolds a long, thick document—an assay claim for one thousand dollars, dated March 1, 1849.

A thousand dollars! They were rich. So that claim was profitable after all.

And then a yellowed death certificate. She squints to read the flowery script.

Lt. J. R. Riddle
July 21, 1861
Manassas, Virginia
Cause of death: bullet to chest

Manassas, Virginia? The Civil War battle? Emma furrows her brow. *How did Riddle get there? And what could have compelled him to leave a wife and family to fight?*

Questions crowd in. How long did it take for Ada to hear the news of Riddle's death? What did Ada do then, alone with two children? Did she move to Nevada City after Riddle's death, or was she already there? There are more questions than answers, and no one to ask.

Beneath the stack of legal papers, Emma feels a small package. The spidery scrawl on the envelopes is unfamiliar to her. She unties the faded ribbon from around the stack of letters and extracts the first one, looking first to the signature: "Mother." She flips through the envelopes: 1879, 1887, 1898, 1904. The last one is dated 1909, post-marked Nevada City.

Emma's heart beats faster. *Ada's letters?* She sets them aside for a moment and opens a file filled with memorabilia: a certificate of midwifery, a pile of newspaper scraps, receipts. And to think Emma almost threw it all away—mounds of records and correspondence and years of memories. If she had listened to her brother, all of this would have gone up in a trail of smoke.

In the jumble, there is one envelope different from the rest. Emma turns it over, unfolds the flap, and extricates a sheet of yellowed paper covered with what looks like a man's ornate scrawl. She looks at the bottom for a signature: "Yours, E. Bryant."

> *My dear Miss Weeks,*
> *Your letter was the most pleasant surprise I have had in months, if not longer.*

How long ago did we stand at the edge of Beaver Creek and wonder what lay before us? When we stepped in that creek and knew, like our great friend Heraclitus, that we'd been changed by that one mere step? My memory burns clear recalling that moment we rounded the corner of that red-rimmed canyon. Did the sight of that wonder not take your breath clean away? The aching beauty of it all? I have been accused (and more than once, I might add) of being a man of great exaggeration, but in this, I have endeavored to be forthright, without luxury of embellishment.

A word about my hasty parting. I loathed to part company, but my boots were itchin' to go West (Have you been watching your g's, Miss Weeks? By now, you have had sufficient time to rid yourself of your convention; I, however, have not been as successful in taming my nasty habit, I am sorry to say).

Crossing the continent was the most rigorous journey imaginable, and not without significant peril, &c. I can only imagine your ordeal. It has been hard to bear the news that emanated from your westering party; forty-some souls lost to eternity. I regret not seeing Mr and Mrs George Donner or Mr and Mrs Jacob Donner again, and now their fate is forever sealed. I have regular contact with Mr Jas Reed, who says he is transcribing his trail journals. I, for one, will anticipate his account with more than a keen interest, having known so many of the departed.

I am kept awake at night thinking of all of these souls and wonder if anything could have been done differently (none other than Mr E A Poe could have rendered scenes as ghastly that gallop through my mind). But I put those thoughts to rest for today knowing that you survived the journey. I have also encountered your Mr P Breen in the city. It is astonishing, is

it not, that not one of his family (nor one of Mr Jas Reed's)
perished? Oh, the human spirit!

Mr J R Riddle tells me you are well. This comes as no
surprise to me, Miss Weeks. It takes a bold man, let alone
a woman, to chance it on his or her own in the wilds of
California. You are the bolder one after all, Miss Weeks (as I
write from a comfortable chair here in the city).

Please indulge me and write to: 6 Commerce Street, San
Francisco. Please don't disappoint me, Miss Weeks. A miss is
as good as a mile.

Yours,
E Bryant

Emma cannot connect all the dots. A lover of Ada's? Or a friend?
It's not anyone she's ever heard about. She folds the letter back into
the envelope and tucks it in the shoebox. *"A miss is as good as a mile?"*
She fidgets in the folding chair as she opens Ada's first letter.

August 18, 1879
Dear Daughter,

It's time I told you my story before I'm gone. Not the eas-
iest telling, I can assure you, but it's got to be told, and told
right . . .

Emma skims letter after letter.

. . . west of Courthouse Rock . . . the Breens are bickering
again. A body could get mighty tired of it.

. . . into the Wasatch . . . a family named Graves overtook
our party today. I think I may have found a new friend, Mary
is her name. She's plain but talks a blue streak. It helps to pass
the hours.

. . . Truckee River . . . finally, water! I hope never to see
another desert again for all my born days.
    . . . at the lake camp . . . a winter best kept under lock and
key (and the key thrown away for all eternity).

Emma's eyes well up as she reads.

    . . . saddest day of my life, and I've known too many. Miz
Eddy just faded away, without a complaint. Can't count on
tomorrow . . .

By now, letters have pooled at Emma's feet. She stops, wipes her
eyes. But she can't help herself. She reads for more than three hours
without budging, even though the hard seat of the folding chair
numbs her backside.

Enma's hands tremble as she opens the last letter in the pile, also
postmarked Nevada City.

December 18, 1909
    . . . some days I couldn't keep count of how many times
we'd forded a river. Nothing I fear more than drowning. I'd
say to myself, you've crossed this same blasted river three
times today, you can do it one more time. I just wanted to get
to the other side.
    I sign off on my story now, Daughter. You know almost
everything now. Some secrets are buried too deep, so I will
leave the rest of them there.
                                                        Mother

Emma gets up, stretches, and climbs the basement stairs, grasp-
ing Ada's letters in her free hand. At the top of the stairwell, Emma
switches off the basement light. The clock on the kitchen stove blinks

4:47 a.m. She puts on a pot of coffee and sits at the kitchen table, watching the morning waken.

Fifteen minutes later, as dawn makes way for the first rays of California sun, Jim rustles into the kitchen. "Gotta get going earlier than I thought, sis. Looks like you've seen to the strong box."

"The basement, too. There's a wad of stuff. You won't believe what I found." Emma waves the stack of yellowed envelopes.

"It'll have to wait. Just got a call from Sunbright. Another crisis with Jim, Jr. Seems he's checked himself out. At five a.m.! Gotta run." He blows a mock kiss across the kitchen.

Emma gives an off-hand wave and rubs her neck. *How many more crises can one family have?* She watches her brother trudge to the car, head down. *Sometimes, it's all we can do to hold it together,* she thinks. *And, over and through it all, we've got to forgive ourselves, and others, over and over and over again.*

When Emma cannot keep her eyes open for another moment, she lumbers to the couch, throws herself down, and pulls her mother's ancient orange afghan over her shoulders. She drowns into sleep, thoughts emptying as through a sieve.

Come, I dare you, the river whispers.

You stand there, arguing with the current. But you know, as well as any, that to stay on shore is only for the faint of heart. Anyone worth her salt is already across. So you dip your toe. Is it enough? Not likely. Sometimes you have to gamble with your life.

I just want to get to the other side!

In you go, calf-high, waist-high. There. Good. You're chest-high, now. In a second of hesitation, you lose your footing. Your head dips below the surface, your mouth fills with murky water, your arms flail. You are suspended in time, debris swirling around your head. Finally—has it been a minute, or a lifetime?—your feet touch gravel.

You drag yourself to the far bank. This is what you hope, as you shake cold, muddy water from your dripping hems and soggy shirt-sleeves and stamp, stamp, stamp your crusty boots on the sandy shore: that someday, in the time you'd make a baby, or bake a hundred pies—*or cross a whole blasted continent*—you'll make it to the far side of that last river and find yourself in a place you call home, a haven of comforts, a respite from the wind.

For now, though, you are spent. You collapse on the river's edge, panting. Perhaps you doze. After a while, when they call you for beans and bread and stale coffee, you rise. You pick yourself up and go on.

One thing's for certain, this won't be the last river to cross. You've survived a hundred; there's surely a hundred more. The bugle sounds and wagons roll, oxen lowing in intolerable heat. It's still seven, maybe eight, miles to camp. You swat at mosquitoes and swipe at your mouth. By late afternoon, your feet swell, your armpits reek. You kick at crusty, bloodshot earth and wonder what's for supper. Someone's whistling. You have to pee.

Always, you migrate westward, ever toward the sun. There is no other way. Like the mockingbird warns, *hurr-eep, hurr-eep, hurr-eep.* Hurry up, hurry up, hurry up. By now, the map is ripped, the guidebook's gone. At times, you doubt yourself, your decisions, your very life. But against all odds, you don't give up. You think, *Maybe tomorrow, somethin' good will come of it, if I can hold on that long.*

So you walk, you stumble, you walk again. In the deepest recesses of your thawing heart, you break into a run.

Afterword

This is a work of fiction. The majority of the characters depicted in the novel are historical, although Ada Weeks and J. R. Riddle are fictitious. I have endeavored to be true to historical record, but have created fictional scenes, situations, and dialogue to move the story forward. Also, to serve the story, I have placed the Breen family with the greater Donner-Reed Party perhaps earlier than history indicates (there are various accounts of when the Breens joined, although they knew the Donner and Reed families from Illinois). Any errors in the novel, intentional or not, belong to the author alone.

A special note: attitudes toward Native Americans expressed in the novel are accurate to the period, and in no way reflect my personal feelings. As a former employee of the Nooksack Indian Tribe in Deming, Washington, and a resident on Swinomish Tribal Community land in Skagit County, Washington, I respect Native American custom, language, and sovereignty and wish, if it were in my power, that history could be rendered differently.

For further reading, see the selected resources below. I highly recommend Michael Wallis's *The Best Land Under Heaven: The Donner Party in the Age of Manifest Destiny*. At the end of the work, readers will find a detailed section on the members of the Donner Party, forty-two of whom perished along the journey, at Truckee Lake, or in the Sierras. Only the Reed and Breen families survived intact; both families went on to live in the greater San Francisco area and some of them spoke or wrote of their ordeal during their lifetimes.

It is interesting in hindsight to mark a lesser known passage of Lansford Hastings's *The Emigrant's Guide:* "Unless you pass over the mountains early in the fall, you are very liable to be detained, by impassable mountains of snow, until the next spring, or, perhaps, forever."

Acknowledgments

I've long been enamored with the stories of women who traveled the more than two thousand miles west from Independence, Missouri, in the mid-nineteenth century along the Oregon-California Trail. I devoured grade school biographies about Tamsen Donner, Narcissa Whitman, and other female American pioneers. Later, I read a plethora of women's journals and scholarly articles when I studied for my college degree in American literature/history at Wheaton College in Norton, Massachusetts. I'm drawn to this period and these women, many of whom never had a voice or left a record of their travels.

To follow in the footsteps of pioneering trailblazers almost 175 years later is but a dim mirror of their travails. It's the same landscape Ada traveled—same but very different. Traveling in an air-conditioned SUV, eating at wayside luncheonettes, being hooked to the Internet, and visiting scores of historical sites makes for more of an educational vacation instead of a life-and-death excursion to points completely unknown. I met storytellers and docents, editors and historians—and read books, books, and more books.

I have been changed by this journey, both the physical one of putting that many miles under our tires, as well as by the writing. The

Oregon-California Trail surprised me in many ways, none as much as walking in original wagon ruts high at the Continental Divide at South Pass, Wyoming, and turning three hundred and sixty degrees to see nothing that the emigrants wouldn't have seen, no cell towers or buildings or fences or roads. It was as if time evaporated and I was standing next to Ada, kicking at the dirt.

Ada Weeks is a figment of my imagination. She was not a member of the Donner-Reed Party, although those whom she traveled with are real. To the descendants of all of those who traveled in the emigrant party in 1846–47, I bow in appreciation to your ancestors. Were any of them perfect? By no means. None of us are. But to vilify them is to do a disservice to humanity. They did whatever it was they had to do in order to survive. I don't know what I would do in a similar circumstance, although I don't think I would have survived what Ada and her companions endured. I'm just not that tough. And I'm not here to judge them. I'm telling their story as best as I can, and honoring their memories.

Ada's character, mannerisms, and outlook on life are drawn from the resilience, demeanor, and spirit of my junior high school friend Ann Thomas Aylesworth, on whom the character of Ada is loosely modeled. Cheers to you, Ann. I see you in Ada and know you would have been tough enough to weather the winter of 1846–47, too.

Writing this novel spanned more than two years. In that time I read hundreds of diaries and journals, firsthand accounts, and newspaper articles to bolster Ada's story. I owe a deep debt of gratitude to my husband, D. Michael Barclay, for his willingness to travel the physical and proverbial Oregon-California Trail with me and for his tireless research and unending support; to beta readers Janet Gifford and Anne-Katherine VanderVeen for being the first eyes on the manuscript; and to loyal critique partners Karen Jones and Michelle Ferrer, who took the manuscript to another level.

Takk skal du ha to Turid Dassel, my Norwegian dialect coach, and to Brett and Rose Mary Hinsch of Mule Power Farm in Tucson for introducing me to their engaging mules. Additional thanks go to Marilyn Allen, Amy Hyzer, Megan Lascik, Ellen Notbohm, Jan Paul, Jane Pekar, Brian Smith, Gerald F. Sweeney, and Nancy Soderlund Tupper, whose collective input was thoughtful, helpful, and necessary before the final draft. I would like to add a very special thanks to the late Greg Finch, a dear friend who asked to read *Answer Creek* two weeks before his death. He was a great fan of *Eliza Waite* and I remain very touched by his request.

In the production phase, a round of applause to proofreaders Katrina Larsen Groen and Frances Simmons; to mapmaker Ruth Hulbert; to She Writes Press publisher Brooke Warner, project manager Lauren Wise Wait, cover designer Julie Metz, and the whole SWP team and sisterhood. Lastly, thanks to my publicist, Caitlin Hamilton Summie, and to sister authors who offered early endorsements.

Deep gratitude to my parents, Gerald F. Sweeney and Barbara M. Sweeney, for creating a home filled with books and music and art and for bolstering my lifelong obsession with words, written and spoken.

This book is dedicated to my four children: Chris, Megs, Annie, and John. You've made my life worth living. To paraphrase Thoreau (and Edwin Bryant): Go boldly, as in the direction of your own unique and matchless dreams.

Selected References

Brown, Daniel James, *The Indifferent Stars Above: The Harrowing Saga of the Donner Party*, Harper Collins, New York, 2009.

Buck, Rinker, *The Oregon Trail*, Simon and Schuster, New York, 2015.

Hastings, Lansford W., *The Emigrants' Guide to Oregon and California*, Shepherd and Company, Cincinnati, Ohio, 1845.

Hardesty, Donald L., *Archeology of the Donner Party*, University of Nevada, 1997.

Hill, William E., *The Oregon Trail Yesterday and Today*, Caxton Press, Caldwell, Idaho, 1987.

Holmes, Kenneth L., *Covered Wagon Women: Diaries and Letters from the Western Trails, 1840-1849*, University of Nebraska Press, 1983.

Kaufman, Richard R., *Saving the Donner Party*, Archway Publishing, Indianapolis, 2014.

Marcy, Randolph, *The Prairie Traveler*, The U.S. War Department, 1859.

McGlashan, C. F., *History of the Donner Party: A Tragedy in the Sierra*, Stanford University Press, 1940.

McLynn, Frank, *Wagons West: The Epic Story of America's Overland Trails*, Grove Press, New York, 2002.

Mullen, Frank, Jr., *The Donner Party Chronicles*, Nevada Humanities Committee, 1997.

Parkman, Francis, *The Oregon Trail*, John C. Winston, Philadelphia, 1931.

Peters, Arthur King, *Seven Trails West*, Abbeville Press, New York, 2000.

Rarick, Ethan, *Desperate Passage: The Donner Party's Perilous Journey West*, Oxford University Press, 2009.

Rhodes, Richard, *The Ungodly: A Novel of the Donner Party*, Stanford University Press, 2007.

Ross, Nancy Wilson, *Westward the Women*, North Point Press, San Francisco, 1985.

Steed, Jack and Steed, Richard, *The Donner Party Rescue Site*, Pioneer Publishing Company, Fresno, California, 1988.

Stewart, George R., *Ordeal by Hunger*, University of Nebraska Press, 1936.

Wallis, Michael, *The Best Land Under Heaven: The Donner Party in the Age of Manifest Destiny*, W.W. Norton, New York, 2017.

Questions for Discussion

1. When do you start rooting for Ada? Is there a time when you do not root for her? When? Why?

2. Discuss the role of leadership in the novel. What makes for a good leader? A bad leader? An ineffective leader?

3. How did you react to the news of Dolan's death? Did you predict it or was it a surprise? Why do you think Ada survived?

4. Describe your thoughts about cannibalism in the novel. What other subjects are taboos in our society? Is there a way to overcome these taboos? How do we start the conversation, especially with those whose worldview differs radically from our own?

5. Is J. R. Riddle a suitable companion for Ada? Or just a convenient one?

6. How do you feel Ada dealt with grief?

7. Piece together the story from the end of the narrative to the present day. Why did Riddle leave California to fight in the Civil War? What did Ada do to survive alone with her children?

8. Have you uncovered any of your own family history that surprised you?

9. Would you have wanted to travel with an overland party? Why or why not?

10. What makes for a good heroine? Name heroines who've stuck with you long after you've finished reading a novel.

About the Author

© Justin Haugen

Ashley E. Sweeney is the winner of the 2017 Nancy Pearl Book Award for her debut novel, *Eliza Waite*. A native New Yorker, she is a graduate of Wheaton College in Norton, Massachusetts, and resides in the Pacific Northwest and Tucson. *Answer Creek* is her second novel.

SELECTED TITLES FROM SHE WRITES PRESS

She Writes Press is an independent publishing company founded to serve women writers everywhere. Visit us at www.shewritespress.com.

Eliza Waite by Ashley Sweeney $16.95, 978-1-63152-058-7
When Eliza Waite chooses to leave a stagnant life in rural Washington State and join the masses traveling north to Alaska in 1898 during the tumultuous Klondike Gold Rush, she encounters challenges and successes in both business and love.

The Vintner's Daughter by Kristen Harnisch $16.95, 978-163152-929-0
Set against the sweeping canvas of French and California vineyard life in the late 1890s, this is the compelling tale of one woman's struggle to reclaim her family's Loire Valley vineyard—and her life.

The California Wife by Kristen Harnisch $17.95, 978-1-63152-087-7
The sequel to *The Vintner's Daughter,* this is a rich, romantic tale of wine, love, new beginnings, and a family's determination to fight for what really matters.

Lum by Libby Ware $16.95, 978-1-63152-003-7
In Depression-era Appalachia, an intersex woman without a home of her own plays the role of maiden aunt to her relatives—until an unexpected series of events gives her the opportunity to change her fate.

An Address in Amsterdam by Mary Dingee Fillmore
$16.95, 978-1-63152-133-1
After facing relentless danger and escalating raids for 18 months, Rachel Klein—a well-behaved young Jewish woman who transformed herself into a courier for the underground when the Nazis invaded her country—persuades her parents to hide with her in a dank basement, where much is revealed.

Portrait of a Woman in White by Susan Winkler $16.95, 978-1-938314-83-4
When the Nazis steal a Matisse portrait from the eccentric, art-loving Rosenswigs, the Parisian family is thrust into the tumult of war and separation, their fates intertwined with that of their beloved portrait.